JOURNEY'S END

JENNIFER SCOULLAR

PILYARA PRESS

ALSO BY JENNIFER SCOULLAR

Brumby's Run (The Wild Australia Stories - Book 1)

Currawong Creek (The Wild Australia Stories - Book 2)

Billabong Bend (The Wild Australia Stories - Book 3)

Turtle Reef (The Wild Australia Stories - Book 4)

Wasp Season (The Wild Australia Stories - Book 6)

The Mallee Girl (The Wild Australia Stories - Book 7)

Paradise Valley (The Wild Australia Stories - Book 8)

Fortune's Son (The Tasmanian Tales - Book 1)

The Lost Valley (The Tasmanian Tales - Book 2)

The Memory Tree (The Tasmanian Tales - Book 3)

Version 1.0
ISBN: 978-1-925827-13-2

Cover Art by Kellie Dennis at *Book Cover By Design*

Pilyara Press
Melbourne

To my late brother Rod, dearly loved and taken too soon

PROLOGUE

The day Kim Sullivan's world ended was disguised as an ordinary Wednesday. She took the kids to school and did some shopping. She came home, put on the washing machine and went to make her bed. Scout poked his head out from behind the pillows. Kim picked up the old border terrier, and set him down on the carpet.

He whined, stiff legs scrabbling to climb back up. On the third attempt he succeeded and nestled down on Connor's jumper, the one she slept with when he was away. His scent was in the weave. Scout had always been more Connor's than hers. 'We won't have to make do with his jumper for much longer.' Kim sat down beside the dog. 'We'll have the real thing home on Sunday.'

Home on Sunday. After years of deployments in war-torn Afghanistan, Connor would be home – home for good. It was hard to believe, a prospect too sweet to be true.

'Daddy will be back from the army in four sleeps,' Abbey had said on their way to school that morning, counting out the days on her fingers. 'It's going to be my show and tell. Mummy, do you think it will be a good one?'

'The best ever.'

Jake had rolled his eyes. 'What would preps know about the army? And Dad's job is supposed to be a secret. You shouldn't go telling everybody, Abbey. The Taliban might hear.'

'I don't think the Taliban will be listening to Abbey's show and tell.'

Jake hadn't looked convinced. He worried so much about his father. Well, he didn't have to worry anymore. In four sleeps Connor would be home and their new life would begin.

Her phone rang from the bedside table. Of course – that's what she'd come in to find in the first place. 'Hi Daisy. What's up?'

'How about I pick your kids up from school this arvo and bring them back to my place? Grace wants to show Abbey her new rabbit, Stuart's been bugging me about having Jake over, and you're always so tailspin busy before Connor gets back. What are you doing now? Cleaning behind the fridge?'

Kim laughed. She'd already done that. 'I want everything to be perfect. You know how it is when they come home.'

'Steve's lucky if I make the bed,' said Daisy. 'What's the point, when the first thing we do is mess it up again? And I'm too scared to look behind our fridge. I think there's a dead mouse.'

Kim shifted her feet as a flush of heat passed through her. Daisy was right. Nothing came close to that coming-home-night passion, or waking up in Connor's arms for the first time in months, or going to sleep knowing the man she loved was safe beside her. She sank down on the bed, dizzy with wanting.

'Are you lot still heading off to your bush block?' Daisy asked.

'Just as soon as we can get away.'

'Sounds like heaven,' said Daisy.

That's exactly what it would be. Connor's grandfather had left him two hundred hectares of land at Tingo, six hours north of Sydney, high on the Great Escarpment. *Journey's End* - a property in his family for generations, although nobody had lived there for years. She could see it now. Stunning views across the mountains of Tarringtops National Park. Sharing a beer with Connor on the farmhouse porch, reconnecting. Watching the kids play on the old willow peppermint, its broad low branches just made for climbing. Talking about their future.

They had grand plans to restore the rundown farm to its natural state. It had been a shared dream since their first visit there, though more hers, perhaps, than Connor's. She was the botanist. He was more interested in the wildlife.

But Kim had quickly fallen pregnant. Connor was promoted and went on the first of many overseas postings. And it had remained just that – a dream. When Jake was two, she started teaching horticulture at Campbelltown College, and then Abbey came along. Their lives were too full, too busy. 'One day we'll take off,' Connor would say. 'Use our saved leave and just go bush.' That day was almost upon them.

Kim wouldn't have heard the knock if Scout hadn't barked. She glanced in the dressing-table mirror, running her fingers through her blonde hair then smoothing her shirt. Good enough. She opened the front door and blinked in surprise. Captain Blake stood on the step. He looked different somehow: sallow and slump-shouldered. Scout appeared at her heels, yapping in short, angry bursts.

'Is Connor home early?' she asked. 'Should I pick him up from the airport?'

He shook his head. A cold stone formed in her chest and slipped down to her belly. 'Is he alright?'

'Let's talk inside.' He rubbed his forehead with his fingers, and she knew. The terrible truth showed in his swift breath, his guarded eyes, how he spoke – the fact he was there at all.

Kim put a hand to her heart. Panic claimed her, like she was walking too close to a cliff. Pain too. Her legs gave way, while white noise drowned out the Captain's voice. Not Connor. Not her brave, handsome, clever Connor. Her best friend, her lover, her soulmate. What about their life together, their future? What about Abbey and Jake? She swayed alarmingly as the ground lurched beneath her. What about her? How would she live?

CHAPTER 1

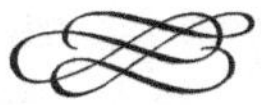

'Scout Sullivan?' The vet nurse smiled and indicated for them to go through.

Scout wheezed more loudly and nestled into Kim's lap. 'Here we go,' she said with a brightness she did not feel. She stood with the dog still cradled in her arms, and went through to the consulting room.

Dr Talbot was a small man, with bushy red eyebrows and a truculent chin. His people skills made Doc Martin on TV seem friendly by comparison, however when it came to his animal patients, Dr Talbot was the soul of compassion. He always held their interests paramount and was an excellent vet.

Kim placed Scout on the stainless steel examination table. The old terrier cried with pain as his legs slipped out from under him. 'Shh,' whispered Dr Talbot, and gathered Scout's limbs into a more comfortable pose. The dog licked his hand, lay down and submitted to the vet's poking and prodding. 'How far can Scout walk?' He shot Kim a suspicious glance as she bit her lip. 'Can he walk from the front door to the street?'

'Sometimes.'

'How old is Scout?'

Kim wished she could simply subtract some years. As if wishing might make it true, and let the dog live a little longer. Dr Talbot consulted a file.

'The Rimadyl doesn't help with his pain anymore,' she said. 'Can we maybe up the dose?'

'If we do his kidneys will fail.'

Scout coughed, a harsh, hacking, hollow sound.

'He can't always stand in the morning, am I right?'

It was more of a statement of fact than a question. Kim was about to lie; she'd done it before. But the expression in Scout's rheumy old eyes gave her pause.

'Yes.' She dreaded what was coming.

Dr Talbot put down the file. 'Scout has severe arthritis and end-stage heart failure.' He fixed her with stern eyes. 'He's on the highest possible dose of inhibitors, diuretics, anti-arrhythmics and pain medication, and his tongue is turning blue.'

'Blue?'

The vet opened Scout's mouth. His gums and tongue were mottled a sickly bluish-grey. 'Scout's lungs are filled with fluid. His heart can't pump enough blood to his body tissues.'

'Isn't there something more you can do for him?'

'Yes,' said Dr Talbot. 'You know there is. He's suffering, Kim. It's time.'

She looked at the terrier, panting and wheezing on the table, and saw him as if for the first time. His breath coming ragged and slow, each one a burden.

'I suppose it is.' Kim tried to imagine life without Scout – without his wise brown eyes, his cold nose against her hand in the morning, his warm presence on the bed at night. And, most terrifying of all, losing the living link he formed to Connor. Connor had loved this dog for as long as Kim had known him. He'd stroked the same wiry head that she was stroking now. He'd walked with him, played with him, missed him. If Scout died, an important piece of Connor would die too. A piece she wasn't ready to let go of, though it had been two years now; two years of the empty space in her bed and a heart that hurt, physically hurt, each day.

Tears stung her eyes. Kim tried to blink them back as she patted Scout's head but it was no use. She dissolved into a sea of weeping, great shuddering sobs wracking her frame. Scout trained worried eyes on her. . 'I want to be with him when . . . '

Dr Talbot shook his head. 'Normally I encourage owners to stay, but you're distraught. Scout is picking up on your fears. It would be best if you let me take care of it.'

Kim tried to compose herself with little success. She ruffled Scout's greying ears one last time, horrified that her weakness had made his last moments harder. 'Goodbye, old mate.' She backed from the room before the tears welled up again, catching one last glimpse of him: Scout trying to stand before Dr Talbot closed the door.

She turned to find all eyes in the waiting room upon her. The vet nurse came out from behind her desk and put a consoling arm on Kim's back. 'At least he won't suffer anymore.'

The waiting clients sensed the truth and held their own pets tighter. The room was stiff with tragedy. Time stretched. Seconds felt like hours.

Eventually Dr Talbot came out and nodded to Kim. 'All done.' Said without emphasis, like he'd put the bin out or made a cup of tea. And with that he called his next patient.

Kim could hear her own heartbeat. No, this couldn't be. The moment was too ordinary. The sun still streamed through the window as it had done before, the clock still ticked on the wall. 'Would you like to take Scout home?' asked the nurse gently. Kim gazed around, her eyes unfocussed. 'Or we could organise it all for you – arrange a cremation and ring when the ashes are ready for collection?'

'Would you?'

'Of course.'

Kim fumbled for her wallet and the nurse shook her head. 'We'll send an account. The ashes come back in a lovely little urn, for you to keep at home, or scatter somewhere special.'

Somewhere special. A scene came to mind: rolling hills and forest ridges. Connor throwing sticks into Cedar Creek for Scout to fetch.

She hadn't been back to Journey's End since Connor died. She'd go there to scatter Scout's ashes, something she'd wanted to do for Connor. But there had been his family to consider, and they'd interred his remains instead at a local cemetery, central to all. The ceremony had brought no comfort, no closure. How could it? Connor had died on some lonely road, a world away, and now she was leaving him in another unfamiliar place. A place that had held no significance for either of them. It still troubled her.

Taking Scout there would help to put things right, ease the feeling that she'd let her husband down. Then she would put the place on the market and try to move on. For the sake of Jake and Abbey. For the sake of herself. But in the same breath, a soft strangled cry escaped her lips. A painful wave of missing Connor crashed down on her, as powerful as on that first day of knowing. She doubted her decision the moment she'd made it. She would try, she really would, but how could a paralysed person be expected to move?

CHAPTER 2

Kim picked up the fruit bowl and tipped the oranges into the overflowing ice box. One of them slipped from her grasp and rolled away. She cursed softly under her breath, then crawled under the table to fetch it. A grubby pair of jeans walked past, and she heard the fridge door open.

'Jake, for the last time – go get your stuff.'

'Where's all the food gone?'

She stood up. Her son was wearing his sulky face. It seemed like he was always wearing his sulky face. Twelve going on fifteen. For the millionth time she was struck by how much he looked like Connor. The same chiselled lips, presently set in a stubborn line. The same high forehead and square chin. The same dazzling blue eyes. Sometimes the resemblance was unbearable. Jake's fair hair curled about the collar of his polo shirt. When had she last taken him to have it cut? She couldn't remember.

'I'm not going,' said Jake. 'I can stay with Stu.'

'Stuart and Grace have gone to their grandparents for the holidays.'

'Why couldn't I go with them?'

Kim added the wayward orange to the ice box. 'Don't be ridiculous. They're not your family.'

'I'll be bored stupid,' he said. 'I bet there's not even any internet.'

'You can live without your iPad for a few days.'

'No,' said Jake. 'I can't. I'm not going.' He slammed the fridge door and slouched from the room.

Should she go after him? What was the use? He wouldn't listen. She started hauling bags out to the car.

Since his father's death, Jake had grown defiant, sullen and quick to anger. The school counsellor said he was still grieving, still missing his dad, as if that was some brilliant insight. Kim rubbed her eyes. Of course he missed his father. But how to help him when she was half-frozen herself? The school had suggested putting Jake on medication, but she'd resisted. It seemed like an admission of defeat. Maybe this trip was what they needed. Laying Scout's ashes to rest, painful as it would be, could provide the closure that neither of them had been able to find.

Kim took a deep breath and resorted to her last-ditch, fail-safe way to budge Jake from his room. She unplugged the modem and swiftly hid it in the tea-towel drawer. An angry shout came down the hall. 'Mum, I know that's you.'

Abbey came in with an armload of soft toys. Seven years old now. A shy girl with golden curls, upturned nose, freckled cheeks – and some mysterious quality that hinted at secret understandings. Sometimes it was hard to believe she'd given birth to this baffling child. Kim braced against the familiar ache that thought always brought, the pain of Connor not knowing his daughter.

Abbey dumped the toys on the floor and tried to stuff them into an open suitcase.

Kim picked up Percy the poodle and stroked his threadbare wool. Abbey prised him from her mother's hands. Kim picked up Raggedy Ann instead. 'How about just taking this one?'

Abbey's eyes widened, and she snatched the ragdoll back. 'Mum, I can't choose.' She went back to cramming toys into bags.

Kim assessed how much room the mountain of stuffed animals

would take up in a car that was already packed full. 'Okay, but they'll have to sit in the back with you.'

'You said I could start out in the front, and then swap with Jake halfway. You promised.'

Kim couldn't remember. Since losing Scout, she lived each day in a kind of fog.

Jake marched in, carrying his bag. That, at least, was something. 'You said *I* could start in the front.' He pulled a face at Abbey. 'Mum, tell her . . .'

Kim waved her hands like startled birds. 'I don't know.' For all she knew they were both right. Too often she simply agreed without thinking. Wanting to avoid arguments. *Parenting through guilt*, Pam, her psychologist, called it. She was right about that. Kim did feel guilty that her children would grow up without their father. No amount of talk could change that.

Kim had stopped attending the weekly consultations organised by the Defence Force. They were too painful, and they didn't help. Pam couldn't understand. She hadn't lost her husband. 'I thought time was supposed to heal all wounds,' Kim had said during that last session. 'I'm more lost now than ever.'

Pam had fixed her with a long, thoughtful look. 'It's not time that heals wounds, Kim, it's what you do with that time. You can't move on unless you want to.'

'Moving on feels like forgetting Connor,' she'd said. 'And I'm not going to do that.'

The kids began a yelling match. 'I'm not sitting in the back with all those stupid toys.' Jake shouldered his bag and headed for the car.

'Mum,' said Abbey, 'stop him.'

Kim ventured out to the driveway, shielding her eyes from the blinding sun. It was unusually hot for an October morning. Haze shimmered over the concrete and baking bitumen beyond. The doors of their old blue station wagon were open, with Jake already in the front seat. He was chewing gum and listening to his iPod through headphones. Time to go before he changed his mind or cooked in the heat.

Kim went into the lounge room, where a small urn stood on the mantelpiece. It had a smooth silver lid with a paw-print design. All that was left of Scout. How could that be? She still didn't understand how a dog or a person could simply be gone. Here one moment, and a pile of ash the next.

At least she knew what had happened to Scout, the details of his death. It was different with Connor. He'd died so far way, in a land unimaginably strange, unimaginably hostile. She had only the sketchiest details – an ambush along some remote track. Kim held the little urn to her heart and closed her eyes. Connor would want Scout to return to Journey's End. It felt good that she could do something for him again.

CHAPTER 3

It was a long drive to Journey's End. Longer than she remembered, and the afternoon sun already hung low in the sky. They'd done the last two-hour stretch without a break. Abbey woke up in the back. 'Are we there yet?'

'No.'

'Are we nearly there?'

Kim negotiated a particularly hair-raising hairpin bend and wished she knew how to answer Abbey's question. The truth was they were lost. She hadn't been to the farm for ages, and back then Connor had done the driving. The GPS was useless. It kept sending her down no-through roads or suggesting she slam into soaring embankments or drive over cliffs. She hadn't thought to bring a map, and her phone had lost reception.

'I need to go to the toilet,' said Abbey.

Hard to hear her over the engine. It was running rough. 'You'll have to wait,' said Kim. The infuriatingly calm GPS voice was giving directions again. *In five kilometres turn left into Bangalow Road.* Maybe this time the turn-off would be where it was supposed to be.

Abbey tapped Kim on the shoulder. 'I can't wait.'

A red light lit up on the dashboard. Darn it, what did that mean? Kim was no mechanic and the car was overdue for a service.

There weren't many places wide enough to pull off the narrow gravel road. At last she found the entrance to a rough track and stopped the car. To their left, tree ferns rose up the sheer hillside. To their right, the ground plunged away to a forested valley. At least it gave them a chance to stretch their legs.

Abbey pouted. 'I need a proper toilet.'

'Sorry. You'll have to go behind a tree.'

So much cooler here, the burning Sydney streets far behind them. Abbey mooched off and Kim trailed after her. This was rainforest. Buttressed trunks towered into the blue, dominating the canopy. Broad leaves and matted limbs meshed overhead, hiding the sun. Black booyong. Scatterings of brush box and tallowwood. And, look, a silver quandong with masses of iridescent blue berries. They hung in colourful contrast to the fresh green foliage and crimson older leaves. Kim turned seed-collector, scouring the forest floor for clusters of fallen fruit.

Abbey emerged from behind a pepper bush, and examined the berries. 'Those are pretty. Can you eat them?'

'They're not poisonous, but I don't know how edible they are.' Kim took a nibble and pulled a face. 'No. Let's take them home as souvenirs.'

When they got back, Kim caught her breath. Jake wasn't alone. He was out of the car and a man stood beside him, hat in hand. Mid-thirties. Tall, very tall, with penetrating, coffee-coloured eyes and a dark complexion. A threadbare T-shirt showed off his powerful build, and a swathe of jet hair fell over his forehead. A scar ran down one cheek. He looked a little wild.

'You are having trouble?' he asked. 'With your car?'

His voice was deep and low, with a foreign inflection she didn't recognise. She wasn't good with accents. Kim moved between Jake and the stranger. 'No, we just stopped to . . . to collect these.' She held out the berries.

His eyes flicked from the fruit to her face with unsettling swiftness. 'They are sour. Better to leave them for the bats and bower birds.'

Jake looked up. 'Bats?' It was the first time he'd shown an interest in anything all day.

'Flying foxes,' said the stranger. 'They have babies at this time of year, and are hungry.'

'Baby bats?' said Abbey. 'They sound cute. Can you show me?' She reached for the stranger's hand.

Kim snatched her daughter away as alarm swept over her. 'We need to get going.' She put a protective arm around Abbey's shoulder. 'Kids, get in the car.' Kim climbed behind the wheel and wound down the window. 'Jake, I said get in.' He shrugged and for once did as he was told.

The car turned over, once, twice, then stalled. She tried again. It shuddered and shook. She switched off the engine and sighed. What did that light on the dash mean? She fumbled in the glove box for the manual.

The stranger appeared at the window and Kim's hands gripped the wheel tighter. 'Your radiator is leaking,' he said. 'You must not drive.'

They all climbed from the car. He pointed to where a slimy green fluid was pooling on the ground.

'Can you fix it?' asked Jake.

'Yes, at least for now. Give me your chewing gum.'

Jake grinned, and fished the gum from his mouth.

'Yuck,' said Abbey, but seemed fascinated just the same.

The man popped the hood without asking. Kim wanted to say *thanks, but no thanks*, and ring the auto club. She tried her phone again, moving around, seeking reception. When she stood in the middle of the road, one bar lit up. Hastily she dialled the NRMA. 'Hello?' The call dropped out.

Kim stood very still, mindful of her surroundings. A breeze sprang up, tossing the treetops. The canopy came alive with its swishing murmur. A crow's mournful *ark ark aaaaarrrrk* sounded in the distance. She tried her phone again. Nothing.

'Mum?' called Jake. 'Come and look at this. He's found a hole.'

Kim hurried back to the car, trying to put her misgivings about the stranger aside. Without his help, they weren't going anywhere.

The man emerged from under the bonnet and straightened. Strength showed in the curve of his spine and the set of his shoulders. He fixed her with dark, unreadable eyes. 'Do you have far to go?'

'No.' She was unwilling to be specific. 'Not far.'

The man dropped the hood and wiped his hands on his jeans. 'That should hold you. I'll fetch some water.' He walked down the track and was swallowed by forest. Ferns by the side of the road shivered and shook, as if something lurked there. No, it must be the wind. Kim tried to pull herself together, but questions crowded her mind. Just where did he expect to collect water from? And what was he doing out here anyway?

Ten minutes later, the man returned with a jerry can and filled the radiator. 'Try it now.' She turned the key. The engine sputtered, then roared to life. 'I've left the cap loose so the gum won't blow out,' he said. 'It needs a proper repair.'

'Is there a mechanic in Tingo?'

'Old Charlie, but he charges a fortune. You'd be better off going to Wingham.'

'Wingham,' said Kim. 'Right, thank you. I was wondering . . . do you know Bangalow Road?'

'You and your family – you are perhaps lost?'

'No,' she said. 'I just thought we would have reached the turn-off by now.'

'It's easy to lose your bearings in these mountains,' he said. 'You don't have far to go. It's next on your left.'

Thank goodness. She could find her way from the turn-off. Kim managed a smile as the kids piled into the car. They wound down their windows and leaned out to wave goodbye. A howling sounded from the forest.

'What's that?' asked Jake.

'Just the wind in the trees,' said Kim, unconvinced.

'That man was nice, wasn't he?' said Abbey. 'And so clever. To fix the car with Jake's chewing gum like that.'

'Yes,' said Kim. 'Very clever.' She sped up, anxious to put some distance between them and the man and the howling forest. *In two kilometres turn left into Bangalow Road.* Not far now. She took the corner too fast, wheels skidding on gravel. That stand of lilly pilly on the left looked familiar. Finally she knew where she was.

Five minutes later they turned into a rutted driveway, marked by a milk-can letterbox and a fading sign hanging precariously on a tree. You could hardly read the words – *Journey's End.*

'Is this it?' asked Jake.

'Don't you remember? You've been here before.'

'That was years ago. How old was I?'

Years ago. Really? It didn't seem so long since they'd spent that last summer holiday here: when Jake was nine, and their future bright, and their family still intact.

The wind almost blew her off her feet as she got out to open the gate. It lay off its hinges and Kim struggled to drag it aside. She reached up to touch the sign, to trace the bleached words with a fore-finger. The slight pressure was too much for the weathered nails. They tore from the bark and the heavy board fell, catching her shoulder on the way down. She cried out. The last time she'd seen that sign, Connor had painted it with shiny black letters, and they'd all trooped down together to hang it up. Now it lay broken in the dust at her feet.

Kim propped the sign up against the tree trunk and climbed back in the car. Please let it start. Why hadn't she left it running? The motor turned over first time. She wrestled with the wheel, struggling to keep the car on course between the washaways and potholes. Across the little bridge over Cedar Creek, then tackling the steep track to the homestead.

'Look.' Jake pointed as a wallaby broke from the scrub and bounded ahead of them. They followed it all the way up to the house, where it doubled back, leaped a sagging wire-netting fence and took off past the dam.

The car shuddered to a halt behind the woodshed. She'd forgotten how ramshackle the place was. Long ago, Journey's End had been a forestry work camp and some historic logging relics lay on the hill behind the house. A rusting, wheeled log-skidder, a dilapidated steam traction engine and what was left of a horse-drawn grader. Rainforest, creeping ever closer to the house, would one day swallow them up. The yard was littered with stuff Connor had thought might come in useful: pipes, wire netting, bricks. More wallabies dashed away from behind a rusting engine block overgrown with blackberries. Weeds were everywhere.

Kim stared at the farmhouse. It looked different from how she remembered: smaller, older. Paint flaked from the weatherboards. A loose piece of roofing iron swayed and rattled alarmingly. Why could nothing stay the same? Houses, marriages, lives, loves – they all fell apart in the end. The wind moaned in the trees and she suddenly wanted to turn around and drive back to Sydney.

'Are we there yet?' asked Abbey.

'Yes.' Kim put on a brave voice. 'We're there.'

Nine o'clock. Kids finally asleep, and the gale had passed. Kim put on a coat, and took her coffee and candle outside where a fat pink moon was rising over the forest. She ran her hand along the rough trunk of an old firewheel tree that shaded the verandah. Thankful that it, at least, hadn't changed. Moonlight though its leaves cast hypnotic shadows on the wall. She saw pictures in the shapes. Here a dog. There a heart.

The evening had gone passably well. Abbey disapproved of the toilet, which was out the back door, beside the dilapidated bathroom-cum-laundry. It required some intensive de-spidering before she consented to use it, and she was disbelieving when Kim flushed it with a bucket of wriggler-filled water from the corrugated-iron tank. The gas and power hadn't been reconnected as promised and without electricity their pump didn't work. Abbey soon got over it. She loved putting the little house in order. Helping to cook pasta for dinner on the ancient wood stove. Making up the dusty beds. 'It's like a giant cubby,' she said, setting placemats for her soft toys at the big table Connor had made that first year from a slab of blue gum. They ate by candle light.

Jake came out of his mood once he discovered the stove and fireplace. Nights were cold in the mountains, even in late spring. He appointed himself master of the flames and did a great job of keeping the wood up, using a tomahawk he found in the shed. This was a surprise. Kim couldn't remember the last time he'd been helpful. The tomahawk went to bed with him. Was twelve old enough to use an axe, albeit a small one? She didn't know. It would be different if Connor was here to teach him.

Connor. She'd grown used to being without him in most places, but never here. This was a new loss. His gumboots still stood alongside her own in the little kitchen, his raincoat on the hook behind the door, his books on the shelves in the hall. How dare they still be here when he wasn't? The air was thick with missing him. Kim swallowed and closed her eyes as grief swelled and built.

A boobook began its soft calling, somewhere in the gloom. The rhythmic *mo-poke, mo-poke* was oddly comforting. She tried to shut out her pain and focus instead on the nocturnal bush sounds. The hooting owl was joined by crickets, a choir of frogs from the dam, a possum's territorial growl. The night was alive. She took a deep steadying breath. A breeze sprang from nowhere, bearing the fragrant scent of eucalyptus. It began to rain. Chilly air caressed her skin and gradually her pain ebbed away.

The candle had burned low when Kim finally went inside. She put a log on the dying fire. It burst back to life and she warmed her cold hands. Dancing flames lit up the room, reflecting on the small urn containing Scout's ashes. Tomorrow she'd find that special place for him.

Kim yawned and headed down the hall. She peeped into Jake's room. He lay sound asleep, with the tomahawk taking up half the bed. She stole in and put it on the floor. Pale hair fell across his face. She swept it back and kissed his forehead, before creeping down the hall to her daughter's room. Abbey was awake. The little girl sat on the old chest beneath the window, hair luminous with moonshine. A line of soft toy animals was perched along the sill.

'Goodness me,' said Kim. 'It's so late. Why aren't you asleep, my darling?'

The girl turned to face her, eyes alight in the soft glow. 'My teddies are talking to the bush animals.'

Kim guided her back to bed and tucked her in. 'Now lie down. Your teddies need to get some sleep, and so do you.' One by one she placed the toys at the end of Abbey's bed until there was no more room.

'What about Percy?'

'He can be our watchdog.' Kim set him back on the sill. She pulled the wide curtains half-shut, revealing a small mural next to the window.

Abbey sat up. 'It's Scout . . . and Percy.' So it was, Kim had forgotten. Abbey couldn't have been more than two when Connor drew a picture of Scout on the wall to keep her company at night. When Kim had protested he'd said, 'It's our place. We can do what we like.'

Our place. Each time they came after that, he added to the picture. A river bank. A tree. A koala in the tree. A pretty waterfall cascading down rocks. Then colour – mellow shades of brown and green, with splashes of blue. Abbey got Percy for her third birthday and Connor drew a poodle on the wall beside Scout. He was a talented artist.

Kim slipped into bed beside her daughter, listening to the soothing patter of rain on the tin roof. Abbey yawned and snuggled close, nestling her head on Kim's arm. The shadow of the toy poodle, silhouetted against the window, looked uncannily real. As Kim dozed off, an eerie howling sounded from the forest. She held her daughter tighter.

'Don't be frightened, Mummy,' Abbey murmured without opening her eyes. 'That's Percy's friends, saying goodnight.'

CHAPTER 4

Kim woke to find Abbey braiding her hair. 'Mum, stay still.' The little girl bit her bottom lip in concentration. Tangles of golden pillow-mussed ringlets framed her face. She looked like an angel in the soft morning light. 'What were those noises coming from under the floor last night?'

'I think we must be sharing the house with a wombat,' said Kim.

'Can we call it Mothball, like the one in the book?'

It seemed like yesterday that Abbey was perched on Connor's knee, listening to him read *Diary Of A Wombat*. Kim closed her eyes. Life was divided firmly into two parts – before and after Connor's death. She referenced each memory this way. Trouble was, the after-Connor ones were multiplying in an untidy jumble, while the precious *before* memories remained finite and frozen in time.

'Can we go exploring?' asked Abbey.

'After lunch,' said Kim. 'A man's coming this morning to talk about selling the house.'

'I don't want to sell it,' said Abbey. 'Neither does Percy.' She jumped up and took the toy poodle from the windowsill. 'We want to live here with Mothball, and get a pony, and grow carrots.'

'Live here?' asked Kim in astonishment. 'What about the outside bathroom and the spiders in the toilet? What about school and your friends?' Abbey shrugged and ran from the room in her pyjamas.

Kim sank back on the pillow. In daylight, Connor's absence wasn't so overwhelming. She'd slept unusually well in spite of the wombat. Bad dreams, so often her night-time companions, had not found her here. She stretched. What was the estate agent's name again? Stan? No – Ben. Ben Steele. He'd be there at ten. She got up and made a face as she caught sight of herself in the wardrobe mirror. Wearing yesterday's clothes and with a crooked crown of unfinished plaits. She'd better tidy herself up but, first, coffee. What time was it anyway? She went into the kitchen and looked at her phone. Dead. Oh well, it couldn't be too late. She never slept in.

Kim checked there was water in the kettle and put it on the stove. Dead. Great. She went outside and took in a lungful of pure mountain air. It was a glorious morning, ringing with bellbirds. Curious wallabies watched her from the overgrown paddock below the dam. A shy half-grown joey dived for its mother's pouch, gangly legs and tail jutting out at crazy angles. Above the trees an eagle traced lazy loops in the sky. The sound of an axe on wood echoed round the hills. Jake must have been up at the crack of dawn. Abbey appeared from nowhere, and together they followed the noise down to the shed.

Jake and his trusty tomahawk were attacking a little log with gusto. 'Yes!' he cried, proudly glancing at his mother. She applauded as the timber fell in half. Jake punched the air in triumph and started on another log. Hard to believe this was the same boy who would barely leave his computer games back in Sydney.

'Can we light the fire?' he asked.

'In the stove – yes,' she said. 'How else will I get my coffee? But not in the fireplace. We'll do that tonight.'

An approaching thrum sounded on the road below, grew quiet then loud again. Clouds of white corellas burst from the treetops as a red land cruiser made its way up the track. Kim combed her hair with her fingers. She would have liked a coffee first. Darn the estate agent for being so early.

The car bumped to a halt beside the shed. A tall, well-built man emerged, dressed in immaculate cricket whites, with thick fair hair tapering neatly to his collar, and a wide, friendly smile. He extended his hand. 'Ben Steele, from Steele & Son, Estate Agents.'

Kim stepped back, a little shaken. Ben Steele bore a disturbing resemblance to her late husband. It wasn't so much the shape of his face – too narrow for Connor's. But the likeness was there in his bright blue eyes, the set of his mouth, the jut of his chin. It was there in his square shoulders and loose-limbed walk.

Jake took a swing at a new log. He dropped the tomahawk as it bounced off the hardwood, barely missing his leg.

'Watch it, mate.' Ben strode forward and picked up the little axe. He wet his forefinger and ran it down the blade. 'Blunt as Old Nick.'

'That's good,' said Kim.

'It might sound odd, but a blunt axe is more dangerous than a sharp one,' said Ben. 'A honed blade bites into the wood and stays there. A blunt one glances off. What's your name, son?'

'Jake.'

'You hit someone with a tomahawk, Jake, even by accident, even if nobody's badly hurt, you don't deserve to own one.' He spun it in the air, deftly caught it, then ran his hand down the handle.

'What are you doing?' asked Jake.

'Testing the wedge is fixed in tight and the haft isn't cracked.' He swung it in mid-air and gave an approving nod. 'Once it's sharpened, you'll have yourself a handy little axe. That's an old blade, though. It needs looking after. Rust-proof the head by coating it in some oil after you use it. And whatever you do, never leave it in the rain.'

Jake was hanging on Ben's every word and nodding furiously. Kim was surprised he wasn't taking notes. Her son was clearly hungry for male mentoring, and she felt a surge of gratitude towards this man; this Connor look-alike – at once familiar and strange.

'Are you going to play cricket after this?' asked Jake.

'Sure am.'

'What are you?'

'Fast bowler-slash-wicketkeeper.'

'I played cricket last year,' said Jake. 'I wanted a turn at wicket keeping, but the coach said I need to learn to concentrate more.'

'Got to listen to your coach,' said Ben. 'Do you bat? bowl?'

'I'm practising to be a spinner, but I'm not very good yet. I never get a go. I'm always put way out in the field. It really bugs me, but my coach says I'm too slow. That a batsman has time to make a sandwich while he waits for the ball.'

'That's a mongrel thing to say,' said Ben. 'Maybe you shouldn't listen to him after all.' He bowled an imaginary ball with easy grace, his arm strong and steady.

'Don't want to play again this year if I never get a turn.' Jake picked up a stone and bowled it. 'It's not fair. I love cricket.'

Jake loved cricket? It was the first she'd heard of it. In fact, this whole conversation had taken her by surprise. Kim hadn't paid much attention last year when Jake joined Stuart's cricket team. Daisy always took the boys and dropped them home. To be honest, she'd thought it was just a phase. She thought Stuart had talked Jake into it and her son was a reluctant recruit. Aussie Rules was the only sport for Connor. She'd assumed Jake would follow suit. Even though he'd told her the game reminded him too much of his dad. Even though he wouldn't even watch it on TV.

'Pity you don't play for Tingo, champ. We're on the lookout for a spinner. I could guarantee you plenty of match practice.' He gave the tomahawk a final twirl and handed it back.

'You don't think Jake's too young to use that?' asked Kim.

'No way,' said Ben. 'How old are you, champ? Eleven? Twelve?'

'Just turned twelve.'

'I was chopping wood for my whole family at eight.' Ben managed to keep a straight face. 'But you need someone to teach you how to do it right. How about your dad?'

Jake turned his back and took a swing at a log.

Kim touched Ben's tanned forearm and took him aside. 'I'm . . . I'm a widow.' It was her standard response when people asked about her husband, and was usually effective in silencing further questions. This time it didn't work.

Ben glanced up to where Abbey was making daisy chains and bouquets of waratahs. 'That's a tough break,' he said. 'Must be hard, trying to raise two kids by yourself. How long … I mean … when did you lose him?'

Kim wasn't used to talking about it. But instead of being annoyed at Ben's audacity, she found herself opening up. 'Connor died two years ago. And yes, it is hard without him. Sometimes it's impossible.'

Kim saw admiration, not sympathy on Ben's face. A refreshing change. 'If there's anything I can do to help, just ask,' he said.

With a final chop Jake split the little log and held up one half to show Ben. 'You look a bit like my dad,' he said. 'Doesn't he, Mum?'

Kim felt her cheeks flame.

'Great work, champ.' Ben gave Jake the thumbs up. 'Now, down to business.' He turned back to Kim. 'Is there vehicle access to the back blocks?'

'A few tracks,' she said. 'They're pretty overgrown. Too rough for my car, even when it's running properly, which it isn't. But yours would manage.'

'Can I come?' asked Jake.

Abbey ran over. 'And me?'

Ben opened the back door of the twin cab. 'Hop in, kids.' He turned to Kim with a grin. There was that touch of Connor again, the slightly crooked mouth, the boyish charm. She found it impossible not to smile back.

It was a grand tour. Surprising, to see how swiftly nature was reclaiming the land. Clumps of wattle, tea-tree and eucalyptus saplings had sprung up all through the unstocked pasture. Weeds too. Camphor laurel, lantana and privet. Wallabies and a mob of forester kangaroos bounded away from the car. 'Cheeky buggers,' said Ben. 'What a waste of good grass.'

'Look,' said Kim. Three horses stood atop a hill to their right. Proud heads raised, still as statues. Dark figures framed by blue sky.

Kim held her breath, captivated by the sight. In a blink they were gone. Had she imagined them?

'Brumbies,' said Ben. 'They must have crossed out of the park. That's what happens when you let a run go wild. It's a magnet for every pest about.'

They followed the winding track uphill along the property's western boundary, pitching and sliding into the worst ruts. Lush weed-free pastures stretched beyond the boundary fence, a stark contrast to the neglected, overgrown paddocks of Journey's End. 'My place,' said Ben, gesturing to it. 'Granite Hills. We're neighbours.'

They left the paddocks behind them, and started up a steep timbered ridge. She'd forgotten how magnificent these forests truly were. Towering stands of tallowwood and blue gum gave way to subtropical rainforest as they climbed. A profusion of tree ferns and bangalow palms. The broad, buttressed trunks of yellow carabeen, red cedar and black booyong – giants that had never felt the axe-man's bite. Elkhorns and bird's nest ferns graced the upper branches. Kim exhaled. What a privilege to see part of the rare Gondwanan rain-forests of eastern Australia that had remained unchanged for millions of years.

It took half an hour to reach the northern boundary, where Kim's property joined Tarringtops National Park. Ben stopped the car and they got out to admire the view. Journey's End stretched out before them. The valley's broad green axis. Winding Cedar Creek, which threaded through the little township of Tingo after leaving her land. The fingers of forest reaching out from the foothills.

'That's our house,' said Kim

Abbey stood on tiptoe for a better view. 'It looks so small.'

'What about over there?' Jake pointed to the east, where slopes of emerald green lay dotted with cottonwool sheep. 'Is that ours too?'

Ben shook his head. 'That's She-Oak Springs. Belongs to a friend of mine, Geoff Masters, your neighbour on the other side. He runs fine wool merinos and a few coloured sheep to keep his wife happy. Top little property. Shows how good this land can be when you look after it.' Kim didn't miss the mild censure in his voice. 'Come on,' said Ben. 'Let's have a look at that creek frontage.'

Afterwards, she and Ben stood on the verandah watching Jake tempt a friendly blue-tongue lizard with bits of ripe banana. Abbey ran after some rabbits. They vanished under a pile of rusty corrugated iron in what was once the garden. The only plants still flourishing were the waratahs, spectacular in a profusion of showy red blooms.

Ben gestured towards the forested hillside, topped by a sky of brilliant blue. Then south to where the creek meandered between blue gums. 'That's a view to die for. Buyers will love it.' He picked at the flaking paint of the verandah rail. 'But I have to be frank, Kim, there's a hell of a lot needs doing.'

'I want to sell Journey's End as is,' she said. 'I'm flexible on price.'

Ben fixed her with his unsettling blue eyes. 'You need to fix this house up, or knock it down. It won't sell *as is* in this market. And as for the land, I could hardly give it away. Your paddocks need new fences. They're thick with regrowth, overrun with rabbits and roos. The place needs a lot of work before it would sell as a grazing run.' Kim's face fell and Ben's expression softened. 'Nice timber, though, and plenty of it: blackbutt, tallowwood, blue gum. Hard to find old stands of quality wood these days – outside of parks that is. It'd be worth a lot to the right contractor.'

Kim shook her head. 'Those forests are why we bought the land in the first place. There's a conservation covenant on Journey's End.'

He frowned. 'That'll drag down the value. Could you remove it maybe?'

'I don't want to remove it.'

Ben whistled through his teeth. 'So, we're looking at the tree change market. You'll still have to spend a few bucks to bring the house up to scratch. But you'll never get top dollar from that sort of buyer.'

'It doesn't matter,' said Kim.

'That's not something I hear very often.' Ben looked as if he hoped she might take the words back.

'Who would I get to fix up the house?' asked Kim. 'I don't know anybody in Tingo.'

'I can help you there.' Ben's smile returned, wide and warm. He certainly was handsome, distractingly so. Or was it just the resemblance to Connor? 'There's a handyman down the road who can turn his hand to anything. Reliable bloke, too. I'll see if he can drop round tomorrow.' Ben got in his car, opened the window and waved to Jake. 'Maybe I'll swing by and sharpen that tomahawk for you.'

Abbey, who was hiding behind her as Ben left, said, 'Jake says that man looks like Daddy. Does he, Mum?'

Kim studied her daughter's upturned face. The freckles dusting her cheeks and the bridge of her nose. The blue eyes, as intense and unfathomable as a Siamese cat. She wrapped her arms around the girl's slim shoulders. 'Yes, I think he does a bit.'

A furrow appeared in Abbey's baby-smooth brow. 'I can't remember enough of Daddy to tell.'

Kim bit her lip. It was these little heartbreaks that kept her sorrow alive. She put on a smile she did not feel. 'Let's go inside and have some lunch. Maybe the power's back on by now.'

They were in luck. Kim made rounds of toasted cheese. She tried to make banana bread, using flour and sugar she found in some old metal canisters. It flopped in the middle, and she couldn't tell if it was the fault of the ancient oven, or the past-their-use-by-date ingredients. The kids ate it anyway.

Kim couldn't put it off any longer, so they took Scout's ashes down to the creek. It had been Jake's idea to scatter them there where the dog had loved to play. They stood on the little bridge, gazing down at a stream so clear they might have counted the pebbles of its bed.

Waratahs and bangalow palms graced the banks, trailing their leaves in the swift-running water. Ancient tree ferns reached for the sky, their soft fronds casting a cool, dappled shade.

The children looked at her expectantly. Even Jake was solemn. Kim wet her lips and thought of some last words. She fingered the smooth metal jar, traced its raised paw-print design, unscrewed the lid a fraction. Her heart thudded against her ribs. That whooshing noise wasn't the creek, but the sound of blood rushing in her ears. Her fingers froze.

Seconds ticked by in silence, except for the chiming of bellbirds. The moment yawned wide. She couldn't do it, wasn't ready to let go. Wasn't ready to cast Scout away and all that would go with him. Abbey shifted impatiently. 'Mum?' Her quiet question broke the spell.

'Let's not do this now,' said Kim. 'Let's go look at the neighbour's sheep instead.' She tucked the little urn safely into her pocket. She could breathe again. A look passed between the children as they moved off the bridge and down the path leading to the eastern boundary.

A flock of newly-shorn sheep grazed in the paddock next door, stretched out in a line beside a bush gully. Stout pine posts strung with taut barbed wire and ring-lock mesh divided the two properties – a stark contrast to Kim's own sagging fences.

'Lambs,' said Abbey.

A pair of snowy, newborn twins played chasey around their mother. A movement in the trees caught Kim's eye. She shielded her eyes from the sun and peered closer. There, a big red fox was crouching in the shadows, ears pricked towards the flock. She stood statue-still, mouth dry, hypnotised by the sinister tableau before her.

'Look,' cried Jake. A big, unshorn sheep was charging for the gully where the predator waited in ambush. The fox turned and fled while the flock crowded together for protection, keeping the youngest lambs at their centre.

'What a brave sheep,' said Kim, breathing a sigh of relief on behalf of the lambs.

'It's not a sheep,' said Jake. 'Look at its tail.'

Kim took a second look. Jake was right – not a sheep at all, but a dog. A large shaggy white dog with a noble head, small high-set ears and a plumed tail. It turned to face them and began a low steady barking. She looked around for its owner. Apart from the flock, the paddock was empty. Kim steered the children away from the fence. The dog seemed satisfied and retreated to where the sheep stood, bunched and alert, in the middle of the paddock. He merged into the flock.

'He may not be a sheep,' said Kim. 'But he seems to think he's one.'

'He's like *Lambert the Sheepish Lion*.' Abbey began to sing the song from the old Disney cartoon about a baby lion that was mistakenly left with a flock by the stork. Lambert lived his life thinking he was a sheep. He only found his courage when forced to defend the flock from a wolf. The show had always been one of Abbey's favourites.

They started back towards the house. 'Can we get a dog?' asked Jake.

A knot tightened in her stomach. It was a fair question, but one she'd been dreading. Scout had died more than two weeks ago. It was astonishing that Jake hadn't asked her before now. Kim took a steadying breath, and tried to see the situation from his point of view. They'd had a pet before, so why not again? And from a practical viewpoint, the love and companionship of a loyal dog could make a big difference to Jake: distract him from his anger, make him more responsible, get him out of his bedroom.

Kim walked faster, making Abbey trot to keep up. Jake ran on ahead, then swung around to face her, blocking her path. 'Well?'

She cringed at the demanding edge to his voice. Normally she gave in when she heard it in order to avoid the inevitable argument. 'We'll see.'

Jake's eyes blazed. 'I'm not stupid. *We'll see* is code for no.'

Abbey moved to stand beside him, set her chin in a determined line and stuck out her lower lip. Kim backed up a step. She had a mutiny on her hands.

'Jake's right,' said Abbey. '*We'll see* does mean no. Why can't we have a dog, Mum?'

What could she tell them? That replacing the little border terrier would feel like a betrayal, not only of Scout but of Connor as well? Saying no wasn't a good answer, or even a rational one. But emotionally, it was the only answer she could give.

'We'll talk about it later.' Kim pushed past the children and hurried down the path, close to tears. Pity about the handyman coming in the morning. Otherwise she'd leave tonight.

When they got back to the house, a woman was standing on the verandah. Mid-thirties, with dark, curly hair escaping from a rubber band, spaniel eyes and a round face. She wore an oversize T-shirt, track pants and a melancholy air. A fluffy white pup sat beside her, a mini-version of the dog that had defended the sheep. This one looked endearingly like a lamb and was, of course, a magnet for the children. They made a beeline for the puppy, stroking its fleecy coat and starting up an energetic game of tag. Kim silently cursed their visitor for her terrible timing.

The woman stepped forward and offered her hand. 'Melanie Masters, your neighbour on the right. Call me Mel.' Kim introduced herself. 'Nice to see a friendly face,' said Mel. 'It gets a bit lonely out here.'

Kim forced a smile. She wasn't accustomed to making small talk, didn't want to. What was the point? They wouldn't be neighbours for long. And these days she shunned company, apart from Daisy. Even Daisy was sometimes too much, urging her to join the committee at Jake's cricket club, telling her to get out more, to meet people. It wasn't going to happen. Daisy was her best friend, and even she didn't understand. How could she? Daisy hadn't lost her husband, her best friend, her lover. Daisy hadn't lost her life. Kim shifted her feet uneasily. She wished the rest of the world could move on without her, and leave her alone with her memories.

Mel didn't take the hint and showed no sign of going. She seemed content to watch the children play with her dog. 'That's a nice puppy,' Kim said at last, for the awkward silence had lasted too long even for her. 'I don't recognise the breed.'

'Snow is a maremma,' said Mel. 'A livestock guardian dog. She's supposed to be living with my coloured flock 24/7, bonding with them. That's how you train them. But since Geoff moved out . . . ' Her voice faltered. 'Geoff's my husband – he left me last month. Found somebody else.' Her tone was almost apologetic. Snow ran to Mel, and put a paw on her leg. 'Let's just say, I need Snow at the moment more than the sheep do.'

Kim smoothed her hair. Had she heard right? Had Mel really confided such a private thing to a stranger? It was beyond belief. Kim had moved after Connor died, and her new neighbours barely knew her name let alone anything about her personal life. By contrast, Mel seemed to be wearing her pain on the outside of her skin.

Mel hugged her pup, and Kim felt a tinge of envy. She'd had that same comfort with Scout not too long ago and craved it again. She stroked the silver urn in her pocket, and said, 'Dogs are good friends.'

Mel brightened. 'Ain't that the truth.' She let Snow run back to Abbey and Jake and circled her toe around a knot in the veranda floor. 'I was wondering . . . ' Her sentence slid to a halt.

'Yes?'

'I was wondering . . . Would you and your children like to come to my place for dinner? Your little girl might like to see the new lambs.'

'Sorry,' said Kim, 'but I've got a lot to do.'

'I want to,' piped Abbey. 'I want to see the lambs.'

Kim tried to ignore her. 'You see, Melanie . . . Mel . . . I only came here to put Journey's End on the market. We're going back to Sydney tomorrow.'

'Oh . . . of course, that's fine.' Kim recognised Mel's determined cheeriness all too well. She was an expert at faking happiness herself. 'I'll leave you to it then.' She whistled her dog and headed off.

Abbey gave up pouting and took up pleading, and jumping up and down. 'Please, Mummy,' she chanted. 'Please, please, please, please . . .'

'Ow, mind my toes. Are you aiming for them?'

'Please, please, please . . .' Her voice grew louder.

Mel heard and turned around, sensing an ally. 'I've got some orphan joeys that the kids might like to see as well. And a baby wombat.' She looked as hopeful as Abbey.

'Okay,' Kim told Abbey. 'You win.'

Roses grew in an ornamental garden by the porch steps at She-Oak Springs. How lovely. Kim had a soft spot for roses. She stopped to smell a large bloom with a swirling centre of ruffled scarlet.

This homestead was quite a contrast to her own rundown farmhouse. Both buildings shared wraparound verandahs. But where Kim's had a rusty roof with leaky nail-holes, Mel's was elegant and bullnosed, with wrought-iron lacework in the corners. The house boasted a fresh coat of paint – federation green with glossy cream accents around solid cedar windows. What was left of the paintwork at Journey's End was flaking away. Kim admired the luxuriant grapevine draping the portico, the broad bird-feeding tables festooned with quarrelsome king parrots, the colourful leadlight surrounds at the front door. She-Oak Springs was beautiful, no doubt about it. But the house was surrounded by sheep paddocks, and didn't have the million-dollar views of Journey's End. Kim was suddenly looking forward to meeting Ben's handyman in the morning. How might her old farmhouse scrub up given the same sort of tender loving care? She put her nose to another flower.

Abbey pulled at Kim's shorts and gave a delighted squeal. A little wombat had emerged from under the deck and was barrelling for them at startling speed.

'Look out.' Mel tried to block its path. The baby dodged and barged into Kim's legs with the force of a mini-bulldozer, knocking her off her feet. She fell sideways into the garden, getting raked by thorns on the way down and grazing her bare knees.

Mel rushed over with a horrified expression on her face. 'Mind Geraldine.'

Geraldine? Who the heck was Geraldine? Kim reached out and took hold of a log to help her up. Something about it didn't feel right – its bark too soft, almost leathery. Help, it was moving. Kim screamed as the log rose on three legs and transformed into a two metre goanna. It hissed loudly and whipped her with its snake-like tail, before racing for the house and scaling a verandah post.

'Cool,' yelled Jake. He ran over and stood beaming up at the indignant reptile.

Mel helped Kim to her feet. 'Sorry. Geraldine was hit by a car and lost a leg. She's become quite a pet, and lives in the rose garden.'

Snow ran to the front door and let herself in by opening the flywire with her teeth. 'Come on,' said Mel. 'Your kids might like to help with the lunchtime feeds.'

They found themselves in a large laundry, where half-a-dozen hessian potato sacks were strung up along the windowsill like Christmas stockings. Mel put her hand into one of them, and drew out a tiny, barely-furred joey. The look of delight on Abbey's face was something to see. 'Can I pat it?' She stroked the baby's dove-grey neck and kissed its muzzle. A little pink tongue emerged to lick her nose. She squealed with delight and Kim smiled. She wanted to pat the joey too.

Before she could refuse, Mel dumped the cute bundle into her arms. 'Hold her while I warm the milk.' She hurried off to the kitchen without waiting for an answer. Kim stroked the joey's skin, soft as fine silk. Enchanting. She cuddled it close and let it suck her finger. The pouch it lay in was made from a printed cotton T-shirt, with the neck and armholes neatly double-stitched. The joey wriggled about, first its tail and then its legs jutting out. Kim wrapped the youngster tighter. Mel returned carrying a baby's bottle, fitted with an odd extended teat. She retrieved the joey from Kim and offered it the milk. Once it was feeding well, she let Abbey have a turn.

Jake moved closer and closer to the joey, until he could feign indifference no more. 'Where's its mother?'

'She was shot,' said Mel. 'Local farmers have permits to cull roos. There's a heap of them round, too many. If shooters find pouch young, they sometimes bring them to me.'

When the bottle was empty, Mel gently prised it from Abbey's grasp, washed the joey with a damp sponge, and put it back in its pouch. She took a long look at Jake, as if she was sizing him up. 'Will you help me feed the next one? He's a lot bigger and stronger. I could do with a hand.'

Jake sprang forward with the sort of physical enthusiasm that Kim had forgotten he was capable of. For a moment she barely recognised him. Her son suddenly looked older than twelve. He was at that mysterious 'twixt-and-tween' age – not quite a child but not yet a youth. She wished Connor was there to see it.

They all pitched in with the feedings. 'Thanks,' said Mel when they were done. 'The kids usually help out, but they're away at the moment.'

'What kids?' asked Jake.

'My daughter Nikki is eight.' Mel ran a sink of hot soapy water and dunked the empty bottles and teats in to soak. 'And I have a son, Todd. He's eleven. They're with . . . their father for the weekend.' A shadow crossed her face. 'Such a shame you guys aren't going to stay on here in Tingo. Our little primary school could really use some new enrolments.' She dried her hands. 'Though I guess Jake might be starting high school next year?'

Jake glared at his mother and thumped from the room. Abbey ran after him, while Mel looked bewildered. 'You've hit on a sore point,' said Kim. 'They want him to repeat grade six. Ever since his father died, Jake's really struggled at school.' Kim twisted her wedding ring, surprised she'd shared this with a complete stranger. Yet something about Mel's own candour had made it easy.

'And I had the gall to complain about Geoff leaving,' said Mel. 'That's nothing compared to what you've been through.'

Kim turned swiftly to the window to hide her face. Yes, Mel's grief was different, very different. But at least she understood about loss – loss of a friend, a lover, a partner for life. 'I suppose, in the end, we're both alone,' she said, managing to look at Mel again. 'However it happened.'

Mel's sad brown eyes grew soft. 'It will be hard for Jake, staying down. Kids can be cruel.'

Kim swallowed. This was her fear. Jake had been told that he risked repeating if his behaviour didn't improve. He'd laughed it off. If anything, the warnings seemed to make him act out more. Jake didn't do his homework, picked fights with other kids, skipped classes, talked back to teachers. There'd been countless conferences, discipline programs, second chances. Nothing had worked.

That final dreadful meeting with Kate Cornish at Sturt Street was burned into Kim's brain. 'Your son is not emotionally ready for secondary school.' The principal's tone was calm and soothing, as though she was speaking to a small child. Kim could hear Jake rampaging around, outside in the corridor. 'He has difficulty taking instruction. He also lacks social skills and the building blocks needed for the more challenging academic tasks that lie ahead. I recommend that he repeats Year 6 here at Campbelltown, and that we put in some extra supports to help him achieve success.'

Kim had felt lost. She couldn't disagree with the substance of the principal's remarks. Since Connor died, Jake had regressed. He *was* emotionally immature. He found friendships increasingly difficult and struggled with schoolwork. But what about the harm repeating the year might do to his already shaky self-esteem? What would Connor say? She wasn't sure, couldn't channel him anymore. In the end she'd agreed.

Jake met the news with an eye roll and a shrug. 'Whatever.' But it was a feigned indifference. Kim had known how much he was hurting.

Abbey came back in and grabbed Kim's hand. 'The lambs. Come see the lambs.'

Kim followed her daughter around the back of the house to a sheltered straw-filled pen. Four lambs were playing king-of-the castle on bales of hay. A greenhouse stood next to the pen. Kim tried to peer through the opaque shade cloth.

'I grow local plants,' said Mel. 'For a bit of a hobby. Geoff thinks it's a waste of time.'

'Can I take a look?'

Timber trestle tables laden with neat rows of tube-stock stood on either side of a narrow centre aisle. Overhead trellises supported a poly-pipe watering system. A great degree of care had gone into the set-up and Kim felt a little jealous. This was a version of what she might have had if Connor had lived. Kim brushed the feathery foliage of a batch of seedlings with the back of her hand. 'Red cedar,' she said. 'And are those black booyong?'

Mel shrugged. 'No idea. Half the time I don't know what seeds I'm growing. I just like doing it.'

Kim's fingertips wandered lovingly over the young plants. 'Yes, definitely black booyong. They're starting to get their adult palm-like foliage. See these seven leaflets with the wavy edges? That's very distinctive.'

Mel cocked an eyebrow. 'How do you know so much?'

'I'm head of horticulture at Campbelltown College,' said Kim. 'Run-of-the-mill stuff, I'm afraid. Basic botany, soil science, pests and diseases – that sort of thing.' She picked up an exquisite little tamarind seedling. 'But my real interest is in rainforest plants like these.' She brushed her hair back from her face. Talking about her passion didn't come naturally. So few people were interested. 'I'm also good at growing vegetables. I know more about sooty mould and mealy bugs than a person should.'

'Plants are all trial and error for me,' said Mel.

'Well, you're doing something right. Your garden's gorgeous, and these seedlings all look healthy.'

'Really?' Mel beamed with pride. 'I have pests that I bet you won't find in Sydney, though.'

'Try me.'

'Wallabies,' said Mel. 'Rabbits. Kangaroos that have been forced from the lowlands by land clearing. Geoff shoots deer up near the national park, and wild goats. We've never had goats before. Whenever I plant my trees out, they get nibbled down in no time.'

'You're right,' said Kim with a smile. 'We don't get deer in Campbelltown.'

'I tried putting up tree guards, but they didn't work. Maybe they weren't tall enough.' Mel picked up a tube and inspected the seedling. 'How am I going to protect you?'

'Mum,' called Abbey. 'Look at this.'

They went outside and found Abbey sitting cross-legged in the straw, with a lamb lying either side of her. It was a sweet scene. Kim snapped a pic with her phone, something she hardly ever did these days. It seemed wrong somehow to take family photos, knowing Connor could never be in them again.

'Come on, kids,' said Kim. 'Time to go.'

'What about dinner?' asked Mel.

'No thanks.' Kim wanted to get away. She-Oak Springs reminded her far too much of her failed dream. 'I've got to get back.'

'How about tomorrow? My kids come home in the morning. They'd love to meet Jake and Abbey.'

'I'm afraid we're heading back to Sydney tomorrow.'

'Oh ... Well, it's been great meeting you.'

'You too.' Kim wasn't just being polite. She didn't often feel a connection with anyone these days.

It took some time to coax the children away from Snow. They set off home along the overgrown track. Kim felt for the silver urn in her pocket, turning it over in her fingers. Abbey slipped her hand into her mother's and gave it a squeeze. 'We are getting our own dog, Mum. He just hasn't arrived yet.'

CHAPTER 5

Kim planned to clean the back verandah when she got home, or maybe clear out the kitchen cupboards, but she didn't have the heart for it. Picking through the leftovers of her failed future was hardly an enticing prospect. The kids got stuck into building a cubby with scrap timber. Jake seemed to have forgotten all about his iPad. She watched them for a while then wandered back inside. Perhaps packing up the hall bookcase would be easier. She found cardboard boxes in the narrow spare room Connor had built by enclosing a section of verandah.

The shelves were stocked with an odd assortment of things, mainly collected from the second-hand shop in Wingham, with rainy days in mind. Old *Grass Roots* and *Earth Garden* magazines. Picture books. Well-thumbed James Patterson thrillers. She selected one with a tattered cover, inhaling its sweet musty smell. *Truth or Die*, one of Connor's favourites. She sighed and willed herself to put it in the box.

Half-a-dozen rural romances came next. *Jillaroo*, *The Bark Cutters*, *Brumby's Run* ... She'd always loved getting lost in these outback tales, imagining that she and Connor might live out their own thrilling country love story, right here at Journey's End.

And look, her botany books. Cronin's *Australian Rainforest Plants*. A booklet on local field management from Parks and Wildlife. Webb's *Rare and Threatened Flora of the Great Eastern Escarpment*. Kim took it off the shelf and flipped through it. The page opened at a full colour plate of a strappy glossy-green plant, perched high on a cliff face. Four nodding flower spikes bore dozens of delicate white blooms with dramatic crimson hearts – the lovely ravine orchid. No record existed of this endangered plant at Tingo, but computer modelling predicted it as 'likely to occur'. Well, if it was here, she'd never find it now.

Kim gave up on her task, too restless to continue, and took the book into the kitchen. Propping it open on the bench against the cracked splashback tiles, she settled into some serious cleaning.

Later that evening, after a tea of sausages in bread, Jake and Abbey were yawning and ready for bed. They'd had more exercise in one day here than in a week back in Sydney. She soon followed them, daring her own bedroom this time. She read a book until her eyes were tired, but sleep would not come.

Kim felt more on her own than usual, lying rigid in the dark. She and loneliness were constant companions. Sometimes it sat in her stomach like undigested food, or crept through her bones. Sometimes it faded to a mere ache, but it never left her entirely, and tonight was as bad as it got. She listened for the wombat to begin work on the foundations, or the scrabble of a possum in the roof. Nothing. She would even have welcomed the strange howling from the forest, any evidence that she wasn't utterly alone. But all was silent. Not even the rhythmic call of a boobook owl to keep her company.

She got up, felt her way to the hall cupboard and found Connor's old Driza-Bone coat. Wrapped in its musty embrace, she went back to bed and waited for morning. The moon had almost completed its journey across the sky before sleep found her.

Kim woke from a fitful sleep, having survived another first without Connor. The last time she'd slept in this old brass bed, it had been filled with him – with them. Filled with joy and sex and plans for the future. She craved his warmth, could still feel his breath on her neck, his weight on her body, his lips on her spine.

Kim set her mind to rewind, searching, snatching at each precious scrap of memory linked to this space: the two of them talking long into the night, sharing a bottle of wine by candlelight, the urgent press of his mouth, the fit of her breast in his hand. Her mind burned with bittersweet recollections. She was running out of first-without-Connor moments. One day they'd be all gone.

The bed's dull knobs shone cold in the morning light. Kim shivered, pulled the blankets tight around her and tried to guess the time. The room's diffuse brightness offered no clue. Still wearing Connor's coat, she threw back the covers, stood at the window and opened the curtains. No wonder she couldn't judge the hour. The world was blank, swathed in a fog that had crept down the mountain overnight.

Kim padded down the hall in bare feet, checking on the children as she passed their doors. Both fast asleep. She went to the kitchen, turned on the little bar heater and warmed her toes. The hot water system should have heated up by now. How she'd love a shower. But when she turned on the hot tap at the sink, the water was icy. She let it run and run. No use. She checked the meter box. Something had tripped the hot water switch. She turned it back on, but her shower was history. It was an off-peak system. There wouldn't be any warm water until tomorrow morning, when they'd be long gone.

Kim put on two pairs of socks, and her old gumboots, after giving them a shake to dislodge spiders. She made a face at her reflection in the window. What a sight; snarled hair, a way-too-big man's coat over fleecy pink pyjamas, and rubber boots. One of the beauties of country living, of course, was that nobody for miles would see or care.

She opened the door and froze. Ben stood there, hand raised, ready to knock. He was making a habit of catching her off guard. No cricket whites today. Instead he wore jeans and a smoky-blue shirt that matched his eyes. She must have looked ridiculous, and his handsome face creased into a grin. 'Love the fashion. Is that what you call *Sydney chic?*' For the second time in twenty-four hours he made the blood rush to her cheeks, but this time she was too surprised to hide it.

'I thought you were coming at nine o'clock?'

'It *is* nine o'clock. I brought Taj with me, as promised.'

Taj? A familiar figure stepped out of the mist. 'We've already met,' he said.

Kim nodded an acknowledgement. 'Taj helped me when I ran into some car trouble on our first day here.'

'Did he just?' Ben raised an eyebrow. 'Told you he was handy. Now, are you going to ask us in? I'd kill for a coffee.'

She stepped aside and the men walked through to the kitchen.

Ben pointed out a mould patch on the ceiling, while she filled the kettle. Such a contrast between the two of them, one as dark as the other was fair. Taj's unruly black hair fell across his forehead. Ben's hair was the colour of wheat and just long enough to be fashionably tousled. Taj's skin had darkened in the sun to a warm shade of mahogany. Ben was tanned too, but his fair complexion had turned pale coppery-brown. Taj's expression was guarded, his eyes watchful like a hawk. Ben's features were as open and sunny as a summer's day. Taj seemed shy, while Ben wore his self-confidence like a badge.

Yet they shared some things. Both roughly her age, around thirty. Tall, well-built and, Kim couldn't help but notice, both heart-stoppingly handsome in their own way. She hadn't seen it when she'd first met Taj. She'd been too unsure of him. But here in the comfort and security of her own kitchen, she made a more objective assessment. The open-necked work shirt, taut over a muscled torso, revealing the tip of a tattoo on his chest. She couldn't make it out. The sun-beaten column of his neck. The square, stubbled jaw and even features. Very attractive, if you liked the tall, dark and brooding type. The scar down his cheek still bothered her. So did his eyes, which were the all-seeing kind, peering from under a broad-brimmed hat that had seen better days. Ben was more her type.

This last thought left Kim a little shocked. Whatever had possessed her? Comparing two men physically, thinking about them in that way? It was an insult to Connor's memory. 'Coffee's ready.'

Ben splashed extra milk in his cup and added a heaped teaspoon of sugar. Taj took his strong and black. 'I'll show you what needs doing, mate. Just the bare minimum – a cosmetic job. And get rid of that old kitchen table. It takes up too much space; makes the room look smaller than it is.'

Get rid of the table? Connor had made that. Its solid, rustic beauty made the kitchen the heart of their home. This wasn't quite how she'd imagined things would work. 'I'm prepared to pay to get the house properly sale-ready,' she said. 'I want to pass it on in good condition.'

Ben flashed her a smile that would level mountains. 'We'll do basic repairs, of course, and give it a new coat of paint. But we don't want to overcapitalise. No point throwing good money after bad.'

'When my husband inherited this place from his grandfather, it was a dream come true for us both. I love Journey's End, and want to do it justice.'

Taj stepped forward and fixed his unsettling brown eyes on her. 'Why are you selling then?'

Kim bristled. It was none of his business. She weighed up her words, and settled on a tried and true phrase guaranteed to close down the conversation. 'My husband is dead.' She waited for the customary response – the embarrassment, the lowered eyes, the muttered apology.

Taj's gaze remained unflinching. 'But you are not.'

Kim swallowed something jagged.

'Steady on, mate,' said Ben. 'Mind your manners.'

Kim walked out. How dare he? She went to her room and sat on the bed for a few minutes, until her breath came evenly again. Then she dressed in jumper and jeans, pulled a comb through her hair, and went back to the kitchen.

Abbey had appeared there in her absence. She sat at the table in her puppy-dog nightie, clutching Percy. 'Look, Mum. The man from the forest.'

Taj was staring at Abbey. Did she really want this insolent stranger to have the run of her house while she was gone?

Ben stepped forward, took gentle hold of Kim's elbow and steered her into the lounge room. 'Cut Taj a bit of slack. He doesn't speak the language too well. Probably didn't even know he was being rude.'

Really? He seemed perfectly fluent in English to her.

'I'm telling you, tradesmen are hard to come by in Tingo, and you won't find a better one.' Kim wasn't convinced. 'I can finish the walk-through on my own if you like?' said Ben.

For a moment she was tempted. 'No, I'll come.'

She followed them from room to room while Ben indicated what work he wanted done. Taj jotted notes down in an exercise book. Abbey trailed after them, clutching Percy. 'That loose floorboard needs a nail,' said Ben. 'This window doesn't shut properly . . . that wardrobe could use new doorknobs . . . replace those splashback tiles, and the chipped ones in the bathroom.' Ben had the quick-fix down pat. He made decisions without hesitation. He was sure of himself. Connor had been like that – a take-charge kind of guy. Even when on deployment, he'd tried hard to stay connected and look after things at home. He'd managed their finances, made sure the cars and house were well-maintained. He even planned their holidays long-distance. Kim loved that about him. It made her feel cared for, cherished. She'd floundered in the last two years, unsure in her new role as the family's unilateral decision-maker.

A welcome relief then, leaving the arrangements to Ben, letting somebody else take responsibility. A way to un-invest in the farm-house, to make the sale easier, both practically and emotionally.

Ben moved to the hall. 'Strip the wallpaper.'

Why? It wasn't old, and it had taken forever to find the design – a stunning botanical print. She and Connor had hung it together that last summer.

'Replace the back door. A cheap hollow-core one will do.'

What was wrong with the door? True, it was crudely made with stout hardwood planks and an old-fashioned lever-handle latch. You could see daylight through the cracks. Yet it had character, it was solid and safe. An intruder would take all day to kick that thing in. Most importantly, Connor had recorded Abbey's and Jake's heights on it in lead pencil. Kim touched their names with her finger, and the smudged measuring marks as well, marvelling at how small the children had been a few short years ago. Abbey stood next to it to show how much she'd grown. Kim's heart melted. If that door went, it would go back to Sydney with her, along with the table. Heaven knows where she'd fit them in their little townhouse.

When Ben told Taj to paint over the mural in the bedroom, Abbey turned goggle-eyed in horror. She tugged at her mother's shirt.

'That painting stays.'

'Buyers want a blank canvas,' said Ben, examining the window frame.

'Well, they can't have one.'

He turned around, hands on hips, looking totally nonplussed. Taj's serious mouth curved into an amused smile. It softened his features, took some of the wildness away.

'Ben . . . I appreciate your help, but I want to go through the rest of the repairs with Taj myself.'

Jake ran in. His eyes lit up when he saw Ben. 'Did you win the match yesterday?'

'Sure did, champ.'

'Did you take any wickets?'

'I took the one that counted. Bowled their tail-ender out with a few runs to spare. Shame our juniors had to forfeit though. We couldn't round up a full side.'

'Mum,' said Jake, 'we should move here. We've already got a house. I could join the team to help them make up the numbers.'

His enthusiasm came as a surprise, considering how determined he'd been not to come in the first place. 'Have you forgotten there's no internet?' said Kim. 'How would you download your *Plants Versus Zombies* updates.'

Jake looked skyward and rolled his eyes. 'Mum . . . that's kid's stuff. I'm getting my tomahawk so Ben can sharpen it.' He raced from the room.

'Might as well go give the kid a hand then,' said Ben. 'If you're sure you don't need me here? Right, I'll leave you guys to it. But remember – a clean slate for the buyers, that's what you're after.'

Kim was beginning to resent these nameless buyers.

'Do you want me to paint this bedroom?' asked Taj.

Kim examined the mural on the wall more closely and saw things she'd never noticed before. A tiny kingfisher on a branch. A possum curled up in a tree hollow. A dingo above the waterfall, staring down at Scout and Percy.

'No, I want you to leave it like it is. And leave the wallpaper in the hall as well.'

'Yay,' said Abbey. 'That wallpaper's pretty. Do you like it, Taj?'

He went into the hall and took a look. 'I like it very much,' he said. 'Silver banksias are lovely flowers.'

It surprised Kim that he recognised them. They moved into the kitchen. 'The back door stays,' she said. 'I don't know about the curtains.'

Taj checked his notes. 'Ben said to take them down and put up a neutral blind.'

'I know,' said Kim. 'But this isn't Ben's house. It's mine. The curtains stay too.'

Taj bowed his head in that oddly formal way he had, a flicker of mirth behind his eyes. He picked up the botany book propped open on the bench. She carefully took it from him. 'That's a ravine orchid,' she said. 'I always hoped to find one here, but it never happened.'

'I have seen this plant,' said Taj.

Kim shook her head. 'You might mean the orange blossom orchid. It's similar and grows all up and down these eastern ranges.'

'It is this one, I'm sure.'

Curiosity got the better of her. 'Where?'

'Not far. I can show you.'

Abbey grabbed her hand. 'Come on, Mum. Let's go.'

Was this possible? Kim studied Taj's face, inscrutable behind a three-day growth. The odds were against it, and she didn't fancy traipsing around the bush on a wild-goose chase with this man. Her fingers released Abbey's. 'No,' she said. 'We have to head back to Sydney. When will you start on the repairs, Taj?'

'Not straightaway.'

'When exactly?'

Taj's expression was apologetic. 'I'm not sure – some weeks.'

Bloody hell. It meant waiting to put the place on the market. She wanted to get the emotional wrench over and done with. Ben came in as Taj was leaving.

'He can't start yet,' said Kim.

Ben shrugged. 'I never said he could. Tradies always have jobs on.'

'Can't we get somebody else?'

'Nobody as good as Taj.'

Jake ran in, brandishing the tomahawk, a devilish glint in his eye. 'Ben says it's sharp enough to shave with.'

'Just a figure of speech, champ. Don't you go trying.

'Take that thing outside,' said Kim.

Jake pointed a defiant chin at her. 'You can't make me.' She reached to take the tomahawk from him. He brandished it at her briefly then hid it behind his back.

Ben frowned and snapped his fingers. 'That's enough. Apologise to your mother.' Abbey ran outside. She hated arguments.

Jake seemed torn. He looked from Kim to Ben, and then back to Kim. 'I'm sorry.'

Ben nodded his satisfaction. 'Now do as you're told. Take the tomahawk outside.' Jake obeyed without a murmur. Kim threw Ben an admiring glance. How on earth had he managed that?

'He's a great kid,' said Ben. 'Anyway, better be off. I'll ring you when we're ready to get on with the business of selling.' He shook her hand, holding it a fraction longer than necessary, then strode out the door with a lanky grace. Kim drew back the curtains and watched his land cruiser reverse from its parking place by the woodshed, and make its way down the rutted driveway. Jake ran after it, waving. Kim stayed at the window long after the car had disappeared from sight.

'What's wrong, Mum?' Abbey waited a while for a response. 'I'm going to look for caterpillars,' she said at last, leaving Kim in peace.

Jake needed a strong male role model like Ben. Apart from Daisy's husband, Steve, he had nobody back in Sydney. No uncles. No male teachers, not once, all through primary school. Connor's father was dead and her own father wasn't good with Jake. He lost patience too easily and the two of them always ended up at loggerheads.

Kim's fingers found her wedding ring. Rubbing it wouldn't help. It wasn't Aladdin's lamp. She dug her nails into her palm. When was she going to stop wishing for the impossible? Connor was gone. He'd never be there for her or Jake again. Never be there for Abbey.

Kim turned and hurried to Abbey's bedroom, throwing things into the bag higgledy-piggledy, averting her eyes from the mural on the wall. What was the point of saving it? New owners would just paint over it anyway.

New owners.

She tried to imagine strangers in the room and couldn't. This house had been in Connor's family for generations. She choked back tears and went to pack up Jake's room. The guilt and grief were too much. She couldn't bear to be there a moment longer.

An hour later she was packed and ready to go. Grey clouds scudded across the face of the range. Rain was on its way. Abbey reluctantly climbed into the car, clutching Percy and wearing her grumpiest face.

'Where's Jake?'

Abbey shrugged and hugged Percy tighter.

Kim swore softly beneath her breath. 'I told him we were going ten minutes ago.' She slammed the car door behind her, headed for the woodshed. 'Time to go.'

'Not yet,' said Jake. 'I just want to chop this last log.'

'We don't need any more wood. We're going home.'

'Just wait, will you?'

'No.' She could feel her stress levels rising, along with her voice. 'I won't wait. We're going – now.'

'All right. You don't have to yell.' Jake left the log half-chopped and headed for the door.

'Leave the tomahawk,' said Kim. 'You're not taking that in the car.'

Jake grasped the handle with both hands. 'It's mine.'

'Put it down,' she said through clenched teeth.

'No.' Anger had flared in Jake's eyes, and he gripped the handle tighter. Kim knew the signs all too well. Often she would give in at this point, reluctant to provoke one of his rages. But this time was different. There was no way she was going to let that axe into the car and, anyway, she was sick to death of tiptoeing around her son's temper.

'Give me that.' She reached for the handle, but Jake jumped backwards and ran from the shed. Kim gave chase. 'Give it to me,' she screamed.

'Here, have it then!' Jake threw the tomahawk.

They both watched in horror as it sailed towards her, the moment slow in time, Kim's movements slow too – she couldn't seem to get out of the way. The blade caught the side of her left boot. Kim's foot buckled beneath her and she wound up on her bottom in the dirt.

Jake's face drained of all colour. 'I didn't mean for it to hit you.'

'What did you expect would happen?' Kim unlaced the boot and eased it off, then the sock. Thank goodness for the thick leather uppers – they'd sustained most of the damage. Blood seeped from a cut in her ankle. She pressed her sock against the wound to stem the flow.

Abbey came to see what was happening. 'Don't worry, sweetie,' Kim said. 'It looks much worse than it is.'

Abbey stared accusingly at Jake. 'Did you hurt Mummy?'

'It was an accident,' said Kim. Jake burst into tears. Kim couldn't remember the last time she'd seen him cry. 'Can one of you please get a spare pair of socks from my suitcase?'

Both children raced for the car. *Now they'll quarrel about who gets them.* Sure enough, raised voices sounded from the driveway. Next minute, Jake arrived with a ball of socks, closely followed by Abbey. She had socks too.

Kim pulled one on, then two more over the top of that. 'Help me up.' Jake and Abbey pulled her to her feet and supported her as she hobbled to the car. She slid behind the wheel.

'Can you drive?' asked Abbey.

'Course I can.' She waved her good leg out the door. 'Mr Right Foot to the rescue.' Abbey giggled. Even Jake managed the ghost of a smile. 'Okay, kids, hop in.'

It began to rain. Fat drops slid down the windscreen. Jake stared longingly towards the woodshed, where Kim's boot and the tomahawk lay discarded out in the open. Neither of them had forgotten Ben's instructions about looking after the blade, not letting it get wet. She took pity on Jake. 'Go on then, put it away.'

Jake ran to store the little axe in the woodshed. She supposed she should be grateful for small mercies. At least he wasn't insisting they bring it home with them anymore. Kim winced as she put some pressure on her injured foot. It hurt badly. Was this the sort of price she'd be paying in the future to win an argument with Jake? It was a terrifying prospect.

The rain grew heavier. Jake started back, head bowed into a strong gust of wind. Kim scanned the skies in all directions. From Tarringtops in the east, right across to the western plains, the sky had turned uniformly grey. The weather was closing in, as if trying to hold them.

Oh no, she'd forgotten about the radiator. Kim struggled from the car. On opening the bonnet, she was pleasantly surprised to find the radiator still full. 'Let's pray this car starts.'

'Don't worry,' said Abbey. 'It will. Taj fixed it.

'Only with chewing gum, darling. I'm not sure that will hold.'

'No, I mean after that. He started the car and poured some stuff in. He said it would save us having to go to that old crook Charlie.'

'When did this happen?'

'When you were saying goodbye to Ben. And look, he gave me a cicada case.'

Kim turned the ignition key and the engine purred to life. Yes, she was relieved that the car had started so easily, and that they wouldn't have to stop at some dodgy repair shop in the middle of nowhere. But it concerned her that Taj had taken it upon himself to fix the car without asking. And Abbey was far too friendly with a man they knew nothing about. Kim wished she'd asked Ben more about Taj: where he lived, where he'd come from, who he really was.

They bumped down the track in pouring rain, across the little bridge and out the crooked gate. She slowed down as they passed the impressive bluestone pillars and wrought-iron gates of She-Oak Springs. Mel would be up there, tending her little rainforest nursery like Kim herself once dreamed of doing. Should she drop in to say goodbye? What was the point? She'd never see Mel again. Ben could organise things from here on. Kim's ankle throbbed as she pressed down on the accelerator.

The kids were quiet during the drive into Wingham. Kim's head was aching now as well as her foot. She braved the rain and stopped at the main street chemist for some Panadol and a bandage. The pharmacist insisted on looking at her ankle. 'Go see a doctor,' he said, as he expertly cleaned and dressed the cut. 'You need a tetanus shot.'

'I will,' said Kim as she stood up. 'Just as soon as we get back to Sydney.'

'Sydney?' The pharmacist snorted, and gave the kids a bag of jelly beans each. 'I feel sorry for you then.' Kim thanked him and they all piled back in the car.

It was only when they reached the Pacific Highway south of Taree that Kim remembered. The tin containing Scout's ashes – she'd left it on the mantelpiece back at Journey's End.

CHAPTER 6

Kim glanced in the mirror as she towel-dried her hair. Every year it turned a darker shade of blonde. When Connor died she'd traded long locks for a no-fuss bob. She hadn't expected it to suit her, didn't really care either way, but now she quite liked it. Daisy said it showed off her cheekbones.

She dressed in jeans and polo shirt – her uniform for working at Campbelltown TAFE. The last week of November, and the term was almost at an end. Exams over, assignments in, and just a few students to see today. Thank heavens for that.

Since returning from Tingo, she couldn't settle back into her old life. She tried to forget about the little house in the mountains, but the harder she tried, the more firmly fixed it became in her memory. At night, scattered images crowded her mind: kaleidoscope visions of buttressed fig trees, soft leaves and bright flowers. Rare orchids. Rainforests of mottled trunks soaring to the sky, tangles of ancient creepers as thick as her arm, the views across the range.

In the morning she woke to traffic jams and smoggy city skylines. Old longings seeped in through the cracks of her life. She thought she'd become immune. She thought that tragedy and loss had destroyed those long ago dreams. There wasn't a way to restore Journey's End without Connor, yet still the idea of wilderness was taking hold - casting its vivid spell all over again. Life in Campbelltown seemed grey by comparison. Pale. Washed-out.

And then there was the growing problem of Jake and school. Word had somehow got out that he was staying down and the teasing and taunts had begun. He had a short fuse at the best of times, but things had never been as bad as this before. Hurt and humiliated, Jake was lashing out, getting into fights and walking out of class. He'd sworn at Miss Wilson when she tried to break up an argument, then kicked her so hard he'd bruised her shin. He should have been suspended.

Kim went into the kitchen, where the kids were eating breakfast. Jake was uncharacteristically quiet this morning, picking at a bowl of Weeties, idly chasing the flakes around the bowl with his spoon. He lowered his eyes and stayed silent whenever Kim tried to make conversation. She studied her son, his hanging head and slumped shoulders.

Abbey was staring now too. 'What's wrong with Jake?'

'Have you finished your breakfast, Abbey? Go get dressed now, sweetie.' When Abbey had gone Kim put an arm around Jake's shoulder. 'Talk to me, mate.'

He looked up with red-rimmed eyes. 'I can't do it anymore, Mum. I just can't.'

'Can't do what?'

'Go to school. I can't. I won't.'

Who could blame him? It broke her heart to see him so unhappy.

'They all start in on me, about how I'm stupid and not right in the head. Amber said my dad was better off dead than having a retard like me as a kid. I wanted to kill her. If Miss Wilson hadn't stopped me, I think I might have.' Now there was fear as well as sadness in his eyes. 'The worst thing is that they're right about me being mental. I get so mad, I can't think straight. I'm scared I'll hurt somebody. And it doesn't help that I'm sorry afterwards, does it? Not after I've done something really bad.' Tears welled in his eyes. 'What's wrong with me?'

Kim thought of the tomahawk in her boot and hugged him tighter.

Then she took his shoulders and turned him to face her. 'There's nothing wrong with you, absolutely nothing. But there's something very wrong with a girl who'd say such wicked things. Don't your friends stand up for you?'

'I don't have any friends.'

'What about Stuart?'

'He's different at school. Stu says the other guys won't be friends with him if he hangs out with me.' Jake must have heard Kim's sudden intake of breath. 'Don't blame Stuart. It's not his fault.'

Anger flared deep inside her. Jake might be troubled, but he was loyal. He'd never betray a friend like that. 'I'll go to see Kate Cornish,' said Kim. 'She'll put a stop to it.' The last bit of colour drained from Jake's face. He was probably right. Complaining to the principal might make things worse. According to her, Jake was the bully who made threats and started fights. It made no difference that he was provoked. A knot formed in her stomach. What should she do? What would Connor do?

'Don't worry.' Kim put on a happy mask. 'No school for you today.'

He gave a you've-just-saved-my-life sort of smile and squeezed her until she thought she'd break. 'Thanks, Mum, you're the best.'

The best, was she? Surely the best mother would have a plan that extended beyond a day off school. She weighed up her own options. Pulling a sickie would be a start. Leaving Jake at home alone in his present frame of mind did not seem like a good idea.

She went to her room and climbed into bed. It might make the lie more convincing. 'Graeme? It's Kim. I can't come in today.' She affected a loud cough. 'Some sort of lurgy. My guys are pretty much finished for the year anyway, but a few are coming in to pick up final assignments. They're on the desk in my office.' Another cough. 'Thanks Graeme.'

Kim fell back on her pillow and tried concentrating on the doona's geometric pattern. It was a modern design, but it lacked soul. Heck, the whole house lacked soul. She'd bought the contemporary town-house six months after Connor's death, and had sold or given away most of their things, even their bedding. As an attempt to move on, to forget, it hadn't worked. She longed for their old patchwork quilt to hide under.

A whoop came from the family room. Jake hadn't taken long to cheer up, but then kids were like that, weren't they? Today was sorted, and that's all that mattered. They couldn't see round corners, couldn't appreciate that dodging a problem inevitably made it ten times worse.

Another yell. Jake was playing RuneScape, losing himself in an imaginary world. A world no doubt more enticing than his real one right now. He loved the online role-playing game, and it was a safe enough pastime. No gratuitous violence or bad language. Not like his previous addiction – Medal of Honor. Jake had downloaded the first-person shooter game without her knowledge and begged her to let him keep it.

'Stuart has it. All my friends do.'

Kim rang Stuart's dad. 'It's tame enough,' said Steve. 'I'll come round and turn off the blood and bad language, if you like.' Blood and bad language? The settings were duly adjusted and she lost her lounge room whenever Jake was playing. Shooting, yelling and explosions, the sounds of war. She couldn't bear it, but she also couldn't bear the inevitable tantrums when she tried to confiscate the game. Jake's rages intimidated her. Kim had no stomach for the fight.

One night she heard him yell, 'Die, you damned Afghan pig!' and found her courage. The game was gone. Jake screamed and swore and threw things. He begged and cried and threatened to run away. It frightened Kim to see her son so out of control. But although she was shaking inside, she stood her ground. The storm finally abated, and now Jake had a new favourite game.

In RuneScape, players travelled through fantasy realms, meeting other avatars, battling monsters, going on quests. Jake's avatar was half-giant and half-dragon. A mighty wizard was his mentor and protector. Poor Jake. At least he had a father figure in the virtual universe.

She told herself that Jake's fixation with the online world was a positive thing. He could talk to hundreds of people his own age, make friends from all around the world. That was okay, wasn't it, even positive? Kim pulled the pillow over her head. Who was she kidding? It was Wednesday and Jake should be at school.

She rang Daisy. 'Can you pick Abbey up on your way to school? Jake's sick, and I'm not much better.'

There was a long pause before Daisy responded. 'Not sure . . . I'm running late.'

Kim couldn't keep the irritation from her voice. 'How much longer would it take you?'

Again, silence. 'I suppose so,' Daisy said at last. 'See you in ten.'

'Ready, Abbey?' Kim finished making a cheese sandwich. 'Daisy will be here in a minute.' At least somebody would be where they were meant to be today.

Jake's words echoed in her head. No friends at school, not even Stuart. Tween years were such an acutely self-conscious time. Kim thought back to what was important when she was in grade six – who sat next to who, who was popular and who wasn't, who went to whose house after school. These things were everything; friendships were everything and betrayal was utterly overwhelming. Stuart and Jake had been mates since grade one. How could Stu turn his back on a friend like that just because of a bit of peer pressure?

Abbey emerged from the hall with Percy under one arm. 'Mum, why doesn't Grace come round anymore?'

'What do you mean? Of course she does.'

Abbey shook her head. 'She's only come over once all this term.'

Kim opened her mouth to argue then closed it again. On reflection, Abbey was right. 'That's because you're always at her place.'

'But I want her to play with my toys. Can she come today?'

If Grace came, Stuart would want to come too, and Kim didn't feel like dealing with that boy right now. 'Not today. Maybe next week.'

Abbey pouted and positioned Percy on the kitchen windowsill, faced to look out of the glass. Since the trip to Journey's End she always did that when leaving the toy at home. Said he was listening for his bush friends, but was too far away to hear them. A knock came at the door.

'They're here,' squealed Abbey, dashing to open it.

'Morning munchkin,' said Daisy 'You ready?'

Kim packed the lunch box in her daughter's bag. Abbey grabbed it and ran to the car. Kim watched her, tight-lipped. She'd give anything to see Jake so enthusiastic to start his day. 'Thanks, Daisy. You're a life saver.'

'How about returning the favour?' Daisy tugged at her dark pony-tail, tightening the band. 'I've got an appointment across town this arvo. Could you pick up the kids after school for me?'

Kim squirmed inside. Could she really cope with Stuart being around, knowing how he'd hurt her son? 'Sorry, Daisy, but I feel like crap today.' She coughed half-heartedly, and wished she hadn't. It sounded fake, even to her. 'Jake's sick. I think we'd better leave it for another day.'

A loud elated cry sounded from the lounge room, followed by laughter. 'He doesn't sound sick to me.' Daisy frowned. 'If you don't want to have my kids, just say so.'

'Where did that come from?'

Daisy shrugged, then made an expansive gesture in the air with both hands. 'You hardly ever have Stuart or Grace round after school anymore. Today I ask a favour for the first time in ages, but appar-ently it's too much trouble to spend fifteen minutes picking them up.' Kim tried to butt in, but Daisy wouldn't have it. 'You expect me to do it for you, though, and I do, all the time. I'm happy to, because we're mates. We're supposed to be best mates, but you never want to go out with me, never want to come over. We don't talk on the phone like we used to. I've been waiting for you to bounce back, waiting for us to be proper friends again, but it never seems to happen. You have to admit, Kim, it's become a bit of a one-way street.'

Kim was stunned. Fourteen years of knowing Daisy, of her barely uttering a cross word – and now this extraordinary outburst. Was Daisy right? Had she really checked out on their friendship? As Daisy stood there, her hands stiff at her side, Kim pondered what she'd heard, each sentence burnt into her brain. Painful as it was, she knew that most of it was true. She *had* become self-absorbed, closed down, careless of Daisy's feelings. It was time to make amends.

But Daisy hadn't finished. 'It's not just me. You've cut yourself off from everybody. When was the last time you came to an army get-together? We had a family day last weekend, as I'm sure you know. Even if you didn't want to go, you could have made an effort for the kids' sake. They would have loved it. This depression of yours is affecting them, especially Jake. He's so angry and unpredictable. Even Stu is struggling to stay friends with him.'

Kim's nostrils flared. It was difficult to keep her voice low so that Jake wouldn't hear them. 'I think you'll find Stuart's given up on that struggle.'

'What do you mean?'

'I mean my son's on the outer with his classmates, and Stu doesn't want to risk being unpopular. So apparently he snubs Jake the moment they walk through the school gates. What sort of friend does that?'

Daisy's expression hardened. 'Jake's only got himself to blame.'

'So you knew about this?'

'It's not as black-and-white as you make it out. Stu feels caught in the middle. Is he supposed to be miserable the whole time and lose his other friends because Jake can't get on with anybody?' Daisy folded her arms across her chest. 'I know better than anyone what you've been through these past two years, Kim. Losing Connor. You had every right to be devastated, of course you did. But at some stage you have to start living again. If this was a hundred years ago, you'd be wearing mourning black until you were an old lady.'

Kim gripped the edge of the bench, her knuckles white. 'How dare you pretend to understand what I've been through – what I'm still going through. Did you lose your husband? Is there a bloody great hole in the middle of your life where Steve used to be? No, your life's just fine. So don't come round here lecturing me, telling me to get on with things. If I'm not good enough for you the way I am, and if Jake isn't good enough for Stu, then maybe you shouldn't bother coming round at all.'

Daisy's face paled and crumpled. Kim found herself putting things away: the bread, the cheese, the knife into the dishwasher. All automatically. She could feel her fingers shaking. Part of her felt justified in everything she'd said. Part of her felt how good it was to let some of the anger inside her out. Part of her wanted to apologise, to take back the hurtful words. But it was a moot point, because Daisy held up her hand. 'Suits me just fine. You won't see me again.'

Then Abbey and Grace came running in together, smiling and holding hands. 'Come on,' they chorused. 'We'll be late.'

Daisy turned and left without a word. Through the kitchen window, Kim watched her drive off past the row of townhouses that were all exactly the same and turn the corner. She was aware of each heartbeat. Aware of the blood in her body. Aware of her very skin. Shattered.

She reached for the reassuring memory of Connor's face, and for once, it wouldn't come. Since losing him, she'd pulled away from her family and most of her friends. She couldn't bear the veiled hope behind their sympathy, the expectation that one day soon she'd get over his death and move on. A sharp stab of anger left her bewildered and breathless. Anger at Connor for leaving her, for abandoning his children. For making her love him so much that she still felt firmly married this long after his death.

Daisy had been her rock, her anchor. The one person who understood grief was a wild and unpredictable beast that wouldn't be hurried. But now? Kim's throat grew tight. She couldn't take the words back, neither of them could. Her legs went weak. The last connection to her old world was slipping away.

Kim sank into a kitchen chair and buried her head in her hands. What to do? Teaching finished next week and the long, empty summer holidays stretched before her. Perhaps she could take the kids to her parent's place at Castle Hill. Kim could see it now. Her mother smiling, well-meaning, serving the vegetables for Sunday lunch. 'Have you been getting out much, Kimmy? I hate to see you moping around on your own the way you do.' Her taciturn father, carving the roast, roaring at Jake for some minor breach of table manners. Abbey, asking if Grace could visit and bake ginger cakes with Grandma. But Grace wouldn't come. Not unless she patched up this rift with Daisy. Could she do that? Could she apologise, say she didn't mean it, ask forgiveness?

Kim got up and marched around the kitchen, filled with a terrible restless energy. The trouble was, she did mean it, most of it anyway. Daisy hadn't lost her husband. She didn't understand what that felt like, how paralysing it was. And no matter how hard Daisy protested, no matter how much she wanted to blame Jake, Stuart's betrayal of his friend was inexcusable. The only thing Kim wanted to take back was the suggestion that Daisy should stay away, and that small concession wouldn't be enough to repair the friendship. Not nearly enough.

Kim wandered into the family room, Jake too deeply absorbed in his game to notice. She studied his profile, drank in each detail. The morning light gleaming on his curly cap of fair hair. His perfect mouth, so much like Connor's, pursed now in concentration. His stubborn chin. A wave of love welled up inside her and made it hard to draw breath. Jake. So young, so vulnerable. So many challenges ahead of him. How could she protect her beautiful boy? Her head started to throb. After coping here for two years, she couldn't cope a day longer.

Kim glanced at the mantelpiece, half-expecting to see the little jar containing Scout's ashes. But that jar was on another mantelpiece, on a peaceful mountainside, a world away from the smog and noise and misery of Sydney. And the answer came, clear as a clarion bell. Take a year's leave. Take the kids out of school. Pick up and move to Journey's End.

CHAPTER 7

Tingo was only an eight minute drive from Journey's End. According to the sign, it boasted an official population of 330, although someone had clumsily changed the 0 to a 3 with a paintbrush. Whether this was in her family's honour or not, Kim didn't know.

She was waiting with Jake and Abbey on a rough-hewn timber bench outside the historic schoolhouse. The entire township of Tingo was historic, every building, all five of them: the general store-cum-post office, school, garage, sports club and memorial hall. Picturesque Cedar Creek wound its way through the centre of town; a perennial water-course that rose in the Comboyne Plateau, eventually meeting the Manning River at Kilawarra, west of Wingham, eighty kilometres downstream.

The schoolhouse had gabled eaves and window boxes spilling pink petunias. It could easily have been the set for a period movie. Very different from the ugly concrete and glass box that was Sturt Street Primary. The children were quiet, a little apprehensive, especially Jake. Kim didn't press them for conversation. Even at her age there was something sobering about sitting outside a principal's office.

They'd arrived at Journey's End three days ago, station wagon piled high with stuff that seemed mainly to belong to the children. Toys, books, clothes, shoes, electronic games, cricket gear, bedding – and of course a mountain of stuffed animals. Bags of Kim's belongings still languished in the hall back in Sydney. She'd been unable to squash them into the overloaded car. No matter. The estate agent who was renting out their townhouse could send them on. The most important thing was for the kids to have what they needed to feel at home.

The move had gone surprisingly smoothly. Kim had informed Sturt Street that her children would not be at school for the rest of term. She hadn't expected any protests and didn't get any. On the contrary, Principal Cornish could barely conceal her delight at seeing the back of Jake. 'I'll draw up the transfer papers right away and have them sent through to the new school. I'm sure you're doing the right thing, Kim. It will be a chance for him to make a fresh start.'

Jake was keen too. Kim hadn't pulled any punches. He understood Journey's End didn't have an internet connection yet, so he'd be temporarily cut off from his RuneScape friends. He understood they'd need a landline installed for reliable phone reception, and a satellite dish before the television would work. The fact that Jake didn't mind was testament to how bad things really had become for him at Sturt Street. But she wasn't fooled. It would take more than a change of school to solve Jake's problems.

Abbey had been less enthusiastic. The prospect of losing Grace loomed large, but she was a willing child and obliging by nature. A mention of lambs and joeys was enough to convince her, though they hadn't paid a visit next door yet. Kim wasn't quite ready for Mel and her disarming honesty.

If the truth be told, she was finding the move harder than the kids. Tingo had seemed like such a good idea. A place to take stock, catch up on some sleep, reconnect with her children. Jake would have room to run. Little head-in-the-clouds Abbey might become more grounded. And they would experience the old-fashioned freedoms that sheltered city childhoods did not allow.

It was all very well to daydream about going bush, but the reality was confronting. Kim had never shared their Sydney townhouse with

Connor. At Journey's End it was different. He inhabited the walls. Sometimes it seemed that if she spun around quickly enough, she might catch sight of him. She'd tried to prepare herself, to caution her heart against his physical absence. Yet all too often the past and present collided, and she was swallowed anew by grief.

Each day she passed the bookshelves he'd built in the hallway. Each morning she used the kettle they'd found together in the op shop in Wingham. The second-hand sash window he'd fitted in the lounge room still jammed. The doggy-flap he'd fitted in the back door went unused. Every room, every stick of furniture, every corner reminded her of Connor, and she could not hide from what had happened.

Scout's ashes remained on the mantelpiece. She'd abandoned even the pretence of scattering them in the creek, feeling less ready now than she had been two months ago. It might bring closure, she told herself. Problem was, she didn't want to close down her old life. She wanted to wedge it open for as long as possible. Kim twisted her wedding ring.

'Look.' Jake pointed to the mountains. An eagle wheeled in high ever-widening spirals. It vanished from sight where the blue folds of the ranges met the blue of the sky. Kim closed her eyes. Somewhere a currawong called. The scent of native mint wafted on the breeze, and she felt suddenly lighter. If she was stuck with this endless grief, Tingo was the best place to bear it.

A voice sang out. 'Come in.'

They filed into the principal's airy office: colourful artwork, dangling sun-catchers, vases of bright flowers. A full-figured, big-bosomed woman with kind grey eyes rose from behind the desk. Kim liked her at once. 'I'm Jean O'Neill.' There was a hint of a Scottish lilt in her voice. 'You've no idea how excited we are for your family to be joining our little school next year.'

'That's very kind—' began Kim.

'Oh, I'm not being kind, dear. I'm being honest. Tingo is a *P six* school.'

'*P six?*'

'A school with twenty-five pupils or fewer. When our Year 6

students move to Wingham High next year, it leaves us perilously short of numbers.'

'How short?' asked Kim.

'The department prefers enrolments not to fall below ten students. And with your children, we'll reach that magical quota.'

'Ten students?' Kim shifted in her seat. She'd never heard of such a thing. Sturt Street had over four hundred.

Jean sensed her reservation. 'For new families, Tingo's low numbers can take some getting used to. But there are many advantages to our unique small-school experience. The beautiful rural setting, for starters. Opportunities to learn and mature in a caring, tolerant, positive environment.'

'So you have composite grades?'

'Small multi-age groups allow for more natural learning – teaching by stages, not ages. Students work at their own developmental level, rather than grade expectations. Children get the sort of personal attention that's impossible with larger classes, and they're encouraged to know each other as people, rather than, *You're in grade three and I'm in grade five, so I'm not playing with you.*'

'But being so small, do you receive enough funding? Do you have enough books and equipment?'

'Oh yes. If anything we're over-resourced. With so few students, each dollar goes a long way. Every child receives an iPad, and has access to their own computer.'

'How many teachers exactly does Tingo have?'

'Well, mainly it's just me,' said Jean. 'But the school has plenty of support. A local lady is helping the kids practice for the Christmas concert this morning. She's a retired music tutor. And we have fully-qualified sports, language and drama teachers, who come in on a part-time basis. This school has been the heart and soul of our community for one hundred and thirty years. We do expect parents to be closely involved in our programs, Kim. I assume that won't be a problem?'

'No problem at all. But just so you know, we only plan to stay for a year so Jake can repeat grade six without the baggage from his old school. When my teaching leave is over, we'll go back to Sydney.'

'Twelve months is a long time.' Jean raised a quizzical eyebrow. 'Perhaps we'll change your mind?'

Connor had gone to a small school at Port Macquarie on the north coast. He'd loved it there. It wasn't as small as this one, of course. Tingo Public School might well be the smallest school in Australia, yet something told her it might also be precisely what her son needed. It felt very good to be wanted for a change.

Jean turned to Jake. 'Delighted to meet you, young man.' She gave his hand a hearty shake. 'I hear you're a budding spin bowler. That's lucky for Tingo. The town's junior side could really use your help.' Was there the hint of a smile on Jake's face? 'Todd and Brent are particularly excited you'll be in their grade next year. Would you like to meet them once we're done here?' Jean's charm offensive had apparently worked, for Jake's smile widened into a shy grin.

'Todd is Melanie Master's boy and roughly the same age,' Jean said to Kim. 'She's your neighbour.'

'We've already met.'

'Splendid. Melanie has a girl too, Nikki, who can't wait to meet your daughter.' Jean turned her attention to Abbey. 'Your mother tells me you love animals. You'll be a big help next year with our new ducklings then.'

'Ducklings?'

'Next year is our *Year Of Sustainability*. We're raising a flock of Muscovy ducks to keep snails and weeds down in the orchard and vegie gardens. Every student will have their own duckling to care for.'

'I *love* ducklings,' squealed Abbey. Even Jake looked pleased.

Kim was impressed, and not only with the duck idea. Jean O'Neill had a knack for saying the right thing, and had won both kids over in record time. This was no mean feat, especially in Jake's case.

'Time for the tour.'

The school grounds were attractive, lovingly maintained and absurdly large for the few children being catered for. Murals adorned every spare wall: bright images of birds and balls and butterflies. Flowers bloomed along a maze of well-trodden paths, dividing play areas from the vegetable gardens and twin ovals. A life-size batsman with a baggy green hat, ready to swing, was sculpted from an old tree stump.

'Chickens.' Abbey ran over to where half-a-dozen red hens were basking in the sun.

'Come and meet our jack-of-all-trades,' said Jean. 'We couldn't do without him.'

A tall, broad-shouldered man on a stepladder was building what appeared to be a chook house. He swung his head as they approached. Kim drew in a quick breath. Those piercing dark eyes. That scarred cheek. Taj stepped down, screwdriver in hand.

'We've already met,' said Kim.

'Lovely.' Jean beamed at them both, as a bell rang. 'Lunchtime,' she said. 'Taj, show Kim the orchard while I take Abbey and Jake to meet the other children.' She took Abbey by the hand.

Kim was ready to argue. Jake would not be confident enough to go without her. But, surprisingly, her son followed the principal without a murmur. She breathed a sigh of relief. So far, so good.

Taj took off his hat. Kim thought back to that first day, when he appeared out of nowhere to fix their car. She'd been cautious of him then, perhaps a little frightened. Even when Taj turned up at the house with Ben she'd had lingering doubts. But seeing him today? Here at this sparkling school, drenched in sunshine, surrounded by adventure playgrounds and flower gardens, and vouched for by the delightful Jean O'Neill? Her earlier misgivings seemed foolish. Still, she hadn't forgotten how he'd challenged her about selling Journey's End.

'My apologies, Mrs. Sullivan. I haven't started the repairs to your home.'

'Too busy building chicken coops, I see.' What was that accent? Would it be prying to ask where he came from? 'You seem to be everyone's favourite handyman.'

Taj bowed his head a fraction, acknowledging the compliment. 'I help Jean out when I can.' He put down his screwdriver and washed his hands under a tap. 'You're moving to Tingo then? This is a fine school. Your children will be happy here.'

'I hope so.'

'Would you like to see the orchard?'

'Please.'

They walked along well-tended rows of mandarins, limes, lychees and assorted nut trees – all thriving on the sunny slope above fern-fringed Cedar Creek.

'When will you start on my house?'

'Next week.'

Kim touched a plump low-hanging orange. Taj stopped, picked the fruit and offered it to her solemnly, as if it was something precious. She slipped it in her bag and kept on walking. 'Could you do more than the quick face lift we talked about last time? I want to make the house structurally sound again.' He nodded. 'And work needs doing on the fences and sheds. Are you available? Will you have the time?'

'I am at your service, Mrs Sullivan, for as long as you need me.'

'Thank you, Taj . . . and please, call me Kim. Now, let's go back. I'm dying to find out how my kids are getting on.'

They walked up the hill, where Taj excused himself and returned to work. A noisy group of children burst from the double doors of a classroom and ran to the old-school play equipment: high steel slides and swings and monkey bars. To Kim's delight, she spotted Jake and Abbey among them.

Jean came over with a self-satisfied smile. 'The introductions went well, I think.'

Kim was growing more optimistic by the minute. 'Jake has . . . since his father died he's had problems making friends and keeping them. He gets angry sometimes.'

'I've read the report by Kate Cornish sent over from Sturt Street.'

'Oh.' That left Kim a little deflated. She'd hoped to put a positive spin on Jake's story before Jean learned too much of his history.

'Don't worry,' said Jean. 'Jake's been through a lot; you all have. His behaviour is perfectly understandable.'

'It is?' Kim could have hugged her. 'Yes, yes, of course it is.' She put a hand on her heart. 'I think this school is what Jake needs right now.'

'Don't forget, it works both ways. Jake and Abbey are also what we need. Tingo Public School might not even have been here next year without them.'

Jake ran over, out of breath, eyes shining. 'Todd's in the cricket club. He wants me to join. He asked me over to his house to practice. He'll be in my class next year.'

'That's wonderful, darling.' Kim put a hand on Jean's arm. 'Thank you.' It was a heartfelt sentiment. 'We've taken up enough of your time.' She looked around for Abbey. 'Where's your sister.' Jake pointed to the half-built chook house. Abbey was creeping up on the hens, but each time she got close enough to touch one it trotted out of reach. Taj stepped off the ladder and the birds flocked around him. He gently scooped up a hen, and knelt down so the girl could stroke it.

'Look at that,' said Jean. 'Taj doesn't have much to say to people, but he certainly has a way with animals.'

'He's going to be doing some renovations for me. Ben Steele recommended him.'

'Couldn't get a better man. He can turn his hand to anything. Carpentry, plumbing, roofing, fencing – he does the lot. And he's reliable to boot.'

'Has he been living in Tingo for very long?'

'About two years, but I think he's been in Australia for a lot longer. He built himself a shack out in the bush, lived like a hermit, and started doing odd jobs. It took folks a while to warm to him. I know nothing about his life before he came here, nobody does. As I said before, he doesn't like to talk. But this town takes people as they find them. I guarantee you won't find a soul who'll say a bad word about Taj Khan.'

Kim watched as Taj placed the hen into Abbey's arms. 'His accent. What is it? Indian? Pakistani?'

'Oh no, dear. Taj is from Afghanistan. He's a refugee from that terrible war.'

Kim felt like she'd been struck. The sunlight faded around her.

Jake frowned. 'My dad was killed in Afghanistan. I hate those people.'

Jean put a hand on his shoulder. 'I'm very sorry about your father.

You've suffered a terrible loss.' She paused. 'But the war isn't Taj's fault. I'm sure he wants peace as much as anybody.'

Jake's eyes flared with anger and he shook Jean's hand away. 'You don't know that. You said yourself you don't know anything about him.'

Kim's throat had grown tight and she coughed to clear it. 'Of course he doesn't blame Taj.' Jake glared at her. 'But, Jean, you must understand, the mere mention of Afghanistan is enough to upset Jake.' *And me too*, she thought.

'I'm getting Abbey.' Jake ran over to where she was playing with the hens. He pulled his sister back by the arm.

'I hadn't finished,' she protested to her mother. 'I still had four chickens left to pat.'

'We're going home.' Jake headed for the car. 'Come on, Mum.'

Jean's smile had turned to a cloud of concern. 'Sorry,' said Kim. 'It's just that Jake's never met anybody from Afghanistan. He'll come around.'

'I'd appreciate you having a word with him,' said Jean. 'Taj is a victim of war too. There's no place for prejudice at Tingo Primary.'

'No . . . of course not. Leave it with me.' She shook Jean's hand. 'Goodbye, and thank you.'

The kids were already climbing into the car. Kim hurried after them, feeling like a fraud. Out the gate, and her steps grew slower and slower until she stopped altogether. She couldn't talk any sense into Jake until she sorted out her own feelings. Taj was from Afghanistan. The very word summoned such powerful emotions – and anger topped the list. Followed shortly by distrust, confusion, fear, and a morbid curiosity about the faraway, alien land that had torn Connor from her.

It bothered Kim to hear Taj described as a victim of war. Maybe he was and maybe he wasn't. Nobody in Tingo knew enough about him to be sure, Jean had said so herself. But one thing was certain: he wasn't as much of a victim as her husband. Connor had travelled to Afghanistan to help people like Taj, and now he was dead.

Kim braced herself against the old familiar pain. She understood very little about Connor's death, despite Captain Blake's words being burned into her brain. *'Your husband sustained critical injuries when his armoured vehicle hit a roadside bomb in Helmand Province. Two other soldiers were also hurt. The men received immediate medical attention and were evacuated by air to the nearby British military hospital at Camp Bastion. Connor suffered a massive head wound and could not be saved.'* That was it, the sum of what she'd been told, and she hadn't asked for more. What was the point? Connor was gone and all the questions in the world wouldn't bring him back.

But now Kim found herself curious about all sorts of things. Helmand Province was in the country's south. Did Taj came from there? Had he once travelled down the same road as her husband did on that fateful day? Connor had sent her photos, some the week before he died. Two in particular came to mind – one of an alien, bombed-out scene, and another with fields of flowers stretching into the distance. She hoped that he'd died among poppies and sunflowers, not in the barren moonscape. Would Taj recognise either view?

Jake opened the car door. 'Mum. What are you waiting for?'

What was she waiting for? Life to make sense again, that's what.

CHAPTER 8

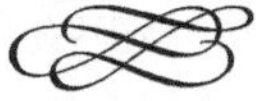

Taj watched Jake come for his sister. There was a look in the boy's eyes that had not been there before, one that Taj recognised all too well. He wasn't surprised to see it there, but it did sadden him.

'Come on, Abbey,' said Jake. 'We're going home.'

'But there are still more chickens.'

'Mum says you have to come, right now.'

Abbey set her jaw into a stubborn line, and for a moment looked ready to argue. Then she handed the hen on her lap over to Taj. 'Goodbye.'

'Goodbye, Abbey.'

The child blew him a kiss and Jake scowled. 'Take care of the chickens for me.'

'I will, little one.' The hen in his arms clucked softly. Taj stroked her ruffled red feathers and gently put her down as the children ran off. Their mother, Kim, was staring in his direction, distracting him, making it hard to return to his task.

He stole another look. She was tall and graceful, with pale-gold hair the colour of ripening grain. Fair-skinned, like many women from his home province of Nuristan, renowned for their beauty and

European complexions. Like Camila. But it wasn't Kim's physical beauty that drew him to her. It was the depth of sorrow in her eyes.

Taj pushed thoughts of Kim aside and hefted his hammer. Time to finish the nest box. Working with wood was better than working with people. Wood was warm and honest, its life truly recorded in the grain. His father, Kadir, who died when Taj was twelve, had been a master wood-carver. More than that, he was an artist and wood his medium. He taught Taj to value pattern and texture, to imagine the tables and chairs hidden in raw lumber.

Taj sorted through the pile of off-cuts, and chose a few likely pieces to whittle later on. Kadir had liked to carve statuettes, miniatures of Nuristani deities banned by the Taliban. Taj sometimes entertained himself at night by carving such figurines.

Curious hens gathered round. Building chicken coops was a far cry from his father's skilled craftsmanship, but it was good honest work. And besides, Taj had never completely embraced Kadir's passion for timber. From the very first his heart had belonged to the living forests and wildlife of his home.

Ariana, the remote and beautiful village where he was born, stood perched on the edge of Afghanistan's last great wilderness. It was a charmed place, a Shangri-La, protected for centuries by inaccessible terrain, and far enough east to be watered by India's summer monsoon. These southern slopes of the Hindu Kush were as lush as Helmand and Kandahar were dry. His uncle grew shady orchards of mulberries and walnuts. His grandfather grazed flocks of fat-tailed sheep on peaceful alpine pastures, watched over by Kuchis, the fearless livestock guardian dogs of northern Afghanistan. Wood-carvers and carpet-weavers traded their wares in the southern city of Jalalabad. To the north lay vast stands of oak, cedar and pine. They reached all the way to the snow-capped summits and craggy passes of the Pamir Mountains, known as the *roof of the world*. Next stop, China. Snow leopards and bears still roamed these wild forests. Wolves too.

Taj gazed up at the peaks of Tarringtops, all clothed in green, and inhaled a steadying lungful of air. It was these mountains that had drawn him to Tingo. They reminded him of home. In their shadow he did not feel so alone.

Taj nailed the last few planks onto the coop and collected his tools. One by one he picked up the hens and released them into their new house. 'Ladies, what do you think, eh?'

Kim's blue station wagon drove past. She didn't like him, didn't trust him – he could tell. Why did he care so much about what this woman thought? He was due to start work on her house next Monday – that was it. So much easier if they could get on. Taj waved goodbye to the kids in the playground. Forget about Kim. He had to meet with Melanie Masters, and see how her maremmas were working out.

Mel had brought two livestock guardian dogs from him after foxes caused heavy lamb losses. Taj was proud of Sultan, the older dog, who was already fully embedded with her sheep. On regular field checks, he'd seen for himself how completely Sultan had blended with the flock. On the last visit, the dog had not acknowledged his former master at all. Instead Taj was greeted with a protective volley of barking.

Hopefully Mel's new pup, Snow, was doing as well. The critical thing in training a guardian dog was to properly bond it to the animals it was meant to protect. The puppy must feel part of the flock and the flock must feel the same way. It was a dual process. Taj had helped Mel set up a large yard with a few orphan lambs, where Snow was to live twenty-four hours a day.

Snow had a few tests to pass. She should be sleeping curled up with the lambs. She should never avoid or run away from them, and a visitor should see her standing with the flock. She should tolerate the lambs nuzzling her, and lick their faces in return. Finally, she should be reluctant to leave them.

Taj had rung several times, offering to help Mel with any training issues, but apparently all was going well. If only more local graziers would embrace the concept of guardian dogs. Maremmas were cheaper, more efficient, and far more humane than haphazard baiting programs, like the ones that had wiped out dingoes from Tarringtops.

Taj had lost his first maremma dog, gentle Farah, to a 1080 bait.

Such a cruel and harrowing death. When she collapsed with seizures, Taj had lifted her into the car and headed for the vet in Wingham. There was no antidote. He would never forget her fear and pain, or the wave of relief when an injection finished her suffering. Bush animals could expect no such mercy.

CHAPTER 9

Kim arrived home from the interview with Jean to find an ancient kombi van parked in their driveway, piled high with camping equipment. A young man sat behind the wheel, listening to rap music. A teenage girl with braided hair emerged from the passenger seat, holding a grubby purple pillowcase. 'Thank god you're here. We found this owl beside the road. I think its wing's broken.'

'Poor thing,' said Abbey. 'Can I see?'

Kim looked at the offered pillowcase. 'Why bring it to me? I don't know anything about owls.'

The girl's face fell. 'But the man at the shop said a wildlife carer lived here. Aren't you Melanie Masters?'

'Melanie lives next door,' said Kim. 'Turn left when you're back on the road, and it's the next gate you come to.'

The horn honked. 'Sorry,' said the girl. 'We don't have time to go anywhere else.' She thrust the owl into Kim's hand, and ducked back into the van 'Don't worry about the pillowcase,' she yelled as they rattled off. 'You can keep it.'

Great, thanks very much. The pillowcase quivered and hissed. Kim opened the neck and stole a peek. Two dark spheres stared back from a silver-grey moon-face, edged in coal. 'Hello there.' Abbey and Jake peered in. The owl clacked its beak, fell on its back and thrust up a pair of rapier talons. It uttered a piercing shriek that almost made her drop the pillowcase.

'We'd better get it to Mel's quick-smart,' said Kim.

'Yay,' yelled Abbey. 'I'll get to see the lambs and the joeys, and Nikki.'

'Nikki will still be at school, sweetie.'

Abbey didn't miss a beat. 'I'll still get to see their wombat, and Snow, and the lizards and . . . '

'Can we please get going?' Kim held the owl at arm's length. 'This thing's hissing again.'

Taj's dusty black ute was parked behind the homestead at She-Oak Springs when they arrived. Unbelievable. It seemed every time she turned around, Taj was right there. Was he stalking her? No, not unless he was a mind-reader. He might think she was stalking him.

Jake's face darkened when he recognised the ute. 'I'm going home.' He jumped the fence and set off across the paddocks. Kim watched him trudge away, shoulders squared, big stick in hand. The war, Connor's death, Afghanistan, Taj – these things were all tangled together in his mind. Tonight she'd have that talk with him, as Jean had suggested: explain how wrong it was to dislike someone purely because of the country they came from. It would help if she knew more about Taj, of course. Jake was sure to be full of questions, and if she had no answers, well . . . the talk would fall flat.

Kim knocked on the back door.

'There they are.' Abbey pointed to a red quad bike, bumping towards them. Mel was driving, while Taj rode in the trailer with Snow.

'G'day,' said Mel, her smile uncertain. She looked brighter than on the first day they'd met, less defeated. 'I've been hoping you'd pay me a visit. Would have popped round myself, but thought you might want to settle in first.'

Kim heard the unspoken contrition behind her words: an acknowledgement that she'd been a bit too much the first time round, an undertaking to respect boundaries.

'How about coming by tomorrow?' Kim said. 'I'll make lunch.'

Mel looked so pleased that Kim was almost afraid to produce the owl, the real reason for her visit.

Abbey made a beeline for Snow. 'She's grown so big.'

'Maremmas grow quickly,' said Mel. 'Livestock guardian dogs have to.'

'Livestock guardians?' asked Kim.

'Dogs that live with sheep or other stock round the clock, protecting them from predators.'

'Like Oddball,' said Abbey. 'The dog in the movie.' Mel nodded.

So that's what the shaggy white dog was doing when he saw off the fox in Mel's paddock. What a fascinating concept. 'Snow just got her six-month report card.' Mel grinned at Taj. 'A miserable fail, I'm afraid.'

'Mel, your dog didn't fail her report,' said Taj. 'You did. Snow can't bond with her sheep if you keep taking her away from them. She must sleep and eat with the flock. She must not look to you for companionship, but to them.'

Mel stroked Snow's ears. 'What about me? Who must I *look to for companionship?*'

Taj's stern face creased into a smile. 'Perhaps Snow is not meant to be a livestock guardian dog. Perhaps she is meant to be your dog.'

'Really?' Mel threw her arms around Snow's shaggy neck. 'Hear that? No more sleeping with the lambs.'

'I find it hard to believe she's been sleeping with the lambs,' said Taj, and Mel shot him a guilty grin. 'Perhaps you should get another puppy, for the sheep this time?'

'Puppy?' Abbey pulled at Taj's shirt. 'Can I have a puppy?'

Taj shook his head. 'No, little one. These are very special puppies, born with a job to do. They are not pets.'

'Except for Snow,' corrected Mel.

'Perhaps Snow has the most important job of all.' Taj stroked the dog's ears. 'Helping to heal your heart.'

A faint flush coloured Mel's cheeks. Kim looked away as a prickle travelled up her neck. What was it with these people? She decided to steer the conversation back to safer waters. She told the story of Lambert and the foiled fox attack on the lambs.

'Yes, yes, that's Sultan,' said Mel, her face aglow with pleasure. 'He's another one of Taj's dogs. I haven't lost a single lamb since he's been living with the hill flock. He passed his report with flying colours, didn't he, Taj?'

'He did, but Sultan was older and already partly trained. If you want another dog, Mel, it's best that we do that again. You are not to be trusted with cute baby puppies.'

Kim and Mel exchanged smiles. This was the right time to introduce the owl.

Mel expertly turned the pillowcase inside out, restraining the owl's feathered legs and razor claws. Out in the open, it appeared larger and more frightening than Kim had expected. 'What a find,' said Mel. 'A sooty owl. Quite a rarity around here.'

'I'm calling her Dotty,' said Abbey. An apt name. The bird's head and wings were smothered in a blizzard of white spots. 'I wish Daddy could see her. He loved owls.'

Kim's heart flipped over.

'I think you're right about this being a *her*,' said Mel. 'Males are usually darker and smaller.' Mel extended the bird's wings one at a time, exploring them with gentle fingers. 'We're in luck. This wing's not broken, only sprained.'

'That's good,' said Kim. 'We'll leave her with you then?'

Mel put the owl back. 'Normally I'd say yes, but right now I'm snowed under with rescues. Two more joeys, and a koala hurt in a logging coupe.'

'A koala,' shrieked Abbey. 'Can I see?'

'I can't keep it,' said Kim. 'I don't know anything about owls.'

'Tell you what,' said Mel. 'Let's do a swap. Your owl for my joeys.'

'I don't understand . . .'

'You take two of my joeys home. That cuts down my workload, and gives me time to bind Dotty's wing and get her feeding properly. Then when the koala rescue people pick up Blinky tomorrow, I'll take the joeys back.'

Abbey's face lit up. 'Please, Mum. You said we couldn't have a dog, but you didn't say anything about kangaroos.'

'Bonnie and Clyde are older joeys and pretty independent,' said Mel. 'They'll be no trouble.'

Abbey was jumping round in excited circles. 'Please, please, please, Mum . . . '

Keeping track of Abbey was making Kim dizzy. 'How would I look after them?'

Mel grinned. 'It's easy. I'll show you.'

Why not? It was only overnight. It's not like she was busy, and therein lay a problem. In theory, twelve months of freedom stretching before her sounded utterly perfect. In practice, it might take some getting used to.

After Connor died, work had saved her. The discipline of turning up each day. She liked fronting students who neither knew nor cared about Connor, and who weren't keeping a sympathetic eye on her. A loud voice inside urged her to keep moving, keep running, keep doing. Death didn't hurt as much when you didn't stop.

But here in Tingo life moved at a different pace. Here, beside the murmuring creek, among the whispering trees, there were no distractions. Too much room to think. Too much time to contemplate what she'd lost. The owl uttered a fierce screech. Mel whistled soothingly and covered its head. Abbey was right. Connor did love owls. He loved all the wildlife found at Journey's End. He would want this.

'Okay, it's a swap,' said Kim. Abbey screamed with delight, and Kim soaked up her happiness. Her daughter was growing more lively, changing from the shy, quiet child, living in a secret world of imagination.

'I'd better take Dotty inside and get her hydrated,' said Mel. 'I'll bring the joeys around later. You'll need a secure pen for them during the day, with a green pick of grass. Do you have somewhere like that?'

'The old chook pen,' said Kim. 'But there are gaps in the wire, and I know as much about fencing as I do about rocket science.'

'Taj will fix it for you,' said Mel. 'Right, Taj? Great. Okay, Abbey, let's put Dotty away and have a look at that koala.'

When they got home, Kim found Jake reading comics in the woodshed, tomahawk by his side. Kim eyed it warily.

'Guess what?' said Abbey. 'We're getting joeys.'

Jake didn't look up. 'Mum would never let us have joeys.'

'I would, actually,' said Kim. 'In fact, they'll be here this afternoon.'

'Seriously?'

'Seriously. Now come inside and have some lunch.'

Jake was full of questions. 'Can I feed them? Can they sleep in my room? Can I name them?'

'I don't know,' said Kim, buttering rounds of bread. 'We'll have to ask Mel.'

Jake devoured his sandwiches in record time, and went down to the gate to watch and wait. Abbey ran to fetch Percy the poodle, and then joined him. Kim watched nervously from the lounge room window, wishing she'd told Jake that Taj was coming over, hoping that Mel and the joeys would arrive first.

No such luck. Kim curled her fingers in the faded lace curtains as the battered black ute bumped up the drive. The kitchen door banged, and Jake burst in. 'What's he doing here? You said Mel was bringing the joeys.'

'She is,' said Kim. 'But they need a safe place to be during the day. Taj is going to fix up the old chook pen.'

'What for? I could do that. Make him go.'

He didn't look like her little boy anymore. He looked like his father. But there was something of herself too, in the set of his stubborn, anxious face.

'Taj just wants to help . . .'

'No, Mum.' His eyes blazed with anger. 'Make him go!'

'Alright. We'll fix up the chook pen ourselves. I'll send him away.'

Jake gave her a sharp nod. 'Good. I'm going for a walk.'

'Thought you wanted to see the joeys arrive?'

'I've changed my mind.' He marched out and slammed the back door.

Kim looked through the window, shielding her eyes from the sun's glare. Abbey was skipping over to Taj as he climbed from the car, chattering away, as friendly and warm as a Labrador puppy. Kim hurried outside. Taj certainly evoked some strong feelings in her children. Abbey, who'd always been painfully shy with strangers, was irresistibly drawn to this man, while Jake despised him. Kim disapproved of both responses. Prejudice wasn't okay, but neither was blind trust.

'Sorry for wasting your time, Taj, but we don't need help with the chook pen after all.'

His searching coffee-coloured eyes held hers, leaving no place to hide. He could see straight through to what she didn't want to say. 'The boy does not want me here.'

'No, it's not that . . . ' Her words petered out. There was no point lying to this man, even to protect his feelings. He already knew the truth.

'Something has changed for him,' said Taj.

Abbey took hold of his hand, her expression kind. 'It's not your fault, Taj. It's because you're from Afghanistan.'

'Abbey,' scolded Kim. 'That's enough.' She tried to fetch her daughter away from Taj by pulling at her other hand. Abbey squirmed free and hid behind him. Why couldn't he just go? She owed him no explanation. But instead he stood his ground, silently requesting one. 'Jake's father – my husband – was stationed in Afghanistan.'

'He was a soldier?'

'Yes.' After all this time, it still hurt to tell. 'Connor was killed, two years ago. A roadside bomb.'

The soft light of understanding shone in his eyes. 'And Jake, he thinks Afghanis are all murderers like the Taliban. Like the men who killed his father.'

Kim gave an awkward shrug. 'I suppose so. Don't worry, I plan to talk with him. Make him understand.'

For one brief moment, a mask seemed to fall from Taj's face, and she glimpsed all the sadness of the world there. 'These things are not so easily explained,' he said. 'I am sorry for your loss.'

'Thank you.'

His mask was back, betraying no emotion. 'Do you still wish me to work on the house?'

'Yes, of course.'

He nodded and turned to go.

'Aren't you going to give Mummy the flowers?' said Abbey.

Kim frowned. Flowers? There was nothing appropriate about Taj bringing her flowers. Her early misgivings about him came flooding back.

'No,' said Taj.

'But she'll love them.' Abbey ran to his ute and snatched something off the front seat, wrapped in a funnel of foil. 'Here, Mum.' She thrust them forward. 'These are for you.'

Taj shifted uneasily from foot to foot, and dragged aside the dark lock of hair that always fell over his face. Kim glanced down and gasped aloud. No, it couldn't be. With extravagant care, she eased the stems from their silver cradle. There was no mistaking the waxy five-petalled flowers: large and fragrant, a dozen or more to each stem. *Sarcochilus fitzgeraldii*, the rare ravine orchid. And these were the rarest of the rare – each perfect bloom pure crimson.

Kim found herself laughing with delight. When was the last time she'd felt like this: this heady combination of excitement and joy?

'I told you Mum would like them.' Abbey was beaming as she danced 'Ring a ring a Rosie' with Percy Poodle. Even the serious Taj looked pleased. Kim's happiness was infectious.

'Where did you find these?'

'On the rocks above the rapids.'

'Are there many plants? Are there clumps?'

'Clumps, yes.' He held out his arms. 'This wide.'

'This wide,' said Abbey, copying him. Kim swept her up in a great giggling hug. 'I *love* it when you're like this, Mummy.'

'Do you, darling?' Kim kissed her and put her down. 'These clumps . . . are they all this colour? Crimson flowers are so unusual.'

'Some are crimson, some are white with scarlet hearts.'

'Both kinds?' Kim began talking so fast it was hard to take breath. 'Ravine orchids have *never* been recorded at Tingo or Tarringtops. Never. Although computer models predicted they'd be here. Do you know how many times I've gone looking for them? I didn't even know there were rapids on Cedar Creek. Are they far?'

'Not far. North of here, on your land.' Taj glanced down at his boots.

He'd been trespassing. So what? Otherwise these exceptional orchids might have remained a secret. She put her nose to the blooms, drinking in their scent. How many people on the face of the earth had savoured the rich fragrance of wild ravine orchids? 'You must show me where you found them.'

'Of course.' The sound of an axe on wood rang through the air. Jake. 'I should go now.'

'Oh. Goodbye then.' How would she bear the waiting? If only the joeys weren't coming. If only Jake wasn't in such a funk. She was filled with the glory of discovery, the way she'd been when she and Connor first explored this mountain paradise. The way she'd never expected to be again.

Kim made an effort to come down to earth. There was still the chicken coop to fix. The joeys would be on their way. She was so excited, so full of news and dying to share it with somebody. Normally that person would be Daisy, but the two of them hadn't spoken since the argument. Not once.

There was her mother, of course. She didn't understand her daughter's passion for rare plants, though she'd do a marvellous job of faking it. But the house was in a black spot, no mobile reception at all. Mel was it, and that was okay.

Kim went to the tank behind the house, and sprinkled the flowers with water. When she got back, Ben's dusty red land cruiser was coming up the drive. He unfolded his long, lean form from the driver's seat. Khaki shorts, a blue shirt with rolled-up sleeves and the ubiquitous Akubra hat – a picture of Aussie bush charm.

'You do remember this place is off the market for twelve months?' said Kim.

'Trying to cheat me out of my commission?'

'Only temporarily.'

'It's a bit of a nuisance. I'd already started on your contract – asked Mandy to search the title and collect info for the vendor's statement. By next year, it'll all need to be updated.'

'No doubt your fee will reflect that,' said Kim.

'Nah, don't worry about it.' Ben stretched his arms over his head and arched his spine. His stance emphasised the strength in his thighs and the ramrod straightness of his back. 'I've just driven home from Sydney. Does it ever feel good to get out of that bloody car.'

Kim was still beaming; she couldn't stop. Ben looked at her curiously. 'That's one hell of a smile. You won the lottery?'

'Better than that,' said Kim. 'Way better.' She wanted to skip and sing the way Abbey did. Where was Abbey? She couldn't see her anywhere.

Jake came pelting up the hill. He looked as happy as she did. 'Ben,' said Jake, a little out of breath. 'I've kept that tomahawk super-sharp like you said. Want to try it?'

'In a minute, champ. In a minute.' His attention remained on Kim. 'So, what's this earth-shattering news of yours?'

'I found an orchid – well, Taj did.' She showed him the elegant stems, with their pendulous, crimson blooms. Ben put his nose to the flowers and inhaled, taking one endless breath.

'Know what they smell like. That crazy expensive French perfume my girlfriend used to like. Cost me an arm and a leg, it did. Bottle those flowers and you'll make a fortune.'

'Sorry, Ben. Your girlfriend will never get to use this fragrance.'

'Never mind. She shot through last month, anyway.' He paused, as if hoping for a reaction. Kim remained blank. She wasn't going to encourage any further sharing. 'Tell me,' said Ben. 'What's so special about your flowers?'

'They might be the only wild ravine orchids this side of Taree.'

Jake pushed in between them. 'We're getting joeys.'

Kim put her hands on his shoulders. 'Ben, you might have these orchids too. If they're there, you'll find them mainly on rocky outcrops along the creek, with their roots clinging to crevices. Ravine orchids is such a perfect name for them. Although sometimes they'll clump around the base of trees. That's uncommon, though. The whole concept of these orchids is uncommon. Promise me you'll look for them at Granite Hills?'

'I don't know.' A smile played around his lips. 'It's not like this matters to you, right?'

Kim brushed his arm in a pretend punch.

'Ow. What if I found them and the government slapped one of those conservation covenants on me?'

'You're an estate agent,' said Kim. 'You know better than anybody they're voluntary agreements.'

'Just winding you up.'

'I think your father organised the covenant on Journey's End for us,' she said. 'Walter Steele?'

'That's him. Must have broken dear old dad's heart to lock up your forests.'

'Not locked up,' she said. 'Protected. It means I can sell this place next year and not worry.'

Ben shook his head. 'I still think you're crazy.'

Kim was too happy to mind. 'Will you look for the orchids?'

'Sure,' he said. 'Why not?'

'Don't waste any time. We're at the end of the season and it's hard to identify them when they finish flowering. You could confuse them with common orchids in the same family.'

'You'd better come with me then,' said Ben. 'Show me what to look for.'

Kim wanted to strike off upstream there and then. 'It's a deal.' She felt lighter than she had in years.

'Ben, Ben . . .' Jake touched his arm. 'My grandad gave me a cricket ball signed by Shane Warne. Do you want to see it? He was a spin bowler like you.'

'I know who he was, champ. Go get it and I'll take a look. Meanwhile, I want to ask your mum a favour.' Jake ran off.

Kim cocked her head at Ben. 'He likes you.'

'Why wouldn't he?' said Ben. 'I'm a great guy.' His grin was boyish, charming, disarming. 'Now, about that favour. How do feel about trivia nights?'

She narrowed her eyes a fraction. 'Why?'

'The local fireys are holding one as a fundraiser Saturday week. We need another person to make up the numbers on our table.'

'What about Jake and Abbey?'

'Bring them along. Mel's bringing her kids. It won't be a late night.'

'I don't think so.'

'Come on. You'll meet the natives, and it's for a good cause.'

Could she? Kim had given up on socialising since Connor died. She didn't do *going out*. But Taj's discovery of the ravine orchids had changed things, woken up some long dormant part of her. Kim sniffed the rare flowers. They made her feel present, alive. 'Okay, I'll come.'

'Great. See you there . . . oh, and ladies bring a plate.'

'Only the ladies?'

'Just a figure of speech.' There was mischief in his bright blue eyes.

And for once, when Kim thought of Connor, her heart did not break.

CHAPTER 10

*T*aj swung his ute down the rough bush track towards home, a troubled man. He thought he was immune to taunts and insults. He thought he'd built an unassailable wall around his heart. So why did the judgement of one small boy disturb him so?

As he neared the house a chorus of howls and barking rose to meet him. Taj checked his watch. Later than he thought. A rare afternoon off, and he'd wasted most of it traipsing up the creek after orchids for Kim Sullivan.

Carla ran to meet him, her silver plume of a tail waving in welcome. He took a moment to admire her. A perfect example of the breed. Elegant, almost feline in her movements despite her large belly, and with the broad head and keen, intelligent eyes so typical of maremmas.

Taj ruffled her soft coat then climbed the rough steps by the house to the shady top pens. More like small paddocks really. Four more maremmas whined and leaped at the gates. A small flock of sheep dozed under the trees behind them. On release, the dogs gambolled about, dashing off here and there, then racing back to him.

Taj led the dogs down a well-worn bush track to where fallen trees had dammed a bend in the creek. A natural swimming hole, dark and deep. Maremmas loved water. The dogs plunged into the shallows, splashing each other and skittering after minnows. Taj stood on a rock and stripped naked, enjoying the feel of cool forest air and dappled sunshine on his skin. He walked along a broad log that spanned the banks and dived in, bracing against the cold. However hot the days became, these mountain streams always remained icy.

He floated on his back, gazing up through a filigree of leaves and branches, shades of brown and green against brilliant blue. Liquid notes of birdsong splashed the air. Taj closed his eyes and let the current empty his mind, dissolve his tension, wash it away He could stay like this forever.

His canine companions had other ideas. Maremmas were strong swimmers. The pack struck out towards the centre of the swimming hole, all except the heavily pregnant Carla. Ava and Bibi reached him first, scrambling for the floating island of his body, dunking him underwater. 'Oh no, you don't.' Taj and the dogs wrestled and played together until they were all tired out. Then, holding onto Saber's collar, he allowed himself to be towed ashore.

Taj settled down in the shade, his back against a blue gum. He loved this place. To the east lay endless fern-filled valleys. To the north rose the cliffs of Tarringtops. However many times he saw those craggy battlements, they always stirred his blood.

He'd had an easier passage to Australia than most, arriving under the interpreter resettlement program. Hundreds of refugee places were set aside for Afghan nationals who'd helped Coalition forces during the war, and when asked to nominate a country, Taj had picked Australia. He'd surprised himself with this decision. Britain should have been his natural choice. When his father died, and his mother shortly after, it was a British aid group that took him in, and sent him to a school where he became fluent in English. The charity rewarded his talent with a scholarship to the University of Leeds, studying envi-ronmental biology. Having grown up in a remote mountain village, he found England overwhelming. He'd never felt at home in its crowded cities and tame countryside.

Instead, a century-old family connection had lured Taj Down Under: stories heard at his aunt's knee of their forebear, Abdul Wade, the intrepid cameleer who had moved to Australia in the 1880s to forge a new life. Those tales had stayed with Taj. Perhaps he could do the same? He'd done his research. Australia was sparsely populated. A country of wild, lonely places where he could lose himself. Where he could find some private corner of the world to grieve.

At first Taj settled in Newcastle under the Rural Australians For Refugees *Welcome Towns* program. Local people sponsored individuals, or sometimes whole families. They took them in, helped them adjust, taught them English and found them jobs. Taj was billeted at the local rectory with an elderly Anglican vicar and his wife. 'Don't worry, young man. We're a tolerant bunch. You pray to Allah wherever and whenever you like.'

Taj hadn't bothered explaining. He soon left the well-meaning vicar and took a job down the coal mines, working twelve-hour shifts and keeping to himself. That wasn't hard. Some of his co-workers were downright hostile. 'You Pakis are all the same. A bunch of bloody Muslim terrorists. Piss off home.' The fact that he was neither Pakistani, terrorist nor Muslim was apparently irrelevant.

He found friendship with Yusuf, a fellow Afghan saving money to bring his wife and son to Australia. And also Hakim, a former policeman with excellent English who'd fled the war in Syria. Taj tolerated the mines for a while, but working down a filthy pit wasn't for him. With some money saved, he went in search of space and solitude.

Setting out on the road like a modern-day nomad, Taj drifted from town to town. Months of wandering brought him to Tingo. So much about this place reminded him of Ariana where he was born. Fat sheep grazed the green foothills. Beetling mountain peaks rose above the tiny township. Even the crystal clarity of light was familiar. Here, with dingoes howling at night, and a vast wilderness on his doorstep – here he would try to heal and make a new home.

Taj found a wild block of land that nobody wanted, deep in the forest. He built a house with rough bush timber and the skills he'd learned from his father. He cleared some land to plant vegetables and an orchard. Kept chickens and sheep. Made his own furniture, installed rainwater tanks, an off-the-grid solar system and back-up generator. Put a sign up at the general store-cum-post office. *Handyman For Hire*. One by one people reached out, accepting him at face value, asking few questions.

Once a week he drove to the library at Wingham, and lost himself in the classics, novels by Tolstoy, Kafka and Mark Twain. He found comfort in volumes of poetry by Wordsworth and Wilfred Owen. He borrowed books about the local environment – the forests, birds and animals – and studied them at night. People called him the Hermit. Taj was proud of the simple, self-sufficient life he'd carved out for himself.

When Taj lost a lamb to foxes, he looked to buy a Kuchi – the dogs his grandfather had used to protect the family flocks from wolves. It turned out the breed wasn't available in Australia, so he bought a maremma instead. Farah, whose name meant *joy*. How he'd loved her. Then came the baiting blitzkrieg on dingoes. When Farah died, Taj picked himself up and purchased a pair of maremmas this time. Two had turned into three, then four . . .

Carla leaped from the stream and bounded to him, burying her big, white head in his lap. He scratched her back. 'You're a good girl, eh?' His dogs were loyal friends and fine companions, and once upon a time they'd been all he needed, but lately something had changed. He wanted more. He was hungry for a human connection beyond chatting to the post office ladies or discussing client's odd jobs.

His friend from the mines, Hakim, had found work at a sawmill north of Taree. Taj had finally responded to his texts and invited him home to share a meal. Their dinners were becoming a regular thing. Last week, when Pat Ryan asked him for the umpteenth time to join the Rural Fire Service, Taj had said yes. This morning, when Jean

O'Neill suggested he lead the Junior Rangers Program at school next year, he'd agreed. He was even looking forward to it. And he was looking forward to showing Kim the orchids.

Kim. Even before today, he couldn't get her out of his mind. And now? Learning of her husband's death in Afghanistan had moved him deeply. There was more to it than a tragic connection to his homeland. Taj recognised himself in this woman's grief, and in her son's blind anger. His heart swelled with feelings he'd thought long since dead.

A clear piping call made him turn his head. An inquisitive willy wagtail sat on a red flowering hakea, within arm's reach. 'You are right, little one. Time to go.' He stood up and gave a whistle. The dogs ran to him, and cocked their ears as a loud howling sounded through the trees. The dingoes were growing impatient for their turn.

CHAPTER 11

'Jake.' Kim lifted the plate of buttered bread out of reach. 'Clyde's in the kitchen again.'

The little kangaroo stood high on his back legs, balancing with his muscular tail, trying to reach the benchtop. 'Scram, you.'

Jake ran in, grinning. 'He wants a sandwich.'

'Well, he can't have one. What would Mel say? Now, take him outside.'

Bonnie and Clyde hadn't stayed for one night as promised. A week later, and they were still there. Mel had taken in two orphaned possums in the meantime, and wanted to settle them before taking the little kangaroos back. Kim didn't really mind. They were rather sweet. Mischievous though, and excellent escape artists. Her makeshift fence repairs were no match for two determined, half-grown joeys. When Taj came on Monday, she would ask him to fix the chook run properly, no matter what Jake said.

Jake shepherded Clyde outside, and Kim went back to the sandwiches. She particularly missed Daisy at times like these. She missed the casual chatter while making kids' lunches, the silly jokes, the shared understandings that only came after years of friendship. Kim shook away the thought and piled the sandwiches on a plate. Damn, the bread was stale and crumbling where she'd cut it. A headache was building behind her eyes. The high she'd been on last week when Abbey gave her the orchids had faded, and she found herself aimless.

During previous stays, when grand plans were still afoot, there hadn't been enough minutes in the day. So much to do: identifying plants, collecting seeds, building terraces for future greenhouses, designing irrigation systems. She and Connor rose together at dawn and fell into each other's arms late at night. Now she didn't know what to do with herself, and each day dragged. The smell of dead dreams lay thick in the air.

Kim missed teaching more than she'd expected to. For the last two years she'd volunteered for summer school, carrying on after second semester almost without a break. Juggling the kids between camps – Daisy and her parents helping – had been tricky and hadn't left them much together time, but they managed. Work was a favourite coping mechanism, and without it she was lost. On top of all that, Abbey was sick, Jake was cranky whenever Taj turned up to work on the house, and her old life still hijacked Kim round every corner.

Night-time was the worst. That damned brass bed was haunted. She couldn't fall asleep without dreaming of Connor. Sometimes she imagined the faces of his killers, and her hatred ran free. She felt herself unravelling as darker fantasies took hold. Frightening nightmares of revenge. And for the first time in her life, Kim was afraid of the dark.

She'd always considered night a blessing, along with summer rain and poetry and silence. Once upon a time, Tingo's midnight sky, ablaze with the Southern Cross, could put things into perspective. She was a traveller on island Earth, adrift in a stream of stars. Part of the great mystery of being. But now? When night closed in, all she felt was her own mortality, hers and her family's. She couldn't concentrate on reading a book. There was no droning television to fall asleep to, no online movies. Not even a radio to fill the emptiness with white noise. So she'd lie awake, wishing life was different. Overthinking everything. Listening to the crickets and frogs, and the eerie forest howling that punctuated the lonely, nocturnal hours at Journey's End.

Abbey came into the kitchen, wearing pyjamas and carrying Percy. Kim tried to shake the gloom away. 'Feeling better, sweetie?'

'I'm bored. I want to go outside and see the joeys.'

Kim took the thermometer down from a top cupboard. 'Put this under your tongue and keep your mouth closed. Wait until it beeps . . . oh good. Normal.'

'That means I'm well enough to come to the trivia night, doesn't it?'

'I don't know.' Kim had planned to use her daughter's cold as an excuse. Why had she ever agreed in the first place? 'How do you feel?'

'Great. Hungry. What's to eat?'

An echo came from behind her. 'Yeah, what's to eat? I'm starved.'

'Sandwiches are on their way, Jake.'

'Is Taj coming today?'

'No.'

'Good.' Jake stood there with Bonnie and Clyde. 'They got out of their pen again. I think they're hungry.'

Kim checked the kitchen clock. He was right; it was time for their milk. Joeys, even older ones, were more work than she'd imagined. Bonnie and Clyde were pretty independent, Mel had said – 'They'll be no trouble.' But the little kangaroos were still on four bottles a day. They slept in the laundry – well, half of the time they slept, snug and warm, in pouches hanging from the door. The rest of the time, like any curious young creatures, they went exploring. They got into the clothes hamper and spread dirty washing everywhere. They pulled open the cupboard and tipped out the laundry powder. They scattered lucerne cubes and droppings all over the floor. They escaped into the house through the door that wouldn't close properly. One morning Kim found them snuggled up together, asleep on the couch.

Each day Kim cleaned up after them, washed their pouch blankets, mixed the day's milk, sterilized the bottles, and joey-proofed the house as much as possible. The kids helped, even Jake. She'd made helping a condition of the joeys' extended stay.

The responsibility had made a difference. Jake was more cooperative, more obliging, less hostile. But he still had his moments – way too many of them. He kept pestering her for a dog, and each refusal provoked a scene. Swearing, kicking doors, throwing things. It would be easier to give in. But the urn with Scout's ashes still stood on the mantelpiece and Kim would not have Scout replaced until she was ready to let him go.

Taj's arrival also triggered tantrums. Either that or Jake would shoot through. The handyman spent three days a week at Journey's End, working his way through the list of repairs: a list that was growing and extending beyond the house. Each day, Kim thought of something else that needed doing. Ben's cautionary comment still echoed in the back of her brain: 'We don't want to overcapitalise.' Wise words. The sale had only been postponed, not cancelled.

However a year was a long time, and she might as well enjoy her time here. The old farmhouse would never be as grand as Mel's gracious homestead, but it deserved more than a patch-up job, and she had the money. Not from the pitifully inadequate military compensation payment, but from Connor's life insurance. She couldn't think of anything he would rather spend it on.

Whenever Kim thought of Connor now, she thought of Taj in the same breath. Yet whenever she mentioned Afghanistan or asked him about his old life, he shut down the conversation. This reticence made her suspicious and more inquisitive than ever. What did he have to hide? Plagued with curiosity, she began grilling other people, but nobody else in town knew any more about him than she did. Except for Winnie Goldsmith, the postmistress and town gossip. 'Every month, without fail, he sends a parcel to Kabul.'

'I don't suppose you know what it is?'

Winnie lowered her voice. 'Taj never tells me anything, but he buys the post pack in the shop, so I see what goes into it. An international money order, there's always one of those. And different gifts: books, toys, pretty soaps and perfume. Do you think he has a family back home in Afghanistan?'

'Who knows?' Kim was more intrigued than ever.

Abbey and the joeys cannoned into her. They were playing a game of chasey round the kitchen. 'Watch out.' Kim lit the stove, took the pre-prepared bottles from the fridge, and started warming them up. Next trip to Wingham, she really needed to buy a microwave and a radio.

Jake began a gentle boxing match with Clyde. 'When are we going to the trivia night? Todd's coming too. I can't wait.'

Oh. Both the kids were looking forward to tonight. How could she disappoint them? 'Who wants to make brownies,' she said, drying her hands on the tea towel. 'We're supposed to bring a plate.'

CHAPTER 12

Kim pulled in behind a row of cars at the Tingo Memorial Hall. It was the first time she'd been out socially among strangers for more than two years, and she felt sick.

Jake grabbed the Tupperware container off the back seat and jumped from the car. Abbey's fingers crept into Kim's hand. 'Mummy, are you alright?'

Kim gave her hand a reassuring squeeze. Trust Abbey to understand. Her daughter was a living, breathing, emotional barometer. 'I'm fine, darling. Let's go.'

The little hall, like Doctor Who's Tardis, seemed larger inside than out. Kim stood by the door, holding Abbey's hand. The interior was a time capsule. Displays of black and white photographs: timber-cutters, plough horses, rows of children sitting outside Tingo's schoolhouse in nineteenth-century clothes. Chintz curtains hung at small square windows, solid cedar benches lined the walls, and a stage stood at one end.

'What do I do with this?' Jake held out the box of brownies. Kim pointed to a trestle table at the back, groaning with cakes and sandwiches. Jake plonked it down and ran off. A dozen people milled about setting up tables and chairs. Kim looked around for Mel or Ben. They weren't there. She didn't know a soul.

A middle-aged Aboriginal man spied her loitering in the doorway. He was large and lean, his warm brown eyes almost lost under a tangle of eyebrows. 'Kim, is it?' He shook her hand. 'I'm Brigade Captain Pat Ryan.'

'This is my daughter, Abbey.' Abbey hid behind her mother. 'And Jake's here somewhere.'

'Come and meet Shirley,' said Pat.

Kim ventured in with an arm around Abbey's shoulder. Pat introduced his wife, a plump, friendly woman, whose dark cheeks dimpled when she smiled. She put a welcoming hand on Kim's arm. 'This stuffy old town needs new blood. We're all thrilled you've come to live here. You've saved the school, you know.'

'Yes, Jean told me.'

Shirley beamed at Abbey. 'Now, who's this pretty little girl?'

'We've got joeys.'

'Have you, sweetheart? Shirley took Abbey's hand and patted it. 'Now come and have something to eat, both of you. The pizzas are warming in the kitchen.'

Kim trailed after them, keeping an eye on the door for Ben. Along the way, Pat introduced her to various people. Old Charlie, the town mechanic, the one Taj had warned her about. Vera, who helped Winnie in the post office, with a beehive bun that seemed lacquered to her head. Des who ran the store, a heavy ginger-haired man with a round face like an over-ripe peach. And Bev, Charlie's wife, small and watchful as a bird.

Kim spotted her son by the food table, helping himself to a lamington. Jake turned round, mouth crammed full and cream-smeared, and his eyes lit up. Ben was in the doorway, weighed down by a slab of beer. He winked at Kim on his way to the kitchen. 'You're on my table.'

Abbey pulled at her sleeve. 'There's Nikki.'

Mel and her children had arrived with a packet of Tim Tams and a bottle of wine. Mel looked different. No shapeless T-shirts tonight. She wore a pretty, floaty top, and her hair was softer and shinier; more wavy than curly. She caught Kim's eye and hurried over, 'I didn't know you were coming.' She gave Kim an unexpected hug. 'This is so great. Are you on my team?'

'I don't know.'

'Well, you are now. Welcome to the Bright Sparks. Come on.' Mel led Kim to a table. 'Sit down. I'll help serve the pizzas, then get us some glasses and open this wine.'

'Should I help?'

'No. You stay here and relax.'

Mel was like an instant friend, just add water. Kim did as she was told, apart from the relaxing bit. Before Connor's death, she'd never been an extrovert, but now even this small gathering made her heart race. She fought the urge to leave.

A few more people were arriving. Jean O'Neill with bags of chips and a bottle of red. A middle-aged man who looked like a farmer, carrying a six-pack of Bundaberg Rum and Coke. Two thirty-something couples, together with a few children she recognised from the school visit. She spent some anxious minutes, wondering how her kids would fit in. Well, look at that. They'd seamlessly joined the gang, laughing and joking, eating cakes and running round the edge of the hall. Jake was making friends here easily, real friends that weren't embarrassed about him.

Ben delivered two big plates of pizza slices. 'Come and get it.' Jake arrived first. 'Got something for you, champ.' Ben pulled a battered cricket ball from his pocket. 'This little beauty took a hat-trick against Wingham last week. Won us the match. It's yours.'

Jake's face split into a wide grin. 'Thanks.' Todd asked to see the ball and Jake proudly showed it off. Kim felt a rush of gratitude towards Ben and the little town that was taking her son to its heart.

Pat set a card table up on stage and rang a bell. 'Questions start in five minutes. There's a list on the noticeboard if you're not sure what team you're on. And the games cupboard at the back is open, so kids, help yourself.'

'I hope you like chablis.' Mel poured the wine. 'To your new life!'

Kim gingerly clinked glasses, uncomfortable with the toast. Twelve months leave was an interlude at best, not a new life.

'Christmas is just round the corner,' said Mel. 'Less than a fortnight. I suppose you have family in Sydney?'

Kim nodded. 'Mum and Dad. My brother's in London. He isn't coming home this year. And then there's Connor's family.' She'd almost mentioned Daisy and had to bite her tongue. Their families usually spent Christmas Eve together. A tradition for years: feasting, drinking and exchanging gifts – her favourite part of the festive season. Since Connor died she'd felt like a bit like a third wheel, yet the tradition had continued. What would she do this Christmas Eve? Her parents would love for them to spend it at their place for the first time in fifteen years. Her throat went tight, and a wave of missing Daisy knocked her flat.

Ben sat down beside her. His long legs took some folding to fit in the chair. 'You two already into the plonk?' He flashed them a devastating smile, and Mel giggled like a schoolgirl. 'Excuse me, ladies. Think I'll grab a beer myself before we start.' He ate a pizza slice in two mouthfuls before heading for the kitchen.

Jean patted Kim's hand as she walked past. 'Watch out for that one,' she said. 'He plays the field.'

Mel waited until Ben was out of earshot. 'Isn't he gorgeous?'

Kim took a swig of her wine. What could she say? Yes, he is gorgeous. He's almost as handsome as my dead husband?

'I know what you're thinking,' said Mel. 'How can I feel that way about Ben when Geoff and I only split up a few months ago, right?'

The thought had crossed Kim's mind. A long time after Connor's death, and she still couldn't desire another man. She still felt married. It was different for Mel, though. Her husband had betrayed her, deserted her. Whoever this Geoff was, he didn't deserve that kind of loyalty.

'Oh god, it's him.' Mel's face turned white. A short, stocky man much older than Mel was walking in the door. People turned to stare and a murmur passed around the room. A plump dark-haired girl hung on his arm; she looked young enough to be his daughter.

'That's Geoff?' Kim surprised herself by putting a comforting hand on Mel's arm. 'Are you alright? Do you want to go?'

'I wouldn't give him the satisfaction.'

Ben came back with his beer, a pen and a notepad. Jean followed and sat down next to him with a glass of red. He passed her the pen and paper.

'Why do I always have to keep score?' asked Jean.

'You know all the answers,' said Ben. 'It cuts out the middle man.'

'I'll do it if you want,' offered Kim. 'I'm not that great at trivia questions, except ones about plants, so I might as well pull my weight some other way.' Jean looked pleased, and handed over the notebook. Kim started to feel better. Their table was filling up, and so far she knew everybody. She passed the plate of pizza around and Jean took a slice.

'It's a good turnout tonight.' Jean said. 'We'll end up with six teams.'

'How many people on a table?' asked Kim, hoping for four.

'Five.'

Oh. There was still somebody to come.

Pat rang the bell. 'Final call.'

Kim looked around for the kids. She spotted Jake playing Uno with Todd . . . and Abbey. How sweet. Back in Sydney, Jake never included Abbey in anything. But here in Tingo, with such a small pool of children to mix with? Well, it was like Jean said. Age didn't matter so much.

Kim turned back to the table to find Taj seated opposite her. It was as if he'd materialised from thin air. Abbey made a beeline for him. 'Taj, I want to show you a bird's nest I found. When are you coming to our house?'

Kim couldn't make sense of him in this kind of social context. She was too used to seeing him in his old work clothes, tools in hand. One thing, though, he sure scrubbed up well.

'Taj,' said Jean. 'Very glad you're here. If this keeps up, we'll have to stop calling you the hermit.' She turned to Kim. 'This is Taj's first quiz night too, so you're not the only newbie.'

Pat rang the bell again, and acknowledged the people of the Biripi nation, the traditional owners of the land where the Tingo hall stood. 'Listen up. Correct answers are worth one point, and no calling out. Six teams, six rounds of questions. Teams nominate a quizmaster, who keeps score and asks one round of questions each so I don't have to stand up here all bloody night. Oh, and there's prizes at the end.'

Ben touched her arm. 'He makes the rules up as he goes. They change every time.'

'Are we ready?' asked Pat. A murmur of assent came from the floor. 'Okay, I'll start us off. The subject for this round is Australian history. Let's see how much you fellers know about the real history of your own country. Right. *What happened in May 1967?*'

'I was born,' said Charlie, and the room laughed.

'No singing out,' said Pat. 'And that's wrong.'

'I should know when I was born,' protested Charlie.

'I'm talking about something historically significant.'

'Being born was pretty bloody significant for me.' More laughter.

'How on earth are we supposed to answer a question like that?' asked Kim.

'Aboriginal people were included in the census for the first time,' said Jean. 'Write it down. I've been to enough of these things to know what Pat's after.'

Kim duly wrote down the answer.

The next few questions were easier, at least in the sense that they weren't impossibly open-ended. But they were pretty obscure just the same, or at least Kim thought so. Pat had bifocals perched on the end of his nose and seemed to be reading from a set of ancient Trivial Pursuit cards. *'What federal electorate did Malcolm Fraser represent from 1955 to 1983? What was the name of the plane Sir Charles Kingsford Smith flew across the Pacific in 1928? What was Al Capone's nickname?'* She was clueless about most of the questions. Ben and Mel weren't much better. Taj stayed quiet. Thank god for Jean. Every now and then, Pat abandoned his tattered quiz cards and slipped in a curly one off the top of his head. '*What happened in February 1965?*'

Before Kim had a chance to complain, Jean said, 'Charles Perkins led the Freedom Rides.'

And so it continued till the end of the round. 'Bloody glad that's over,' said Ben, sculling his drink and pushing back his chair. 'Who wants a beer?'

Taj raised his hand. 'I'll have one.'

'Righto.'

Kim looked up from tallying the points, straight into Taj's eyes. She forced a smile. His gaze always left her a little tongue-tied, especially without Abbey as a go-between. She tried to look away, but couldn't seem to.

When Taj worked at the house, they talked about walls and windows. Nothing more important than that, not even the orchids. Why? Perhaps she didn't want to upset Jake. Perhaps knowing the hidden place where the ravine orchids grew would anchor her too firmly to Tingo. Perhaps Taj's brooding brown eyes were simply too disturbing.

Kim took a gulp of wine, searching for some small talk to break the awkward silence between them. 'I didn't think Muslims drank beer.' Had she really blurted that out? What was wrong with *Have you been busy lately?* or *Wasn't it warm today?*

His eyes softened with amusement. 'I didn't think they did either.' He delivered the remark, cryptic as it was, with considerable warmth.

Jake came over, eyes blazing. 'What's he doing here?' His constant mantra where Taj was concerned.

'Honey, Taj is on our table.' Kim's stomach tightened, and she drank her glass dry. Please, please don't let him have an outburst. Not here in front of half the town. In front of Jean. In front of all his new friends.

Jake glared at Taj. 'I don't want you on my mum's team.'

Jean and Mel stopped talking. Conversation ground to a halt at the next table as well.

'That's enough,' said Kim, knowing how futile it was reprimand to Jake, going through the motions anyway. 'Say sorry to Taj.'

'No damned way.'

Ben arrived with the drinks. 'Whoa, what's going on here?' He moved Jake aside with a hand on each shoulder. 'You can't use that sort of language in front of your mother. Apologise right now, or you and me – we're going to have a problem.'

Oh no. Jake didn't respond well to ultimatums. Any moment now he'd launch into a fury, alienating everybody. It would be like Sturt Street all over again, and it was her fault. Not realising Taj might be here as a trigger. Coming here at all.

'Well?' said Ben. 'I'm waiting.'

Jake scowled and breathed harder, his fists balled at his side. His face went red. All the signs were there. Kim tensed in readiness . . . but the explosion didn't happen. Instead Jake examined the floor and mumbled something beneath his breath

Ben's frowned. 'I can't hear you.'

Jake looked up at his mother. 'Sorry.'

'That's better,' said Ben. 'Now beat it. Round two's about to start.' He plonked a stubbie in front of Taj. 'There you go, mate. Get that into you.'

Jean leaned forward and whispered, 'Kim, it's Taj who deserves the apology.'

'Yes, of course.' Kim's heart rate was returning to normal. 'I'm so sorry, Taj'

Jean frowned. 'No, I meant Jake needs to . . .'

'Let it go,' said Taj, who'd remained impassive throughout.

Kim wanted the floor to open up and swallow her.

The bell rang. Team two, the Village Idiots were up next. A spindly teenage boy acted as quizmaster and the topic was sport. Ben came into his own this round. *How many gold medals did Australia win at the 2000 Sydney Olympics? Who is Australia's all-time leading run-scorer in one-day internationals? How many Australians have raced in the Formula One world championship?* Kim didn't know or care, and found it hard to concentrate. Mel had given up trying to answer questions altogether, and spent most of her time glaring at Geoff. She'd found another bottle of wine, and was giving it a nudge.

'*Which batsman helped India make one of the best comebacks in test history by scoring 281 in the second innings, on the 2000–2001 Australian tour of India?*'

'Sachin Tendulkar,' said Ben.

'How do you spell that?' asked Kim.

'No.' Taj drained his beer. 'It's VVS Laxman.' This was the first time he'd offered an answer.

Kim looked up. 'What do I write?'

'Don't ask me,' said Jean. 'I've no idea.'

'I'm team captain,' said Ben. 'Put down Tendulkar.'

She hadn't realised their team had a captain.

Geoff passed by their table with two cups of coffee. 'How can he bring that woman here among all our friends?' said Mel. Her voice wavered and a sheen of sweat showed on her cheeks. She went to top up Kim's wine.

'No more for me,' said Kim. 'I have to drive.'

Mel had to drive too, but the hint fell on deaf ears. Mel refilled her own glass instead, and Kim went back to scoring. Keep your head down, she told herself. Don't get involved. Just survive the night and get out of there.

The rounds kept coming: geography, films, entertainment. Jake stayed away. Abbey returned occasionally with scraps of childish gossip: Nikki was getting a pony. Aiden's mother was having twins. Todd could wiggle his ears. 'Jake said Dad could touch his nose with his tongue,' said Abbey. 'Could he Mum?'

Kim searched her mind, but for some reason couldn't remember. How could that be? How could she have forgotten something like that? Abbey gave up waiting for an answer, and ran off to join the other children.

Kim felt Taj's eyes upon her, and turned away. He wasn't being much help, which was understandable. How was he supposed to know Marilyn Monroe's real name or what city Beyoncé was born in?

To be fair, she didn't answer many questions either. Neither did Mel or Ben. They didn't have to. Jean was a walking encyclopaedia.

At the end of the fifth round, their team was neck and neck with Geoff's Sock Puppets, and Mel was distraught. 'We can't let them beat us. Geoff thinks I'm stupid. Look at him, gloating. He thinks that without him we can't win.' She glared at Ben. 'If we'd gone with Taj instead of you on that cricket question, we'd be ahead right now.'

'Hang on a minute, Einstein,' said Ben. 'How many questions have you answered tonight?'

Jean tried to give him a swift kick under the table, and connected with Kim instead. Ouch.

Pat approached their table. 'Sorry to do this to you, Bright Sparks, but Jean's hubby has rung in. Apparently Bessie's gone down. He reckons she'll calve any time, and that Jean would want to be there.'

'Of course I want to be there,' said Jean. 'How exciting.' She found her bag. 'Sorry to leave you in the lurch like this, but it's Bessie's first calf.'

'We'll never win without Jean.' Mel glanced miserably across to where the Sock Puppets were smiling and clinking glasses.

Pat stepped up to ring his bell. 'So, final round, with two teams neck and neck for first place. Hold onto your hats, folks.' A few whoops. 'Now let's make Kim welcome, quizmaster for the Bright Sparks.' A smattering of applause.

'Knock 'em dead,' said Ben.

She stepped onto the stage, burning with self-consciousness. Pat handed her the cards. Oh no, science and nature. Finally a subject she was good at, and she wasn't allowed to answer any questions. Poor Mel. Geoff would have a clear run.

Kim began. *'Which native Australian tree lives the longest? How many million years ago did Gondwanaland split apart? "Aurum" is the Latin name for what precious metal?* Damn, she knew all of them so far. She glanced over at her table and was surprised to see Ben writing furiously and Mel smiling. The quiz grew harder, too hard even for her. *What is the Latin name for a Moon Bear? Which native animal did scientist Dr David Peacock successfully reintroduce to South Australia? What is a* '*trophic cascade*'? Where on earth did Pat get these questions? Kim finished the round and returned to her table, where the rest of the team were joking around with each other. Mel's grin was the widest of all.

'What are you guys so happy about?'

'Taj here's a dark horse,' said Ben. 'Answered every one of those questions.'

Pat rang the bell and began reading out the answers. Ben picked up the scoresheet and his pen. 'Now we'll see if he was feeding us a load of bull.'

'You weren't, were you Taj?' Mel clutched dramatically at his arm. 'I'll die if those bloody Sock Puppets win.'

'Nah, it's all good,' said Ben, ticking off line after line. 'He's acing it.'

'That's the finish,' said Pat. 'Add up your scores.' He collected the tally sheets from each table, headed back to the stage and balanced his glasses on his nose. 'Well done everybody. For much of the evening, it was very close, but one team ran away with the game in that final round.'

Mel couldn't contain her glee. 'Look at him.' She pointed to Geoff, who was high-fiving one of his teammates 'He thinks he's won.'

'And without further ado,' said Pat. 'The winning team is . . . the Bright Sparks.' Cheers, applause, and disbelieving glances from Geoff's table.

Kim looked at Taj askance. 'Those were tough questions. You did very well.'

Taj shrugged. 'I like biology.'

'It must be more than that,' she said. 'Who the heck knows the frequency of a wolf's howl?'

'Leave him be,' said Ben. 'The man's answered enough questions for one night.'

The skinny teenager emerged from the kitchen with a side of lamb slung over each shoulder. 'First prize is a prime lamb,' said Pat. 'Donated by Geoff Masters of She-Oak Springs.'

'What a nerve,' said Mel.

Pat looked over to where Geoff sat. 'Looks like you won't be winning it back tonight, mate.' The rest of his team laughed, but not Geoff. 'Now, we do have a prize for the runners-up.'

'That's a shame,' said Mel.

The teenager dropped the lamb sides to the floor with a thud, ducked from the stage and returned with a milk crate. 'Second prize is a vintage record collection,' said Pat. 'You Sock Puppets will have to argue among yourselves over these little beauties.' The moth-eaten sleeve of *Val Doonican's Greatest Hits* peeped out the top. Mel chuckled and drained her glass of wine. 'Don't laugh,' said Pat. 'Vinyl's making a comeback. These records will be worth a fortune in a few years. Anyway, thank you all for coming. We've raised almost a thousand dollars towards the purchase of our new fire truck.' Everybody clapped. Mel hooted and cheered.

Kim turned to Ben. 'I'm a bit worried about her driving.'

Ben sized Mel up for a few seconds. 'Come on, mate. Call those kids. I'm driving you lot home.'

'I'll be okay—' began Mel.

'No, you won't.' Ben strode off to find Nikki and Todd.

'I didn't know he cared,' giggled Mel. 'Hope Geoff's watching.'

Jake appeared at Kim's side, all smiles now. 'I don't want to go yet. Todd and I are having the best time.'

'It has been a good night, hasn't it?' said Kim. 'But everybody's going home now, even Todd.' It would be an even better night if she could talk Jake into saying goodbye to Taj. Baby steps.

But when she turned around, Taj was gone.

Ben arrived with the kids trailing after him. Nikki and Abbey were holding hands and yawning.

'What about the sides of lamb?' asked Kim. 'How are we supposed to share them?'

'Taj said he'll slice them up and drop them off for us,' said Ben. The very mention of Taj's name was enough to wipe the smile from Jake's face. 'Now, let's get going. These girls look like they could go to sleep standing up.' Ben put out his hand. 'Keys please, Mel.'

Sweet of Ben to look after her like that. Mel was plainly quite taken with him, and why not? Drop dead gorgeous. A larrikin on the outside, with a heart of pure gold. Connor was like that. Kim looked over to where her son was laughing and arm wrestling with Todd. Jake respected Ben. Nobody else could have headed off his outburst the way Ben did. She couldn't be both father and mother, no matter how hard she tried. Jake needed a man to teach him how to be a man. Maybe that man was Ben.

CHAPTER 13

Taj whistled as he packed the ute and did a final tool check. A week into the new year and Kim was finally back from spending Christmas with family in Sydney. Her two-week absence had seemed much longer. Taj prided himself on self-sufficiency. He'd schooled himself to be grateful for what he had, to require no more. So why did his thoughts turn to Kim on waking and when he closed his eyes at night? Why had he counted down the days until she returned?

He'd spent a lonely Christmas, lonelier than usual, and was glad the holiday was over. The loss of Camila always loomed large in this season, her favourite time of year. She'd loved their secret Christmases in Afghanistan: white-capped peaks, fir forests heavy with glazed snow, decorating their cabin with a tiny tree that could swiftly be hidden from visitors.

Her parents, Kamal and Amira, had converted to their own vaguely understood version of Christianity, after being helped at Camila's birth by UN medical aid workers. Camila survived because an American surgeon performed an emergency caesarean on her mother. However he extracted a heavy price in return – an undertaking that the family convert. Such was the depth of their gratitude that her parents raised Camila and her sisters as secret Christians.

There was no such thing as religious freedom in Afghanistan, and for Taj, the doctor's demand was just another example of control. It was an unfair and dangerous ask, yet Camila would hear no criticism of the man who'd saved her life and that of her mother.

Her parent's understanding of this new foreign faith was imperfect. However they tried their best, using objects and ideas gleaned during the American's short stay. The English language bible he'd given them remained a mystery, so they relied on a wall poster written in Dari. Camila had shown Taj where it hung in the back of a cupboard, hidden by furs. He still remembered it. The bright colours. The three quotes. *'Do unto others as you'd have them do unto you.' 'Do not judge so that you will not be judged.' 'What do you benefit if you gain the whole world but lose your own soul?'* Next came an injunction to prayer and to tolerance. A picture of Jesus on the cross. *From the cross, through the church, to the world.* And a children's story of the first Christmas tree, a tradition that her family had embraced. Camila had been gone for eight years now, and he'd accepted the reality of her passing. Yet he still wished she could know one of the sunny summer Christmases of his adopted country. Maybe she did know. From time to time he felt her spirit smiling down on him.

This year Taj had cut a little tree in her honour, from a plantation in the next valley. The trees grew on the bones of a dead rainforest, clear-felled to make way for the rolling green desert of pines. Taj found evidence of the forest under his feet: fragments of mahogany, tulipwood, white beech – even a stump of ancient red cedar, three metres across. All premium cabinet timbers. He collected this waste wood and used it to whittle gifts for Jean and her students, and for Kim and her children. A carved cow and calf for Jean. A poodle for Abbey. He fashioned a cricket bat for Jake, from one of the willows that grew as weeds along Cedar Creek. And for Kim, a mahogany figurine of a Peri, the beautiful winged fairies of Nuristan folklore, who represented everything bright and good in nature. He wrapped the gifts and placed them beneath the tree, which was decorated with sprigs of flowering lilly pilly, gumnuts and the colourful fruits of tamarind and blueberry ash. And there they remained.

As Christmas dragged into New Year, his desire to see Kim grew into a kind of nagging background hunger. A homesickness – not for a place, but for a person.

Taj had suffered more than his fair share of homesickness. When he moved to Parun, he'd been homesick for Ariana. When he moved to Kabul, he was homesick for Parun. But although it had taken some time to creep up on him, it was when he moved to England after winning an academic scholarship that he'd suffered the most.

The move from Afghanistan to Leeds plunged Taj into a brand-new fast-paced world of busy streets, endless shops and girls in jeans and short skirts. Overwhelming. Too much to see. What to do? Where to look? The vibrant student town, buzzing with eclectic people and diverse ideas, opened his eyes and his mind. The contrast really hit home the first time his classmates took him out on the town for his birthday – an Afghan restaurant in his honour.

The rather plain sign outside on the street read *Kabul Express*. The narrow staircase was plastered with clichéd posters of desert scenes, camels, and caravans of Afghan women in traditional dress – no hint of the country's vast mountainous north. Upstairs was all faded glory – 'a seventies hotel lounge gone wrong', his friends called it. Gold accents, black glass, and red fabric seats lining the bar. The food had been good, surprisingly authentic, and speaking Dari to the expatriate owner had eased his homesickness. But in every other respect, it was unlike any night Taj had known.

There was wine, for one thing: copious amounts of cheap chianti, scoffed by the bottleful. And there was talk lasting into the morning, ranging from philosophy to politics, art to religion. 'Are you a Muslim?' they asked him.

'For thousands of years Nuristanis followed an ancient form of Hinduism,' he told them. 'In the 1890s a conquering Emir, Rahman Khan, converted the people to Islam by the sword. But swords cannot conquer people's hearts. Some of us retained our old customs and beliefs in secret.'

'So you're a Hindu?' asked a girl.

'I said some, not all. Why must you label me? I lost any faith I had long ago.'

'They say there are no atheists in foxholes,' said another. 'When death threatens, everybody prays to some god or another.'

The conversation moved on to a lively debate on the pros and cons of atheism. Taj hadn't imagined this kind of dazzling intellectual freedom could exist, and he hoped England might become his second home.

But this new life came at a cost. The initial thrill of city-living swiftly waned. He gazed up at a smog-filled, hazy night sky, and wished for inky blackness, for the blazing moon and stars of the Hindu Kush. He walked along the River Aire, flowing meekly within its manicured banks, and wished for a rough slatted bridge, no wider than a man, swinging high above a furious alpine torrent. He ventured into the green and pleasant Yorkshire countryside to view mediaeval abbeys and Norman castles. Yet before long, he was seeking out the wide moors, broad-leaved woodlands and limestone cliffs of national parks. It wasn't enough, though. He couldn't connect with this tame landscape. He longed for the wild mountains of home.

After finishing his studies, Taj returned to Afghanistan with a master's degree in environmental biology and a new understanding of the dangers facing his country's wilderness. Decades of war had devastated the forests and unique wildlife of Nuristan. Bears, wolves, ibex and snow leopards were being driven to extinction, and when villagers sold pelts and timber rights for a pittance, they also suffered.

Taj found himself in the right place at the right time to secure his dream job – head ranger at Afghanistan's new Hindu Kush National Park. It encompassed an area twenty-five per cent larger than Yellowstone. Taj was charged with protecting traditional communities inside the park's borders and recruiting local people in the fight against poachers and illegal logging.

It was there he met Camila, a health worker helping to establish the area's first medical clinic. She stood out among her darker companions, with pale hair, skin the colour of ivory, green eyes, and a delicate, chiselled face that would have made Botticelli proud. 'My mother says I'm descended from Alexander The Great,' she said, when Taj boldly complimented her on her flawless complexion.

'Alexander the Great himself?' he'd teased. Alexander's invading armies were a popular explanation for the presence of fair-skinned people in Nuristan, but it was the first time he'd heard someone claim direct descent from the great man.

Camila was beautiful on the inside too: gentle, wise and brave enough to teach girls and women about their rights. Even when it antagonised the corrupt local mullah, who had links with the Taliban. Within a year they were married, and together they made quite a team. Taj's proudest accomplishment was the Wildlife Hero program he'd started at the local school. He enlisted the children as carers for bear and wolf cubs orphaned by poachers. He sought their help in wildlife mapping projects, and taught them how trees stopped the erosion of rivers and pastures. They in turn taught their parents. Thank goodness the program had continued after his sudden exit. After all, the future of Nuristan's wilderness, of all the world's wildernesses, lay with the next generation.

Taj picked up the little pup playing at his feet, and put him on the seat beside him. He checked that he'd packed the presents for Kim and her children. 'Come on, Dusty,' he said, feeling an unfamiliar surge of excitement about the day ahead. 'We have work to do.'

CHAPTER 14

*K*im trailed her fingers along the freshly painted verandah rail. Taj had done a good job. Journey's End was starting to look cared for again. He certainly was a hard worker, having arrived before she was up. She could hear him hammering away, putting a new roof on the hay shed.

It was as beautiful a morning as she'd ever seen. Diamond-bright. Fragrant with satinwood and peppermint. Above her, the firewheel tree's crimson flowers sparkled with dewdrops, and a flock of lorikeets burst from its branches in a rainbow of colour. The mountains beyond, framed by the blue span of sky, seemed to hang within reach. Heaven and earth had conspired to create a masterpiece – and yet she found no comfort in all this loveliness.

Just a week into January and she and Jake were already at each other's throats. At this rate it was going to a very, very long summer. Kim rubbed a hand over her eyes. She wasn't proud of herself. How had she let this morning's argument turn into a shouting match?

Christmas without Connor was always difficult, but this year had been a nightmare. Staying with her parents, with no Daisy to act as a circuit breaker. So much confected cheer, trying to make things fun for the sake of the children.

Her mother believed that the key to happiness was keeping busy, and had arranged all sorts of outings and activities, bless her. But Kim didn't want to go to the beach. She didn't want to swim and make sandcastles and feel the sun on her skin. She didn't want to play back-yard cricket, or even keep score. She didn't want to have Christmas at all. There was too much sorrow in the ordinary moments. In the fake plastic tree, because Connor wasn't there to organise a real one. In the empty chair that Jake kept in his father's honour at the table. In the confusion over who would carve the turkey. Kim had fled town as swiftly as courtesy allowed.

The children didn't mind. They'd soon grown bored in Sydney without Daisy's kids for company. Suburban backyards and city parks had lost their appeal when compared to the joys of running wild in the country. Jake was eager to resume training for his first cricket match with Tingo Juniors. Abbey couldn't wait to see the animals. And Kim had hoped things would be better when they got back.

But the tension had followed them home. This morning's clash with Jake continued the longstanding row that had flared in such an ugly way between them at Christmas and still festered. It was simple. Jake wanted a dog. No, it was more complicated than that. Jake was desperate for a dog, possessed by the idea. For some reason he had it in his head that Kim was buying him a puppy for Christmas. His pain and disappointment when one did not arrive was terrible to see. Yet although Kim would do almost anything for her son, she couldn't give him the thing he most wanted. Not yet. Scout and Connor were inextricably linked in her mind. She could no more replace Scout, than she could bring a new man into her life.

She'd tried, she really had. She'd tried so hard to let that little dog go, but she could see him everywhere. Sleeping in the shade of the firewheel tree. Barking comically, half-in and half-out of the doggy door. Making a collection of his favourite sticks on the verandah. She'd tried to strip away these images of him, layer by layer, hoping to reveal a clean place beneath where fresh memories might grow. But the scar tissue ran too deep, and it hurt too much, and she wasn't brave enough.

Jake would have to wait until she was ready. It wasn't like he didn't have any pets. Mel's unofficial wildlife sanctuary had well and truly overflowed into Journey's End. Bonnie and Clyde were back on the doorstep the minute they returned from Sydney, along with a few extra additions to the menagerie. Abbey's shirt currently harboured a baby possum curled up next to her heart. Two fledgling magpies lived in Jake's room, and the bath was home to an injured water dragon, complete with an island of river sand and smooth water-worn rocks for him to hide behind. But her son had his heart set on a dog.

The ring of steel on timber woke the echoes. Jake had graduated from the tomahawk to a light axe, courtesy of Ben. He was taking out his anger on the wood heap. Well, at least he wasn't taking it out on her. At this rate, there'd soon be no logs left to chop. His fascination with heavy blades troubled her. Axes and angry adolescents were a dangerous mix, and she had the scar on her ankle to prove it.

Yesterday Kim had picked up the axe herself. She wasn't very good. Couldn't judge the right place to strike, and wound up just denting the stumps or making useless chips, too small to burn. But she understood her son better for trying. Kim imagined him, red-faced, swinging the blade high and letting it fall, using gravity to increase his power. She could feel the strain in his aching shoulders, the shock in his wrists when steel met wood. Hear his ragged breath. And she suddenly longed to be the one with that axe in her hand. It was what she needed right now.

Abbey came running from the house, prising a bundle of soft grey fur from around her neck. 'Stop it, Hush, that tickles.' The little possum took refuge down her pyjama top, provoking a peal of giggles. Abbey held out a handful of glass gems. 'These are a present for the bower bird. Is Taj here yet? He promised to show me when we got back.'

Kim took a moment to *ooh* and *aah* over the shiny blue beads. How on earth could her children have such diametrically opposed opinions of Mr Taj Kahn? Kim touched Abbey's rosy cheek. Tingo had brought her pale waiflike daughter out into the sunshine. At Journey's End Abbey slept soundly, ate well and played hard. She even looked different, with her face sporting a healthy layer of dirt, nut-brown skin, and curls brightened to white-gold by the sun.

And Kim had to admit that Taj was a big part of this transformation.

A surprising friendship had sprung up between the shy girl and the quiet handyman. Kim had been uneasy about it at first, finding reason to stay close, keeping watch like a good mother should. What she discovered touched her deeply. With Taj, Abbey found her voice. The pair talked of frost and rain, of trees and birds, of clouds and rainbows. Of chainsaws and septic tanks and water pumps. They talked of why the sky was blue, and how the forests grew, and where the eagles flew. Taj seemed to enjoy these conversations as much as Abbey did. This unexpectedly tender side of him only added to her curiosity about the man.

The house phone rang and she hurried inside. Maybe it was Telstra or the TV people? At a pinch they could live for a year without television. That might even be good for them. But they couldn't live without internet access, and the Olympic Games were in August. It would be unfair if the kids couldn't watch, so Kim had decided to get a satellite dish. The sooner the better. Cranky Jake could use a distraction from arguing with her.

But instead of the hoped for technician, it was Mel on the phone. 'Want to come for a drive today?' she asked. 'It'll be fun, I promise. Right up your alley.'

'Sorry. I'm waiting on a call from the TV people, and Taj is here.' Kim felt a twinge of guilt. The call could wait, and Taj didn't need supervision. She could get away if she wanted to. But she was in too dark a place, in no mood to share, and sharing was Mel's favourite pastime.

'Please, Kim. There's a rainforest nursery holding a closing-down sale and I could really use your expertise as a botanist.'

'A rainforest nursery?' Kim had never heard of such a thing.

'The bloke who runs it – Dougy Henderson – had a stroke. He's gone to live with his daughter in Taree. Such a shame, all that local knowledge lost. Doug was an old hippy at heart, a grassroots conservationist. For forty years he grew plants endemic to the mid-north-coast forests and sold them on to home gardeners, farmers and land care groups. Now all his stock has to go.'

Kim was intrigued. 'What are you looking for? Anything in particular?'

'That's just it,' said Mel. 'I don't know. There's a huge eroded gully in my top paddock, the one that abuts the national park. I've always wanted to fence that land off and replant it, but Geoff would never agree.'

'But now you can,' said Kim.

'Yes, but I have to know what to plant. I can't ask Doug anymore, so I thought . . . '

'There are some candidates right in your own greenhouse,' said Kim. 'But you need a broader selection – a mix of fast, medium and slow-growing plants.'

'Like what?'

'First you'll want to establish a forest canopy as quickly as possible. You need quick-growing pioneer species like silky oak, blue fig, red ash and tulipwood.'

'What then?'

'Once you have part shade, you can start on your understorey. Smaller rainforest trees like lemon myrtle and tuckeroo. Shrubs like rosewood and pepper bush. Palms and lilies like cordyline, burrawang and cunjevoi. That's the way to get a naturally layered and diverse forest.'

Mel giggled. 'You'll come then?'

'Yes.' Kim was laughing at herself now. 'I suppose so.'

'Right. Tell Abbey that Nikki's coming with us.'

'What about Todd?'

'Sorry. He's gone fishing with Geoff. Pick you up in half an hour.'

'Yay,' said Abbey when she heard. 'I get to see Nikki. Do you think Taj will mind if I see the bower bird next time?'

'I don't think he'll mind at all.'

Kim made Abbey breakfast and took some toast outside for Jake. The world had fallen silent. He'd either worked out his frustration or run out of wood. She called him from the back verandah, still astonished at how a voice carried in these mountains. She didn't really expect him to respond. She'd probably have to go looking. But no, there he was, pelting back from the sheds, covered in dirt. What had he been up to?

Jake accepted the offered toast. He must have forgiven her. The hammering started up again from the hay shed, and another sound too. A soft animal sound, halfway between a yap and a whine. Taj must have brought one of his dogs with him.

Kim studied Jake's sun-flushed face. What to do about him? He'd be bored stiff going to look at plants, especially without Todd for company. But she didn't much like the idea of leaving him alone with Taj either.

'I'm going with Mel and the girls to look at a nursery,' she said. 'Want to come?'

'Nah.' Jake's face showed no trace of his earlier anger. It was a puzzle given his capacity to hold a grudge. 'I'll stay and look after the animals.'

Kim considered her options. 'I don't want you starting anything with Taj.'

'Don't worry, I won't.' He was shovelling toast in his mouth so fast she thought he'd choke. 'Promise.'

'Thank you, Jake. That means a lot.' Two pieces of toast left and he took them both. 'Can you give the joeys their lunchtime feeds? Just warm the bottles in the fridge.' He nodded. 'And answer the phone if it rings.'

'Sure, Mum.' Jake was already walking away with the toast when something caused him to stop and turn around. Was that a smile? 'And Mum . . . '

'Yes?'

'Have fun.'

Kim stared after him. How astonishing. Maybe the mountains *were* working their magic. Maybe the stress and strain of Sydney was seeping away, taking all that poisonous tension with it, leaving them room to breathe again.

A bold willy wagtail darted down from the firewheel tree right in front of her: Connor's favourite bird. 'Hello,' she said. 'Aren't you lovely?' As if in response he danced closer, a poser in a black and white tuxedo, wagging his tail and chanting *Sweet pretty creature, sweet pretty creature* over and over. 'Flatterer.' Tears pricked her eyes, but for once they were happy tears. Journey's End worked in mysterious ways.

CHAPTER 15

Taj nailed the corrugated iron ridge cap onto the new roof, and stepped back to survey his handiwork. He'd rebuilt the old hay shed almost from scratch, replacing rotten beams, rusty struts, missing tin. This was the kind of work he loved. Restoring things. Creating something intact from what had been broken. The shed should last Kim another hundred years.

From his vantage point on the roof, Taj could see the rear of the homestead. Jake was talking to his mother. Another argument perhaps? It was impossible to spend very long at Journey's End without realising how very alike mother and son were. Jake was a handful, no doubt about that, but Taj recognised where the antagonism stemmed from. As a child he'd been just as lost, just as angry, when his own father died. Furious with the world, needing somebody to blame. For him, that part had been easy. A Taliban commander had murdered his father. The enemy had a face, a name. How different it must be for Jake, with no tangible target for his bitterness, no picture in his mind of the man responsible. Nobody to hate. Not until now.

Down on the ground, Dusty ran about, not looking where he was going, his gaze fixed skyward on Taj. He kept tripping over his own feet and running into the ladder. 'Hold on, little one,' said Taj. 'I'm coming.' He climbed down, finding it hard not to step on the excited pup as he reached the ground. Taj picked Dusty up and hugged his wriggle-happy body.

Dusty was one of three orphaned puppies Taj had found before Christmas up in Tarringtops. He was collecting bush seeds and fire-wood, when Saber picked up a scent and wouldn't let it drop. Taj shouldered his rifle and followed him along an animal track that ran up a scrubby slope. The dog normally only showed such keen interest in foxes or wild goats, and either one was fair game.

The trail led to a mass of big boulders near the top of an incline, all overgrown with bangalow palms and climbing wombat berry. Saber thrust his way forward, nose to ground, then disappeared abruptly. Taj stopped just as suddenly. Where had his dog gone? He investigated the pile of rocks, edging his way in, methodically parting the leafy screen. There, a flash of white fur just ahead of him. He pushed through the tangle of vines. Beneath the dead stump of a forest giant lay the yawning mouth of a wide den. Saber stood to one side, whining and wagging his tail.

Huddled near the entrance were three little puppies, suckling in vain at the belly of their dead mother. They couldn't have been more than a week old; their eyes still closed. There was no pungent smell of death. The she-dingo had only recently lost her fight for life. Taj examined her body. She'd been shot in the hip and the wound had not proved immediately fatal. There'd been time to struggle back to the den, agonising as that crawl must have been. Time to wrap herself around her pups. She'd died with her head bowed and tongue extended, in a last attempt to clean and comfort her young.

Taj had seen a lot of human suffering in his time, more than a man had a right to. He'd lost a lot of people he loved. Not much made it through the shield he wore. Yet something in this mother dingo's devotion and courage moved him to tears. Tenderly he covered her body with branches, and sprays of rose myrtle. And though he wasn't a religious man, he offered a prayer to Imra, as his father might have done. Then he bundled up the whimpering babies, two girls and a boy, and brought them home.

Carla was delighted. She eagerly adopted the orphans, adding them to her own litter of newborn pups, suckling all ten of them. But it had been more than a month now, and the physical demands of her growing family were taking their toll. Carla was tired, losing weight. It was time to wean the cuckoos from the nest.

Like wolf cubs of his native Nuristan, the dingo puppies were developing more rapidly than domestic dogs. At around five weeks of age they were as forward, physically and mentally, as a maremma pup at eight weeks. And although they were all thriving, the little male, Dusty, had grown much faster than his littermates. He was different from his sisters in other ways too. They had sandy fur and white-tipped tails. Dusty bore the dark black and tan coat of the forest dingo. He soon learnt that the sound of an opening fridge on the verandah meant a meal was close, and would sit by his bowl. He learnt to climb up the netting to the roof of his kennel, and stash food there out of reach of the others. He learnt that by working at the joins in the wire with his teeth, he could squeeze out of his pen altogether. Such a smart dog. In many ways Dusty reminded him of Aakil.

Yesterday Taj had moved the pups to a nursery yard adjoining the dingo enclosure. Here they could safely meet the four other young dingoes, all orphans themselves. In time, he hoped they might bond and form a functional pack.

The adult dingoes showed a lot of interest in the little newcomers. Red, the alpha male, especially so. He greeted the female pups with friendly overtures, wagging his tail and yodelling in excitement. But with Dusty it was a different story. Red honed in on the little male with snarling intent, never taking his gaze off him. He prowled the fence-line, testing it with teeth and claws, then almost succeeded in scaling its three-metre height.

Taj frowned. Things were not going to plan. He knew of the dingoes' famous problem-solving ability. Some said they rivalled that of the wolf. But if he hadn't seen what happened next, he wouldn't have believed it. Red sat down for a few minutes, looking around the enclosure, for all the world like he was deep in thought. His intelligent brown eyes settled on the tug-of-war toys that lay several metres from the fence – old car tyres with lengths of tow rope attached. He bounded to the closest one, seized the rope between his teeth and dragged it towards the boundary. By the time Taj realised what was happening, Red had made a new run at the fence. And by using the tyre as a springboard, this time he scrambled to the top. He teetered for a moment at the apex, balancing himself for the leap down. It gave Taj a few precious seconds. He sprang into action, unlatching the gate and scooping Dusty into the air, just as Red snatched at him with bared teeth.

The three other dingoes trotted over to examine the tyre, then as one, gazed up at the fence top. Dingoes were observational learners. If he didn't remove those tug-of-war toys, they'd all soon be out of their enclosure. Taj had hugged Dusty to his chest, mindful of Red's baleful glare. 'Bad luck, my friend. This little one's coming with me.'

Taj kept glancing towards the house, toying with the idea of going up to see Kim. Finding the courage to hand out the gifts he'd made was proving harder than he thought.

He felt a tug and looked down. Dusty had seized his bootlaces, growling comically, and thrashing his head from side to side. Taj wiggled his foot, provoking a fresh flurry of growling. He picked Dusty up. 'You're a fine strong pup, aren't you?' He was rewarded with a lick on the nose. Dingoes, like wolves, were intensely social animals, fiercely loyal and bonding strongly to their *family*. They needed that. Without a dingo pack for Dusty to join, he'd need a substitute human family. Yet raising the pup with his own maremma dogs would blunt their guarding instinct, their natural protective response to predators. Perhaps there was another option for Dusty, a better option.

Taj had spotted Jake early that morning, after the boy became bored with chopping wood. He'd been lurking in a yellow-flowering cassia thicket above the hay shed – eyes trained on Dusty. Occasionally he dropped to his knees, crawling partway from cover, calling the pup at a whisper and clicking his fingers. Dusty needed little urging, as curious about Jake as Jake was about him. Soon the pair were rough-and-tumbling together in the shade. Caught up in play. Forgetting all about Taj on the roof. It was only when Kim called to Jake from the house that the spell was broken and he remembered he was supposed to be hiding.

The boy quickly backed into the thicket and out the other side, waving the pup away. Dusty had other ideas. He pounced after Jake, grabbing at his jeans and whining. 'Shoo, shoo.' It was no use. Dusty was determined his playmate should not escape.

Taj smiled and took pity on the boy. Climbing noisily down the ladder, he called the puppy, pretending not to know what was happening. This was just the distraction Jake needed, and he managed to slip away. A disappointed Dusty trotted back to the hay shed.

'So,' said Taj, chucking the pup under the chin. 'You've found a new friend, eh? Somebody more fun than me?' Taj fetched a shallow dish from the car, filled it with water and gave the pup a meaty marrowbone to chew on. 'Now, you stay put. Something tells me your friend will soon be back.'

As if on cue, Dusty turned his head and pricked his ears. Moments later Taj could feel the boy's eyes upon him.

'That's a nice dog.' Taj turned to find Jake standing out in the open, watching him warily. 'What's his name?'

'Dusty.'

'Can he have some toast?' Taj nodded and Jake dropped two triangles of vegemite toast on the ground. The pup scoffed them down.

'Would you like to hold him?' asked Taj.

The boy moved restlessly from one foot to the other. 'I suppose.'

Taj picked Dusty up and stepped towards Jake, who flinched but held his ground as he took the pup. Jake's guarded expression changed to one of pure joy. He gazed into Dusty's topaz eyes, transfixed. The pup squirmed closer, resting his head on Jake's heart, making contented rumbles in the back of his throat like he was purring.

'That pup likes you,' said Taj. Jake clutched him tighter. Dusty proceeded to wash Jake's face with his neat pink tongue. 'He's yours now.'

Jake blinked in confusion. 'Mine?'

Taj shrugged. 'Only if you want him.'

'Oh, I want him,' said Jake. 'I want him more than anything.'

'You'll have to ask your mother.'

Jake's eyes narrowed. 'I don't get it. Why would you give me a puppy?'

'He needs a home.'

'This won't change anything,' said Jake. 'You can't make me like you. I'll never like you.'

'Suit yourself.' Taj took a swig from his water bottle and began collecting up his tools. When he turned around, Dusty and Jake were gone.

CHAPTER 16

'I'm Lizzie,' said the plump young woman with the baby on her hip. 'You're welcome to browse, but I'm afraid I don't know much about the stock. There are more than five thousand plants, and lots of them aren't labelled. Plants aren't my thing. Grandpa's the only one who knows what half of them are, and I'm afraid he's not here.'

'I heard about Doug,' said Mel. 'So very sorry.'

Lizzie gave a sad smile. 'It will kill Pa to see this place go, but what else can we do?' She looked from Mel to Kim as if hoping to find the answer written in their faces. A soft sigh. 'Tube-stock's one dollar. Everything else is two dollars. Oh, except for the orchids. They're three dollars, but all the big ones have already sold. You get a twenty-five per cent discount on bulk purchases – that's twenty plants or more.'

The baby smiled and cooed. 'She's so sweet,' said Nikki. Abbey tickled her plump, pink feet.

Lizzie beamed. 'She's about to have her bottle. You girls can come and watch if you like, give your mums time for a proper look round.'

'Can we?' chorused Abbey and Nikki.

Mel looked at Kim, who nodded. 'Go on then.'

Lizzie looked as pleased as the girls. It would be lonely, stuck out here all day in the middle of nowhere, with a baby and hardly any customers. That's if you weren't interested in plants, of course. Kim surveyed the cluster of broad shade-houses. For her it would be heaven.

'Let's grab ourselves a trolley,' said Mel.

Kim wandered around the soon-to-be-defunct Cedar Creek Rainforest Nursery, unable to believe her eyes. It was simply magnificent. A cornucopia of subtropical rainforest species. Some very rare, all of them endemic to the Great Eastern Escarpment and Manning Valley. Bleeding-heart, blueberry ash, booyong and cassowary pines. Snow-wood, sassafras, figs and flame trees. Even with every ounce of her botanical knowledge, Kim found it hard to recognise some seedlings. Many were too young. Even the labelled ones were tricky, with cryptic tags written in a kind of shorthand.

'Thank god you're here,' said Mel. 'Otherwise I wouldn't know where to start.' They wandered the shade-houses, finding fresh treasures around every corner. What a man this Doug Henderson must be. How heartbreaking to leave behind what was clearly the work of a lifetime. 'What did I tell you?' Mel grew more smug with each new discovery. 'I knew you'd like it.'

Like it? That was an understatement. Kim loved it. How would she ever drag herself away? She wanted to take every single plant home with her, all five thousand of them.

They set to work loading up their trolley. Mel took notes. 'So I know what to buy when I come back with the truck,' she said. 'I won't be able to fit all the plants in this trip.'

Kim couldn't conceal her enthusiasm. Such fun, planning a mass planting like this: the sort of thing she used to dream of doing. 'I'm getting another trolley,' said Mel.

Kim wasn't listening. She'd found the orchid house.

Hundreds of tiny pots, full of strappy green mysteries, stood on double rows of trestle tables. All tiny, far too tiny to identify by leaf structure or growth pattern. She picked up the nearest pot and inspected the label. The letters, written in marker ink, were faded and hard to read. *Gracs*. What on earth did that mean? Kim examined some more labels. None of them made sense. They were in some sort of code that no doubt only the tragically silenced Doug Henderson understood. *Specd, Falcs, Kingd, Austs*. Kim tilted her head, as if looking from a different angle might make a difference. There was a pattern here, there had to be. It was just a matter of thinking logically.

Kim examined another pot. This orchid had a companion: a tiny, self-seeded staghorn fern. What a sweet thing. She ran her finger down a channel in the orchid's jade-green leaf. The same colour as the tree frogs frequenting the ferns at Journey's End. Delicate aerial roots spilled out, reaching for her. She felt the pot – way to dry. 'Lizzie needs to water you guys.' The label had fallen out, but what did that matter? She wouldn't be able to read it anyway. She'd take this pot home, separate out the staghorn, and give them both a fighting chance.

As Kim turned to go she spotted a little white tag on the ground. Picking it up, she wiped away the grime with her finger. Her heart beat a little faster. *Fitzs*. Surely that must stand for *fitzgeraldii*. *Sarcochilus fitzgeraldii*. She stared at the pot in astonishment. This was a baby ravine orchid.

Kim carefully put it down and started sorting through the pots in a kind of controlled frenzy. In a minute she had half-a-dozen more *Fitzs*, and the key to the code. The *S* after *Fitz* stood for the genus, *Sarcochilus*. She read another label: *Falcs*. So if the *S* stood for *Sarcochilus* . . . of course. *Sarcochilus falcatus*. An orange-blossom orchid.

She read another label: *Specd*. And the *D* stood for the genus, she knew that now. So . . . Kim laughed aloud as it suddenly made sense. *Dendrobium speciosum*. This was a rock orchid, a species found all up and down the eastern coast, including at Tarringtops. The names on the other tags weren't so obvious. She should have paid more attention during *Native Orchids 101*. Kim gazed around the tables – all those orchids, and she had the key to their identity. It was like discovering the Rosetta Stone. Once they had internet access at home, she'd be able to track down their names and decipher every label.

'What have you found?' asked Mel.

'Orchids.' Kim's arms were overflowing with pots. 'I'd better get a box.'

It was after five when they arrived back. Taj's ute had gone, and Jake was nowhere to be seen. 'Why not let Abbey come with me?' said Mel. 'Jake too, if he wants. Todd will be home soon. I'll drop them back after dinner.'

'Can I?' asked Abbey.

'Okay, run and find Jake. See if he wants to go too.' Abbey trotted off. She always seemed to know where to find her elusive brother.

Kim carried the box of orchids to the back verandah, found a watering can and gave the plants a good soaking.

Abbey came running back. 'Jake doesn't want to go.'

'Did you say Todd would be there?'

'Yep,' She was shuffling about in an odd fashion, not meeting her mother's eye. 'Mum . . .'

'Yes, sweetie?'

'I don't want to go either.'

Kim looked up. 'But you just said you did?'

'I've changed my mind.'

'Why?'

'Hush will miss me.'

'He'll be fine,' said Kim. 'I'll look after him.' Abbey squirmed. 'Did Jake say something to you?'

'No.' Abbey was glancing longingly towards the sheds. Something was definitely up.

'I'll go see Jake,' said Mel. 'See if I can talk him into coming.'

'No, you can't,' yelled Abbey, growing wide-eyed with alarm. She tried to push Mel back. 'He doesn't want you to.'

'Right.' Kim started for the sheds. 'Where's Jake?'

Abbey blocked her path and began to cry. 'Please, Mum . . . don't go down there.'

By now Kim was getting worried. She thought about the awful row she'd had with Jake that morning. He seemed to have calmed down before she left. Yet Abbey's tear-stained face showed that something was seriously wrong. What could have happened? She should never have left Jake alone all afternoon.

Kim pushed past her daughter. 'Jake,' she called. 'Where are you?' She strode around the corner of the woodshed, saw a flash of brown. Jake was hugging something to his chest, chin thrust out, wearing his most defiant face. Thank goodness he was all in one piece. 'What have you got there?' Kim edged closer. How extraordinary – a puppy.

Mel and the girls arrived, and Jake rounded on his sister. 'I told you not to say anything.'

'I didn't.' Abbey's lip trembled. 'Mum guessed somehow.'

'What a lovely pup,' said Mel. 'Can I see.' She advanced as if approaching a frightened colt.

When she reached out her hand, Jake pulled away. 'Dusty's mine.'

'I'm not going to take him, Jake,' Mel said. 'I just want a look.' This time when she reached for Dusty, Jake let her hold him. 'Hello, sweetheart.' She stroked his broad head. 'A kelpie, right?' Jake shrugged. She held the pup up for a better look. 'I know a kelpie pup when I see one. What a beauty. We had a black and tan one just like Dusty when I was a kid. Best sheepdog we ever had.' Mel handed him back to Jake.

'What did I say about getting a dog?' said Kim. 'Where did it come from?'

'Dusty's mine.' Jake's voice dripped with challenge. 'I'm keeping him.'

Kim knew better than to provoke an argument with him all het up like this. 'Let's go to the house,' she said. 'That little dog is probably hungry.'

Jake looked down at the pup with sudden concern. It had fallen limp in his arms. 'What's wrong with him?'

'Don't worry, he's just asleep,' said Mel. 'That's a very young puppy. Only six or seven weeks old at a guess. Your mum's right. He needs a feed.'

Jake looked from Mel to his mother, as though he was struggling with his decision 'What should I give him?'

'There's a bag of puppy food at home,' said Mel. 'From when Snow was small. I'll go get it. In the meantime, you could give him some porridge, or Weet-Bix and milk. He'll love it.'

Kim pressed her lips together for a moment, and then managed a smile. 'Weet-Bix and milk it is.'

Mel went home for the dog food while Jake prepared a bowl of cereal. He set it down in the kitchen and Dusty scoffed the lot. 'He's still hungry.'

Kim looked doubtful. The pup's tummy was so fat it looked ready to burst. He rolled over on his back, and she gave his belly a rub – it wasn't pink and bare like Scout's, but fully furred. She'd never seen that before. 'I think he's had enough. Take him outside for a wee.' One wee and ten minutes later, Dusty was curled up fast asleep on Jake's bed.

Mel arrived back, complete with a frozen casserole, a bag of puppy food and Todd. It looked like she'd invited herself for tea. 'It's lamb.' She was stating the obvious. Mel never seemed to cook anything but lamb.

'Where do you think that dog came from?' asked Kim.

'Won't Jake tell you? Well, Taj was here. Why not go and ask him? I'll hold down the fort.' Mel opened the pantry. 'Now where's the rice?'

CHAPTER 17

Still broad daylight, yet Kim missed the turn-off, twice. There was nothing to mark it. Nothing to indicate that the patch of gravel and rough bush track leading into the forest was the entrance to anyone's house.

Kim pulled over and wound down the window. It was the same place she'd stopped on that first day. How suspicious she'd been of Taj, completely thrown by how he'd turned up out of the forest. Troubled by his wild appearance, his foreign accent, his interest in Abbey. Apprehensive about being alone with him. Her skin tingled at the recollection and she rubbed her arms.

Kim got out of the car and glanced around the looming trees, all senses alert. There was no furtive rustling in the ferns this time. No flash of a sandy hide in the bushes. Yet she still felt uneasy, a little spooked. She took a deep, steadying breath. It didn't help. Her imagination was running away with her. Behind the fragrance of eucalypt and peppermint, she fancied she could smell the odour of decay, of a billion leaves rotting on the ground. The bush took on a sinister quality. Take a walk in this remote forest, and blood-sucking parasites might hitch a ride: land leeches and paralysis ticks. Wait-a-while vines, armed with hooks, might tear her clothes. Touch the graceful heart-shaped leaves of the stinging tree, and her skin would burn for days. Get back in the car and keep going, she told herself. You're scaring yourself silly. And there was nothing to be scared of, was there? Not Taj, not anymore.

She seemed to drive for ages. The house was set further back in the forest than she expected. Would he be home? The rutted track narrowed, and narrowed again. There was that damned howling. At least this time she knew it was only the maremmas.

Finally she reached an oddly shaped mud-brick building, set back into the hillside. With its pitched iron roof, irregular angles and rough bush timber, it seemed to have grown organically from the earth itself. Terraced vegetable gardens, paddocks, animal pens and a young orchard extended up the slope behind the house. Below lay dog runs, a hay shed, chook house and various other outbuildings. Quite a compound.

Taj stood on the verandah. He beckoned her in, for all the world like he'd been expecting her. The front door bore a beautifully engraved name plaque, *Wolf Hall.* Inside, the illusion of organic growth was even stronger. The split-level floor, a combination of hardwood and natural rock, rose and fell with the lay of the land. Forked blue gum trunks supported central beams carved with images of animals – wolves and bears and strange mythical figures. Wide windows, some at odd angles, featured rainforest scenes in leadlight. The effect was stunning.

'It's gorgeous.' Kim admired a stained-glass vine twining from the corner of a window. The burgundy trumpet-shaped flowers seemed to hang in three dimensions.

'These windows are reclaimed from the wrecker's yard,' he said. 'I used odds and ends of coloured glass to repair cracked edges and corners.' He ran his long finger down a seam separating tinted glass from clear, then looked up. 'You'd never know this used to be damaged, would you?'

She tried to turn from the intensity of his gaze, but couldn't look away. The man really did have the most mesmerising eyes.

'Sometimes,' he said, 'things are more beautiful when they are broken and mended.' She found herself staring at the fragment of tattoo visible through the open top buttons of his shirt. He cleared his throat. 'Would you like coffee?'

Taj took their coffee to the verandah, which overlooked rolling hills of rainforest, and handed Kim her cup. His hand was large, strong and work-worn, his forearm heavily muscled, yet he had the long, slim fingers of an artist. For a while they stood in silence, gazing at the view.

'When I arrived home today,' said Kim. 'Jake had a puppy.'

'Boys and dogs are a natural fit. They will be brothers.'

Kim wondered again if he had his own boy in a faraway land, waiting each month for a parcel. Wondered if he had his own wife. 'So you gave him the dog?' Taj turned his dark, searching eyes on her. 'The thing is . . . ' She was suddenly all too aware of his physical presence: the set of his shoulders and arrow-straight back. His powerful thighs. The maleness of him. 'The thing is, you'll have to take him back.'

Taj frowned. 'Why? That will hurt the boy, hurt him badly.'

'It's complicated,' said Kim.

'Then help me understand.'

The request unsettled her. She didn't have to justify herself to him, or anybody else. Yet something about those eyes drew her in, made her want to explain. 'Our dog died a few months ago, at sixteen years of age. My husband, Connor . . . he owned Scout before we were married. That old dog was very special. I don't want to replace him.'

'One dog never replaces another. Dusty will build himself a new home in your heart.'

'I'm not ready.'

'Jake is ready.' Taj's voice, though soft, rang loud with feeling. 'You are head of the family now. Your duty is to lead him out of his anger, out of his sadness. Yet for Jake to live again, you must live again.' His eyes flashed, bold with challenge. 'Will you stay forever married to a ghost?'

Kim started to tremble. She was right to have been wary of this place, this man. Her chest ached like he'd punched her in the heart, and she was tempted to fling the coffee in his face. 'You have no idea. You know nothing about my life, or my marriage, or my son.' The words came in an angry, outraged rush. 'If Jake is hurt by giving Dusty back—'

'*When* Jake is hurt,' said Taj.

'Okay. *When* Jake is hurt, because he will be, you're right. But that's because you didn't ask me in the first place. And as for me not living my life . . .' She paused for breath, overwhelmed anew by the audacity, the rudeness of Taj's comments. This conversation was taking her to an intensely painful place. 'Not that it's any of your business, but the reason I moved here in the first place was so that we could do just that – live our lives. Make a fresh start.'

'I don't think so. You haven't truly moved to Journey's End. You're camping round the edges, scared to put down roots, to venture past the sheds.'

Kim's heart beat fast, and her cheeks flamed. She should go. She should turn around and walk away.

But Taj wasn't finished. 'What about your grand plan?'

Kim took a step backwards. A *grand plan* – that's how she and Connor used to describe their dreams for the farm. 'Who have you been talking to?'

'Don't you know?'

Kim shook her head.

'Abbey.'

Her mouth went dry. She had no idea Abbey had ever heard that expression, let alone understood its meaning. For the first time in a long time, Kim allowed herself to think about those long-lost plans. 'Connor and I, we wanted to regenerate the rainforest, remove the weeds, plant—'

'You wanted to rewild Journey's End,' said Taj.

'Rewild?' It was a term Kim wasn't very familiar with. She'd heard it once before, in relation to a Scottish highland estate. Its millionaire owner had replaced pastures and plantation pines with broadleaf natives like oak, aspen and rare black poplars. Controversially, he'd also brought back wolves to keep down the deer who browsed on the seedlings. 'Well, yes, I suppose so,' she said. 'Although doesn't rewilding mean restoring animals as well as plants?'

A quick pulse started in his cheek. 'Plants and animals evolved together. They rely on each other,' said Taj. 'If the web of life is broken, the rainforest will not return as it should.'

Kim's anger was waning, replaced by astonishment at her daughter and a renewed curiosity about Taj. Who was this man? 'I'm afraid that grand plan died along with my husband,' she said. 'I can't do it alone.'

'What if you didn't have to?' He searched her face. 'What if I could help?' He did not hide the hope behind his measured words. 'Eradicating weeds and feral animals, propagating native trees, planting them out. There are some in my greenhouse all ready to go. You'll need tree guards until the goats and deer are gone, but that's doable. The whole plan is doable. Wouldn't your husband want that?' She should slap him, What did he know of Connor? 'I'd work for nothing. Fencing. Clearing out the privet and lantana. Although it might be worth leaving that patch of camphor laurels above the dam. Use the canopy to protect shade-loving plants like burrawang and native ginger, then rip out the laurels once the seedlings have established.' He paused as if awaiting a response.

How could she respond? She was too overwhelmed.

'Wait here.' He gestured for her to stay, palms held out in supplication. 'I have a journal article about it.'

He went inside, leaving Kim bewildered. Part of her was stirred by his proposal, a part long-dormant, yet not dead. But his voice came again and again: Will you stay forever married to a ghost? Will you? Will you?

Would she?

And Jake and Dusty. It was too much.

Her arms goose-bumped, and it crossed her mind that she could simply leave. Walk away before he came back. At first, she couldn't lift her feet. As in a nightmare, they seemed to have taken root along with the house. Kim willed them to move, feeling more and more panicked.

She could hear Taj now, heavy footfalls on the wooden floor, coming nearer and nearer.

The dogs began their eerie howling, and suddenly the spell was broken. Kim took flight down the verandah. She reached the car, looking back once before turning the ignition key. Taj stood staring at her. Kim took a last lingering look , then sped away. In her mind's eye, she could still see his tall figure, silhouetted against the sinking sun.

CHAPTER 18

Kim tore down the road in a cloud of dust. She made sure she was well out of sight before she pulled over, let her head fall onto the steering wheel. She could feel the pulse in the tips of her fingers, her heart louder than usual. Her head spinning.

Was she Jake's problem? Kids reflected their parents – everybody knew that. What sort of a mirror was she for Jake? Clinging to yesterday, unable to let go of a partner who was gone. Unable to even let go of his dead dog.

If the truth be known, Connor was slipping away from her, in spite of her best efforts to hold him. When she reached back as before, searching for that place where he still lived, he felt less and less real. And when she seized onto a memory, sometimes she wasn't sure if it was true anymore or some sort of composite, cobbled together from a jumble of similar recollections. There was a time when she could summon up conversations, family breakfasts, romantic dinners, nights of lovemaking – all with a blinding clarity. But not so much now. Sometimes the memories wouldn't come at all. It was like reaching for a mirage, or a rainbow, or fragments of a fading dream. Taj's words still rang in her ears . . . *Will you stay forever married to a ghost?*

She gunned the car again, startling a flock of rosellas from the trees. If she drove fast enough could she keep ahead of the question? Could she make it so it never had to be answered? When she reached Bangalow Road, she took the turn too fast and cannoned across the intersection. She fought for control, wrestling with the steering as her wheels spun uselessly on gravel. Dammit. Sliding sideways now. Everything happening in slow motion. The sky wheeling. A tree. She shut her eyes. The seat belt dug into her flesh as the force of the impact jerked her sideways. Something slammed the right side of her head, and she couldn't breathe. The car came to a shuddering halt.

Kim opened her eyes to find the side airbag had exploded in her ear, releasing a cloud of choking white powder. She slid across to the passenger side, coughing and spluttering, her eyes streaming. Bursting out the door, she stumbled straight into Ben Steele's arms.

'Kim. Are you all right?' He hugged her close, held her upright. 'Lean on me.'

Her head swam as her legs gave way. He swept her up, supporting her, cradling her in both arms. Kim found herself seated in the back seat of his land cruiser, Ben's impossibly handsome face coming close, his solicitous eyes gazing into hers. For an impossible moment, she thought he was going to kiss her.

Kim reached out and touched his cheek. 'How's the car?'

Ben burst out laughing. 'Forget about the damned car. Let's get you home.'

Mel topped up Kim's glass of riesling for a second time.

'Go easy,' said Ben, helping himself to a Coke from the fridge. 'She might have concussion or something.'

'Didn't the airbag go off?' said Mel. 'What did that feel like?

'Like being punched by a fist wrapped in cottonwool.' Kim took a sip of wine. 'But I'm all right, a bit sore is all. I don't need a doctor.'

Abbey had pushed between Kim's knees, and even Jake seemed concerned.

'Will you stay for dinner, Ben?' Mel stirred the pot on the stove.

'Lamb casserole. I'm making more rice so there's enough to go round. How about a glass of wine?'

'No thanks. I'll shoot home and pick up some beer and steaks – proper tucker.' Mel's shoulders slumped a little and she turned away. 'Then I'll see about towing your car back, Kim.' Ben spied Jake lurking nearby, carrying Dusty. 'Just the man I want to see. A few of the lads are having a knock at the nets tomorrow after work. You'd better come, champ, get your eye in. That's if you want to play on Saturday. We need a good spinner.'

'What about Liam? Isn't he your spin bowler?'

'He's still on holidays. We could really use you.'

Jake's face lit up. 'Did you hear that, Mum?'

Kim shot Ben a grateful smile, and he winked. 'I'm glad that's sorted. In the meantime, do you want to come for a ride to my place? Pick up some steaks and snags?'

'Can Dusty come?' Jake held out the squirming pup.

'Sorry, mate, just cleaned the car.' Ben took a closer look at Dusty. 'Where'd that mutt come from?'

'He's not a mutt,' said Mel. 'Looks like a kelpie to me.'

Ben turned to Kim. 'Come to your senses, have you? Going to put some stock on the place?'

'Well, I'm not sure . . . '

'If you're looking for a farm dog, I could get you a pup with top bloodlines. Or my brother-in-law could sell you an older dog, already trained up. You don't want to go buying any old puppy.'

Dusty was trying to scratch behind his ear and chew Jake's finger at the same time - a comical sight.

'If you don't know its breeding,' Ben said, 'it's likely to be more trouble than it's worth.'

Jake's face fell.

'I'll look after Dusty if you want to go with Ben,' Kim said.

Jake seemed torn, staring at her suspiciously while she stroked the pup's ears. 'Don't worry, he'll be here when you come back.'

'Really?'

'Really.'

Jake's mouth moved into a half-smile. He bent over to kiss her, a rare enough thing, then deposited Dusty on her lap. 'Thanks, Mum.'

'Let's go get those steaks.' Ben fished car keys from his pocket. 'I could eat a horse.'

Abbey made a small noise of alarm and pressed in closer to her mother. 'That's just an expression,' said Kim. 'Ben didn't mean it.'

Dusty yawned and licked Kim's chin. Then he curled up, buried his nose in his tail and went to sleep. '

'We can keep him, can't we, Mum?' asked Abbey.

Taj's words echoed in Kim's ears. Painful home truths. It was unfair to deny her children just because she wasn't over Scout's death. This wasn't about her. Dusty sighed and rolled onto his back, eyes still shut, fuzzy tummy exposed. He really was very sweet, and the kids loved him already. 'We can keep him.'

Abbey screamed with delight and squeezed Kim's cheeks so tight she thought they'd pop. 'I'm going to tell Nikki.'

Kim smiled in disbelief as she ran off. She couldn't remember the last time her quiet daughter had shouted.

Kim picked up the sleeping pup and placed him on a pile of spare wallaby blankets in the corner. Dusty barely stirred, sleeping with the deep, innocent trust of the very young. She went into the lounge and picked up the jar of Scout's ashes from the mantelpiece. Kim could still picture him in this room. Asleep on the faded burgundy rug, paws scrabbling as he chased dream rabbits. Sitting on the frayed empire chair. Basking before the fire in winter, soaking up the warmth.

Kim sank down on the couch. 'Oh Scouty, forgive me. Nobody will ever take your place.' Her eyes brimmed with tears, and she could almost feel the touch of his cold nose on her bare leg. So real. Out of habit, her hand dropped to fondle the old dog's head.

She jumped at the feel of silky soft fur and looked down. Dusty was nuzzling her. He wagged his tail and flopped on her feet. On impulse she picked the pup up. He snuggled down on her lap, his topaz eyes trained on hers. Eyes that unexpectedly reminded her of Taj. 'I wonder what Scout would have made of you, eh?'

And then something strange happened. She felt compelled to tell

Dusty all about Scout. How he would chase cats up the backyard peppercorn tree, and climb right up after them. How he would shake himself, as if wet, after the car went through the car wash. How he joined in the Easter egg hunt every year, piling his share in his food dish. And how Scout loyally stood guard in the children's bedrooms whenever they were sick, barely eating or sleeping until they were well again.

Dusty regarded her with an earnest intensity as if her stories were the most important thing in the world. Kim didn't feel foolish for long, and soon she was laughing through her tears. It felt good to remember Scout like this. Remembering the joy of his long life, not the pain and sadness of his death. A burden flew from her shoulders. 'So you see, you've a lot to live up to.' The pup whined and lay his head between his paws, as if the responsibility was all too much. From the kitchen she heard the clattering of plates and felt grateful to Mel that she'd allowed her this time alone.

'Mum?' Jake stood in the doorway. 'Who are you talking to?'

She put the puppy down and replaced the ashes on the mantelpiece. Jake shuffled in, unsure and fidgeting. Dusty hurled himself at the boy in an ecstasy of welcome, all waggling tail and wriggling body. Jake bundled him into his arms, finding it hard to speak through Dusty's determined efforts to lick his mouth. 'Is it true, what Abbey says? Can I really keep him?'

His forehead was creased with worry, his eyes guarded. The resemblance to Connor struck her, like it so often did, and she braced herself. But for once the familiar pain didn't come. In its place was a kind of epiphany. Connor had given her the gift of this wonderful child. How fortunate she was. How very blessed.

'Yes,' she said. 'You can keep him.'

Jake chewed on his bottom lip, the way he used to do when he was little. His expression didn't change the way Abbey's had when she heard the news. Jake didn't believe her. Well, why should he? She'd said *no* so often, put her needs ahead of his for so long. It was troubling to see how little he trusted her.

She got up and put a hand on his shoulder. 'Jake, you *can* keep him. Dusty's yours now, all yours.'

A smile found its way through the mask of his uncertainty, and he ran from the room, no doubt before she changed her mind.

Happiness settled on her skin and, for once, it wasn't bittersweet. For once it wasn't brought on by thoughts of the past. She had to stay living in the present for Jake's sake, and for Abbey, however hard it might be. More than that, she had to think of the future. What about her grand plan? She had a whole year, enough time to get it off the ground. The prospect was exciting and frightening at the same time. Why did Taj want to help her? What was his angle?

If only she hadn't run away from Wolf Hall like that. She should have stayed to talk to Taj, find out more about him, discover what was driving him. He must have some sort of background in ecology; that much was clear from the trivia night and their conversation today. She'd never really thought about the breadth of Taj's life, never tried to imagine him before he came to Australia. She'd been curious about Afghanistan, of course. She'd asked him about his country, but only because of Connor. She hadn't cared about Taj at all. It reminded her of a taxi ride she'd once taken: a long trip, chatting with the driver to while away the time.

'Where are you from?' she'd asked him.

'Syria.'

'Do you like driving taxis? Is that what you did back at home?'

His answer had been slow in coming. 'I was an orthopaedic surgeon, but my qualifications and experience are not recognised here. This is the only work I can get.'

'Mum?' Abbey came in. 'Jake won't let me play with Dusty. I said he could have a turn of Percy' – She held up the toy poodle – 'but he wouldn't swap.'

'I'll make sure you get a turn later,' said Kim. 'Meanwhile, come and talk with me for a bit.'

'Can I sit with you on the empire chair. It's the prettiest.'

They both squeezed into it.

'You like Taj, don't you?' Kim said.

Abbey's face lit up. 'Oh yes. Taj shows me beetles and things, and tells me stories. He's my second-best friend after Nikki.' She frowned. 'And Grace, of course, but I don't see her anymore.'

'Does Taj tell good stories?'

'The best. All about when he was a ranger in Afghanistan. He has wolves and bears in his forests, not like here. Even leopards. And deer with fangs like vampires. We have deer here too, Mum. I hope they're not vampires. Anyway, Taj used to keep them safe from poachers, and stop bad guys from chopping down the trees. Did you know he had his own wolf pack? ' Kim shook her head. 'He raised some baby cubs, and when they were grown up enough he taught them how to live in the wild again. They thought Taj was a wolf, like them.'

Nikki came in. 'Mum wants to know if there's tomato sauce.'

Abbey bounced to her feet. 'I'll come show you.' She kissed her mother on the nose. 'Don't forget to tell Jake it's my turn for Dusty next.'

Kim sat there for the longest time, considering Abbey's words. Taj must have been spinning tales. Wildlife in war-torn Afghanistan? Connor never talked very much about his time overseas. It left a frustrating gap in her understanding. The country didn't have forests, did it? Let alone bears and wolves and fanged deer. The images in her mind were of deserts and barren, bombed-out landscapes.

Kim went to her room and opened her iPad. May as well get some mileage from their brand new internet connection. She googled *Afghanistan, forests* and *wolves*. The results confounded her. An astonishing range of wildlife survived in the country's remote northern forests, including wolves and rare deer with tusks like sabres.

How blinkered her knowledge of Afghanistan really was. She scrolled through the images on her screen. It seemed there was more to the country than desolation and violence. More than the death and roadside bombs shown on the nightly news. There was also a mythical beauty – ancient forests, rugged snow-capped mountains and wild rivers. A landscape Connor would have loved. He did not die, as she'd imagined, trapped in a place of unrelenting ugliness. Perhaps his spirit had found sanctuary and peace in Afghanistan's last wilderness. It was a comforting thought.

Ben poked his head round the door. 'Are you hungry? Grub's up.'

'Yes,' she said. 'I'm starved.'

Ben's perfect white teeth gleamed in a devilish grin. She returned his smile. Despite her aches and pains from the accident, this was the lightest she'd felt in years. She was suddenly looking forward to an evening of talking and drinking with friends. Of meeting her son's eyes with hope. Of sharing a joke with the charming Ben, a man who Jake adored, and who'd swept in after her crash like a knight in shining armour.

Kim changed into clean jeans and a silk shirt of the softest green. She went to the bathroom, washed her face, brushed her hair and stared at her reflection in the mirror. Then, hesitatingly, she found a lipstick . . .

CHAPTER 19

Kim hoped it wasn't too early on a Sunday morning to ask her new friend a favour. 'Knock, knock.' Kim pushed in the back door at She-Oak Springs, and found Mel chasing a half-grown kookaburra around her kitchen. 'Any chance of borrowing your truck?' She threw a convenient tea towel over the bird as Mel cornered it in the sink. 'For the whole day, if possible.'

'Sure.' Mel quietly caught the squawking youngster and placed it in a crate. 'What's up?'

'You know that rainforest nursery?'

Mel put on the kettle. 'I heard it's closed down now. Somebody bought out the entire stock, the whole kit and caboodle. Pity that – I wanted some more tamarind seedlings.'

'You'd better ask me then.'

Mel turned to stare. 'You mean—'

'Yep. That's why I need the truck.'

'Oh my god! What are you going to do with all those plants?'

'Give you as many as you need, for starters,' said Kim. 'A few more understorey species wouldn't go astray in your gully.'

'That would be wonderful, thank you. But what about the others. How many are left?'

'Thousands.'

Mel put two cups of coffee down on the table, and gestured to a chair. 'I know you've got a lot to do,' she said, 'but there's always time for a cup of coffee. Now sit and tell me what you're up to.'

Kim hesitated, then sat down. 'You know I'm a botanist, right? When Connor inherited Journey's End twelve years ago, we talked about a project of broad-scale rainforest regeneration. When he died, I gave up on the idea. Didn't think I could do it on my own.' Kim sipped the hot brew. 'Well, I've changed my mind. I'm going to restore the original, pre-European vegetation cover.'

Mel looked confused. 'You mean over the whole two hundred hectares?'

'That's the plan.'

'What about pasture for stock?'

'In case you haven't noticed, I don't have any stock. Unless you count goats and brumbies and the odd wild pig.'

Mel shook her head as though she couldn't quite believe what she was hearing. 'You'll lose your improved land value. What if you want to reclaim the paddocks down the track? Clearing costs a fortune in steep country like this. And when you sell, who's going to buy two hundred hectares of bush? Especially if it's locked up with conservation covenants.'

'Someone like me.' Kim put down her half-drunk coffee and stood up. 'Now can I borrow the truck or not?'

'Of course,' said Mel. 'Don't get me wrong – I just want to be sure you know what you're doing.'

'Right.' Kim bit her tongue. It wasn't the reaction she'd expected. She thought they were on the same page, that Mel would be as excited as she was about the plan. After all, visiting the nursery had been Mel's idea in the first place, and she had her own greenhouse full of natives.

'I wasn't criticising,' said Mel. 'It's just I've never heard of anyone converting their land back to wilderness. Regenerating creek banks maybe, or putting in shelter belts. But not their whole farm.'

'Well, now you have.' Kim sat back down. This wasn't the time to get in a huff. She needed to explain this to Mel, get her on side.

'What does Ben think? I can't imagine he'll be happy.'

'I haven't told Ben. Only you and Taj.'

'But I thought you and Ben were . . . you know.'

'Well, we're not.'

But Mel would not be deterred. 'Admit it, ever since that crash a few weeks ago, Ben's been spending a lot of time at your place. I see his car there all the time.' This wasn't entirely light-hearted teasing. Kim knew full well Mel had a crush on Ben. 'You realise he's the town catch, don't you? Tingo's most eligible bachelor.'

That made Kim smile. How many people were there in Tingo again?

'Don't be silly. He's a friend,' said Kim. 'And Jake likes him. Ben helps him with his cricket.' Mel did not look convinced. Time to get the conversation back on track. 'What I'm planning isn't very different to what you're doing with that gully, Mel, just on a larger scale. Think how great this will be for your orphans. You can release them right next door.'

'That does sound good,' said Mel, her tone still uncertain. 'But if you let the place run wild, won't feral animals take over? I've got enough problems with foxes as it is.'

'I'm starting an eradication program, with Taj's help. Did you know he's got a master's degree from the University of Leeds in environmental biology?'

'You're kidding,' said Mel. 'Wouldn't a qualification like that be recognised in Australia? I wonder why he's working as a handyman.'

'Taj says these mountains remind him of home – that's why he stays. I know,' said Kim as Mel raised her eyebrows. 'I thought Afghanistan was all ruins and desert.'

'Didn't your husband . . . didn't Connor talk about it?'

'Not much and, anyway, he was stationed in the south – Helmand Province. Apparently the mountains are miles away, in the north-east.' Kim drained her mug, surprised at herself. It wasn't often she could talk about Connor so matter-of-factly. 'So, back to the truck . . .'

'I'd better drive,' said Mel. 'It's got a few quirks, like no door handles. You need to use the needle-nosed pliers in the glove box when you want to get out. And reverse gear is tricky. If it doesn't take then you have to keep the clutch in and quickly go through first and second, then very slowly back to reverse, and . . . '

'Okay,' said Kim. 'You drive.'

Nikki ran in. 'Drive where, Mum?'

'Kim's bought herself a baby rainforest. We're going to pick it up.'

'Cool. Can Todd and I come?'

'Sure.' Nikki ran off to find her brother.

Kim gave Mel a grateful smile. 'I'll bring the kids in my car, if you like. They can help us load up.'

'Deal.' Mel put the mugs on the sink and grabbed some keys from a hook behind the door. 'Come on,' she said with a grin. 'Let's go get your forest.'

Even with Taj's help, it had taken them all day to collect the stock. This was their final load. Taj took off his hat and wiped the sweat from his brow. 'That's it.' He handed down the last plant to Kim, then jumped from the tray of the truck, landing beside her with the easy grace of an animal. The feathery fronds of a tree fern poked out the top of the pot, along with a wilting seedling. She felt the soil. Bone dry. 'You poor thing.' The rightful occupant of the pot had almost been smothered by the self-sown fern. Kim was constantly amazed by the sheer fecundity of life in Tingo.

Kim trailed her fingers along the seedling's nondescript leaves. No label. It could be anything. She looked up at Taj. 'What do you think this one is?'

Taj bent close, and she could hear his steady breathing, almost taste the salt on his skin. He plucked the pot from her hand and studied the young plant with great care as if examining something precious and rare. He rolled a leaf-tip between thumb and forefinger. Closing his eyes, he brought the fingers to his nose and inhaled. Kim waited. The moment swelled and built. Finally he opened his eyes.

'*Cinnamomum oliveri*. Cinnamonwood.' He handed the pot back as though he was giving her a gift.

Dusty bowled into her legs and the moment was lost. 'Well hello, sweetie.' She put the little pot down in the shade with the others, and tickled the excited pup. In the few weeks they'd had him, Dusty had tumbled, romped, snuggled and charmed his way into all their hearts. She'd loved Scout, but the border terrier was all grown up when she first met him. She'd never raised a puppy before. And according to Mel, Dusty was rather a special one. 'He's so clever. You can see his mind ticking away, working things out. I kicked a stone behind the gate today to close it because my hands were full and I couldn't do up the chain. Well, Dusty sat there and looked at that rock awhile. Then he picked it up in his mouth, moved it aside, and swatted the gate with his paw. It swung right open. It was the darnedest thing.'

Kim had learned to take her friend's stories with a grain of salt. Mel had a nickname in town. Mel-odramatic, because she tended to exaggerate. But Dusty did seem to be very smart, though Kim had no basis for comparison.

It shouldn't have come as a surprise. Connor had told her stories about the bravery and intelligence of military dogs. 'Dogs can understand two hundred and fifty words and gestures,' he said. 'They can count to five and are as intelligent as two-year-old children.'

Kim didn't doubt it. Dusty could already undo the catch on the crate Mel had loaned her for house-training. He'd learned to open the pantry door, hide quietly under Jake's bed when she wanted to put him out, and unlatch the chook pen so Bonnie and Clyde could come out and play with him.

Kim picked Dusty up. 'What have you been up to, eh? Where's Jake?'

Taj, who was fitting a hose to the tank, indicated the house with a jerk of his head. Kim turned to see Ben's red land cruiser parked in the drive. Jake was bound to be with him.

That explained why Dusty had deserted Jake. The pup knew Ben didn't like him. His overtures of friendship were always rebuffed, and he ended up slinking away with his tail between his legs. 'Why is Ben so mean to Dusty?' Abbey had asked her. Kim hadn't known what to say. Maybe Ben only liked dogs with a pedigree, and Dusty didn't cut the mustard.

Taj tested the hose. Kim put Dusty down, and the pup leapt and snapped at the water stream. Taj let him play with it awhile, then turned it on the pots. Kim watched with a smile of satisfaction as curtains of spray rained down on the thirsty seedlings. This unique collection, these thousands of subtropical rainforest plants – all safe, all hers. She could still hardly believe it.

'What do you say now?' Kim asked him. 'Am I still living around the edges?'

Taj turned to her with a grin. 'No.' The warmth of his smile was reflected in his voice. 'You've well and truly moved in.' He picked up a little Moreton Bay fig. 'Half of these seedlings are too small to plant out yet. They need re-potting and time to grow. In the meantime, I'll bring you some advanced trees from home.'

'Mel has some bigger ones too. We have plenty to get started.'

The sound of Ben's voice calling Mel from the house interrupted them.

'Time I went.' Taj turned off the tap, and a disappointed Dusty pawed at the lifeless hose. 'Make sure they all get a good soaking. Tomorrow I'll put up shade cloth and connect an automatic spray system to the pump on the creek. Otherwise your tanks will run dry.'

'Why not stay for dinner?' said Kim. 'Mel and the kids are coming back once they feed the animals. We can have a barbeque.'

He shook his head. 'I'm camping out at the yards again tonight.'

A local brumby group had lent them a set of steel passive trapping yards, to catch the mob of wild horses who'd moved in from Tarring-tops over summer. Taj had set them up on Kim's land, beside the bill-abong on Cedar Creek, where it was shady and flat, with access for trucks. The lay of the land formed a natural funnel, helping to channel the brumbies towards the trap.

'They seem a bit flimsy,' Kim had said when she first saw the yards. She shook a section of fence. 'Wouldn't it be better to reinforce these panels with timber posts?'

'Too dangerous. They need a bit of give in them.'

For the last few weeks he'd been baiting the yards with salt blocks, molasses and hay. Once the brumbies were used to coming in, a trip-wire would be rigged up to a counterweight, swinging the gate shut behind them. But so far the wild horses had proved too clever, avoiding the yards whenever the trap was set.

Some nights when she slept, she dreamed of Taj out there, in his swag by the billabong beneath the stars. Once, after waking from a restless sleep, she went out on the verandah, and saw the wild horses on the hill, slipping wraith-like through the moonlit trees.

'Good luck,' she said. 'Let me know if you catch them.'

Kim watched his ute swing round and drive away, wheels spinning on gravel. Was that the real reason he was leaving? Taj always disappeared pretty promptly when Ben arrived. She was beginning to think he shared Abbey's dislike for the man.

Kim's thoughts kept returning to Mel's words earlier in the day. *Ben's been spending a lot of time at your place. I see his car there all the time.* Kim had called her silly, but was she? Ben swung around after work most nights now. At first it was to check on her after the accident. But the visits continued after it became clear that she was okay. Sometimes he brought little gifts picked up in Taree, where he had his real estate office. Flowers or a bottle of wine. A new cricket ball or comic for Jake. Sticker books for Abbey or a horsey postcard to add to her collection. Not that she was very receptive. Not like Jake.

Her son hero-worshipped Ben, and since he'd been coming round, Jake's behaviour had improved out of sight. Even Abbey noticed. 'I almost like Jake now,' she'd whispered, when he made a pond for her turtle. However Abbey didn't agree with her mother's explanation for the turnaround. 'It's not Ben that's made Jake nicer,' she said. 'It's Dusty.'

Abbey was just a child. She didn't understand.

Kim was lonely living in this remote place, especially at day's end, and she looked forward to Ben's visits. She checked the clock more frequently as the afternoons wore on, listening for his car down on the road. What she made for dinner and what she wore became a more carefully considered affair. Ben often stayed on to share the wine he brought. Sometimes he casually brushed against her, or picked a leaf from her hair. There was no doubt they were growing closer.

There was also no doubt that there was something very seductive about Ben's resemblance to Connor. Not just physically, but in personality as well. Ben was a take-charge kind of guy, naturally confident. His presence brought a comforting sense of security along with it. He sorted things for her. When the satellite television people were giving her the run-around, Ben stepped in and dealt with them. The house was hooked up within days. He arranged for her car to be fixed promptly, dealt with the insurance company and lent her a replacement vehicle. He dropped off her mail and took Jake to cricket practice. After managing alone for so long, it was nice to be looked after again.

The similarity didn't end there. Like Connor, Ben was entertaining and gregarious, a perfect foil for her serious side. He told her jokes, made her laugh. Charmed her from her introversion. Although on one point there was no comparison. Connor would have loved Dusty, she was sure of it.

Mel's car pulled in behind Ben's just as Taj was leaving. Todd ran off to the house, carrying a bottle of soft drink, Nikki following. Mel emerged more slowly, with a salad bowl in her hands, and a smug *I told you so* expression on her face. 'Ben's here again. How did I guess?'

Kim gave her a wry grin and took the offered bowl.

'Greek salad,' said Mel. 'Except with cheddar cheese, because I don't have any feta. And capsicum instead of cucumber.'

Kim peered into the bowl. 'Is that bacon? I don't remember bacon in Greek salad.'

'The bacon's instead of the olives. I didn't have any olives.'

Kim laughed. 'So it's a Greek salad with no cucumber, feta or olives.'

'And no onion. Nikki doesn't like onion.' She headed into the house.

The boys and Nikki came round the side of the house with Ben.

He must have come straight from work. She liked how he held himself. She liked the pride he took in his appearance. Connor had been like that. He'd used their iron more than she had. Ben's muscles showed beneath his fitted, short-sleeved business shirt. Sandy-blond hair ruffled by the breeze. Knife-edge crease in his trousers. He looked too well-groomed for the bush. Kim glanced down at her soiled jeans and sweaty singlet.

'What have you got here?' Ben pointed to the pots. 'Looks like you're starting up a nursery.'

'That's not a bad idea,' said Kim. 'Maybe I will one day. But for now, I'm doing some replanting.'

'Replanting? You'd be better off doing the opposite. Getting the tractors and chains in, reclaiming some of that scrubby hill country.'

Dusty crept towards Ben, smiling and wagging his tail. Ben ignored the pup at first, then pushed him away with his foot. Kim saw Jake flinch, then gather himself.

Abbey was watching from the seat of the old steam traction engine. She clapped her hands. 'Dusty.' He pricked up his ears and trotted off to friendlier territory. Jake looked torn but let him go. The lure of his hero was too strong.

'Let's get some practice in before the match tomorrow,' Ben said, and Jake and Todd ran off to get their stuff.

'Why don't you like Dusty?' Kim said into the quiet that fell.

Ben frowned. 'I happen to believe dogs should be useful, earn their keep round the farm. You need solid bloodlines for that. You won't think he's so cute when he's all grown up and running amuck with Mel's sheep.'

Kim looked to where Dusty was now playing chasey with the girls. Was Ben right? Would the pup become a problem?

Ben strolled off to help the boys set up a makeshift pitch. Kim went back to watering, careful not to miss a pot, stopping frequently to examine this one or that one. Lengthening shadows crept over the sea of plants. She should go help Mel with dinner, but she couldn't tear herself away. Each pot came with the promise of something wonderful, something unexpected – a botanical lucky dip. She owed

Taj a lot. If it wasn't for his goading, she'd never have found the courage to follow her dream.

'How's that!' Ben's voice rang out across the paddock. Taj and Ben. Two men, different as night and day. Two men who, each in their own way, were teaching her to live again.

CHAPTER 20

$\mathcal{A}$ knocking summoned Kim from the fog of sleep. She rubbed her eyes. It was barely light.

'Kim? Kim, wake up.' Taj stood in the doorway to her bedroom, as wild and alarming as the first day she met him. Gum leaves and hay clung to his clothes. For a moment she thought she was dreaming.

She sat up with a start, aware of the swell of her breasts beneath the thin cotton nightie, and a tingle in her nipples. They were unaccountably erect. Taj took her in with fathomless eyes, before retreating to the hallway.

'We've caught the whole mob,' he called. 'The brumby people are on their way with a truck.'

'That's marvellous.' Kim's arms were goose-bumped, and she pulled a wrap around her shoulders. 'I'll wake the kids.'

Abbey yawned. 'Is Nikki coming?'

'No. Mel's busy today. Now, can we go?' They ventured outside, into the early morning chill. Late summer, and there was already a touch of autumn in the air.

'I think we should leave them,' said Jake. 'I like seeing brumbies on the place.'

'We can't,' said Kim. 'They're trampling our plantings and caving in the creek banks.'

'Can I keep one as a pet?' asked Abbey.

'I'm sorry, sweetie. These are wild horses, not children's ponies.'

'Can I bring Dusty?' asked Jake.

'No dogs,' said Kim. Today's task might not be a straightforward one. Safely loading wild horses onto a truck was bound be stressful, and she wondered about the wisdom of bringing Abbey along. Of course it would be hard to leave her behind. Word had somehow got around. There was plenty of local interest in the brumbies, and apparently half the town was turning out to watch.

The scene at the yards was more confronting than she'd imagined. The mob's black stallion had cut his foreleg and was pacing the fences. He tested them occasionally by hurling his shoulder into the panels. They rattled and shook, yielding a little to the force, but held firm. Kim felt a shiver down her spine.

'What happened to his ear?' she asked.

'He's the victim of a sport called tagging,' said Taj, his voice low so that the children didn't hear. 'Young brumbies are chased on horseback, roped, and then have half an ear cut off as a trophy. He may have led his herd to Journey's End to escape his tormentors.'

Kim blanched. 'They will be all right, won't they, when we put them on the truck?'

'They'll be well cared for,' said Taj. 'Hayley has devoted her life to the protection of these wild horses.'

Abbey and Jake approached the yards. The mares milled along the fence: two bays and a buckskin. They kept the two taffy foals between them, shielded from sight. 'Come away,' called Kim, as the stallion charged the fence, all rolling eyes and flattened ears.

Abbey screamed and darted back to hide behind her mother, but Jake held his ground. 'Whoa, boy. Nobody's going to hurt you.'

'That's right,' said Taj. 'Show him no fear.' The stallion's ears snapped forward and he lowered his head. The grinding of gears cut through the still air. 'Here come the troops.'

The horse truck was followed by half-a-dozen cars. Quite a crowd was gathering. 'What happens now?' asked Kim. 'Do we try to load the horses?'

'That will be hours away,' said Taj. 'We let them settle down first. Next we encourage them to walk through the cattle crush. Then we get them used to standing in it for a few minutes at a time. This must all be done very slowly, so they are not frightened. Once they will stand calmly in the crush, we halter them. Each horse is taught basic pressure and release.'

'All that with wild brumbies?' said Kim. 'How long will it take? I thought you'd just rope them or something.'

Taj gave her an amused look. 'Like in the cowboy movies?'

Kim smiled back. 'Just like that.'

'A wild horse's first encounter with man leaves an indelible impression. Take that black. His trust has already been broken. If we chase him with ropes, if we panic him, he will hurt himself. Brumbies are like us. They learn more quickly when they are calm, so we give them time, remain patient. Only when they are leading – learning our language – only then will we load them on the truck.'

'How do you know so much about brumbies?'

Taj shrugged. 'I have a way with wild things.'

'He bloody well does.' A fresh-faced girl with messy blonde hair and a pierced lip interrupted the conversation. 'G'day, I'm Hayley. I manage the wild horse sanctuary.' She gave Kim a quizzical look. 'You seem surprised.'

'It's just . . . you look so young.'

Hayley laughed and tossed her hair back from her eyes. 'I'll take that as a compliment. I might be young, but I've been fanatical about brumbies since I was fourteen years old.' She put her arm round Taj's shoulder. 'What this man doesn't know about horses isn't worth knowing.'

Taj certainly was full of surprises. Kim couldn't stop looking at the girl's arm round his shoulder. For some reason it annoyed her.

Hayley turned and studied the horses in the yards. They seemed to have settled somewhat. Even the stallion had stopped his restless pacing. 'They sure are beauties. Do you have a name for the black horse, Taj?'

'One-Ear.'

She grinned. 'Perfect. Let's get to work.'

It was an intriguing day. Taj was true to his word. To Jake's disappointment, there were no *yee ha* cowboy tactics employed with the horses. The volunteers worked quietly and calmly, never rushing or making sudden movements. Slowly and surely, the mares learned to walk through the crush, then stand quietly inside for a few minutes with the gates closed.

The taffy filly-foal was braver than the others, and very inquisitive. Despite the herds' best efforts to guard her, she refused to stay put. She played with the water trough. She tugged at the halters hanging on the fence with her teeth. She almost gave her poor mother a heart attack by trotting up to Taj and chewing his shirt.

These antics went down well with the watching children. A party atmosphere had developed among the two dozen or so people who'd come to watch. The cricket club had a bye that week, and it seemed for some that the brumbies were the alternative Saturday entertainment. A reporter had arrived from the *Wingham Gazette*, with a cameraman who was madly snapping photographs. Mothers spread out blankets for picnics beneath the shady red gums. Kids swam in the billabong and swatted flies. Shirley and Pat Ryan, who Kim had met at the quiz night, were there with their grandchildren. The men were swapping stories about sheep and tractors, and arguing about who had the best bull. They leant on the yards, offering advice, being shooed away by frustrated volunteers.

Hayley insisted on giving the brumbies frequent breaks between teaching sessions, only working with each animal for stretches of ten minutes at a time. 'Stop mucking around, love,' said one farmer, when Hayley stopped for lunch. 'Get a rope on those buggers and I'll winch them into the truck for you.'

Hayley politely refused his help. 'That's one way to make a horse head-shy for life,' she told Kim beneath her breath. 'Or break its neck.'

Kim opened her little esky. 'Want a sandwich? There's ham and tomato, or egg and lettuce.'

'Thanks,' said Hayley. 'I forgot to bring lunch.'

'How long have you known Taj?'

'He's been volunteering for about two years. Takes on the tough cases, ones that have already had a hard time from some other bastard.' She pointed to the rearing, crop-eared stallion in the yards. 'Like him.' She lowered her voice. 'Taj is quite a babe, don't you think?'

'Well, I—'

'And what about that accent?' Hayley put a hand to her heart. 'Gets me here every time.' She pointed to the yards where Taj was working with One-Ear. 'Look, he's about to get the halter on.'

People were stopping to watch.

One-Ear stood in the crush, a-tremble from the tip of his nose to the end of his tangled tail. Taj had one hand on his sweat-streaked shoulder. The other held a rope halter. He was crooning something soft and lyrical, in a language Kim didn't recognise. In one sure movement he slipped the noseband on, passed the crown-piece over the stallion's neck, and knotted it. The horse plunged forward, but the cramped crush brought him up short. He stood with nostrils quivering, eyeing Taj, who still crooned his soothing song.

Slowly One-Ear relaxed. His head came down. He licked his lips, allowing Taj to rub his withers. 'That's a bonding move,' said Hayley. 'Horses mutually groom each other in that spot.'

'What's he doing now?' asked Kim.

'Breathing into his nose,' said Hayley. 'A little horse-whisperer trick of the trade. It's a sign of friendship. See there? Rubbing his ears?' Her eyes shone. 'Amazing. The last time a man got near that horse's ears, they sliced one off.'

Ten minutes later, Taj had One-Ear following him around the yards without a rope. It was a remarkable accomplishment. Even Jake was impressed. 'Can we keep that horse, Mum? I want to try what Taj is doing.'

By three o'clock the brumbies were loaded and, as Taj promised, it had remained a calm affair.

'Bye-bye, brumbies,' said Abbey. 'I'll miss you.'

As if in response, the stallion stomped his feet, shaking the truck, and letting out an ear-splitting neigh.

'I think One-Ear's trying to tell us something,' said Hayley. 'Time to get this show on the road.'

Kim shook her hand. 'Thank you for your help, Hayley. I'll put a donation into your account tonight.'

Hayley smiled. 'You and your kids can visit the brumbies whenever you want, if I can come and have a look at your rewilding project.'

'It's not proper rewilding,' said Kim. 'More like rainforest regeneration. But you're welcome to have a look.'

'But what about the dingoes?' asked Hayley. 'Taj said—' A furious kicking came from the truck. 'I'd better go. Taj is coming home with me. Nobody can handle One-Ear like he does.'

A surge of irritation hit Kim, and she shook it away. Why shouldn't Hayley have a crush on Taj? He was charismatic and ruggedly handsome. A little wild, but that was part of the attraction. An excellent horseman. Self-assured, good with his hands, enigmatic. Some women might be attracted to that.

'Excuse me, I couldn't help but overhear you talking before.'

It was the journalist, a tall woman with a stylish black bob and intense green eyes.

'Adelaide Fisher from the *Wingham Gazette*. I'm the environment reporter You can call me Del.' She shook Kim's hand. 'I'm also the rural, fashion, arts and entertainment reporter. Oh, and the literary editor, but that's neither here nor there. I'm interested in your rewilding venture. If there are fashions in conservation, rewilding is certainly the big one at the moment. It's fascinating to think we have a local project happening.' She gave Kim her card. 'You own the run next to Ben's place right, Journey's End?'

'Yes, but—'

'Would *love* to visit sometime.' The truck fired up, and began its precarious journey across the rough paddock to Bangalow Road. 'Got to go,' said Del. 'Don't want to miss the unloading. I'm making a documentary about this lot, following their lives through from bush brumby to riding horse.' She flashed Kim a brilliant smile. 'I'll be in touch.' And with that, she hurried off after her cameraman.

'Are our brumbies going to be movie stars?' asked Abbey.

'Looks that way, sweetie. Now, we'd better get home. Hush will be ready for a feed.' Abbey spun round and around until her legs went wobbly. 'What are you doing?'

'Making myself dizzy with happiness. I *love* living here, don't you? Don't you love it, Mum?'

Kim looked around at the golden summer afternoon, at the fern-fringed billabong, and darting blue kingfishers. She could smell the peppermint gums on the breeze, hear the squeals of children as they swung over the water on overhanging branches then let go with a splash.

'Kim.' It was Shirley. 'Come and have a cuppa.'

Kim smiled. Maybe she could stay a bit longer after all. Shirley poured her a mug of coffee from a thermos. Pat found her a chair. Somebody passed her a biscuit. Life was simpler here than in Sydney, each day a lesson in mindfulness. And the catastrophe of losing Connor did not loom so large. Nobody walked on eggshells around her or cast pitying glances. In Tingo you were accepted for who you were – right here, right now. It didn't matter what had happened before. She could see why Taj was so drawn to this place. Perfect for Jake, and for her too.

'Yes,' she said, giving Abbey a hug long after the girl had forgotten her question. 'I do love it here.'

CHAPTER 21

The first day of autumn. Taj slowed the quad bike as it reached the crest of the ridge, expertly negotiating a winding animal track up to the lookout point. All too aware of the press of Kim's slim arms round his waist and the sandalwood fragrance of her hair. The bike hummed to a halt and the weight of her arms fell away.

'Come.' He beckoned her to follow him, scrambling up between clustered rocks and onto a stone ledge.

Kim took in the view with shining eyes, her wind-whipped hair framing her face.

When she went closer to the cliff edge, his muscles tensed involuntarily. Taj moved to stand beside her. He could feel a vibration where their arms touched, the slightest shiver of skin. The narrow stone table offered a spectacular view across the range, which was in turn blanketed by forest and scarred by jagged bluffs. A pair of eagles wheeled across the sky, riding the updrafts, and the sun sailed overhead, high as heaven. This was his favourite vantage point to look out over Tarringtops. With a little stretch of the imagination, he could be gazing at a mountain pass in the Hindu Kush.

'All these years and I've never been to this spot,' she breathed. 'It's by far the best place to see the waterfall.' Across the valley, Devil Falls plunged two hundred metres down Echo Gorge, a silver ribbon breaking in a rainbow of spray on the rocks below. The special clarity of early autumn light made the cascading water seem almost close enough to touch. 'It's the loveliest thing I've seen.'

Taj nodded. Lovely, yes, but with a dark past. It was rumoured that during colonial times, local Biripi people had been dispossessed of their land and thrown to their deaths from the top of the falls. Beauty and violence went hand in hand here just as they did in his native Afghanistan.

'See to the left of that line of trees?' He moved behind her, closer now, pointing down the valley. 'That's where our last planting is.'

'Or was,' said Kim, with a rueful smile.

Removing the brumbies had succeeded in stabilising the creek banks, but it hadn't solved their main problem. As fast as they could plant the trees out, they were nibbled down by browsing animals. Wallabies, deer, goats, even rabbits took their share. Heartbreaking. Plastic tree guards proved too flimsy, and fencing such large areas wasn't practical. Taj went spotlighting most nights, much to the delight of the locals. He'd supplied them with enough venison to last for months. But as fast as he eradicated one pest, another took its place. He was only one man, and targeting ferals didn't dent the wallaby and kangaroo population.

'Look.' Taj pointed to a troop of goats with half-grown kids, emerging from a gully. They spread out across the replanted paddock to graze.

'Cheeky beggers,' said Kim. 'We'd better get down there before they clean up what's left.' Her shoulders sagged. 'I feel like when we plant out we're just sacrificing the poor seedlings to an army of chompers.'

A strong gust of wind caused her to step back, pressing against him. Taj steadied her with a hand to her waist, and a spark passed through him. Surely she could feel it too? He guided her back down the rock scramble, reluctant to let her go. Wanting to take her hand. 'I have an idea,' he said. 'But first, I must show you something.'

. . .

Kim stood with a hand clamped to her mouth, staring at the ravaged plants on a slide of lichen-covered rocks above the rapids on Cedar Creek. 'The orchids. The ravine orchids you were going to show me .. . was this them?'

'Yes.' His eyes brimmed with sadness. 'I'm sorry.' The orchids once grew here in a glorious profusion, forming broad mats across the moist rock face, many metres wide. Now the ancient clumps had been reduced to a few clusters of fleshy grey-green roots. They clung precariously to high stone fissures above the turbulent water.

'What happened?'

'I thought the cliffs would protect them. But I hadn't counted on sure-footed goats.'

He had wanted to *give* her this view of the orchids, the beauty of them tumbling down the rocks, an image she could see over and over against her eyelids as she fell asleep. Why hadn't he brought her here sooner? All this while he imagined them safe and beautiful, and now... It broke his heart to see her disappointment.

'We have to do something.' She choked back a sob. 'Tell me your idea?'

CHAPTER 22

Kim sat on the verandah of Wolf Hall. For the second time that day she was left open-mouthed. 'Dingoes? Your plan is dingoes?'

'Hear me out. Do you know what a trophic cascade is?'

A trivia night question that she couldn't remember the answer to.

He ran his fingers through his hair and tried again. 'Have you heard of the wolves of Yellowstone?'

'No.' He wasn't making any sense. 'What have wolves got to do with anything?'

Taj laced his fingers together. She'd never seen him so tense. 'In the 1930s,' he said, 'wolves were wiped out from Yellowstone National Park.'

'That's sad, but how is it relevant?'

He held up his hand. 'Elk and deer populations exploded. They ate the grasslands down to nothing, ringbarked trees, killed the young cottonwood and aspens . . .'

'Go on.'

His voice, low and lilting, took on the rhythm of a tale-teller. 'It wasn't just the forest that suffered. Elk trampled the river banks. Without wolves, coyotes thrived, decimating small mammals and

168

birds, in turn depriving owls and eagles of their prey. With food trees stripped bare, and no chance to steal kills, the bears starved. Beavers vanished, along with the river willows.'

Kim sat forward in her chair.

'Then, after more than seventy years, they brought the wolves back. Just thirty-one of them, in a park of nine thousand square kilometres. Within months, elk deserted the valleys and streams where wolves could easily ambush them, which allowed the trees to regenerate. Coyote numbers plummeted, and as the forests staged a comeback, so did the birds and little mammals, the beavers and their dams. Rivers flowed more slowly, recharging water tables, creating wetlands for moose and otters.' Kim's scalp prickled. 'Wolves restored Yellowstone. They brought the ecosystem back to balance.' Taj paused. 'And dingoes can do the same here if you give them half a chance.'

For the longest time she sat there. Not moving, not speaking, barely blinking: her mind awhirl with new concepts and ideas. Everything he said made perfect sense.

Taj must have mistaken her silence for misgiving, for he redoubled his efforts to convince her. 'Imagine a creek flowing through the forest – then it comes to a cliff, like at Devil Falls. It drops over the edge of the cascade, hits a rock and splits. Then each of those streams hits another rock and splits again. The single stream at the top scatters into many. An apex predator is like that creek. Its influence splinters out over the entire ecosystem. That's a trophic cascade. It starts at the top of the food chain and tumbles all the way down.'

'I get it,' she said. 'It's brilliant. Is there any evidence it will work with dingoes?'

Taj leaped to his feet. A breeze stirred the overhanging tamarind tree, and lifted the lock of hair from his eyes. 'Yes, absolutely.' He paced about, unable to keep still. 'I worked as a boundary rider on the dingo fence, based at Katunga Bore north of Broken Hill. Mungo Station was on the southern side, the dog-free side. Boonda Station lay to the north. The manager there had a soft spot for dingoes, left them alone. I saw what happened on both sides of the dog fence.'

'And?'

'Dingoes were common at Boonda, and I often came across their kills. Sometimes a calf or wild goat. But ninety per cent of the time they hunted kangaroos. I never shot a single fox there, and only saw one cat. But small native animals were thriving. Dunnarts and hopping mice. Echidnas and jacky dragons. Lots of birds. The dingoes didn't bother with small fry when large prey was plentiful.'

'And on the southern side, on Mungo?'

'No dingoes, not a lot of birds, but tons of goats and kangaroos. The bush was grazed bare. Cats and foxes everywhere. I shot dozens a night. And little animals were missing, even the lizards.'

'Dingoes eat cats and foxes?'

Taj nodded. 'Even the scent of their scat keeps ferals away.' He sat back down. 'Bring back dingoes and the rainforest will practically restore itself.'

Kim turned the idea over and over in her mind. This plan went way beyond anything she'd dreamed of. Bringing back a top-order predator – that was real rewilding. Taj was pacing again.

'It's an amazing idea, Taj. Original. Ground-breaking.' She thought back to the conversation with Hayley on the day they caught the brumbies, and gave him a shrewd, side-ways glance. 'You've been planning to spring this on me for a while, haven't you?'

'Yes.' His honesty was disarming. Taj plucked a leaf from the tamarind tree, rolling it between his fingers. A pulse started in his cheek. 'You must be sure,' he said. 'It won't be easy. Many people will be against us.'

'When it comes to protecting rainforest, I'm tougher than you think. One question – where would we get dingoes?'

He dared to take her hand. 'Come with me.'

'I don't believe it.'

Six dingoes paraded up and down the cyclone-wire fence in a pen above the house. Wagging their tails and yodelling a greeting. Their cries swelled and built into a synchronised chorus of howling. So that's what she'd heard that first day when she met Taj. A wild, eerie sound. No wonder she'd been a little frightened.

The dingoes were medium-sized and muscular, with short coats, erect ears and broad, angular heads. Two half-grown pups looked very much like Dusty, except for their sandy colour and the white tips at the end of their bushy tails.

A big male jumped up at the fence near to where she was standing. She shrank back. 'I've never seen a dingo, let alone been up close to one. Aren't they supposed to be dangerous?'

'You're ten times more likely to be bitten by a domestic dog than by one of my friends here.' Taj stroked the animal's nose through the wire. 'And you are mistaken about not having met a dingo before. One lives in your home. Dusty is a dingo.'

Kim gave him a sharp, disbelieving look. 'That can't be. Mel says he's a kelpie.'

'Then Mel is wrong.' He pointed to the pups. 'These are Dusty's sisters. I found them in a den on Tarringtops with their dead mother curled around them. She'd been shot.'

'Why didn't you tell me?'

'Would you have wanted Dusty if I did?'

'If you remember, I never *wanted* Dusty in the first place. But thanks to you, I got him anyway.'

Taj frowned. 'Does the pup displease you in some way?'

Did he displease her? Hardly. Dusty was a gem: funny, affectionate, heart-tuggingly beautiful and loyal to a fault. Utterly adorable. And since she'd enlisted Mel's help with training, obedient as well. He was more independent than usual, apparently. A bit of a deep thinker, but he learned quickly and was easy to teach.

'No, I'm completely in love with him – we all are. I can't imagine life without him. But I take your point. I may have unfairly judged him if I knew he was dingo.'

Taj's face relaxed from its frown. 'We need to give dingoes a public opinion makeover, but there'll be a lot of prejudice to overcome at first.'

Kim couldn't help thinking that he was talking about more than the dingoes. 'Don't you need some kind of a permit?' Probably a silly question. Taj wasn't the type to bother with red tape.

'Not in New South Wales.' Taj squared his shoulders, looking implacably determined, but vulnerable at the same time. An oddly appealing combination.

This project clearly meant the world to him, and his passion was contagious. She was keenly aware of the strength and warmth of his body beside her. He turned to speak to the dingoes and the dappled sunlight caught his face in profile. The stubborn set of his jaw. The shadow of his stubble. The jagged scar that ran down his cheek. Not for the first time, she wondered how that scar got there.

Taj opened the gate, and the dingoes streamed out.

Kim pressed back against the fence. 'You could have warned me.'

'They're perfectly friendly, as friendly as Dusty. Even a little shy.'

Slowly Kim relaxed, exhaled, found her confidence. The dingoes dashed about, bushy tails waving. Their coats gleamed with good health and their almond-shaped eyes shone with intelligence. They greeted Taj with high-pitched yelps, filled with joie de vivre. Soon she was laughing and romping along with them. It was impossible not to be won over – they were simply magnificent.

The smallest dingo sidled up to her and she bent to stroke it. 'So you're Dusty's sister. Pleased to meet you.' The pup licked her hand, showing a flash of bright white teeth. 'I can see the family resemblance.' She glanced at Taj with sudden concern. 'You don't mean Dusty too, do you? You don't want to send him off into the wild?'

'Dusty doesn't belong to this pack. He belongs to yours. Dingoes bond more powerfully than domestic dogs. His love and loyalty will always be for you and your family. He'll never be happy anywhere else.' It was silly, but Kim felt flattered, honoured even. Though Dusty had no monopoly on love and loyalty. That worked both ways. She was as committed to him as he was to her.

Kim offered Taj a slow uncertain smile. Their eyes locked and something passed between them – an acknowledgement that this was an alliance, that together they could accomplish something important, 'Well, we've got our dingoes,' she said. 'So what happens now?'

Taj's face split into a winning grin, dazzling against his olive skin. 'I haven't got that far.'

CHAPTER 23

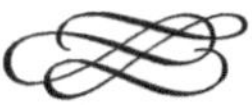

Kim cut herself another piece of chocolate mud cake. Mel had brought it over as a bribe. 'These babies won't be any trouble,' Mel mumbled, her own mouth full of cake. 'They're off milk feeds and eating meat now.'

Kim looked dubiously at the three little tiger quolls climbing the kitchen curtain. They looked a bit like mongooses, except for the large white spots extending right to the end of their tapering tails. Another quoll explored the bread bin. 'Why can't you keep them?'

'I need their cage for the sugar gliders,' said Mel. 'Your old chook pen's free now, isn't it?'

'Only because Abbey's brought the three possums into the house.'

'Don't let her do that with these quolls,' said Mel. 'They need a hands-off approach. I'm trying to keep them as wild as possible to prepare them for release.'

'Does that mean they bite?'

'No. Well, hardly ever. They domesticate quite easily, so it's important not to encourage tame behaviour.' The bread bin quoll came to sit on Kim's knee. She gingerly stroked the baby's ginger fur, and it sniffed her chin with its twitching, pink nose. 'Which can be very difficult,' said Mel, 'when they're so cute.'

'Okay,' said Kim. 'The more the merrier, I suppose.' The quoll jumped onto her shoulder and sat there, cleaning its face with tiny hands. Cute was an understatement. 'Abbey will go nuts over these when she gets home from school. Maybe Taj can rig up a pen away from the house. It might stop her corrupting them.'

Dusty scratched at the door. 'I guess the poor thing's lonely now Jake's back at school,' said Mel. 'How's that going do you think? Todd says Jake's fitted right in.'

'He has,' said Kim. 'I've never been so relieved about anything in my life. He comes home happy, excited about his day. He's off those stupid computer games. He's doing homework, and getting reasonable grades for the first time in two years. He's like a different boy.' The quoll investigated her ear. 'It's early days, but I have a feeling your little Tingo school could be the making of my Jake.'

'I'm so pleased.' Mel licked some chocolate icing off her fingers. 'I don't suppose you'd think about staying on, after this year, I mean? Jake could catch the bus to Wingham with Todd in the morning.'

'I can't,' said Kim. 'My job's in Campbelltown. I can't afford to take more time off.'

'There's a TAFE at Taree. It's an easy hour's drive. Ben does it. You could work there.'

'It's not that simple.' The quoll was licking Kim's ear now. She could feel the tickle of its tiny tongue. 'I'm head of horticulture at Campbelltown. You can't just walk into a position like that.'

'No, of course not.' Mel fiddled with a spoon on the table. 'What about all the trees you're planting? Don't you want to see that through? The new owner might cut them all down.'

'They can't,' said Kim. 'Journey's End is protected by a conservation covenant. And, anyway, I'll sell it to somebody like me.'

'There isn't anybody else like you,' said Mel fiercely. 'I'm sorry. It's just . . . It's just I don't want you to go. I've never had a friend like you.'

Kim felt a catch in her throat, thinking of all the times she'd dismissed Mel as a bit of a dill or tried to avoid her. 'I'm not going anywhere,' said Kim. 'Not for ages. Ow!' Her hand flew to the side of her head. The inquisitive quoll had nipped her ear.

'I'm so sorry.' Mel plucked it from Kim's shoulder. 'Huey was just playing, weren't you, baby?'

'Huey?'

'That's right.' Mel pointed to each quoll in turn. 'Huey, Dewey, Louie and Minnie.'

Kim laughed. 'They all look the same. How do you know which is which?'

'It's easy,' said Mel. 'Huey has a big, blotchy spot – right here. And Minnie's smaller, see? And she has a spot right at the tip of her tail. Louie—'

'Should I be taking notes?'

'As a matter of fact, yes. You'll need to weigh them once a week so you'd better learn who's who.'

'I'll make a point of it,' said Kim. 'Now how about we take these monkeys up to the chook pen? I can't wait to see how they like it.'

The quolls explored their new quarters, climbing effortlessly up the chicken wire, snapping up a few disturbed moths and snails as they went. One by one they discovered the old possum nesting box, and vanished inside. 'Quolls are mainly nocturnal,' said Mel. 'They'll come out again after dark.'

The two of them examined every inch of the enclosure for weaknesses and holes. Dusty poked his nose into everything, trying to help, making them laugh with his antics.

'We really should have done this *before* we installed the new residents,' said Kim.

'I was thinking that myself.'

'Where did the quolls come from?'

'A dairy farmer shot their mother in his chook house,' said Mel. 'His wife found babies in the pouch and brought them here. It makes me so mad. Last week I heard some locals in the Wingham pub complaining about a quoll plague. When I asked, it turned out they'd seen three quolls between them the lot of them in three years. Only three bloody quolls. A few sightings like that is enough to make people think they're still common. Or someone will hear a shriek in the night and say it's quolls. There are plenty of other things that shriek in the night – possums, feral cats, a rabbit taken by a fox.'

Kim put down the fencing pliers and turned to Mel. 'This really matters to you, doesn't it?'

'Of course it matters.' Mel's voice rose a notch. 'What did you think? That I accept all these half-dead, orphaned animals because I'm lonely, or a soft touch, or have some over-developed maternal instinct?'

Kim looked hard at a small hole in the chicken wire. The comment was a little too close to the truth.

'That's what Geoff thinks,' Mel went on. 'That it's some silly, sentimental hobby. But he's wrong. I've studied and taken courses. I'm a registered wildlife carer, and a bloody good one too. I'm just as committed to what I do as you are to your plants.'

'I don't doubt it,' said Kim, impressed by her friend's passion. 'These animals have really found their champion.'

Mel's expression softened. 'That means a lot, coming from you. In some ways, you're everything I wish I was. Smart, educated, independent. Beautiful . . .'

'*You're* smart, educated, independent and beautiful,' Kim said. Why couldn't Mel see it? She'd blossomed in the short time Kim had known her. She was coming into her own. But Mel continued as if Kim hadn't said anything.

'No wonder Ben likes you.'

Kim felt her cheeks flame and she looked away. Time to change the subject. 'I have a favour to ask.'

'Anything.' Mel's eyes held a touching eagerness.

Kim had no idea why Mel was so determined to put her on pedestal. She had the feeling that Mel would have agreed to almost anything. Thank goodness this favour would be right up her alley – sort of.

'At the moment there's no safe forest passage for animals from Cedar Creek up to Tarringtops,' said Kim. 'But if we take down some fences between my place and yours, and plant trees all the way from your timbered gullies right down to the creek, well . . . we'll have a wildlife corridor that connects the remnant bushland of the river basin with the national park.'

'Like a nature highway?'

'Exactly. Taj has been telling me about a concept called Cores and Corridors – restoring connections between core wilderness areas.' Kim wasn't being entirely honest. This was an edited version. The concept was actually known as Cores, Corridors and Carnivores. She hoped Mel wouldn't google the term for herself. It called for the reintroduction of top-order predators as well. This might not be a sheep farmer's favourite thing.

'It's a brilliant idea. I love it,' said Mel. 'Getting rid of the fences between us. Joining up like we're proper partners.' Mel put down the wire she was holding and wrapped Kim in a heartfelt hug.

'We need to celebrate,' said Kim, moved by Mel's trust in her. 'There's some bubbly in the fridge. Though Taj should be here. It was his idea in the first place. I told you he was a biologist, right?'

'Are you ever spoilt for choice,' said Mel. 'The two hunkiest men for miles around, and they're both falling all over you. How do you do it?' She turned back to the pen. 'Play hard to get?'

'I'm going to pretend you didn't say that.'

'Fair enough.' Mel sighed. 'Keep your secrets. Now, about these fences – we can't take them all down. What about my sheep?'

'Of course not,' said Kim. 'Just where your gully abuts my boundary, and again where it meet Tarringtops. Then we'll fence the length of it. I'm happy to pay for materials, and we can all help with the work.' The full enormity of what they were proposing hit her. 'Just think,' said Kim. 'Animals will be able to pass freely between the creek flats and the rainforest again for the first time since timber-cutters cleared these hills.'

'That was over a hundred years ago.'

'We'll be righting a century-old wrong then,' said Kim.

Solemnly they shook hands.

Mel finished patching a tiny hole in the chicken wire. 'That's the last one. Those quolls will need magic to get out of here now. Let's break out the bubbly.'

'One more thing,' said Kim. 'Somebody's been spotlighting here. I've heard rifle shots after midnight and seen lights on the hill. The last thing I want here is hunters. Any idea who it might be?'

Mel picked up her tools. 'Could be almost anybody. Most blokes round here go rabbiting and this place used to be fair game. I guess it's all right if they're picking off ferals. Doing you a favour, really. They should ask permission, though, now you're here.'

'Bloody oath they should,' said Kim. 'This is a nature reserve. I don't want anybody but Taj shooting here. Where are they getting in, do you think?'

'Well, not through She-Oak Springs, and Ben wouldn't put up with trespassers on his side, but there are plenty of other places. That track by the billabong where Taj built the brumby yards. Or maybe they're crossing in from the national park.'

'Might have to hold a stake-out one night,' said Kim. 'Catch them in the act.'

'And maybe get shot in the process.'

'That's a bit melodramatic,' said Kim.

'Make fun of me if you like, but I'm warning you – drunken bogans, guns and darkness are a dangerous combination.'

'Okay, Mum,' teased Kim. 'I'll brush my teeth and go to bed early instead.'

Dusty put a paw on Mel's leg, and she gave him a pat. 'He's growing into a good type, Kim. Old timers always say the best dogs have a touch of dingo in them.'

CHAPTER 24

Today was the seniors' cricket grand final. Tingo against Wingham – the first time the local team had ever made it through. Abbey helped pack the sandwiches and cold chook in the esky, along with the coleslaw they'd made the night before. Kim added butter and a loaf of sourdough from the freezer. It would defrost by lunchtime. A packet of Chocolate Royals. Some bananas, oranges and a sorry-looking bunch of grapes that Abbey had been picking at. A second esky held the drinks and ice. Two folding chairs leant against the wall. Pity she didn't have any more. Maybe Mel would bring some?

Kim closed the lid, and studied the esky like she had x-ray vision. Would there be enough food? Taj would be there as well. Maybe she should have made some extra sandwiches? Kim glanced at the clock. There might still be time.

'Mum.' Jake pelted into the kitchen, Dusty at his heels. 'Ben's here.'

Okay, no extra sandwiches. She pointed to the eskies. 'Can you take one of those please?'

Jake picked up the heavier of the two in one easy motion. The physical aspect of life in Tingo had been good for him. He was stronger, with muscles that weren't there a few months ago. Tanned and fit and brimming with confidence.

Jake put the esky back down. 'Can Dusty come?'

'I don't think so, darling. It will be too crowded in the car.'

Since Taj had made the astonishing confession that Dusty was a dingo, she'd been loath to take him out in public in case somebody guessed. He didn't come on the school run anymore, or to the store. He stayed out the back when visitors came. She was probably worrying about nothing. A Google image search for *black and tan dingoes* brought up multiple pictures of dogs that looked a lot like kelpies – and Dusty did too. However she wanted to err on the side of caution.

'Ben wouldn't let him in his car anyway,' said Abbey. 'He hates Dusty.' Jake glared at his sister, but held his tongue. 'Why not ask Taj to bring him?'

Jake looked even more surly. 'Is Taj coming today?'

'Yep.' Abbey was wearing her triumphant face. 'That's why we made corn beef and pickle sandwiches. They're his favourite, aren't they, Mum?'

'Wayne Stevens rolled his quad bike and broke his collarbone,' said Kim. 'He can't play. Taj is making up the numbers.'

'Great,' said Jake. 'Now we're bound to lose.'

'Well?' said Abbey. 'Are you going to ask Taj to bring Dusty or not?'

Kim waited, hoping Jake would make the decision to leave the pup himself, so she wouldn't have to weigh in. He pulled at his ear and looked out the window, as if the answer might be there. Since getting Dusty, his level of hostility towards Taj had gone down a notch. But not enough, Kim suspected, for Jake to ask him for a favour.

'I guess he can stay here,' said Jake at last. 'Can he have a bone?'

Kim smiled. 'The biggest, juiciest marrowbone I can find. He'll hardly notice you're gone.'

The back door swung open and Ben strolled in. He was Tingo's top bowler and a handy bat – the sort of talented all-rounder that country sides dreamed of. Cricket clothes whiter than white, and perfectly pressed. He looked like the lead model in a laundry-powder ad campaign. Why didn't Jake's whites ever look like that?

'Ready, folks?' Ben flashed Kim a brilliant smile, and picked up an esky. 'You want this in the car?'

'Yes, thanks.'

'Bye Dusty.' Jake picked up the other esky and followed Ben out the door.

Dusty whined. Kim hugged his shiny black mane. Four months old now, and growing fast. Mel said the size of his feet meant he'd be bigger than the average kelpie. 'Don't grow too much more,' whispered Kim. He whined again. 'Cheer up. Let's get you that bone.' He trotted to the fridge, his whole body aquiver with anticipation. 'You understand me perfectly, don't you?' Dusty pointed his nose to the roof and gave a funny, yodelling bark, making her laugh. And to think there was a time she didn't want this little dingo.

Ben poked his head round the door. 'Tie that mutt up and let's get going. Will I pack these chairs?'

The pup shot out the back of his own accord. Kim took him a bone, almost as big as he was. Such a pity Ben didn't like Dusty. Maybe with time that would change.

Ben cruised round the sports ground for a minute or two, then nosed the land cruiser into the guardrail. 'You'll get a good view of the pitch from here.'

Jake jumped out and hauled Ben's sports bag from the back. 'Can I carry this for you?'

'Sure thing, champ.' Ben did an Aussie salute, waving a crowd of sticky bush flies from his face. It was shaping up to be a scorcher, one of those hot, humid days that sometimes turned up in late March, summer's last hurrah. Ben turned to Abbey and fished a few dollars from his pocket. 'Here you go, sweetheart. They sell chips and cold drinks at the canteen, that's as long as your mum doesn't mind.'

Abbey's angelic face creased into a frown. She put her hands on her hips, and drew her seven-year-old self up to full height. 'No, thank you, Ben.' It was as good a cold shoulder as Kim had seen.

Ben shrugged. 'Suit yourself. Come on, Jake.' The pair of them headed off towards the change rooms.

Kim sighed. Jake didn't like Taj. Abbey didn't like Ben. Ben didn't like Dusty. Why on earth couldn't everybody get along?

A honk from behind. Mel, trying to squeeze her car in beside them, without much success. At last she gave up, reversed out, and parked under a spreading peppercorn tree. What a lifesaver. Kim wasn't much of a cricket fan. Without Mel, it could be a very long day.

A carnival atmosphere was developing, as more and more cars entered the ground. The rural fireys ran a sausage sizzle. The brownies had a fairy floss cart, which proved endlessly fascinating to Abbey and Nikki. The high school sold half-melted paddle pops from a rattling freezer on the sports club verandah. People with cans of drink sat in their cars or on their bonnets. Watching the game. Tooting their horns when a player made a good shot or went out. Cheering at every run.

It seemed like the entire population of both towns had turned out to spur on their teams. Men and women, young and old – they were all there. And, to her surprise, Kim was enjoying herself. She thought back to the trivia night, just a few short months ago. First time in a room full of strangers for two years, and she'd been terrified. What a long way she'd come. Although she wasn't surrounded by strangers, not anymore. Every second person greeted her, called her by name. The cricket club was tightly woven into the social fabric of the community and she loved feeling that she belonged. Kim spotted Jake with Todd on the far side of the ground. The boys had put the greatest possible distance between them and their mothers.

Mel arrived with cans of Fanta for the girls and two beers. Kim stared at her friend's stylish, slim-fit jeans. At her black, tucked-in shirt, bearing the RM Williams longhorn emblem on the pocket, and revealing an enviable waist. At the swept-back hair with copper highlights. Plain little Mel was turning into a hot item. 'Look at you.' Mel reddened, her face a charming mix of pleasure and embarrassment. 'What about that hat?' Mel's fingers reached for the brim of her brand-new, white Akubra. 'And those.' Kim pointed to Mel's dark-red, calf-length, embossed-leather boots.

'Cowgirl boots,' said Mel, a little shyly. 'Ariat. I've always wanted a pair, but Geoff didn't like them.' She smiled. 'I guess now I can do what I like.'

'I guess you can,' said Kim. Together they burst out laughing.

Horns honked, and the Tingo player walked from the field, a picture of dejection. 'Just in time.' Mel handed Kim a beer, and cracked her own. She moved her camp chair into a patch of afternoon shade and settled down to watch. 'Ben's up next.'

It was turning into an entertaining match, and Kim was looking forward to Ben's innings. He strolled out to the pitch, emerald-green courtesy of artificial turf, a tall, confident figure owning the field. His clothes somehow remained blinding white, despite a morning's bowling. Except for a red stain on his trousers. Mel groaned. 'How *hot* is he? I wouldn't mind being his cricket ball. Did you see the way he polished it when he was bowling? Rubbing it up and down his pants . . .'

'Stop it.' Kim stifled a laugh. 'The girls will hear you.'

Ben was coming into bat at number six. Tingo were chasing a score of one hundred and twenty-seven, and still needed eighty runs. Not too hard a target, and they had Ben to thank for that. He'd kept Wingham's two star openers quiet with his showy spinners, and then bowled them both out. Tingo had its hopes pinned on him coming through for them as a batsman as well.

Ben started off well, batting with easy precision, taking the score to sixty-five and putting on a show. Jake and Todd came back to the car when they were hungry. They sat on the bonnet, eating oranges and watching the game.

Jake cheered and horns honked as Ben hit a six and held his bat aloft. The next shot wasn't so pretty. The ball went up in the air, and seemed to hang, teasing them all. But when it finally plunged to earth, the Wingham fielder dropped an easy catch.

'He's leading a charmed life,' said Mel. 'At this rate, Tingo will win before we finish our beers.'

But it wasn't to be. The next ball was spun to leg stump. Ben faced it squarely and made a huge swing, a slog sweep, going down on one knee in dramatic fashion. Once again, the ball hovered in mid-air. This time, however, it fell straight into a fielder's hands. Ben was out.

'Oh no.' Kim looked at the scoreboard, but it hadn't been updated since lunch. 'Where does that leave us?'

For an admitted scatterbrain, Mel was a surprisingly accurate score-keeper. 'We're forty-five runs down, with five batsmen to go. But to be honest, we don't have any good ones left.'

'What about Taj.'

'I don't know. He's never played before, but he was handy in the field this morning. Maybe he can bat a bit. He'll come on last, so hopefully we won't need him.'

They hadn't seen much of Taj during the day. He hadn't joined them for lunch. He'd brought the girls back to the car a few times, and stayed once for a cold drink. Jake had been rude, asking him if he'd played cricket before, helpfully reciting the rules in a sarcastic voice that made Todd laugh. Kim had told Jake off, and Taj politely ignored him.

The next batsman up, and the crowd were paying attention. This was the pointy end of the game. People stopped chatting in the shade, stopped buying sausages in bread and cans of drink. They wandered back to the sidelines, to their chairs and cars, and settled in for the final chapters.

The score crept up to one hundred and three before disaster struck. The Wingham bowler was on fire. He took a hat trick, sending one batsman after another back to the change room without scoring.

Ben arrived back at the car, swigging a lemonade, and they all congratulated him on his innings. 'What about that six?' said Jake with a grin. 'You were fantastic. We'll win, won't we?'

Ben frowned. 'Two wickets left. We should be okay if Nick can keep the strike.' Nick did just that, taking six from one over.

Drinks came on, and Tingo still needed seventeen runs. The first delivery of the next over was fast and straight. Too fast. Nick's middle stump cartwheeled out of the ground. Horns blared and cheers went up from the Wingham side of the ground. 'That's it,' said Ben, 'We're screwed.' Jake's face fell.

'It's up Taj now,' whispered Mel.

Taj wandered out to the middle wearing borrowed cricket whites. He looked different, more civilised. Kim found herself wondering if the polo shirt hid his tattoo, or whether the top still showed through the open neck

'Think he knows which end to hold the bat?' said Ben.

Taj took guard and the field closed in. Kim flinched as he faced a bouncer. Who said cricket was safer than football? He ducked, and regained his balance. The next ball was full and wide. He planted his foot, swung hard towards mid-off – and missed.

The crowd groaned. 'That wasn't a bad shot,' said Mel. 'He was unlucky.'

Next he met a ball like the one that undid Nick. With a classic straight drive he sent it back over the head of the bowler. It went for six and Tingo cheered. It wasn't over yet. Eleven needed.

Kim watched Taj swing his bat in a sure practice stroke while waiting for the fielder. Her pulse quickened and a quiver ran through her. Kim cleared her throat and glanced at Mel, afraid she would somehow guess.

Last ball of the over, short into Taj's ribs. Kim's hand flew to her mouth.

'Yes!' yelled Todd. 'A leg bye.' They scampered through for a run. 'Ten to go.'

'Idiots,' Ben said, 'Why did they take that run? Now when the bowlers change ends, Taj is on strike again.'

'And you think that's a bad thing, why?' asked Mel.

The next ball thudded into Taj's pads. An appeal of *Howzat!* The bowler spun around, imploring the umpire to raise his finger and give

Taj out. A roar came from the crowd, then silence. Kim's heart was in her mouth. It was as if the world, not just this match turned on the outcome. The umpire's hand started upward then halted. He shook his head, said something to the bowler, and clasped his hands once again behind his back.

The entire ground held its breath. The next ball was almost identical, just a touch more down the leg side. Taj was masterful, owning the pitch. With a deft flick of the wrists, he sent it for four. The crowd cheered and beeped their horns. Only six runs needed now.

'Lucky edge,' said Ben.

'That was no edge,' said Mel. 'He can play. We can win this.'

The field scattered. Gone were the three slips and short leg. It was game on.

The next ball rose towards Taj's throat. He stepped back, pivoted and sent it flying. The fielder at deep mid-wicket watched it sail over his head.

The umpire raised both hands. Six. Horns blared and Tingo erupted. Even Jake bounced up and down. They'd won. They'd beaten the favourites, and Taj was a hero. A flush of pleasure coloured Kim's cheeks. That man was full of hidden talents. Was there anything Taj Kahn couldn't do?

It was late when Ben brought them home from celebrations at the Tingo sports club. Abbey and Jake were finally in bed. Kim stood with Ben on the verandah, staring into the night, abuzz from too much champagne. Such a gorgeous evening, alive with nocturnal sounds, and the warm wind whispering through the branches of the firewheel tree. Ben was quieter than usual: serious, thoughtful. She studied his rugged face in profile.

They'd said goodbye in the kitchen some time before, yet still he lingered. There was no need for the outside light. The moon and stars blazed as they only did in the bush, patterning Ben's shirt with shifting shadows. Kim was in no hurry for him to go. After a day of fun and friends, she wasn't looking forward to being alone.

Ben turned to her, such a familiar face, handsome in the soft moonshine. He came close, closer still, until his tall figure blocked out the starry sky. All she could see was him. He swung her into the circle of his arms, and Kim's head began to spin. The wine? Something more? Ben pressed his mouth to hers, coaxing, questing, his lips warm and sweet. She responded instinctively, swept up in the moment, reliving a hundred kisses with Connor on this very spot. Dizzy with remembering. It was only when Ben kissed the pulsing hollow of her throat, that she pulled away.

He drew her back, and she stiffened. 'I'm not ready for this'

A sigh escaped him. 'I'll just have to wait then.'

'I might never be ready.' she said. 'Don't wait.'

'Let me make up my own mind.' He took hold of her hand, stroked her palm with his thumb. 'Let's just see where we go. Okay?'

Her thoughts raced, searching for an answer. Where was the harm? She liked the feel of his fingers, the solid nearness of him. 'Okay.'

He raised his eyes to heaven and whispered, 'Thank you, God.'

She smiled. 'You're a good man, Ben Steele, did anybody ever tell you that?'

'Only all the time.' He kissed her again, this time chastely on the cheek, before vaulting over the verandah rail.

'Show-off!'

Twin blades of light pierced the dark, as he swung the car round and headed down the track. She stayed watching long after he'd disappeared from sight, thinking of all that had happened. Taj surprising them all, winning the match for Tingo in such style. Celebrating with their friends at the sports club. The warm sense of belonging. Ben kissing her, saying he'd wait. What a day it had been.

CHAPTER 25

Taj dragged the mangled carcass through the gate and escaped before the dingoes had a chance to greet him. They turned their attention to the fresh kill, yelping in excitement, licking and tearing at the bloodstained fur.

'Poor thing,' said Kim.

The truck in front of her had hit the wallaby on Bangalow Road the night before, and hadn't even stopped. The animal was still jerking and trembling when she got out to help, and found a baby in its pouch. She'd taken the joey straight to Mel. Then she'd dragged the mother's bloody body to the side of the road for Taj to collect in the morning. Life here was a far cry from suburban Sydney. Simpler, yes, but also tough and uncompromising – even brutal at times. The wallaby's death had not been entirely in vain. Wallabies, wild goats, roos and rabbits were the only food the dingoes were allowed to eat.

The pack had been living in the acclimation pen for more than a month now. Taj, with Kim's help, had fenced off fifty square metres of land, high on the remote northern boundary of Journey's End. Each day Kim dropped the kids at school, and by the time she arrived home, Taj would be waiting for her, his battered ute piled high with tools and materials. It had been a steep learning curve, but by the time they'd strained and stapled the last section of mesh, Kim was a pretty handy fencer. She could wield a post-hole digger and strain wire with the best.

She'd also learned a bit more about Taj. Her desire to talk to him about Afghanistan was matched by his reticence on the subject, but he'd let some things slip. Intriguing snippets about his former life in Nuristan, meaning *land of light.* Like the fact that he'd once run a junior ranger program for school children, teaching them about the importance of wilderness. And that he too had reason to hate the Taliban, although he wouldn't tell her why. This admission came as a relief. Connor's death was never far away, and Taj's silence had fuelled her own fears about where his loyalty might lie.

He had experience with carnivore release projects. Not with dingoes, but with wolves in Nuristan. Abbey was right. Taj had raised a group of orphaned cubs, held them in an acclimation pen for several months, and then successfully reintroduced the pack into the wild.

'Okay, so you're a wolf-whisperer,' said Kim. 'But how do you know your talents will stretch to dingoes?'

'I don't,' he said. 'But wolves and dingoes are both keystone predators, they fill the same niche. There's a good chance they'll react in the same way. Dingoes are smaller, though, so we won't have to build this fence so high.'

Even so, the enclosure stood three metres tall, with a ground apron to prevent digging and an inverted top to prevent climbing. It contained a permanent spring and rocky outcrops to serve as potential den sites.

Taj laced lamb carcasses with the nausea-inducing chemical thiabendazole, and put them in the pen. 'It's the same concept biologists use to teach quolls not to eat cane toads,' he said. 'I trialled it back in Afghanistan to help keep the wolves away from flocks. If predators eat a certain type of animal and get sick a few times, they stop seeing that species as prey. They even teach their young to avoid it.'

Kim had been dubious about this theory, but it seemed to be working. The last sheep he'd given to the dingoes hadn't been touched.

After a few days, she'd insisted he remove the stinking, flyblown body from the corner of the pen. If only she could tell Mel how hard they were trying to keep her sheep safe. But on this point she and Taj were in firm agreement – the dingo project must remain secret, at least for now.

They only visited the pack twice a week to provide a feed of rabbits, goats or roadkill. Keeping human contact to a minimum was difficult for Kim. She hated ignoring the friendly animals. But the dingoes were already wilder, less interested in their human jailers, more attuned to their environment.

'It's called a soft release,' said Taj. 'Slowly getting the dingoes used to their new surroundings, and less reliant on us. Hopefully it will also reset their homing instinct, so they won't head straight back to my place.'

'What happens when we let them go?'

'We'll open the gate, and walk away. The rest is up to the dingoes.'

That day was finally here, and this wallaby carcass would be their last offering to the pack.

'Do you want to do the honours?' Taj asked.

Kim gave him a sarcastic smile. 'You just want me to take the blame when this goes horribly wrong.' She was only half-joking. Now the moment of release had arrived, her courage was failing.

Taj must have sensed her misgivings. 'Think of these dingoes as the guardians of Journey's End. Defending the forest, just as my maremmas defend Mel's flocks. They can't protect anything if we keep them locked up.'

A hush fell on the bush. Kim stared at Taj, couldn't look away. She could feel the throb of anticipation in his veins, and her body pulsed in time with his. One by one, the feeding dingoes stopped their meal and turned to watch.

'Now,' said Taj. Kim opened the gate, and he laid his big hand on her shoulder. An undeniable charge passed between them. 'Back in the car.'

The curious dingoes trotted to the open gate. They paused, puzzled. The two smallest ones, Dusty's sisters, ventured outside the pen. With wagging tails they trotted to the ute and jumped up at the windows, seeking attention.

'Ignore them,' whispered Taj.

It was hard. Apart from their sandy colouring, they looked very much like Dusty – not like wild animals at all. She wanted to reassure them, tell them it was for the best, give them a final cuddle. But Taj laid a hand on her arm and pressed a finger to his lips. 'Shh . . . don't speak.'

Once again, Kim's body betrayed her. She could see ink on skin through the open neck of his shirt. How would it feel to undo those buttons, one by one, and reveal the whole tattoo? She closed her eyes, wanting him to touch her again, wishing that she didn't. His presence swelled, filling the cabin. Pushing everything else away.

Why was this happening? If Ben had caused her to respond like this, she might have accepted it. She might even have welcomed it, taking it as a sign that she was finally ready to move on. That her valiant efforts to let go of the past were working. But it hadn't happened with Ben. In spite of his resemblance to Connor. In spite of his help with Jake, and his movie-star good looks and the way he made her laugh. It hadn't happened during the nights they'd stayed up late playing cards, or watching television. Not even when they'd shared that drunken kiss on the verandah after the cricket final. Ben had made his feelings plain. He was the natural choice if she were to let herself love again. He was right for her and especially right for Jake. A familiar face. Caring and protective. A soft place to fall.

Taj, on the other hand, was an unknown quantity. A man of a faith she knew nothing about - a man disturbing in every way. A loner. From a different culture and the country that took Connor. And with, she could feel it, shadows in his past. Jake loathed him. Even Ben seemed to dislike Taj these days. His attitude had changed from friendly – if somewhat patronising – to veiled hostility.

Taj touched her arm again and she lashed out, striking his chest with a sideways fist. 'Don't do that,' she said. 'Don't touch me.'

'Forgive me. I said your name, and thought you didn't hear.'

Had Taj spoken? Was she so lost in tangled thinking that she didn't hear? Taj subtly moved his body away from her. 'I thought you might have wanted to say goodbye.'

'Goodbye?' Kim looked out the window. The pen was empty. She opened the door, hoping to give Dusty's sisters a final hug in spite of Taj's warning. They were gone too.

'Will we see them again?' Her mouth was dry, and thick with fear for them.

'I don't know.'

'Catch them. Bring them back.' Her eyes filled with tears as she got out of the car. 'They might be shot, or poisoned.' Her voice cracked. 'They might starve.'

'Kim—'

'What's wrong with you? Don't you even care?'

This was why she hadn't wanted another dog, why she hadn't wanted Dusty. Why she didn't want to get attached. She should never have agreed to this stupid plan in the first place, sending the young dingoes into who-knew-what kind of danger. Why hadn't she insisted they stay with Taj? Why couldn't she keep the things she loved safe?

Kim knelt down and sobbed, a wild, primal howling that didn't sound like it came from her own throat. In the forest to the north, the dingoes answered, adding their voices to the song of despair. When Kim raised her swollen eyes, Taj was weeping too.

CHAPTER 26

They drove home from the release site in silence. Taj stole the occasional glance at Kim. Each time she was staring out the window. He hadn't realised what a wrench it would be for her to let the dingoes go, and his mind was awash with unfamiliar feelings. Kim's raw torrent of emotion had flooded his defences, exposing the jagged, long-submerged rocks of his own grief.

When they reached the house, Kim sat awhile, blinking back tears and staring into middle distance. Taj handed her a dusty tissue he'd found in the centre console. She blew her nose, rubbed her blank eyes. He wanted to reassure her, tell her the dingoes would be safe, that she had nothing to fear. But that would be a lie. Risk was the price of freedom; he knew that better than anybody.

Taj glanced at the clock. 'Are you okay to drive? Would you like me to pick Abbey and Jake up from school?'

Kim shook her head. She seemed entirely forlorn, like a lost child. Taj burned with words that wouldn't come, hating that he'd added to her misery. He'd dreamed of doing the opposite, dreamed of lifting the sadness from her eyes. Whether on full show or lurking beneath the surface, it was always there. Taj recognised it all too well. He saw it in the mirror each morning.

How lovely she was, even now, with her blue eyes rimmed in red, and her lips ending in a tremulous downward curl. She blew her nose again. A slender nose, somewhat crooked at the tip. It spoiled the symmetry of her face, giving it an irresistible charm.

Dusty came pelting over. Kim shoved open the door and exited without a backward glance. Taj watched her go, wrapped up in her anger and hurt, powerless to help. Her anguished plea for the dingoes played over and over in his mind. *They might be shot, or poisoned. They might starve. What's wrong with you? Don't you even care?'*

Of course he cared. The raising of each pup had been a labour of love. He'd fed them through the night, nursed them when they were sick, taught them to howl and to hunt. He'd considered their welfare before his own, been both mother and father to them. Prepared them as well as he could for the threats they would face: snakes, snares, baits, men with guns. There was another threat too, one that he hadn't shared with Kim. Taj had found fresh dingo scat by the creek. An exciting find, yet he hoped it belonged to a lone animal, Dusty's father perhaps. If a wild pack had moved in to Journey's End, well . . . dingoes were territorial, and the youngsters would come off worst in a fight. But now they were grown, he could not deny them their birthright. He hated that Kim thought him callous.

But worst of all was her furious, 'Don't touch me.' He'd misread things badly. For the last few weeks the two of them had been working together nearly every day. Planting, clearing, weeding, planning. Arguing about which seedlings were big enough to plant out, and which ones needed re-potting. Laughing at the mischief that Dusty got up to. Marvelling at the sheer size of the task ahead. Two people born worlds apart, brought together by a magnificent shared vision. Striking sparks off one another.

A long-dormant feeling grew within him, unrecognised at first. A warm physical energy that lit up his body and radiated out. The attraction between them was tangible, and he'd been sure she felt it too. Kim had become his ally, his muse, his creative inspiration. Sometimes he imagined she was already his lover. He couldn't take his eyes off her, any more than a man in the desert could take his eyes off a distant mirage, although he knew he'd never taste it.

What did Jean say to the children? *If wishes were horses, beggars would ride.* His confidence had been nothing but wishful thinking.

A honking horn startled Taj out of his thoughts.

'Get out of the road, mate.' Ben in his land cruiser, yelling and waving. Jake glared at Taj through the back window. Why on earth was Ben picking up the kids?

The horn honked again and Taj moved his car a few metres before stopping. Ben shook his head and squeezed past.

Taj had never viewed Ben as a rival. He'd seen how Kim was with him – friendly, yet aloof, as she was with everyone. Though Ben often visited, there was no connection, why should there be? Kim and Ben had nothing in common. He had no feeling for the forest, no interest in wildlife or wilderness. He was a businessman, with no poetry in his soul.

Taj watched him in the rear-view mirror, striding towards the house with Jake at his heels. Kim came round the corner, still visibly upset. He wished he could hear what they were saying. Then . . . Ben had Kim in his arms.

Taj's fingers tightened on the steering wheel and his knuckles showed white. A shudder ran through him as he pulled away and he drove faster than necessary onto the road.

What a fool he'd been.

Of course Kim and Ben had something in common – it was staring him in the face. Something vast and all-pervasive, which he could never compete with. They were shaped by the same society, the same culture. They shared a set of assumed values that, as an outsider, he could only guess at. For that's what he was, and would always be. An outsider. This remote place, with its wild mountains and easy-going people, had lulled him into a false sense of belonging. He was accepted here, but only up to a point. There was a line he could not cross.

For the rest of the drive, Taj struggled with a sudden and profound homesickness, a longing for the life he'd left behind in Afghanistan. But even as the memories struck home, one after the other, emptying him out, he knew he'd find no comfort there. That world was gone; utterly, tragically changed. There was no going back.

His throat was tight with disappointment, so tight he found it hard to breathe. He might not have Kim. He might not be the one to help her heal. But he knew one thing for certain. If Ben wanted to be that man, Taj would have his eye on him.

CHAPTER 27

Winter came soft-footed, bringing mild blue-sky days, and crystalline views across the range. The forest showed a different face: muted, gentler. Gathering strength for the fertile eruption of spring. Kim had forgotten how much she loved this time of year in Tingo. Clear mornings, cool night. No more uncomfortable humidity. Leeches and ticks in abeyance, mosquitoes and flies as well.

Kim and Taj still worked together. Their passion for the job of rewilding remained, and the dingo project was proving to be a success. Since their release a month earlier, the animals remained elusive, but all indications showed they were thriving. And they weren't just living on rabbits. Taj had shown her several kills: wallabies and a goat. Her fears for the dingoes had so far been unfounded, yet Kim still missed them.

She also missed her old relationship with Taj. Although physically there, he wasn't available in the same way as before. He stuck strictly to business. He didn't stop to point out sleepy koalas or decorated bowers or roosting owls. He didn't forget himself and indulge her boundless curiosity with snippets about his old life. He found no excuse to touch her.

She wanted their old rapport back, the close connection and easy banter. This new Taj was tightly controlled, formal, always on his best behaviour. It was what she'd asked for, she knew that, but perversely it was driving her mad. She even missed their arguments.

'Should we go get another tankful?' she said, spraying the last seedling of the waving field they'd just planted.

Taj shook his head. 'They've all been well watered.'

Kim stuck her finger in the soil. 'I'm not so sure. Winter's our driest season. It might not rain for a while.' Taj stopped spreading mulch around the roots of a little cassowary pine and headed for the ute. 'Where are you going?' asked Kim.

'To get another tank of water.'

'But you said we didn't need it.'

He swung to face her, his expression unreadable. 'And you said we did.'

'For goodness sake, Taj. Since when do you do what I say?' She lightly punched his arm in frustration. There it was, that inexplicable frisson of excitement that always happened when they touched. Surely he felt it too. Was that why he stepped back so swiftly? Kim dragged her fingers through her hair. She could hardly blame him.

She groaned and looked at her watch. 'Don't bother. We should get back anyway. It's almost school pick-up time.' Taj nodded and wordlessly began collecting tools. 'I have to hand it to you,' she said. 'The dingoes are already making a difference – to the creek flat plantings anyway. The goats are leaving them alone, and even the wallabies are steering clear. Do you think that's because the pack has found a new den site lower down, closer to the creek?'

Taj loaded the mattocks onto the ute. 'Perhaps.'

Kim tried again. 'The creek's much closer to Mel's boundary. I hope they don't start bothering her sheep.' He began gathering up the trays of empty pots that were scattered over the ground. 'What do you think? Will they go after Mel's sheep?'

'I don't think so.'

'When you released the wolves in Afghanistan, did they ever go after local farmers' flocks?'

'No.' He climbed up on the tray, and began securing the tools with jockey straps.

Argh . . . she hated this! The way he shut down. She hadn't realised how much their conversations had meant, how special they were. Nobody else could fill that space.

Ben was witty, endlessly entertaining, and made her laugh. She felt relaxed and safe with him, happier than she'd been in a long time. But he didn't intrigue her the way Taj did.

She could talk to Mel about dogs and orphans and the wildlife corridor. But Mel didn't possess the breadth of vision or the encyclopaedic knowledge of ecosystems that Taj did. Nobody else understood the true significance of what they were trying to achieve.

But Kim didn't just miss shoptalk with Taj. It was so much more than that. She missed discussing politics, art, philosophy – all manner of things. She missed his out-of-the box thinking and questions that came from left field. 'If you could go back to any moment in history, when would that be?' he'd ask, as they toiled side by side, ripping the earth into furrows for planting. The conversation that followed would make time fly. Or he'd gaze at the sky and say, 'I wonder if you see blue the same way I do?'

Once, when they'd spent all day clearing a waterway choked by lantana, Taj asked her, 'Is there anything people do that isn't selfish?'

'What do you mean?'

'I look at that stream and wonder – did we work so hard to help the stream, or to help ourselves because it makes us happy to bring it back to life?'

'Does it matter why we did it?' asked Kim. 'As long as we did it?'

'Maybe it does,' said Taj. 'Maybe intention is everything.'

'Seen that way, even love is selfish,' said Kim. 'We want to protect our loved ones because they bring us joy. Because we can't afford to lose them.'

'And what if we can't protect them?' he said. 'What then?'

Something intensely personal in his tone put a lump in her throat. 'All we can do is our best,' she said. 'Then we have to move on, without guilt. We owe it to them. We owe it ourselves.'

Taj had pondered her answer for a long time. 'That is wise advice,' he'd said at last. 'Perhaps you should follow it.'

These conversations remained with her, sometimes keeping her awake until the early hours. Pondering. The stillness of night helped Kim see things more clearly. Slowly, tentatively, she'd been piecing together the broken pieces of her life, making sense of them. And now, without Taj to act as a catalyst, she'd come to a dead end.

Taj stowed the last rake onto the tray, and put up the gate. 'Are you ready?'

No, she wasn't ready. Not for this. Not to be cut off from that other part of Taj's life. The part that knew where the lyrebirds danced and the brumbies ran. The part full of richness and meaning that challenged how she saw the world. His stories of Afghanistan, which connected her in some small way to Connor. When would she ever be ready for that?

el pulled Huey from his hollow log. 'Lucky last.'

Kim reached over and stroked the quoll's soft fur. Huey craned his neck towards her and hissed, his mouth gaping impossibly wide. 'How old do they have to be before we can release them?'

'At least a year,' said Mel. 'Old enough to have a fighting chance against predators. The zoo let seven young quolls go at Devil Falls last year. They were wearing tracking collars. Cats killed five of them within a month.'

A year. Kim watched as Mel deftly measured and weighed the feisty quoll. She'd grown very fond of her rare charges. It saddened her to think she would not be there to see them released.

'You've done a wonderful job with them,' said Mel, putting Huey back in his log. 'He's put on three hundred grams since I last weighed him.'

'They ought to be growing,' said Kim. 'You should see the amount they eat. Taj can barely keep them supplied with rabbits.'

'Tell him to come to my place,' said Mel, as she pulled Minnie from a nest box by her spotty tail. 'Plenty of rabbits at home. Too many. Or ask Ben to help out. He loves a bit of spotlighting. Dropped off a goat for my dogs last week. Said he's shot a few on his place in the last fort-night.' She weighed the quoll, released it, and wrote down the results in a notebook. 'Was he ever cranky about it too. He said . . . no, I shouldn't say.'

'You can't start to say something and then change your mind,' said Kim. All she had to do was wait. Mel couldn't keep a secret to save her life.

'I don't want to cause any trouble.'

'That's it,' said Kim. 'You have to tell me now.'

'He said the goats got through from your place.'

So that's why the new plantings were doing so well. The goats had cleared off next door. This was wonderful. The first tangible proof that the presence of dingoes was fundamentally changing the behaviour of their prey.

'I don't know why you look so happy about it,' Mel said. 'Feral goats are a bloody nuisance. They'll play havoc with your seedlings.'

'I have a feeling the goats won't be a problem here much longer.'

'Don't know how you figure that,' said Mel, as she began packing the set of scales away in its box. 'Not unless you get somebody to clear them out for you.'

Kim was bursting to explain that she'd done just that. That she had her own roving squad of native guardians that were targeting the ferals, keeping the kangaroo and wallaby populations down, giving the rainforest a chance. But Taj was dead against telling anybody yet. Next time she saw him she'd ask if they could bring Mel in on it.

'By the way,' said Mel. 'Ben reckons he spotted a dingo down on the road. Next week I'm laying some baits along my boundaries, so you'd better keep Dusty locked up.'

'You can't,' said Kim, with a shiver.

'Why not? Sultan can't be everywhere at once. I've got enough trouble with foxes already, without dingoes as well.'

What should she say? How could she convince Mel to change her mind without revealing the secret? 'Isn't baiting cruel?'

'Not as cruel as having my sheep ripped apart by wild dogs.'

'Has that happened before?'

'No,' admitted Mel. 'But Parks and Wildlife used to run wild dog eradication programs. That was before dingoes in Tarringtops were protected. Now the programs only happen if landholders report stock losses.'

'Why don't you wait?' said Kim. 'See what happens?'

'What, wait until I lose sheep? That's ridiculous.'

Kim stepped back. She'd hit a sore point. It was the first time she'd seen mild-mannered Mel angry with anybody except Geoff.

'Journey's End is just a hobby for you, Kim, but I'm not playing at being a farmer. I took a real financial hit when Geoff left. The bank only let me hold onto She-Oak Springs, because there's a niche market for premium fleeces from craft groups and hand-spinners – the coloured ones especially. My flock is the result of years of careful breeding. They're my livelihood. I can't afford to lose a single sheep.'

Kim frowned. She'd been too caught up in her own plans to give much thought to how her friend was travelling, financially or otherwise. Despite her grand garden and homestead, Mel was the definition of asset-rich, cash-poor.

'Sorry, I've been selfish.' Kim reached out to grasp Mel's hands. 'But this is important. Please, *please* don't lay down bait. If you lose any stock, I'll compensate you, I guarantee it.'

Mel looked confused. 'Just tell me what's going on. I thought we were friends.'

Kim let go of Mel's hands, sighed. Knew what she had to do and knew that Taj wouldn't like it.

'Kim?' Mel put a warm hand on her shoulder. 'What's wrong?'

She pulled herself together. 'Have we finished with the quolls? Come to the house then. You might need a coffee after my news – or something stronger.'

'Let me get this straight,' said Mel. 'You and Taj have released an entire pack of dingoes, right here, at Journey's End.'

'Just six animals, but . . . yes.' Kim poured them both coffees and sat down opposite Mel at the kitchen table, ran her fingers over the rough wood.

'Why would you do that?'

'To protect the regeneration sites. To get rid of the ferals and reduce the number of roos and wallabies. To restore balance to the ecosystem.'

Mel stood up and moved away from the table to the window. 'What about my sheep? Didn't you think about how this would affect me?'

'Of course we did,' said Kim. 'Taj laced lamb carcasses with a chemical that made the dingoes sick, to put them off killing sheep. He raised them on goats and deer, rabbits and roadkill. He released them into an area filled with plenty of game.' She stood up too. 'It's counter-intuitive, I know, but Taj says the dingoes will actually help you. Your sheep will have less competition for grass. Taj says the reason you're overrun by foxes in the first place is because the dingoes were wiped out.'

'So dingoes kill foxes?'

'That's right, and cats too. Taj says even their scent and scat are deterrents for feral predators. Journey's End will be a much safer place to release the quolls.'

'Taj says this, Taj says that.' Mel tapped a fretful finger on the windowsill. 'How much does Taj actually know about how things work in Australia?'

'He's very well qualified – lots of field experience.'

'In Afghanistan? I've seen the news reports. The only animals over there are overworked donkeys and half-starved mangy dogs.'

'That's what I thought too,' said Kim. 'But we're wrong. The north-east of the country, where Taj comes from, has big forests. Taj worked with wolves. He says dingoes are our version of wolves.'

'That's comforting.' Mel looked less convinced that ever. 'Sorry, Kim, but I can't get my head around this.' She sat down again, drained her coffee. 'I won't bait your precious dingoes, but don't expect me to be happy about them either. At the end of the day, I'm a farmer. I have to report stock losses directly to the Rural Lands Protection Board whether you compensate me or not. It's the law. After that, it won't be up to me what happens.'

'The dingoes will improve things for everybody,' said Kim. 'Just give me a chance to prove it.'

'You'll get your chance,' said Mel. 'But you can forget about the wildlife corridor. I've got to be honest, Kim, I hate dingoes.' Dusty put his paw on her knee and she stroked his soft ears. 'I won't be party to building them a direct highway to my sheep.'

'It wouldn't be like that—'

'Stop it.' It was almost a shout. Dusty whined, and lay down in the corner. 'You have no idea how it will be, Kim. This is just an interesting experiment for you.' Mel's tone was taut. 'You weren't going to tell me, were you? You only said something because I mentioned the baits.'

The silence yawned between them – Kim unable to meet her eye – then her phone rang from under a pile of papers on the table. The theme song from *Lambert, the Sheepish Lion*. The caller's timing couldn't have been worse.

Mel dragged a hand over her face. 'You'd better answer it, and I'd better go.'

Kim turned off the phone. 'Whoever it is, they can ring back.'

But Mel was already leaving. She turned at the door. 'We were never partners, were we? Not really. Maybe not even friends.'

And before Kim could think of a response, she was gone.

Kim felt hollow, empty. Mel had become an important part of her life. Had she betrayed her? The thought was unbearable.

CHAPTER 29

Kim put the little quoll back in its log with a few meal worms, refilled the water bowl and shut the gate. They were doing so well. Louie had put on a record amount of weight. Mel would be pleased . . . if she knew, that was. Two days since she'd told Mel about the dingoes, and Kim hadn't seen her since.

The rhythmic sound of an axe on wood rang out. Jake's enthusiasm for chopping firewood was really paying off now it was winter. Kim went back to the house, passing the woodshed on the way. She found Abbey trying to teach Dusty to collect kindling. He had the hang of finding and picking up sticks okay. Bringing them back was another matter, and involved a vigorous game of chasey.

Jake was piling evenly-sized logs into the wheelbarrow. He'd become an expert at using the splitter wedge that Ben had given him. Kim watched her son for a while unawares – so strong and sure of himself. What a difference Tingo had made to Jake, and much of it was due to Ben. Kim was becoming more and more open to the possibility of Ben. Handsome, charming, reliable. He made sense in so many ways. He helped fill the gap left in her life since Taj had pulled away.

Better get a move on. Ben was coming round tonight for dinner. Time to chop the vegetables, get the roast on, have a shower.

When Kim got back to the house she rang Mel, but the call went to voicemail. It was funny. How many times had she wished her neighbour wasn't quite so eager a friend? And yet now, when Mel was staying away? Kim missed her terribly. She toyed with the idea of dropping by unannounced, but decided against it. Mel needed some time to adjust. She'd come round. As long as she didn't tell anybody else, there was no harm done.

'Dingoes?' Ben said, when she opened the door. 'What sort of crazy idea is that? Taj should know better.' He put down the loaf of bread he was carrying on her bench and gestured to let Kim know it was for her. 'I'm running steers, not cows and calves, so I should be right. Wouldn't want to be Mel, though. Her sheep will be sitting ducks.'

'I don't think so,' said Kim.

Ben smiled. 'So now the Sydney girl's an expert on sheep, is she?'

'I'm serious. A maremma dog guards Mel's weaners, and Taj has trained the dingoes to avoid sheep by lacing carcasses with a chemical that makes them sick. There's plenty of natural prey, so there's nothing to make them turn into stock killers.'

'It's instinct.' Ben put his hands on her shoulders and looked deep into her eyes. 'Steer clear of Taj from now on, will you?' His voice brimmed with concern. 'You'd best be ready to cop some flack. Tingo's a tiny town full of big opinions. Everybody's going to want their two bob's worth on this one.'

How right he was.

The next morning Kim went to the store to collect the mail. 'Mel told me what you're doing,' said Winnie. 'Bringing back the dingoes. I saw a *Landline* program about it. The cattle station up north – Evelyn Downs – they're leaving the dingoes alone to keep the roos and foxes down. Cats too. It's working apparently.' She turned to her husband. 'You should have seen the puppies, Des. Cutest things ever.'

'Cute?' said Des. 'Bloodthirsty killers, more like. Kill for fun, they do. I'm sorry to say it, Kim, but it's a crime, what you're doing. Bad enough the government lets the mongrels breed up in Tarringtops, without letting them wreak havoc in farmland as well. Just wait until Mel Masters starts losing sheep. You'll soon change your tune.'

Kim refused to engage in the argument and went home. She needed to stay positive. It had been weeks since their release and the dingoes hadn't caused any trouble yet, unless you counted wild talk as trouble. So long as they continued to behave there was every chance that the interest in them would blow over.

As she pulled into her drive, her phone sounded in her pocket. She sprinted up the hill to a spot near the dam that sometimes had reception. 'Hello.' The caller hung on the line without speaking. 'Hello? Who is this?'

'It's me, Kim. Daisy.' A hesitation. 'How are you?'

'Daisy? Oh my god!' Kim felt a loosening of something within her that she hadn't known was wound tight. 'I've never been happier to hear anybody's voice in my life.'

She and Daisy launched into exhaustive accounts of their lives since they'd last met. Sometimes taking turns. Sometimes talking over each other in a jumble of words, eager to make up for lost time. Neither of them mentioned the fight that had torn them apart. There would be time for that later.

When Kim came up for air, an hour had passed, but she was loath to end the conversation.

'I was thinking,' Daisy said, 'school holidays start next week, and Steve's away. Do you have room for visitors at your country hideaway?'

'Do I ever.'

A wave of relief and joy washed over her. She would see her best friend again; for that's what Daisy was, in spite of their differences, in spite of the ugliness that had marred their last morning together. There would never be a substitute for Daisy. Old friends, shared histories, common understandings. She walked back to the house, past the firewheel tree, now empty of its whorled flowers, and thoughts of Taj flickered into her mind. How sad for him to never know these things again.

Dusty sensed her excitement. He gambolled about, acting the clown, stealing Kim's hat and making her laugh. She couldn't wait for Daisy and her children to meet him – and the joeys and quolls and the rest of the menagerie. Couldn't wait to show them round Journey's End – Cedar Creek, the rainforest, Devil Falls. Couldn't wait till after school to tell Abbey and Jake about the coming visit. She wished already that the week would fly by.

It didn't. The days dragged. Mel stayed away. Kim made overtures of friendship, inviting her round for lunch one day and on a shopping trip to Taree the next. Both times Mel declined. Todd and Nikki stayed away too. Fortunately the kids were so excited by the prospect of Daisy's visit, they didn't take much notice. Abbey chattered away to Grace on the landline for what seemed like hours each night, making plans and seamlessly picking up their friendship.

Taj came by mid-week. So far it had been a particularly warm, dry winter and they spent the morning carting water to the regeneration sites. Since reintroducing the dingoes, the improvement in the plants' growth and survival was staggering. They could almost see the seedlings grow.

They went about their work in silence, each in their own private world. If Taj knew that their secret was out he didn't say. She needed to explain why she'd told Mel, but kept putting it off. Only when they came across a freshly killed wallaby above Cedar Creek, did she pluck up the courage.

Taj listened in silence to her story, his face grave. 'So Ben saw a dingo?'

'That's what Mel said. Down on the road. She was going to put down baits. I had to tell her.'

'How did she take it?'

'She thinks we betrayed her and don't care about her sheep. Then she told Winnie and Ben. Word's getting around.'

Taj frowned. 'Let me talk to her. I hoped the dingoes would stay up near Tarringtops, where we released them. They're far too visible down here by the creek.' He inspected the earth around the wallaby carcass, and then knelt down for a closer look. 'See here?' He pointed to a large paw-print. 'This is not one of our dingoes. They have been joined by a wild one.'

Taj was an expert tracker. She'd seen him track wombats to their burrows, and foxes to their dens. She'd seen him follow the trail of a deer injured by hunters, so he could put it out of its misery. And he had an uncanny ability to recognise the spoor of each member of the dingo pack.

'A wild one. Is that good or bad?'

'Good, I think. Right now, our dingoes are babes in the woods. A wild adult will show them how to stay out of sight, how to hunt more effectively as a team. Teach them the way of the pack.'

'Did this ever happen in Nuristan?' asked Kim. 'Did wild wolves ever join the cubs you released?'

But he would not be drawn. They got back in the ute, and drove to the next site in silence. He'd shut down again.

Kim gazed out the window, arms crossed over her chest. Taj wouldn't talk to her. Mel wouldn't talk to her. The dingoes weren't a safe subject to bring up with Ben or any of the townsfolk. Daisy on the other hand? She was an outsider, with no stake in any of this. What a relief it would be to have her there.

CHAPTER 30

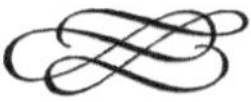

Kim yawned and itched her nose. She might be half-asleep, but she still knew what day it was. Daisy day.

Jake poked his head in. 'I can't find Dusty. He wasn't in my room when I woke up.'

Kim rubbed sleep from her eyes and checked the time. Eight o'clock. 'He probably got sick of waiting, and took himself for a walk. You should get up earlier.' It had been an unseasonably warm night for late June, and she'd left the back door open to catch the breeze. Dusty had long since learned to open the screen door for himself.

She fell back on the pillow, still tired. It had been a late night, cooking, cleaning – making sure everything was perfect for Daisy's arrival at lunchtime. There was still plenty to do. Sweep. Make up mattresses on the floor for Grace and Stuart. Put clean sheets on the bed in the side verandah room for Daisy.

Abbey came in, sleepy-eyed and clutching Percy, something she didn't do so much anymore. She climbed into bed with Kim and snuggled close. 'I want to go back to sleep, so when I wake up, Grace will already be here.'

How very Abbey. On Christmas Eve she always wanted to go to bed at lunchtime, to make Santa come more quickly.

'None of that.' Kim wrapped her arms around her daughter, inhaling the sweet scent of her silky curls. 'You've got to help me get things ready.'

'Can we make chocolate crackles? They're Grace's favourite.'

'Of course we can,' said Kim, tickling Abbey into peals of musical laughter.

'Does this mean you and Daisy are friends again?'

'We were always friends,' said Kim.

'Grace says you weren't. Grace says you and her mum had a fight.'

Kim sat up, facing Abbey, who hugged her knees to her chest. 'Remember that time when Grace stayed the night and hid Percy in the laundry cupboard when it was time to go to bed.'

Abbey nodded solemnly, and snatched Percy up from the pillow. 'She thought it was funny.'

'But you're still friends, right, even though she made you sad by hiding something that meant a lot to you? Even though you were mad at her for a while?'

Abbey twirled a finger in her hair. 'Did Daisy hide your wine?'

Kim smiled. The sheer enormity of her love for Abbey threatened to overwhelm her. 'Never mind. Let's get chocolate crackling.'

It was past two o'clock when Daisy's silver Tarago bumped its way up the long driveway. Abbey, who'd been waiting down by the gate, had hitched a ride to the house. She and Grace tumbled from the car, laughing and talking over each other.

'Those two have certainly taken up where they left off,' said Daisy.

Kim stepped forward and gave her a long, heartfelt hug. 'Remind me to never argue with you again.'

Jake and Stu were more circumspect. They greeted one aother with grunts, then stood around, eyeing each other off as Daisy unloaded an unnecessary number of bags.

Stu looked around. 'Where's your dog?'

Kim looked up. 'Hasn't Dusty come home yet?' Jake shook his head. A worm of concern turned in her stomach. It wasn't like the pup to wander away for so long. 'Why don't you take Stu and go have a look for him?'

Jake nodded. 'There's an old tractor,' he told Stu. 'And a grader. Want to see?' The boys went off, side by side. Kim felt a lump rise in her throat as she watched them go.

Daisy touched her arm. 'Now that's a sight for sore eyes. Stu's really missed Jake, although he'd never admit it. He could hardly sleep last night.'

'Jake was the same.' Kim laughed. 'To tell you the truth, so was I.' She gave Daisy another hug. 'Come on. Let's get your stuff inside.'

Kim showed Daisy where to put the bags, and gave her a tour of the house.

'Oh, look at this wallpaper,' Daisy said as they moved through the hallway with the silver banksia print. The two women stood in front of Connor's mural in Abbey's room for a long time, Daisy with a soft hand on Kim's arm.

'Kim, this place is so very you.'

It didn't hurt to look at the mural anymore; it hadn't for a long time. As they went back to the kitchen, Kim felt light and free. Ben would be here soon, and she was looking forward to showing him off. She could hear a car slowing on Bangalow Road, and then making the turn.

But when she went outside to see, it wasn't Ben. An ancient Dodge truck was parked in the drive. Kim's stomach lurched. The body of a black and tan dog was strung up to the back of the tray by its hind legs. Its plumed tail hung down, hiding its face. Half-a-dozen foxes and three huge tabby cats dangled beside it. A foul odour wafted towards her.

A man in a blue singlet leaned out of the driver's window, smoking a cigarette. Lean face, pockmarked with scars, eyes almost hidden by a grimy bush hat. 'Afternoon, love. Just shot this dingo down by the creek. Better keep an eye out. Where there's one of these buggers, there's bound to be more.' He flicked his ash onto the ground. 'I could do a bit of shooting on your place if you like.'

Ben's car came into sight. He parked behind the pick-up, and got out, taking in Kim's ashen face and the bloody bodies in the truck. 'What's going on here?'

'I was telling your missus . . . '

'Mum?' Jake and Stu came round the corner of the house, and stopped dead. Dusty trotted at their heels, and Kim's legs went wobbly with relief.

'Take Dusty inside and give him a feed,' she said.

Jake frowned and pointed to the truck. 'Who's that?'

'Just take him inside, quickly.'

Jake hesitated. He set his jaw as if he was ready to argue, but the urgency in her voice had the desired effect. Dusty and the boys left.

Ben went over and leant on the tray of the truck. 'Where'd you shoot that feller?'

The driver managed to talk without letting the cigarette fall from his lips. 'About a hundred metres from your front gate, mate.'

Kim tried to avert her eyes from the dingo, but couldn't. It looked like Dusty. Larger and heavier, true, but nobody seeing the two of them together would miss the resemblance. 'We have young children here. I don't want them upset, so . . . '

The pick-up driver flipped his butt out the window. 'Just trying to be neighbourly, love. A *thank you* wouldn't go astray.'

Kim stepped forward. If he wanted thanks for killing the dingo, quite possibly trespassing to do so, he had another thing coming. Ben moved to diffuse the situation. 'Better go, mate. A house full of city kids – you know how it is.'

The man cast her a last baleful glance, grunted something incomprehensible, and wound up the window. The truck rattled and swayed off down the drive.

'Who on earth was he?'

'A fox scalper. Professional shooter. He'll make a few bucks selling those skins.'

Kim shuddered. 'What sort of person does that?'

Ben wrapped strong, comforting arms around her. 'It takes all kinds. You said yourself that foxes and cats are wiping out the wildlife. He's doing you a favour.'

'If you'd thanked him, I would have slapped you.'

Ben laughed. 'I guessed as much.' The clean, fresh smell of his aftershave cut through the stink lingering in her nostrils. 'He thought we were hitched, you know,' said Ben. 'Called you my missus.' He kissed her lightly on the mouth. 'Perks of marriage.'

'Oh really,' said Kim, stifling a laugh.

Neither of them moved. She could easily have leaned in, touched his lip with her fingers. Did she want to kiss him back? Yes and no. She wished she could figure out her feelings. An image of Taj flickered into her mind, unbidden. She chased it away, and then took a step backwards. Had Daisy been watching through the window? The kiss could take some explaining.

'Thanks for getting rid of him.' Her voice was deliberately casual. 'I owe you. Now come and meet my friend.'

Ben was a hit with Daisy and her kids, as Kim knew he would be. Grace, unlike Abbey, was endlessly amused by him. He pulled a dollar from behind her ear, did a clever card trick, and knew what colour crayon she picked from a box, just by feeling it behind his back.

'I run my finger along the wax to get a bit of colour under my nail,' he confessed to Kim in a whisper.

'Do that trick again with Abbey,' demanded Grace, 'to prove it wasn't a fluke.' But when they turned around, Abbey wasn't there. She'd probably run off with Dusty somewhere.

'I'll find her,' said Kim, and slipped down to the sheds. It would give her a chance to ring Taj and tell him about the scalper. But when she tried, there was no reception. Darn these mountains and their dead spots.

She found Abbey and Dusty, sitting together on a broken bale in the old hay shed.

'What's wrong, sweetie?'

'Is Ben still here?'

Kim sat down beside her. 'He's staying for a barbeque.'

Abbey snuggled close and peered at her mother, her eyes like searchlights. 'Do you like him – the way you like Daddy, I mean?'

'No, darling. Not the way I like Daddy. But I do like him a lot.'

'I don't.'

'Why is that?' asked Kim. 'Has he ever done anything to hurt you, to make you feel uncomfortable?'

'No.'

'Then what?'

'He's devious,' said Abbey.

'Devious?' Kim smiled. 'Do you even know what that means?'

'Of course I do. Don't patronise me, Mum.'

Kim suppressed her smile. What did she ever do to deserve a child like this? 'Okay, then – tell me exactly how Ben is devious.'

'He cheats at magic. You know that disappearing coin trick? He sneaks it into his other hand. I saw him.'

'That's not cheating. That's an optical illusion. All magicians do it. It's just some are cleverer at getting away with it than others.'

Abbey pouted and kicked the ground. 'Well, I still don't trust him. Neither does Dusty.'

Kim pondered the best way to lure her daughter back to the party. 'Grace will be looking for you. How about we go up to the house and you can show her how we feed the joeys.' Abbey's stubborn mouth relaxed a little. She was wavering.

'Can we have bowls of ice-cream with Milo?'

'Yes.'

'And can we scrunch up chocolate crackles and sprinkle them on top?'

Kim frowned. 'You drive a hard bargain, but okay.'

Dusty's ears pricked up; a moment later his tail was furiously wagging. Abbey cocked her own head to the side, listening with a very dog-like expression. 'Taj is here.' The girl and dog ran off.

Taj. That solved the problem of trying to ring him. Kim wandered after the pair under the afternoon sky, a sky almost white with clouds. What would he make of the scalper's visit? Of the dead dingo that looked so much like Dusty?

Kim was surprised to discover Taj and Daisy deep in conversation on the verandah. Stuart was listening in, while Jake hovered nearby. Kim had to tap Daisy to get her attention.

'Daisy, can I steal Taj for a bit?'

'Righto. I'll go talk to Ben instead. Here I was feeling sorry for you. Worrying you'd be lonely living way out here all by yourself. Turns out you're up to your ears in handsome, eligible men.' Daisy winked at her. 'You're a dark horse, Kim Sullivan.'

Kim felt the beginnings of a blush, made a face and a shooing gesture with her hands.

'Okay, okay. I'm going.'

'There's good news.' Taj glanced around, making sure they were alone. 'The pack has moved back up to the original release site. Either something frightened them or the wild dog has led them away.'

'Have you seen it, this new dingo?'

'An older female. Tawny with a limp. Joining them will save her life, and perhaps the lives of them all. She offers them native-born wisdom and they offer the protection of a pack.'

Kim told him about the fox scalper and the dead dingo. 'It looked just like Dusty.'

'His father, I think,' said Taj. 'Did anyone else see?'

'Everybody saw. Well, not the girls, thank goodness. They were in the house with Daisy.'

'Ben too?'

She nodded, and a shadow crossed his face. 'We must hope the dingoes remain up near the park. I will leave them a kill twice a week again, to encourage them to stay.' Taj's eyes darted to the door, and he put a forefinger to his lips.

Ben was strolling down the verandah towards them, a curious gleam in his eye. 'What are you two in a huddle about?'

Kim shot him a nervous smile, although she had no idea why. Ben already knew about the dingoes.

'Will you stay for the barbeque, Taj?' She didn't expect him to say yes. He didn't spend his down time at her place anymore. But this was proving to be a day of surprises.

'Thank you … yes.'

The pleasant afternoon wore on. Food was plentiful and delicious. Beer and wine flowed freely. The clouds began to clear, revealing the cool blue sky. Jake and Stu were soon laughing and joking as if never apart. They began building a tree house in the old willow peppermint. Abbey and Grace were in their element with the animals, and Kim couldn't stop smiling at Daisy. Everybody appeared to be enjoying themselves.

Yet there was an undeniable undercurrent of tension between the two men. Abbey wasn't the only one stonewalling Ben today. Taj was guilty too. Nothing overt. Kim sensed it in the odd, scathing glance. In the hostile set of his shoulders when the two by chance bumped into one another. In the sarcastic curl of his lip when Ben told a funny story about his latest property deal.

Not that Ben was innocent either. It could have been an accident of course, but he overcooked Taj's steak and then dropped it on the ground when passing it over. Ben speared the meat with a fork, dusted it off and handed it to Taj. 'It'll be okay, won't it, mate? You'll have had worse back home.'

A friendly game of backyard cricket warped into something else as Taj stepped up to the rubbish-bin wicket. He whacked Ben's first ball, an attempted yorker, high and long towards the trees.

'Watch out for snakes,' said Daisy, as the boys hared after it.

He struck the second hard back at Ben, who managed to parry it away.

'Ooh, dropped,' the boys sang out.

Ben's next ball flew fast and straight at Taj's face. He couldn't react in time, and the tennis ball thumped into his ear.

'Sorry, mate,' said Ben. 'She slipped.'

'No ball,' called Stu. 'Above waist high. Free hit.'

Kim walked over, picked up the ball and put it in her coat pocket. 'I think perhaps that's enough cricket for today.'

Almost midnight. Taj and Ben had gone home, and the kids were in bed. Kim sat with Daisy out on the verandah. The moon hung in the sky – a giant lantern, beaming bright above the trees. The night was quiet, apart from the rhythmic hooting of an owl, and the soft flutter of Bogong moths against the kitchen window. A half-empty bottle of red wine stood between them on an upturned milk crate. They nursed their glasses. A little drunk, enjoying being together without anybody else around.

'I had no idea how beautiful it was here,' said Daisy. 'No wonder you want to stay.' Moonlight through the firewheel tree was working its magic, casting patterns in the shape of butterflies and birds on the wall.

'It's beautiful all right.'

'But there's something I don't understand. You're with Ben now, right?'

'No . . . well yes, sort of.' She'd been expecting this interrogation, but even so, Kim's face flushed with warmth. 'We're taking it slowly.'

Daisy's eyes gleamed darkly in the moonlight. Kim tried to read her expression. No, surely not. Was that disapproval she saw?

'I don't get it,' said Kim. 'For months you tell me, *'Go out. Have some fun, Stop moping around.'*

Daisy giggled. 'I wasn't quite as insensitive as that, was I?'

'And then when I finally put my toe in the water . . . what gives?'

'Don't read me wrong,' said Daisy. 'I'm proud of you, I really am. It's just—'

'What?'

'You've got the wrong man.'

'I thought you liked Ben?'

'I do. I like him because he's funny, charming and gob-smackingly handsome.' She pretended to swoon. 'Don't tell Steve I said that, by the way. But my question is, why do you like him?'

'Well, I suppose for all the reasons you just mentioned.' Kim's head was swimming, and not just from the wine. This conversation had taken a decidedly unexpected turn.

'I don't think so,' said Daisy. 'Those reasons wouldn't wash for you. They might be the icing on the cake, but they wouldn't be enough by themselves.'

'Okay, miss psychology professor. Why do you think I like him?'

'You really want me to tell you?'

Kim swigged the last of her wine, and poured herself another. 'Hmm. Let me see – yes.'

'You like Ben, because' – Daisy sipped her wine, seemed lost in thought – 'because he reminds you of Connor and because he pays attention to Jake. You don't feel so guilty about Jake not having his father when Ben's around.'

Kim laughed: a high, nervous laugh to hide how thrown she was. 'Don't be ridiculous. There's more to it than that.'

'Tell me, then. Tell me why you like Ben?'

'Like you said, he's funny and good-looking.'

'And?'

'And—' Kim stopped short. She couldn't think of anything else to say.

Daisy topped up her glass. 'Here, I'll help you. What do you guys have in common?'

'Well, he lives next door.'

'Very funny. Is he interested in plants, for instance? Does he love dogs? Does he help you with your orphans? Is he a nerd, like you, or a mad reader? Is he artistic at all?'

'I'm not artistic.'

'Maybe you don't have any talent yourself—'

'Thanks, Daise.'

'But you like looking at arty things. Remember all those galleries you dragged me round? Carvings and sculptures and things? You're a culture vulture, Kim. Is Ben like that?'

'Jesus Christ, I've only just started seeing him'

'And I only just met him today,' said Daisy, 'but I can tell you, he's not. I know somebody who is though. Taj, that's who.'

'You're drunk.'

Daisy thought about it for a while. 'Yes. Yes, I am.' They both burst out laughing. Daisy finished her wine, and stood up, a little unsteadily. 'I'm turning in.'

'Goodnight, Daisy, and thank you.'

'What for?'

'For ringing me when I was too stupid and stubborn to ring you. For calling me a nerd, and saying I have no artistic talent.'

Daisy started giggling again. 'Any time, mate. Now I'm going to bed.'

Kim smiled, feeling giddy, surrendering to the red wine buzz. How she loved having Daisy back in her life. Daisy with her unbridled enthusiasm, her wacky sense of humour, her zany ideas. Crazy Daisy, Connor used to call her. Crazy in the nicest way, but crazy just the same. She hadn't changed.

Kim lifted up the bottle of wine. Empty. Just as well, she'd have a headache in the morning as it was.

Kim picked up the empty glasses, took them to the kitchen and piled them with the rest of the dirty dishes. She peeked into Abbey's room; the girls were fast asleep, so beautiful when they were sleeping. In the boys' room, Dusty was stretched out beside Jake, their heads together on the pillow. Stu was on the floor, one foot out of the doona, the way he'd always slept. It was so good to see Grace and Stu again.

Dusty opened his eyes and wagged his tail. She crept in, meaning to make him get down. But the beseeching look in his big brown eyes melted her resolve. She kissed Dusty and Jake on the head. 'Goodnight boys.'

Kim got undressed, leaving her clothes in a pile on the floor. Shivering, she pulled on pyjamas and dived beneath the doona. The old bed had never felt so comfy. Despite her weariness and all the wine, sleep would not come. That last tipsy conversation kept coming back. Why was she with Ben if they had nothing much in common? That was the question Daisy had asked her, wasn't it? It was all mixed up in her mind. Or maybe that wasn't it. Maybe the real question was, if they had nothing much in common, why did Ben want to be with her?

CHAPTER 31

'Kim?'

She looked up from repotting a seedling to find Mel standing there. 'Hi.' Kim wiped dirty hands on her jeans. 'It's good to see you.'

The school holidays were drawing to an end. Daisy and her kids had gone home, casting Kim into a depression. She'd been thinking about Mel a lot, trying to pluck up the courage to go see her, given she'd had no luck on the phone. Hoping that, like Daisy, Mel might come around first.

'Jake and Abbey are down at the school helping Jean dig the veggie garden. But they'll be back soon if you want to bring your kids around.'

Mel didn't look her in the eye. She shuffled her feet, making lines in the damp earth. 'I'm afraid this isn't a social call.'

'Oh?' Kim put her trowel down. She'd never seen Mel look so serious.

'Your dingoes have killed my sheep.'

Kim felt the ground shift beneath her. She reached back for the old trestle table to steady herself.

'Two of my best ewes. I found them this morning. They'd been

224

dead a couple of days. Milly and Panda. Pregnant with their first lambs.'

'Pregnant? Oh no . . . '

Mel's mask of control was slipping. 'If only Sultan had been there.'

'He wasn't?'

'No.' Mel's voice cracked. 'He was running with the weaner lambs. Maybe it's just as well. What hope would he have had against a pack?'

'Can I . . . can I come and see?'

Mel nodded. 'I want you to. Taj as well. I want to prove what a mistake you've made.'

Three crows flapped away as the jeep approached. It was an awful sight. The corpses lay not far from each other, hollow sockets staring skyward. The birds had picked out their eyes. Great holes gaped in their fleece where their flanks should have been, exposing blood-flecked bones.

Mel and Kim stayed by the car while Taj went for a closer look. He made a thorough examination: inspecting the bodies, taking photographs, studying the ground for many metres around. Kim had to look away when he rolled one sheep over, and a slimy, purplish mass of entrails spilled out. She should look – her dingoes had done this – but she couldn't.

When Taj returned to the car, his face was grim. 'I'll email you those photos, Mel, and come back later to remove the carcasses.'

She gave him a thin smile of thanks.

'And I'll pay you compensation,' said Kim. 'For the sheep. For the unborn lambs. For emotional distress, whatever you want.'

Mel didn't seem to be listening. 'Panda was a real character,' she said. 'Hand-raised as a lamb, so very tame. And she loved Sultan. So did Milly. They saw dogs as friends.' She blinked back tears. 'They wouldn't even have been scared of the dingoes - not to start with ...'

Kim could feel her own tears coming. 'Oh, Mel, you warned me and I didn't listen. I'm so very sorry. We'll do anything to make up for it, won't we, Taj?'

Taj remained strangely stony-faced and silent.

'There's only one thing you can do for me.' Mel wiped at her eyes. 'Get rid of those dingoes.'

Taj sat in Kim's kitchen with Dusty's head pressed against his knee. She bustled about, making coffee, wiping down the bench, finding biscuits – anything to avoid opening the emotional floodgates.

'Come and sit down,' he said at last.

She collapsed in the chair opposite him. 'You told me this wouldn't happen, that the dingoes would leave the sheep alone. What are we going to do? Mel's bound to tell people. What if she reports the attacks? What if—'

Taj held up his hand. 'The dingoes didn't do it.'

Kim grasped for understanding. 'You mean it was domestic dogs?'

'I mean it wasn't dogs at all. Dogs and dingoes kill by biting throats, damaging the trachea and major blood vessels in the neck. Or they attack fleeing prey from the rear, causing hind leg wounds. Mel's sheep had no such injuries.'

'No, just bloody great holes in their bellies.'

Taj fixed her with those piercing eyes. 'That's not what killed them.'

'You could have fooled me.'

'Those sheep were already dead when the scavengers came.'

'Already dead?' Taj was making less and less sense. 'How could you possibly know that?'

Taj gulped his coffee, swirling the dregs, inspecting his cup as if the answer might lie there. 'I can't be certain until I skin the carcasses. The size and location of wounds in the hides will tell the true story. But there were no prints around the kills other than foxes and eagles. I tell you, our dingoes aren't to blame.'

Kim tried the theory on for size. 'So how did the sheep die? If some illness is going around we have to tell Mel.'

'We will, once I examine the bodies. But, until then, please don't share my suspicions with anyone.'

Kim gave him a wry smile. She had no intention of peddling his crazy notion around town.

Taj rose to leave. 'There's one more thing.' The clock on the wall ticked loud in the silence. 'I want to take Dusty home with me,' he said. 'Just for a while.'

Kim stiffened. 'Whatever for?'

Taj didn't answer, his expression guarded.

'No,' she said. 'Absolutely not. Dusty's part of the family. It would break Jake's heart to spend even a night apart from him.' Mine too, she thought.

'Very well.' His dark eyebrows slanted in a frown. 'But don't let him wander.'

Kim followed Taj out to his car. Dusty seemed agitated, trotting at his heels and leaping into the driver's seat when he opened the door.

Kim called him down. 'No, Dusty, you stay here with me.'

As they watched Taj rattle off down the drive, the pup raised his nose in a spine-tingling howl that seemed too big for his body. A howl full of infinite sadness.

Later that night Kim sat on the couch before the TV, leaning against Ben, listening to the rain on the roof. He pumped the air as another English wicket fell. With her new-found interest in cricket, the Ashes test series had turned into compulsory late-night viewing, especially since Australia was trouncing the English team.

Kim reached for her beer. Beer and sport on television. Not football, true, but it still took her back. How many nights had she spent like this with Connor? And Daisy was wrong. She and Ben did have something in common. They both barracked for the Giants.

Ben settled back with a contented sigh. She liked the easy weight of his arm draped round her shoulder. She liked his male smell, his solid presence beside her. Being with Ben felt right: familiar, safe, a guaranteed cure for loneliness.

She'd told him about the dead sheep, so there would be no secrets to poison their fledgling relationship. But not about Taj's theory that the dingoes were innocent. Of course Ben said 'I told you so', but otherwise he'd been relaxed about it – surprisingly so, considering that he disapproved of the whole rewilding thing.

'Those dingoes aren't my problem,' he'd said with a philosophical shrug. 'But don't expect everyone to feel that way. Some blokes will take it as a challenge to shoot the beggers.'

'They're protected up in Tarringtops,' said Kim. 'And there's no hunting here or at Mel's.' She shot Ben a pointed look.

'Okay, I won't let people shoot at my place,' he said. 'But that doesn't mean they won't try. You said yourself people have been spot-lighting here.'

Kim didn't need reminding. Just the week before she'd seen lights, high in the hills behind the house, and heard the crack of rifle shots in the night.

'Bloody ripper,' yelled Ben, as another wicket fell.

Kim put a finger to his lips and he nipped at it playfully. 'Shh, you'll wake Abbey.' She had only one ear on the television, listening for the pitter-patter of small feet in the hall. There they were. Kim ducked out from under Ben's arm just as Abbey came into the lounge room, sleepy-eyed in puppy pyjamas, holding Percy by one ear.

'Hello, sweetheart,' said Ben. 'What are you doing up?'

Abbey stared at him with a steady, unblinking gaze that seemed to look through and beyond him. Then she turned to her mother. 'When's he going home?'

Her daughter was getting as rude as Jake. 'Don't mind Abbey. She's tired.'

Kim guided her back to her room, sat on the bed, and drew her daughter onto her lap.

Abbey yawned. 'I can't get to sleep when he's here. Will you read me some more of *The Silver Brumby*?'

'Okay. Hop into bed.'

Abbey's rosebud mouth turned up in a smile, and she snuggled under the covers.

Kim took the book off the shelf, and lay down. 'I wish you'd try a bit harder to like Ben,' said Kim, stroking Abbey's hair. 'He's been a good friend to us, and it would mean a lot to me.'

Abbey took the book from her mother, turned to the bookmarked page. 'Read.'

'Will you at least think about what I asked?'

'Maybe.'

It was not a convincing response. Kim kissed her baffling daughter. In some ways she was as mysterious and exasperating as Taj. 'Come on then.' Kim tucked Percy in between them. 'Let's see what Thowra and his herd are up to.'

Two chapters later, and Abbey was finally asleep. Kim glanced at the bedside clock. Almost midnight. The hum of the television had stopped. Kim kissed her daughter goodnight, and bumped into Ben in the hallway.

'I'd better go.' He indicated Abbey's room with a point of his chin. 'She asleep?'

Kim nodded, linked her arm through Ben's and walked with him to the back door. 'I don't know why she's got such a set against you.'

'Kids are funny things.' Ben drew her in for a tender, searching kiss. For a moment she let herself be swept away, surrendering to a quick pulse of desire. But the image of Abbey's sweet, disapproving face swam before her, and she pulled away.

Ben groaned and licked his lip, as if savouring what was left of the kiss. 'I haven't met a woman like you before.' He ran his finger down her cheek. 'A woman who plays such a slow game. We've had an understanding for a while now . . . '

'It's no game,' she said. 'I want this to go somewhere . . . for us, to go somewhere.'

'You're doing it again.' He gently took hold of her hands and lifted them from the shadows. 'Playing with your ring.'

'Was I?'

The gold band on her finger glowed soft in the faint porch light. That old, unconscious habit of feeling for it was hard to break. Such a comfort to touch it, to twist its solid warmth between thumb and forefinger.

Ben leaned close, and whispered in her ear. 'Take it off.'

Kim's breath caught in her throat. How could she not wear Connor's ring? She might as well live her life naked. On the other hand, if she wanted to move on. If she truly wanted to move on with Ben . . .

Her fingertips found the wedding band as they had done thousands of times before. Exploring, tracing its smooth strength, spinning its endless arc. An unbroken, eternal circle. The symbolism seemed suddenly hollow, and she tried to wrench the ring off.

'Careful.' Ben eased it over her knuckle, massaging the finger as he went. With one final twist it came free.

He dropped the band onto her outstretched palm, and she examined it with new eyes. How peculiar it looked from this angle. How strange. Smaller, humbler, not the same ring at all. Its promise of undying love nowhere in sight.

He closed her hand over the ring. 'Now, let's try it again.' She shut her eyes. Ben's kiss was more persuasive this time. His lips recaptured hers, feather-light, then harder. They left her mouth to found the hollow of her throat. When they moved down to the soft swell of her breasts, she eased herself away.

Ben scrubbed a hand over his face. He wore a smile of part amusement, part frustration. 'Jesus, Kim, you sure know how to get a man going. I'd better leave before I explode.'

Kim watched Ben go, his headlights slicing a path through the rainy darkness. The time was coming when she would not send him off into the night. When she would lead him instead to her bed. But not yet. Abbey's disapproval weighed too heavy on her heart, and the wedding ring was too heavy in her hand.

Kim checked in on Abbey, Jake and Dusty, then went to her room, slipping the ring into a drawer. When she flicked out the light, the darkness was all-engulfing. She crawled into bed as the rain grew louder.

The storm strengthened. Howled like a monster through the black night, roared through the forest, rattled the windows. She normally loved the sound of rain on the roof, but tonight was different. This was a bombardment.

Kim buried her head in the pillow to block the deafening noise. Her fingers reached automatically for the ring. When they didn't find it her heart lurched alarmingly. She got up and padded surely to the dresser, despite the inky blackness. Her hand dived into the drawer, connecting with the ring as if it was a magnet and she was iron. Kim slipped it on her finger and exhaled. Back under the covers, and the ferocious peak of the storm was passing. The wailing wind was replaced by the distant cry of dingoes. How things had changed. That eerie sound, once so disturbing, was now a promise that all was well. Reassured by the howling, and by the familiar feel of Connor's ring on her finger, she drifted off to sleep.

CHAPTER 32

*K*im woke early to a rosy, rain-washed sky. She'd endured a restless night, and half-remembered dreams hovered just out of reach. Only their vague, unsettling emotions remained. The kids were still asleep. She dressed quickly, called Dusty from Jake's bed, and went out to meet the morning.

Just what she needed. A brisk uphill walk past the dam, and a great lungful of fresh mountain air. Notes of mint, eucalyptus, laurel, and the rich earthy smell of damp soil. Leafy bouquets of wind-whipped twigs and branches littered the ground, evidence of the storm. Bull ants scavenged for drowned insects, and toiled to rebuild their flooded mounds. Glossy satin bowerbirds bathed in puddles, their iridescent blue-black plumage gleaming in the cold morning sun. The bush revelled in the rain's aftermath.

Dusty was enjoying himself too. He bounded on ahead, plunging into the brimming dam, snatching at reeds and floating bark streamers as he dog-paddled about. Kim sat down on a fallen log to watch. Seven months old now, and acquiring the strength and grace of an adult. Was it just her, or was the mountain dingo in him showing more and more? In his cat-like agility, and the dexterity of his paws. Dusty used them like hands to turn doorknobs; his rotating wrist-bones were unique in the canine world. In his soft, dark double-coat that kept him warm on the coldest nights and allowed him to slip unseen through the shadowy forest. And in the keen, almost human intelligence shining from his eyes. If she could see the growing resemblance to a dingo, so might others. Dusty was due to be desexed the following week when the kids went back to school. Perhaps she should take him farther afield than the vet in Wingham where he'd had his vaccinations.

Dusty leaped from the water and galloped towards her. Kim jumped to her feet and ran for the house, knowing what would happen next. It was a futile escape attempt. He overtook her in a few strides, propped in front of her and shook himself, showering her with a rainbow of spray until she was as wet as him. 'I'll get you for that,' she said, shaking with laughter. He smiled – she could swear he smiled as warmly as any person – put his tail between his legs and scooted away, inviting play.

Then it was on. They tore through the trees, taking turns to chase each other in a gloriously silly game of tag. When she finally collapsed on a green carpet of moss, Dusty dropped down beside her. They lay together in companionable silence. Panting, happy, filled with the joy of young things, although Kim was no longer young. It didn't matter. With one wave of his plumed tail, the dingo could transport her back to the untroubled days of childhood. Then Dusty raised his head, pricking his ears towards the house. It was very early for visitors.

The car bore the words *Wingham Gazette* on its door. Two people stood beside it. The man held a camera and the woman looked vaguely familiar. Dusty kept his distance. He was always cautious with strangers.

'Del Fisher.' The woman shook Kim's hand. 'And this is Andy, my cameraman.'

The penny dropped - the reporter she'd met at the brumby catch. What was she doing there?

'I didn't have contact details for you, so thought I'd just rock up.

I'm still interested in doing a piece on your rewilding project. Especially now you're bringing back dingoes. That's a fascinating angle and, may I say, quite a controversial one.'

Oh no. Time to shut this thing down. 'Sorry, I'm not interested.'

'I can promise you a fabulous feature,' said Del. 'Double page spread, lots of photos, and syndication in newspapers throughout rural New South Wales. I wouldn't be surprised if the nationals picked up a story like this.'

'I don't want publicity.'

'Publicity could bring in funds, sponsors.'

'At the moment I'm funding the project myself.' Del took a pen and notebook from her bag, and started scribbling. 'Put that away,' said Kim. 'I said no story.'

'Look, Kim, I have to be honest. This piece will go to print, with or without you.' As Kim opened her mouth to protest, Del held up her hand. 'Don't blame me. Not my call. But if this article is a done deal, which it is, wouldn't it make more sense for you to be part of it?'

Kim knew when she was being wedged. But Del was right. She couldn't afford to let the story get out without putting her side as persuasively as possible.

'Okay,' she said. 'Let's do this.'

'Do you have time now? Otherwise we can—'

'Now's fine.'

Del was as good as her word, asking intelligent questions, and taking lots of photographs. Kim showed her the rows and rows of seedlings under shade cloth. She showed her the seed propagating igloos and the orchid house. 'These are endangered ravine orchids.' Kim put two tiny pots into Del's hand, and the cameraman took a close-up. 'Wild goats devastated the only site where they're known to grow locally, a rock face above Cedar Creek. But when the dingoes moved in, the goats moved out, and the orchids are starting to recover.'

'Great,' said Del. 'People love orchids. After we finish here, can you show me the site?'

Kim nodded. At least she seemed to be getting a fair hearing.

Del loved the orphaned wildlife: the joeys, possums and new baby wombat. She seemed particularly charmed by the little quolls. 'Surely if you plan to release native animals like these, bringing dingoes back is foolish?'

'It's counterintuitive, I know,' said Kim. 'But dingoes actually improve the survival of small mammals.'

'That makes no sense.'

'In the past two centuries, thirty mammals have become extinct in Australia, animals that had lived quite happily with dingoes for thousands of years. That's half the mammalian extinctions in the world. Eastern hare-wallaby? Gone. Lesser bilby? Gone. Broad-faced potoroo? Gone. Dingoes aren't the problem. It's the explosion in fox and cat numbers when dingoes are exterminated.'

'That's fascinating. Can you cite studies to prove it?'

'Sure. Come inside.' The kids were in the kitchen making toast. 'This is Abbey and Jake.'

'Nice to meet you,' said Del. Dusty padded over to Jake. 'Is that is one of your dingoes?'

Andy snapped a photo.

'Dusty's not a dingo,' said Jake. 'He's a kelpie.'

'Ahh,' said Del. 'My mistake. He's certainly a beautiful dog.'

'Come through,' said Kim, anxious to take the focus off Dusty. They followed her into the lounge room, where Kim had her laptop set up at a desk in the corner. She showed Del studies by Chris Johnson at James Cook University, Dr Thomas Newsome of Sydney University, and half-a-dozen more. 'I'll send you the links,' she said. 'Dingoes don't just protect native animals. They protect plants too. Take a look at this.'

Kim clicked through to the photos of her regeneration plots, before and after the dingoes' release. 'See the damage caused by browsing animals in these first shots? We had massive problems: deer, goats, wallabies, roos. They ate everything down, knocked over fences and tree guards. Rabbits nibbled the fresh shoots and dug up roots.'

She scrolled through to the *after* shots of thriving plantings and healthy saplings, bursting with vigorous new growth. The contrast was plain.

'All because of dingoes,' said Kim. 'Herbivores are much more wary now. They don't hang round the flats, but keep to the cover of gullies and ridge tops. It makes regenerating the rainforest so much easier.' As Del dutifully took notes, Kim relaxed a little. How great to make this sort of information public. The article might be a good thing after all. 'If you like, I'll take you and Andy out to see for yourselves.'

'Brilliant,' said Del. 'But there's another side to this, isn't there? The farmers' side. You know that old saying – the only good dingo is a dead dingo.'

Kim did not know it, and it gave her a chill.

'Emotions run pretty high on the subject. So much so that people have even warned me against writing this article.'

Kim turned off the laptop and wished Del had taken that most excellent advice.

'I heard the dingoes have already killed some of your neighbour's sheep.'

Kim's mouth went dry. She hadn't expected news to travel so fast. Damn Mel and her big mouth. 'Two sheep at She-Oak Springs were found dead yesterday,' she said. 'But there's no proof that dingoes were responsible.'

Del tilted her head and gave Kim a knowing look. 'But it's likely, isn't it? The carcasses were partially eaten.'

'Well, yes, but . . . ' The answer wasn't coming out the way she meant it to.

'I think we've finished here.' Del closed her notebook. 'How about we go bush now, and you can show me around?'

Del spent a good two hours out in the field. She wanted to see everything. The creek, the regeneration sites, the soft-release pens and the tracts of pristine rainforest along the northern boundary.

'Will we see dingoes?' she asked.

'I don't think so,' said Kim. 'They're elusive at the best of times, and very shy of strangers.' The tour finished at a vantage point on the border of Tarringtops National Park. A wild luxuriance of virgin forest stretched southwards, clothing the hills in a mottled cloak of green. There was something timeless, almost holy about the view, and it never failed to send a tingle down Kim's spine.

'Magnificent.' Del's voice was husky with emotion. 'These forests feel ancient.'

'I'll show you a red cedar on the way back that's at least three hundred years old. If people had built these rainforests, they'd be national treasures.'

'There must be a fortune in timber here,' said Del. 'The trees are lucky to have you as their protector.'

A warm glow of pride passed through her. *Protector of Trees.* A title worth fighting for.

It was three o'clock before Kim waved Del and Andy goodbye, with a promise the article would be out the following Wednesday. As they left, they passed Taj coming up the drive.

'Why was the *Gazette* here?' Taj had a grim line to his mouth.

'They're doing a piece on rewilding Journey's End. I didn't have much choice but to talk to them,' said Kim. 'They were doing the story anyway, and at least people will get to hear our side. It went pretty well, although the reporter knew about the sheep killed next door.'

'Dingoes did not kill them. I found this lodged in the spine of one of the sheep.' Taj took something from his pocket and handed it to her.

A bullet sat, small and deadly, in the palm of her hand. Kim stiffened. 'It was shot?'

'They both were. In the body, not the head. Blood trails quickly bring foxes.'

Kim tried to process what she'd heard. 'The sheep . . . did they die straight away?'

Taj shook his head and held out two empty shell casings. 'I found these on the ground a hundred metres away, near a faint set of tyre tracks.'

Kim blanched as the full horror hit her. Pity and anger vied for top place. 'Come on,' she said. 'We have to tell Mel.'

When they arrived at the She-Oak Springs homestead, an unfamiliar Land Rover was parked outside, and Mel's car was nowhere to be seen. Snow's barking summoned a woman from the house. A few years older than Mel, but the family resemblance was plain: same dark curly hair, same round cheeks. 'Mel's away for a while. I'm Nicole, her sister.'

'It's very important that I reach her.' Kim spotted Todd and Grace watching from the back door, and waved.

'Have you tried her phone?'

Kim nodded. 'She's not answering.'

A shadow passed over Nicole's face. 'And you are?'

'Kim Sullivan from next door.'

Her eyes hardened. 'So you're the crazy woman from Sydney, who set dingoes loose next to a sheep station.'

Kim took a step backwards. 'Please, I have to talk to Mel.'

'You've done quite enough damage to my sister already. Mel's had a hard time this year, what with Geoff leaving and everything. The one bright spot was this new friend who'd moved in next door, with kids the same age. She talked about you all the time, admired you, trusted you – and then you go and stab her in the back.'

'You've got it wrong. Dingoes didn't kill her sheep.'

'Like hell they didn't.' Nicole's nostrils flared with anger, and she was suddenly in Kim's face. 'You and your mangy dingoes should be shot. Now hightail it out of here, and take Muhammad with you.'

Taj gently took her arm. 'Come. This will not help.'

Nicole sneered. 'That's right. Better listen to your muzzie friend.' She was so close Kim could feel spittle on her cheek.

'Come,' Taj urged again.

This time Kim allowed herself to be led away. The barrage of hostility had left her shaken, adding to the dark pit in her stomach when she thought of the sheep slowly dying.

'I can't believe that woman is Mel's sister,' she said once they were safely in the car.

Taj put the ute in gear. 'Nicole is different to Mel. Her mind is closed. Once she makes it up, she will not be swayed by facts, or truth, or reason.' His tone was solemn, like he was delivering a much broader wisdom. A muscle twitched in his jaw.

How did he bear it? *Muhammad. Muzzie.*

'We should tell nobody about the sheep being shot,' he said. 'Not until we can talk to Mel. If she hears it from somebody else, without the evidence or the first-hand account of what I found – she will not believe it.'

'What about Ben?'

The muscle in his jaw twitched again.

'Nobody.'

Kim studied his face in profile. Dark, watchful eyes that missed nothing. Unruly hair sweeping back from a high forehead. A square, striking face, full of strength. Inscrutable. That scar. For all their old conversations, which she still missed, in some ways Taj remained as enigmatic as on the day they first met.

'I bloody well hope Mel doesn't stay away for too long. I don't know how long I can stomach living next door to her sister.'

'I will be away too,' said Taj. 'A fencing job north of Taree.'

'How long?'

'Two weeks, maybe less. When I return, we will convince Mel together that the dingoes are not a threat.'

Two whole weeks … Kim forced a smile she did not feel.

CHAPTER 33

Taj returned to Wolf Hall more concerned than he cared to admit. An article in the paper was a very bad idea, even a balanced account. For every convert, there'd be ten more readers who still saw dingoes as public enemy number one and would want to wage a war against them. A government order to cull the pack was a very real threat.

The maremmas greeted him, tails aloft, soft eyes gleaming. Saber, more aloof than the females, soon returned to his sentry position by the door. Taj knelt down to give Ava and Bibi a hug – both of them pregnant, but not showing yet. They would give birth in the spring. Carla's pups had sold quickly, and he already had bookings for these new litters, some from interstate. Taj only permitted pups to go to farmers and the demand was strong – elsewhere. Only one pup had sold so far in Tingo. If dingoes and farmers were going to coexist locally, livestock guardian dogs should be part of the mix.

He fed the chickens, collected eggs, and picked some salad greens from the garden. On the way back, he stowed his fencing tools into the ute: wire spinner, strainers, post drivers and ring-lock mesh. The dingoes had been tracking west along a ridgeline into Ben's place, and he planned to fence off their main access point before leaving for

Taree in the morning. Not that they posed a danger to Ben's cattle. It was more that Ben posed a danger to them.

Taj prepared a plate of boiled eggs and thick slices of homemade bread for lunch. He didn't have much of an appetite. The situation with the dingoes wasn't the only thing bothering him. It wasn't even at the top of the list. That honour went to Kim, and her growing attachment to Ben Steele. Taj didn't trust him. He cared for Kim, more than he'd thought it possible to care for a woman again, and he was determined to protect her.

Taj glanced at the small, framed photo on the wall – a laughing fair-haired woman, with mischief in her eyes. He hadn't protected Camila. That failure had left him lost and broken for years. He'd cut himself off from friends and family, leaving Nuristan to work with the Australian forces in their fight against the Taliban. High-functioning by day, surrendering to private demons at night. By the time he reached Australia, he'd grown numb: immune to loneliness, and the bigotry and prejudice that sometimes came his way. Compared to the pain of losing Camila, nothing could hurt him. Better to be a log or rock and feel nothing.

Her death still haunted him, poisoning his dreams. Yet here in Tingo he was healing, slowly coming back to life. He had his animals. He had the wild forests. He had the grand beauty of his adopted mountain home, and the respect and acceptance of the community. Tingo had rescued him, and it could do the same for Kim, if she let it.

Kim. The image of her lovely face and serious blue eyes was never far from his thoughts. Although she didn't know it, they shared something profound, something he'd recognised in her that first day. They'd both lost parts of themselves. She'd suffered like him, grieved like him, hated like him. Her children had suffered too. Jake, stubborn and proud, full of misguided bitterness. Abbey, elfin and ethereal, too wise for her years. Taj had been drawn to her from the start. If Camila had lived, their child would be the same age.

His admiration for Kim had grown stronger as he came to know her. Here was a woman, beautiful inside and out, who had no idea how special she was. A woman who challenged expectations and acted in defiance of convention. A champion of the wild, supporting the dingo project when nobody else would. He'd never met anyone quite like her, and she deserved better than Ben Steele. The bond growing between them disturbed him beyond measure.

Taj had lived with wild animals for so long he'd developed a sixth sense for danger. Only once had it failed him. Sometimes it was mere intuition, an urge to trust his hunches. Sometimes it came as a visceral spasm, a snake slithering deep in his gut, and it had saved his life more once. Warning him before a deadly avalanche took out the bridge he was about to ski across. Warning him before armed bandits attacked him on a mountain road. And he'd felt the same belly-clench on that first day, when Ben introduced him to Kim.

His misgivings had strengthened as Ben ever so slowly moved in on her. Using his good looks and charm to ingratiate himself into Kim's life. Taking advantage of her loneliness. Targeting Jake and his need. Taj had made some discreet enquiries about Ben. There were rumours of dodgy real estate practices: kickbacks, under-quoting, dummy bidders and exorbitant up-front expenses. But nothing concrete.

Ben had no police record. He wasn't secretly married, although he'd left behind a string of broken hearts. There were no stories about a gambling problem, or drink or drugs. No evidence that Ben was a threat other than the fact that he was a player, the kind of man who found any beautiful, hard-to-get woman an intriguing challenge. At night, Taj could see Kim's house shining across the valley. Sometimes he'd sit outside with his last coffee before bed, drawn by the light on the hill, waiting for it to go out. His insides twisting at the thought that Ben might be there when it did. His mind drawing troubling pictures.

Was he on a futile witch-hunt, motivated as much by jealousy, as anything else? Taj had begun to think so, begun to think that his sixth sense was playing him false. Until that morning, when he received a fascinating text from Hakim. If what his friend said was true, it meant Ben might be dodgy in a way he'd never dreamed of. Taj pushed his half-eaten plate of food away. There was a lot to do before leaving. But first he'd head up to the ridge country and build a bloody big fence between Journey's End and Ben's land.

It took Taj a week of backbreaking labour to finish the contract fencing job that should have taken two. At last he was free to follow up on that damning text.

His ute rattled into the lumberyard where Hakim worked, the three maremmas on the tray at the back, barking wildly. Valley Saw Mill was a smallish concern: a main mill shed where the sawyers worked, machinery and storage sheds, drying kiln and manager's office. Taj had seen bigger operations in Nuristan.

He took a look around, savouring the sweet, spicy smell of sap and sawn wood. For a small mill, they held a lot of inventory. Vast stacks of raw logs, all different grades and sizes, stood ready for processing. Further afield lay racks of milled lumber, and piles of woodchips and sawdust. The largest logs were on the left, gnarled forest giants of impressive girth. No plantation trees there.

Taj approached a big-bellied man, who was loading a massive log onto his forklift. 'Hakim? He's due for morning smoko.' Taj followed him across to the main shed, where the man dropped the log on the mill, expertly positioning it at the best angle.

An ear-muffed Hakim, who was adjusting logs on the hydraulic saw, looked up and grinned. Then he set the mill to work, squaring off the log, and cutting it into three big beams. The forklift set about moving the milled timber.

Hakim wiped his hands on his trousers. 'Better than working down a stinking hole, eh?'

The two of them spent a few minutes catching up, then Hakim fetched a thermos of Turkish coffee to share. Taj took a sip of the thick brown brew. 'So, mister ex-policeman, tell me what you've found out about our friend?'

Hakim looked around to make sure nobody was near. 'To buy trees, the mill needs proof that landholders have the right approvals.'

He took some photocopied forms from his wallet. The first one was a log purchase order. Under *Name of Vendor Landowner* it read *Ben Steele. PVP/Council Approval Number – PNF-PVP-03903.* Then it listed the address of the logged property, species and volume of trees, harvesting area, docket numbers and a seriously impressive purchase price. It was dated a month ago.

'This form's dodgy.' Hakim leant over. 'See here, where it says spotted gum and blackbutt? Not true. Saw the trucks come in myself. They were something different. I've never seen logs that size.'

Hakim lit a cigarette. 'And this Mandanga address on the order doesn't match the one on the truck-driver's ticket.' He showed Ben a crumpled delivery docket: same date, same reference number, same landholder, but showing the pick-up address as Wombat Road, Yarram. 'Found this in the bin, and then did some snooping. The docket on file's been doctored.'

'When did the trees come in? Can I take a look?'

Hakim shook his head. 'They were processed three weeks ago.'

Taj studied the documents. There was only one conclusion. Ben and the mill were in cahoots, using false addresses and approval numbers on purchase orders for illegally harvested logs. A slow grin spread across his face. 'You haven't lost your touch. This is gold.'

Hakim let out a great belly laugh, and slapped him on the back. 'There could be more where that came from, my friend. Ben Steele is the listed landowner on half-a-dozen more orders.'

'Could you get hold of them?'

'No worries.'

'You might lose your job.'

Hakim shrugged. 'Plenty of other jobs for me. The bosses all love me. They say Aussies are lazy buggers.'

Armed with this new information, Taj set out to see for himself. First he would visit the property listed on the purchase order, in Mandanga, an hour's drive north-east of the mill. This was where the logs had purportedly come from. The approval number was legitimate. He'd found it via the online public register, and the location seemed to match. Was Hakim wrong?

Taj arrived at the address before lunch. A crooked gate, and an unremarkable stretch of woodland, dominated by spotted gum and blackbutt, the very species listed on the purchase order. He let the dogs loose, jumped the gate and went for a walk. A few hundred metres in, he came to a logging coupe. Regrowth grew tall here. Friendly yellow robins flitted at his feet. An echidna was demolishing a broad bull-ant mound, and the understorey of acacias, palms and cycads was beginning to make a comeback.

Taj spent a few hours exploring. Wherever he went, it was the same. This land hadn't been logged in several years, which meant the purchase order Hakim showed him was wrong. No consignment of timber had left here last month for the Valley Saw Mill. So where had the logs come from?

Taj whistled the dogs, returning to the car with a spring in his step. Lovely Carla, always so full of joy, leaped up and tugged at his shirt, causing the truck driver's delivery docket to fall from his pocket. She seized it, tail awag, and deposited it in his hand. 'Clever Carla.' He checked the address. 'Wombat Road, Yarram, here we come.'

The two-hour trip to Yarram took them on a winding journey up the Great Escarpment. As they negotiated the narrow, poorly-graded roads, eucalypt woodlands gave way to pockets of rainforest, which grew more extensive as they climbed. Hairpin bends offered spectacular views across the range. Taj was in his element.

He took an obscure turn-off, driving slowly, concerned the place might be hard to find. But he was wrong: 300 Wombat Road was difficult to miss. A broad, bulldozed section swathed through the forest to his right, splintering tallowwood and spindly tea-tree alike. The old stock fence had been ploughed into the ground. The tread of giant tractor tyres had gouged the damp soil into strange, geometric shapes.

Taj parked the car, called the dogs, and followed the mud trail through the rainforest: soaring stands of corkwood, sassafras and booyong, with a smattering of majestic yellow carabeen. This was standard for logging coupes – a buffer zone left standing to shield the destruction from the road. He rounded a kink in the track and stopped dead.

Taj had been prepared for the sight, but it was still heartbreaking. A splintered bombsite of woody debris, churned earth and shattered roots. Levelled pedestals of giant trees, broad as billiard tables, dotted the devastated scene. He'd seen this type of destruction before in Nuristan. Rebel loggers tearing down ancient stands of oak and pine, exposing fragile soils to winter storms, decimating the wildlife and causing farms to be washed away.

Taj spent most of the afternoon exploring the clear-fell, taking notes and photographs, estimating the number of hectares logged. It was eerily quiet. No musical birds in the upper canopy. No wind in the trees, or calling frogs. Just a vast, silent space.

The damage was recent and tallied well with his timeline. Old-growth trees like these were worth a fortune, hard to come by, and large enough to mill big-dollar items like overhead beams for homes, fireplace mantels and solid slabs for high-end conference tables. This was Ben Steele's land. It shouldn't be hard to prove that Hakim's mysterious logs had come from here, not Mandanga, and that Ben had no approval to harvest them.

Taj took a last look at the dead place where an ancient Gondwanan rainforest had once reigned for thousands of years. Kim needed to know.

CHAPTER 34

'Time to go.' Kim popped mandarins into the kids' lunch boxes. First day of third term, the beginning of their final six months in Tingo. Already she was feeling nostalgic. It was hard to imagine going back to Sydney, but that's where her work was, and it was time to start planning. She'd need to rent a house with a big backyard for Dusty, and choose a new school for Jake. Daisy hadn't been happy with Campbelltown High and had switched Stuart to a small independent college nearby. That could be the perfect choice.

Kim had changed her mind about selling up. She owed Journey's End too much. It would be a holiday house for now, and later on, who knew? Maybe a permanent home in Tingo was on the cards. They were all so happy here, and Jake was a different boy.

Abbey was more problematic. She remained implacably set against Ben. It would make moving forward difficult, but that's what Kim wanted to do – move forward with Ben, however slowly, in spite of moving back to Sydney. See where it led. Time at Journey's End had changed her, helped her see Connor's death differently. The rainforest on her doorstep burst with an abundance of life, yet death was never far away. Death, decay and rebirth – the circle of life confronted her every day here. One thing she knew for sure now – she would not be defined by grief. She wanted to live.

Jake came into the kitchen, dressed and ready in plenty of time. Eager for school. Kim took a photo of her smiling son. What a difference from the sad, angry child of six months ago. 'Will Todd be there? I haven't seen him for ages.'

'I think Todd and Abbey will both be there,' she said, 'although Mel's still away.' Kim popped a fun-size pack of smarties in the lunch boxes, gave Abbey a hurry-up, and glanced out the window. Another perfect winter's day, with a sky blue enough to swim in. She was looking forward to today in every respect but one. Del's article would be out.

Kim dropped the kids at school, and then went to the general store to pick up the paper. 'Morning, Des.' She looked about for the pile of *Gazettes*. They weren't in their usual position on the shelf. 'Isn't the local paper in yet?'

'All sold out.'

'Sold out? It's only nine o'clock.'

Winnie hurried in from out the back, flourishing a single newspaper. 'Well, my girl, you've certainly set the cat amongst the pigeons.' Her face was flushed with excitement. 'Here, I've saved you a copy.'

Kim took the offered paper. Blazoned across the front page in big letters she read: *WHO'S AFRAID OF THE BIG BAD WOLF? DINGOES – FRIEND OR FOE?* The headline was accompanied by a photo of a snarling dingo captioned 'The Killer Among Us'.

She could have cheerfully strangled Del. 'I didn't realise the article would be quite so prominent.'

'Prominent?' Des laughed. 'That's an understatement. It's all people are talking about.'

'I'm afraid he's right,' said Winnie. 'Opinions are running pretty high. Some people can't see past the headline.'

'But my Win's been sticking up for you.' Des grinned and rubbed his hands together.

'I certainly have,' said Winnie. 'When Geoff Masters said you should be run out of town, I told him what a silly old fool he was.'

'Run out of town?' asked Kim. 'What is this, the wild west?'

Des whooped with laughter. He clearly found the whole thing hilarious. 'Well, you can hardly blame him. It's his stock them dingoes are killing.'

Kim bristled. 'No, it's not. It's Mel's.'

Des shrugged. 'Doesn't make it any more fun for the sheep.'

'You don't understand. The dingoes aren't killing anybody's sheep.'

'But you just said—'

'Oh, shut up, Des.' Winnie gave Kim a reassuring smile. 'Here's your newspaper, love. Maybe it's just as well we've sold out of them.'

Kim turned on her heel with as much dignity as she could muster. Going out the door, she overheard Des say, 'Hold the fort, Win. I'm doing a run into Wingham for more copies.'

Kim drove home, too dejected to look at the article. Only after she'd made a strong coffee did she sit down to read, prepared for the worst. But once she got past the sensational headline it actually wasn't so bad. You could even call it balanced.

'Cutting-edge research is questioning the logic of culling dingoes, and wondering whether they shouldn't, in fact, be re-introduced into regions where they're locally extinct. Botanist Kim Sullivan is doing just that as part of an innovative rewilding project on her property at Tingo.'

Then they quoted her: *"Dingoes play a vital role in protecting small native animals and birds, by getting rid of cats and foxes."*

It then outlined the risk of attack and stock losses attributed to dingoes, and the various methods used to cull them.

'Yet according to Kim Sullivan, culling is counterproductive. It increases predation, by destroying pack structure. *"Juveniles without leadership are much more likely to target livestock and interbreed with domestic dogs. If you kill the alpha pair, breeding goes ballistic."* She denied that her dingoes were responsible for the death of two sheep on neighbouring land, stating there was no conclusive proof.'

The article went on to discuss livestock guardian dogs, and other ways to deter attacks. *'Dingoes help graziers by providing 24/7 pest management,'* Ms Sullivan said. *'They kill or drive away kangaroos, rabbits, pigs, and goats, reduce competition for grass, and help farmers' hip pockets.'*

It finished with before and after photos of the rainforest plots and a last comment: *'Putting away the guns, traps and poisons might be the best way forward, for forests and farmers alike.'*

Kim reread the article several times. The more she read it, the more she liked it. Surely anybody reading this would understand what she and Taj were trying to do? She really should have mentioned Taj. After all, this was all his idea. She couldn't wait to show him.

The problem was, Taj still wasn't back from his out-of-town fencing job. Of course he had to earn a living. She sometimes wondered how he managed, spending so much time working at her place for free.

No Taj. No Mel. Daisy a five-hour drive away. The kids back at school. It was getting a wee bit lonely at Journey's End. Thank goodness for Ben. Dusty pushed through the screen door, and laid his head on her knee. 'Oh, and you of course.' She tugged at his ears the way he liked. 'Who could forget you? How about a slap-up breakfast of bacon and eggs.' At the word *breakfast* he trotted to the fridge.

Dusty hadn't been in Jake's room this morning when she woke him for school. She thought back to Taj's advice – 'Don't let him wander.' It was easier said than done. Dusty was a clever escape artist. A dingo's broad head was the widest part of his body, which meant if his head could fit through, so could the rest of him. Dusty had quickly learned to use the doggy door. She'd had to board it up. The screen doors didn't stop him, and neither did the main doors unless they were locked, and she'd lost the house keys a few weeks earlier. It hadn't seemed important at the time. Nobody locked up in Tingo, but it meant she couldn't secure him inside. The outside runs were full of possums and wallabies and other assorted wildlife. When she tied him up, the kids complained, and it wasn't just them. Who could withstand his sad eyes and pitiful howls? She needed a locksmith. In the meantime, she'd have to put safety chains on the doors, front and back. The dingo article could make life more dangerous for wandering dogs.

Kim spent the day fertilising tube-stock and transferring root-bound plants into larger pots. Spring wasn't far away and soon there'd be a burgeoning of new growth. Dusty was good company, copying everything she did. When she fetched empty pots from the shed, so did he. When she dug in the mulch pile, so did he, showering her in pine bark. Kim had to draw the line, though, when he started pulling plants out of pots. 'No Dusty, you'd better let me do that.' He reproached her with a furrowed brow.

Time slipped away. It always did when she was working with the plants. She forgot lunch and was late feeding the currawong chicks and joeys. Bonnie and Clyde were quite big now and no longer needed milk, but she still gave them bottles as a treat when she fed the others.

'Done,' Kim told Dusty at last. 'Stay here while I go get the kids.' The pup cocked his head at her, and then went to lie down on the porch. He never wandered during the day. Ben thought it strange that she had conversations with Dusty, but to her it seemed entirely natural. He was as much a member of the family as anybody.

She found her car keys and took off down the drive. As she approached the gate, her stomach lurched. Taped to the fence was a white sheet, with the words *Dingo-Loving Bitch* scrawled across it in red paint that looked like blood.

Bile rose in her throat. Kim scanned the road in both directions. Empty. Feeling a little shaky, she climbed from the car, ripped down the sheet and stuffed it under bracken at the side of the road. She'd come back for it later. The main thing was not to let the kids see it. The forest took on a sinister feel as she drove the short distance to

Tingo. An unfamiliar car on the side of the road near Ben's place filled her with suspicion, and she memorised its number plate.

For some reason Jake and Abbey were waiting fifty metres down the road from the school gate. She hadn't expected them to be so prompt. First day back, seeing their friends again after the long holiday break? She thought she'd have to have to go looking.

Abbey seemed happy enough, but Jake was a mess: face like thunder, grazed cheek, torn collar. He climbed in without a word, volunteering for the back seat. As she drove, Kim observed him in the rearview mirror with a cold creeping sense of déjà vu: the bowed head and knitted brow. The hunched back. How many times had she picked him up from his old school looking like that?

'What's up?'

'He had a fight with Todd,' whispered Abbey.

'Shut up!' Jake savagely kicked the back of his sister's seat. Jake and Todd were best buddies. What would it take for them to fight?

Abbey turned round in her seat, made a face at her brother, and then said in a stage whisper, 'It was about the dingoes.'

Kim slammed on the brakes as she missed the Bangalow Road turn-off.

Damn Del Fisher and her stupid article.

Jake's foot crashed into the back of Abbey's seat again. 'I said, shut up.'

'That's enough,' said Kim. 'We'll talk about this when we get home.'

She parked the car and Jake called Dusty and headed for the sheds. The hollow sound of an axe on wood soon echoed round the hills.

Abbey frowned. 'Aren't you going to yell at him?'

'No, I'm going to talk to him.' Kim put an arm round her daughter's shoulder. 'But first, I'm going to talk to you.'

They sat in the kitchen, suitably fortified with choc-chip biscuits and milk. 'Now,' said Kim. 'What happened at school?'

Abbey launched into a blow-by-blow account of her day from the moment she entered the schoolyard. Kim let her talk. But after ten minutes, Abbey had only made it as far as recess, and Kim interrupted. 'It certainly sounds like you've had a good day. What about Jake?'

Abbey rolled her eyes. 'That's what you wanted to know about all along, isn't it?'

'I want to know about you too, of course I do. But you're much better at telling me things than Jake is.'

Abbey took another biscuit. 'How much better?'

'Heaps better,' said Kim. 'Now when did this fight happen?'

'After school. I didn't hear the first bit, because me and Nikki stayed behind to help put the library books away.'

Abbey paused so Kim could congratulate her for helping. It was clear she was going to milk this for all it was worth. 'Then what?'

'Well' – she dipped the biscuit in her glass of milk – 'I went to look for Jake, because Jean wanted to know if he'd brought back his holiday books.'

He hadn't. Kim knew exactly where those two *Deltora Quest* novels were – on the shelf above the outside loo.

'Then I heard all this shouting. Todd was showing Jake a newspaper, and then they were, like, wrestling around on the ground beneath the pine trees.'

'Is Todd alright?'

'As alright as Jake is. Anyway, Todd was yelling that the dingoes were sheep-killers, and his dad was going to shoot them all. Jake said he'd better not try it and that Todd's dad was wrong. Then Todd said, "What would a townie like you know?" And they started punching each other again.'

'What did Jean do?'

Abbey finished her milk. 'Jean didn't see. Can I go play with Dusty now?'

'Better not, sweetie. He's with Jake. Steer clear of your brother for a bit, okay?'

'Then can I watch TV? They're showing *The Saddle Club* again, right from the beginning.'

'Go on.' Abbey took one last biscuit and ran off. Soon the televi sion was blaring away in the lounge room. Kim sat for the longest time, grappling with her thoughts. Why had she let Taj talk her into releasing dingoes at Journey's End? Ben was right, she must have been out of her mind.

She tried Mel's mobile. No answer. She tried the She-Oak Springs landline. Nicole picked up. 'Oh, it's you. If your thug of a son so much as goes near our Todd again, I'll call the police.'

'Let's keep things in perspective,' said Kim. 'Two boys had a dust-up at school, that's all, and, from what I hear, Todd was as much to blame as Jake. Now, is Mel there please?'

Nicole hung up.

Kim tried Taj, but he was out of range. She left a message for him to call her. Her anxiety was coalescing into smouldering anger. This was his fault. Sure, she'd gone along with the dingo plan, but that was because she hadn't understood how whacky it was. All that talk of wolf-whispering and top-order predators and trophic cascades. She was a botanist from Campbelltown, for goodness sake. What did she know about dingoes or the tidal wave of feeling they stirred up in the bush? She was losing friends over this; her kids were suffering. And what about the vile sign on the fence?

Kim fought to calm her jangled nerves. For the first time in a long time she craved Connor. Automatically she felt for his ring, but it was in her bedroom drawer. She was in the habit of taking it off each morning now. But she always put it back on at night, otherwise she couldn't sleep. A stiffness in her throat made it hard to swallow. Wine would help, but she didn't have any. What about that bottle of Baileys Mel had given her for Christmas? There it was, in the top cupboard. She mixed it with a bit of milk in a mug, and took a swig. The creamy liqueur went down well, easing her tight throat. Just what she needed before tackling her son. She'd give him a bit longer. Let him vent his anger on the logs for a while.

The back door slammed, making her jump. Jake marched in with an armload of firewood, dumping it into the corner wood-box with a thud. He swung to face her, eyes wild and red. He'd been crying.

'Mum, it's like you're deliberately trying to get people to hate me,' he said. 'Did our dingoes kill Todd's sheep?'

'Taj doesn't think so.'

'I don't care what he thinks. What do you think? Is Todd's dad right?'

Kim patted the chair beside her. 'Sit.'

Jake ranged around the room for a while. Finally he plonked down beside her, eyes trained on the floor.

'Whatever you may think of Taj,' she said, 'you have to admit he's a good bushman.' Hesitation, then a begrudging nod. 'And Taj didn't find dingo footprints anywhere near those carcasses. Plenty of fox tracks, crows, even eagles. But no dingoes. What he did find were bullets and spent rifle shells.' Jake glanced up. 'The sheep were shot, and eaten by scavengers later. Our dingoes had nothing to do with it.'

Jake let out a long breath. 'You have to tell Mel.'

'How?' said Kim. 'I don't know where she is. She won't answer her phone or my texts, she's not on Facebook, and her guard dog of a sister won't give her my messages.'

Jake frowned, the way he did when puzzling over a Chinese checkers move. He put his elbows on the table and rested his chin on his hands. They sat awhile in silence. Slowly the fury leaked out of him, like air from a pricked beach ball, leaving him merely sad and deflated. 'What do I say to Todd tomorrow?'

'How about sorry?' Kim pushed the plate of biscuits across, and dipped one in her Baileys.

Jake ate two while pondering her suggestion. 'I'm sorry about the fight, but I'm not sorry about sticking up for the dingoes.'

Kim moved her chair close, and rested a hand on his shoulder. 'Why not make it a kind of non-specific apology? Just say sorry and leave it at that.'

'I suppose.'

'Do you want us to try and catch the dingoes so Todd's dad isn't bothered?'

'What would happen to them?'

'I don't know, a zoo, or something?'

A fierce glint showed in his eyes. 'They've done nothing wrong. They shouldn't be locked up just because Todd's dad is an idiot.'

Tears threatened a comeback. Jake was loyal to a fault. How she hated having put him in this position. She gave his shoulder a squeeze and got up to light the fire, but not before pouring herself another drink.

'Ben's coming round tonight. That should cheer you up.'

But it didn't. Jake went to his room. Ben was no fan of dingoes, and her son knew it.

Night had wrapped the little house in darkness, and the roast was dry and overcooked when Ben rang to say he couldn't make dinner. Oh. Disappointment on top of disappointment. She tried to sound like it didn't matter. 'I could still come round later, after nine.' he said, his voice warm. The cloud of loneliness that had been moving in cleared a little.

Ten o'clock. Kids in bed. Ben still hadn't arrived and Kim was drunk and bored. Maybe he wasn't coming. She left the cosiness of the fire and went to the kitchen, where the window gave a good view of the drive. Nothing. This was as good a time as any to go down to the front gate, pull that disgusting sign out of the bushes, and get rid of it.

A mist had crept down the mountain, smothering the moon and stars. Blackness swallowed the torchlight a few metres from her face. It must be cold, because she was shivering, but with a belly full of Baileys she couldn't feel it.

Kim started down the track, stumbling on the rough ground, crossing the bridge over Cedar Creek's black, rushing waters. She'd almost reached the gate when something stirred out in the dark. A rustling in the ferns. The wind, or something else? Kim stopped. Nothing showed in the torch beam, except an owl, gliding through the night like a grey ghost. Still the sense of being watched was growing. Her skin bristled with the ancient fear of what lived in the night, beyond the fire-glow.

The noise came again. Kim held her breath as a dingo stepped out of the shadows, then another and another, lining up side-by-side like soldiers. Next moment they were all around her, greeting her with the joy and affection owed to a lost member of the pack. Fear turned to wonder as they slipped like wraiths in and out of the torchlight. Pressing their warm, soft bodies against her legs, yodelling with quiet excitement. It was hard to tell them apart in the dark, but she recognised Red, the alpha male, pushing his wet nose into her hand. And Dusty's sisters, gambolling around her, a jumble of pouncing bodies and wagging tails. A darker dog approached, and a prickle of fear returned. Could this be the wild dingo that had joined the pack? It came closer. No, not a wild dingo at all. Dusty.

Red briefly touched noses with him. Kim watched in dismay as Dusty joined in their play, romping around, chasing his sisters, even cheekily pulling Red's tail. This was not his first encounter with the pack. They knew him, accepted him.

A car was coming on Bangalow Road. Headlights pierced the gloom as it swung in at the gate. Kim and the dingoes froze for a moment in the headlights. Then the pack melted into the night, all except Dusty. Kim kept a hand on his collar, just to be sure.

Ben jumped the gate and ran to her. 'Bloody hell, are you okay?'

'I'm fine.'

A low rumble sounded in Dusty's throat and Ben backed away.

'Come and look at this,' he said. She followed him back down the track. Wired to the gate was a piece of old tin bearing the words *Piss Off Dingo Lover*.

CHAPTER 35

'I'm not going,' said Jake as they pulled up at the school.

'Yes, you are.' Kim's patience was nearing its end. 'Out you get. I've got things to do.'

Jake threw her a mutinous glance, grabbed his bag, and slammed the door behind him.

'You too, sweetie.'

Abbey's frown showed her own reluctance to leave. 'Don't be late picking us up,' she said as she climbed from the car.

Kim watched until the bell went and they trooped inside. Jean, standing at the classroom door, gave her a wave. Yesterday Jake had jumped the fence before school and walked all the way home.

A mere week into third term, and Kim's new life was collapsing around her. The dingoes, that nobody had actually seen, were dividing the town into two rough camps. Old hippies and tree-changers, who'd come to Tingo as a lifestyle choice, saw them as iconic animals, romantic symbols of wild Australia. Farmers, with a few exceptions, saw them as vicious vermin. She couldn't walk down the main street without somebody voicing an opinion.

Kim needed bread and milk and weighed up the pros and cons of shopping at the general store. It was either that or drive all the way to Wingham and back. What the heck. It was right around the corner. She'd be in and out before you knew it.

Kim began the short walk to the shop. Oops, bad idea. Old Charlie had pulled up outside. He might be a mechanic now, but apparently he used to be a farmer.

'It's criminal, what you're doing,' he said, spotting her. 'I spend half me life getting rid of bloody dingoes, and you go bring them back on purpose? The blood, sweat and tears that goes into raising livestock. You've no idea. Sleeping out in paddocks at lambing time, a rifle perched on your knee. Weeks of baiting wild dogs and checking traps. Then one morning there's a dozen lambs wandering round with their guts hanging out. Or a calving cow with her insides eaten.'

Kim couldn't count how many of these horror stories she'd heard. And her escape path to the car was blocked now, because Shirley Ryan was coming up behind her.

'I'm afraid I agree with Charlie, dear,' she said.

Didn't anybody say hello anymore?

'It's not until you see what they do to the poor sheep that you realise. All that time and money lost. It gives me the jitters, just knowing they're out there somewhere.'

Kim could scream. Everyone was an expert. Everyone wanted their say on the subject, even if it didn't affect them at all. Shirley was retired and lived in the cottage behind the fire station, for heaven's sake. What could the dingoes do to her? Slaughter the snapdragons? Maul the delphiniums to death?

Lurking close was the thought of the obscene signs left at her place. There'd been anonymous texts as well. It was making her paranoid. Who was it? Geoff Masters? Old Charlie? It could be more than one person. It could be almost anybody. Suspicion was poisoning her relationship with the people of Tingo.

'Sorry, Shirley, but I forgot something.' Kim hurried past her, back to the car, back to safety. Compared to visiting the general store, a long round trip to Wingham for milk and bread seemed like an attractive deal.

Kim took her time, visiting the library and post office, not arriving home until lunchtime. The afternoon was a write-off. She couldn't concentrate, couldn't settle at anything. The kids, the dingoes, the person – people? – who'd left the sign. Ben, Taj, Mel – what to worry about first? Was Mel alright? Where was she? Even Dusty's clowning couldn't distract Kim today.

She set about preparing some seeds for planting, but her mind wasn't on the job. She forgot to wear gloves when opening the flame tree pods, and hundreds of irritating guard hairs pierced her fingers. She accidentally soaked the tuckeroo seeds, instead of the lacebarks, in scalding water. No chance of them germinating now. And she sneezed when opening a paper bag of red cedar capsules, scattering their tiny winged seeds to the wind.

In the end she gave up and went inside to watch daytime television, something she hadn't done in years. *The Doctors* talked about stress and how it could shorten your life. *Dr. Phil* was about the damage to bereaved children when their mother found a new man too quickly. The cooking shows made her feel inadequate. As the afternoon dragged on, her concern for the kids grew. How were they getting on? She checked the clock for the umpteenth time.

When it was finally time to pick them up, Jean was waiting with Abbey and Jake outside the school gate. 'A word please, Kim?'

Good grief, what now? They followed the principal round to her office.

'I want to talk to your mum on her own.'

Jake slumped on a bench, face blank, eyes fixed on the wall. Abbey seemed upset too, avoiding Kim's gaze, picking at a scab on her knee. It was beginning to bleed.

'We've had an unfortunate day,' said Jean when they were alone.

'The other children made a silly decision. Sending Abbey and Jake to Coventry, so to speak - refusing to talk to them. I didn't realise until halfway through lunchtime, when Abbey was sensible enough to come and tell me.' Jean paused. 'You have to understand, these children are mainly from farming families.'

'I can't believe it. All this over a few dingoes on my land, next to a national park, where, I might add, they're protected by law.'

'Geoff Masters says they're killing stock at She-Oak Springs,' said Jean. 'He's pretty het up. It hasn't helped that Todd's mother is away and the boy is staying with Geoff. He's picking up on his father's anger.'

Kim wanted to tell her about the bullets Taj had found. Why had she ever promised to keep that secret? 'We're talking two sheep, and I don't believe for a minute that dingoes killed them.'

'That's not really the point, is it?'

Kim liked Jean, she really did, but right now the principal was getting on her nerves.

Jean continued, 'I'm afraid it's all about perception, what people think.'

Kim's composure wasn't only slipping; it was ready to crash on the floor. 'So if the truth stands for nothing, what's your plan?'

'I've spoken to the children, of course. At such a small school it's hard for any one child to resist the tide of peer pressure.'

Kim's mouth fell slack as the penny dropped. 'So what you're saying is, you can't promise that this won't happen again?'

'Promise? No. It's a very fluid situation. However I'm ringing all the parents to request that they talk to their children tonight.'

Kim shoved her chair back. 'A fat lot of good that'll do. It's the kids' parents who've set this up. They're not going to do anything.'

'I'm hopeful—'

'Hopeful won't cut it.' Kim rose to her feet. 'If you think I'm going to drop my kids off here on Monday, to be humiliated all over again .. . then you're insane. They'll come back when you can guarantee them fair treatment by everybody at this school. *Guarantee* it, you hear? Not before.'

She turned on her heel and marched from the room.

Abbey sprang back from the door – she must have been listening. And, uncharacteristically, Jake wrapped his arms around his mother.

'Group hug,' said Abbey, piling in too.

Kim held them tight, the embrace touching a warm place in her chest, reserved only for her son and daughter.

Evening came, masquerading as a lovely painting. The setting sun sent pale streamers of purple and gold across the sky. Mountains peaks burnished in bronze glowed to the north like beacons. The rainforest, poised between light and darkness, took on an eerie beauty. Yet for once Tingo's splendour failed to move her. The encroaching forest was more claustrophobic than enticing. Watering the plants was simply a chore. She didn't stop to count the new leaves unfurling to the promise of spring. Feeding the possums and quolls was an unwelcome distraction. She didn't wait, as night brought the little creatures to life. She just wanted to get it over with.

Dusty sensed her sadness. He put on a show: sitting up and waving, rolling over and over, chasing his tail as he tried to make her laugh. But he annoyed her too. 'Nick off.' She shoved him away with her foot. 'You and your mates are the reason we're in this mess.' Dusty whined and slunk away.

The only bright spot on the horizon was the prospect of Ben coming around. In spite of his aversion to dingoes, he only occasionally badgered her about them.

When she rang to tell him about the debacle at school, he hadn't criticised, or said 'I told you so.' He'd simply insisted she needed cheering up, and offered to drive them all into Wingham for a pub dinner. 'You don't want to be bothered with cooking after the day you've had.'

She was looking forward to it. Getting out of Tingo was exactly what she needed.

Ben was good for her. His easy charm, his ready smile, the way he brought her out of herself. And, yes, it was true, although she'd denied it to Daisy – she liked that he reminded her of Connor. Sometimes, when he turned his head or flashed a smile, she felt for a precious moment that her husband was back. And if, as rumoured, Ben had been a bit of a ladies' man, that was clearly in the past. It was flattering really.

Kim wandered back to the house, thinking about the evening ahead. Abbey might be a problem. She didn't like going places with Ben, which was why he always came to their house. Granite Hills homestead was far more spacious and comfortable. Ben had grown up there, and when his parents downsized and moved to Taree he'd taken the place over. Foxtel. A billiard room. Even a swimming pool. Jake loved it, of course, but because of Abbey they'd only visited twice. She didn't even like being in the car with Ben. Well, tonight Kim would put her foot down. They would all drive to Wingham, have a lovely meal, and Abbey would enjoy herself. This was non-negotiable.

However Kim had underestimated the strength of her daughter's opposition. A taste, perhaps, of what was to come when Abbey hit adolescence. Her sweet, adorable girl had turned into a screaming and rather melodramatic monster, raging in the kitchen.

'I hate Ben. I'd rather die than go anywhere with him.'

'Don't talk nonsense. Just this once we're doing it my way.'

Abbey ran off.

Kim found her in her room, zipped inside a sleeping bag, head and all. A curious Dusty lay beside her, pawing at the girl's wiggling body, making her giggle. Kim tapped lightly where she imagined Abbey's head was. 'Knock, knock. It must be hard to breathe in there. You'd better come out.'

'I can't,' came the muffled reply. 'It's my cocoon. I'm turning into a butterfly and then I'll fly to heaven to find Daddy.'

Oh Abbey.

Ben arrived, looking casually handsome in narrow jeans, a vintage Rolling Stones T-shirt and the hint of a spike to his hair. He looked out of place in her rustic kitchen, but that suited her fine. She was fed up with country anyway.

'She won't come,' said Kim.

'You're kidding me?' Ben ran his hand through his hair. 'I swear, I've never done a thing to that kid, other than bring her presents and pizza.'

'Aren't we going after all, Mum?' asked Jake, coming in from the lounge room. Disappointment lay heavy in his voice.

'I'm sorry, love. Your sister's being difficult.' He'd had such a terrible day. What a shame. Bloody Abbey.

'Can't Ben and me go by ourselves?'

'The plan was to give your mum a night out,' said Ben. 'Not leave her behind. I'll go talk to Abbey.'

Kim followed him to the bedroom, Jake trailing behind them, and pointed to the sleeping bag on the floor.

'Abbey, honey. Come on. We're all going out for a pub meal.'

'Not me.'

He moved closer and Dusty growled. 'Get that dog out of here,' Ben said to Jake. 'And teach him some manners while you're at it.'

Before Jake could do anything, the sleeping bag began to thrash around and Abbey's head popped out. 'Leave Dusty alone. I hate you.' Her arms emerged next, and wrapped themselves tight around the dog's neck.

Ben's face reddened. 'Are you going to let her get away with that?'

Kim guided him gently from the room. 'Abbey's had a very rough day. I don't want to push her. Why don't I make dinner here? There are chops in the freezer and beer in the fridge.'

'No way,' said Ben. 'I said you weren't going to cook, and I meant it. Come on, Jake. We'll drive into Wingham, pick up some drinks and take away.'

It was late, almost midnight. Kim and Ben sat together on the couch in the lounge room, his arm draped lazily across her shoulder. A dying fire lay in the grate. An empty bottle of shiraz stood on the coffee table. Ben topped up their glasses from a second bottle.

The closing scenes of *Ghost* played out before them. Kim, who hadn't seen the movie before, was entranced. A dead husband returning to protect his wife. What an intriguing concept. Molly's grief at Sam's death was painfully personal, and Kim lived every moment of their tragic love story right along with her. Molly was asking the same questions that Kim had been grappling with for two and half years. Is there an afterlife, and where do lost loved ones go? Will they be okay? Will we all be okay?

One scene in particular moved her. The eerie frisson of Sam's spirit possessing Whoopi Goldberg, so he could share one final dance with the grieving Molly. It moved Kim to tears. Would she recognise Connor if he came back like that? She had no doubt she would.

Ben was caught up in the show too, although for different reasons. *Ghost* wasn't just a love story. It also meshed crime and action and had some great comic lines. They were lost on her, but Ben was getting plenty of laughs; he'd seemed oblivious to the way the movie was affecting her. The haunting strains of The Righteous Brothers' *Unchained Melody* sounded as the credits rolled. 'Now that,' Kim said as she drained her glass, 'was one amazing love story.'

Ben trailed a finger down her cheek. 'We could make an amazing love story of our own, you know.'

Then his arms were around her, sure and hard. His hand slipped beneath her shirt as he kissed her with exquisite softness, velvet smooth, his tongue tracing the fullness of her mouth. Then more hungrily as she pressed her lips to his, responding to the passion in his kiss. He tasted of aftershave and wine. She wanted to want him, wanted to be swept away with desire. Wanted to reclaim a libido which she sometimes thought lost forever.

Ben's breath became ragged, and he nuzzled her neck. 'Come to bed.'

She let him take her hand and lead her down the hall. When Kim reached Abbey's door, she hesitated. 'I should check . . . '

'Shh.' He tugged at her hand. His simmering urgency swayed her, and she followed him. The curtains were open and the moon shone through, highlighting the bed, leaving the rest swathed in darkness. It didn't look like her room at all, which was probably a good thing.

Ben undressed her with extravagant care, as if she was a costly gift. First her shirt. Buttons coming loose, one by one, exposing the soft swell of her breasts, her belly. Her jeans came down. She stepped out of them, on display before him in a black bra and knickers. His gaze roamed admiringly over her body. Surreal, to be an object of desire again. She slipped the T-shirt over his head. Running hands down his muscled chest, his ribbed belly with its trail of fair hair heading south. Making unavoidable comparisons. How long had it been since she'd touched a man other than Connor?

Ben stood stock still as she explored his torso, his skin. Undoubtedly a beautiful body, and he knew it. In perfect proportion, pulsing with desire for her. Magnificent. So why did she feel at a loss? Here she stood, almost naked, with this gorgeous man who cared for her. Yet where was the jolt of electricity, the hammer in her heart? Where was the overwhelming need? Instead she felt strangely detached. Flattered, yes. Curious, certainly. But that was all. The only buzz was from the wine. This wasn't Sam returning to Molly. Ben was a poor copy of Connor.

Kim squeezed her palms to her eyes. 'I can't do this.'

He took her hands in his, separated each finger, and kissed the tips, one by one. 'I know it's been a while, but don't worry. We'll take it slow.' His voice sounded strange and loud in the dark.

She jerked away and turned on the light. 'You don't understand. I don't want to. I thought I did, but I don't.'

Ben gave her an I-don't-believe-what-I'm-hearing kind of smile. He stripped off his jeans and fell back on the bed, the picture of lazy confidence. Raising himself on one elbow, he said, 'We've got all night for you to change your mind.'

'No, we don't.' Kim pulled on her jeans. 'I'm serious. You have to leave.'

His expression shifted from self-assured to disbelieving to astonished. 'What? You mean you really want me to go?'

'Yes. ' Kim shoved his clothes at him. 'Could you please get dressed.' She pulled on a dressing gown and headed for the kitchen to put on the kettle.

A few minutes later, Ben emerged from the hall, buttoning his shirt - his face stony. 'If I'd known I was going home, I wouldn't have drunk a whole bottle of wine.'

'You're welcome to sleep in the spare room.'

'The spare room.' Ben shot her a sour, sarcastic smile. 'You're a piece of work, you know that?' He picked up his wallet and keys from the bench. 'Beauty of Tingo, eh? No booze buses.' She didn't know what to say, tried to smile.

'Anyway, I'm too stirred up to sleep.' He squeezed his eyes shut for a moment. 'Before I go, I think I deserve a reason.'

'I can't give you one,' she said. 'It just wasn't working.'

'Speak for yourself.' He rearranged the crotch of his jeans. 'You sure know how to take the wind out of a bloke's sails. Well, I guess that's it. See you.'

Kim waited until she heard his car leave before making herself an extra milky hot chocolate and taking it to bed. She turned on the bedside lamp. It cast a familiar shadow on the wall. The room was her own again – lonely, but all hers. It seemed inconceivable that ten minutes before, Ben had been lying in this very place, naked.

She finished the chocolate, turned out the light and snuggled down. Mel would never believe she'd turfed the dazzling Ben Steele from her bed. She could barely believe it herself. Would she regret her decision in the morning? She was too drunk to tell, and didn't dare think about Jake. Abbey would be happy, at any rate, and Dusty. Daisy too.

What had Daisy said? 'You've got the wrong man.'

Kim felt for the empty place on her finger. For once she didn't feel compelled to put the ring back on. Tonight she could sleep without it. Kim closed her eyes and drifted into a wine-induced slumber, and at the edge of dreaming she saw Taj's face.

CHAPTER 36

A loud banging jarred her from sleep. Barely light, and someone was knocking on the front door. More like pounding, or was that just her head? No, there it came again. Loud, angry, out of control. She checked the time. Seven o'clock on a Saturday morning. What on earth?

Kim shuffled down the hall in her dressing gown, with furry teeth and a headache.

Geoff Masters stood on the porch, his legs planted wide. Water dripped from his hat. Yesterday's sunshine had given way to grey skies and rain.

'A friendly warning to you, Kim. My wife comes home on Monday and I don't want you filling her head with any more garbage about dingoes. Wild dogs are the natural enemy of livestock, it stands to reason. But my Mel's gullible, always has been, and for some reason you seem to be able to talk her into all kinds of crackpot schemes.'

'Your Mel?' Kim could just imagine how furious Mel would be at this characterisation.

'And another thing – leave my boy alone while you're at it. Todd was spouting some nonsense about wolves saving Yellowstone. He could only have got that from you.'

Kim did her best to appear imposing, which was difficult with pillow hair and a pilled dressing gown. 'You're wasting your time, Geoff. I'll speak to whoever I like, whenever I like, and that includes Mel. You don't run her life, and you certainly don't run mine.'

His fleshy face reddened. 'Why don't you close your goddamned mouth?'

Kim didn't respond at once. Mel had warned her about Geoff and his anger. 'Once he starts, you have to shut up. He's like a string of firecrackers. You have to let each one explode until it's through, and not let it touch you.' What must it have been like, being married to such a man?

Geoff thrust his face closer, a mask of contempt and rage, and something else . . .

'Was it you, Geoff, sneaking around here in the dark? You don't scare me. If there's one more sign on my gate or one more harassing text, I'll call in the police.'

'You stupid bitch.' He spat on the ground.' Those dingoes are as good as dead.'

Kim slammed the door in his face, too shaken to remember exactly what she'd said - apart from the lie. He did scare her. How he must have scared Mel.

A long shower took away some of the fear, along with strong coffee, toast and Panadol. What her mother said was true: things did look better in the morning. Kim felt more positive, almost human. Her thoughts turned to Ben. How was he feeling this morning, she wondered? She'd been afraid of waking up full of regret. But no, her decision about Ben had been the right one. He wasn't the man for her.

Jake emerged from his room, sleepy-eyed, and looked around the kitchen. 'Mum, where's Dusty? He's not in my room.'

A wave of guilt swept over her. Last night she hadn't checked in on the kids as usual. And in the confusion of Ben leaving, she hadn't fastened the dog-proof safety chain on the back door. She had no idea when Dusty might have gone walkabout.

'He'll be back when he's hungry.'

Dusty had wandered overnight before and come back safely. There was no reason to suspect this time would be any different. Yet in the back of Kim's mind was a haunting vignette – the dingoes circling around her, shadowy figures shrouded in mist. Dusty shifting at their centre, the darkest shadow of all.

She wished Taj was back. It felt as if he'd been gone forever. She tried ringing him, but it went to voicemail.

The weather closed in further as the morning wore on. Jake had gone looking for Dusty in the paddocks and neither of them were back yet. Kim and Abbey sat on the verandah, staring out at the grey curtain of rain, the firewheel tree dark and sodden, the willow peppermint slumped under the weight of the water.

'Aren't we going to look too?' Abbey asked

'I thought we should wait for Jake to get back.'

'We could leave him a note?'

'Okay. Go get your coat.'

Kim gazed hopefully down the track. No dingo, no boy. Just a wet sky. Wait, there he was, trudging up from the sheds, shoulders hunched against the rain. Thank goodness. Kim prayed for the figure of a dog to be trotting at his heels: wanted it so badly that for one glorious moment she could see Dusty, clear as day. But it was a trick of the light.

'We'll start down on the road,' Kim said, resolving to not say anything about Jake's red eyes.

She turned left out of the gate and drove a few kilometres. Nothing. Back again and past their drive. A couple of kilometres on, her heart froze as a dark shape loomed on the verge. She slowed – a dead wombat. She felt ashamed for being so pleased.

The downpour redoubled its efforts. Poor Dusty, he was a sook with rain. Even with the windscreen wipers working overtime, it was hard to see. She pulled over for an oncoming car. Bangalow Road was too narrow for overtaking at the best of times, let alone when the runoffs each side ran like rivers.

'Look, Mum. It's Taj.'

Abbey was right. The familiar old ute, caked in mud, piled high with tools. She closed her eyes and sagged with relief. Taj stopped his car. He came across to her, took her hand, his dark eyes the brightest thing in the rain-soaked day, his hand full of strength. Taj would know where to find Dusty.

Taj did find Dusty. His body lay in plain sight, in a paddock above the billabong. Too late to keep the kids away. The four of them stood and stared. The rain had stopped, and as if in tribute, blue bands of sky appeared. A shaft of sunshine reached the ground.

Kim knelt down, blood thundering in her ears.

Dusty seemed smaller in death, sweeter, like a puppy again. His open eyes still seemed to see. He must be cold, with his fur all flat and bedraggled like that and his plumed tail lying in a puddle. She knelt down, reached out, touched him. It felt holy, like a psalm. An electric charge filled the space between them: expanding, intensifying, until she was sure the air itself would explode and jolt Dusty back to life. She waited, but it didn't happen. The bloody hole in his head saw to that.

Abbey began to cry. Kim gazed at her children, her own heart breaking, thinking of that last day and how she'd pushed Dusty away. Jake's lip trembled. With buckling knees he fell on Dusty, stroking his still form, pulling his ears and tickling his tummy the way he liked. Jake looked at her, beseeching, disbelieving. His pain unbearable. Kim shook her head. No, this couldn't possibly be happening.

Taj swept Dusty up, and cradled like a babe in arms, carried him to his car. Jake walked beside them, a hand on Dusty's collar, while Kim and Abbey trailed behind. Taj laid the dingo with tender care on a tarpaulin in the back. He covered Dusty with a blanket and folded a T-shirt to pillow his head.

Jake jumped in beside him.

'No darling, you need to come in our car.'

'Leave him,' said Taj. 'The boy must say goodbye.'

Kim hesitated, then nodded. Taj fastened the side-gate, and cleared a place for Jake to sit. She laid a hand on Taj's arm. Her pain was his pain too. 'Thank you.'

His hat lay low over his eyes, but there was no hiding his silent tears. This could break them all.

CHAPTER 37

aj watched Kim move around the kitchen, going through the motions, making coffee and hot chocolate. Her face was deathly white. This wasn't the time to tell her what he'd discovered about Ben Steele.

He sat with the children at the table. Jake quiet. Abbey weeping in a steady stream, as if it was now her normal way of being. Without thinking, he opened his arms. She moved into them, and buried her head in his shoulder. Poor child, she must be nearly out of tears.

'Dusty loves you, little one. He wouldn't want you to cry.'

'But he doesn't want to be dead,' she said between sobs. 'He wants to come back. He's lonely.'

'No, no. He misses you all, but he isn't lonely. He's happy, playing with his mother and father.' He gently lifted Abbey's chin. Kim had stopped to listen. 'It is you who are lonely without him, yes?'

Abbey nodded.

He gave her a tissue from a box on the table, and she blew her nose.

'Our daddy's dead. Is he happy too?'

'Of course. He has plenty of friends in heaven, right?'

Kim sat down, a little more colour in her cheeks.

'There's Grandma, and Poppy, for starters. And Ron and Macka. Auntie Joan.'

'And Scout,' said Jake. 'He was our first dog. I wish he could meet Dusty. Do you think Scout will meet Dusty?'

Taj's smile was one of infinite reassurance. 'Oh, I'm sure they will meet,' he said. 'Since you have wished it, Jake. Heaven is a magical place where wishes come true.'

'How do you know so much about heaven?' asked Abbey.

'Many people I love live there.'

Abbey had stopped crying. 'Mum, why didn't you ever tell me that heaven was magical?'

Kim looked bewildered. 'I don't think I knew myself.'

'Does it make you feel better, Mummy, now that you know, I mean?'

'Why yes.' Kim pulled Abbey onto her knee. 'Yes, it does.' She hugged her child for the longest time. 'Why don't you finish your cocoa, sweetheart, before it grows cold,' she said at last. When Abbey hopped off, Kim gave Taj a meaningful look. 'Could I talk to you alone please?'

He followed her onto the verandah, wanted to take her in his arms and comfort her, the way he had done for Abbey.

'Dusty was shot in the head, wasn't he?'

Taj took two empty shell casings from his pocket. 'I found these, and tyre tracks.'

'Of all the vile, despicable acts.' She ran her hand over the railing of the verandah, the painting he'd done worn in now, no longer new. 'Geoff Masters was here this morning, making threats.'

'What sort of threats?'

'Against the dingoes. There've been signs left on the gate as well, some awful texts.'

Taj felt sick. What was wrong with him? Why wasn't he ever there when people needed him? 'Have you called the police?'

'That would really endear me to the town, wouldn't it?' She searched his face. 'Is there any way you can tell who killed' – she struggled to say the words – 'who killed Dusty?'

'Maybe. I'd need the—'

She held up her hand. 'I don't want to know. Take Dusty's body if it helps.' Her voice broke. 'We can bury him later.'

This was his fault. He should have been there to protect Dusty. To protect them all. 'Shall I stay?'

'No, I need time alone with the kids – to decide what to do.' There was that haunted smile again. 'What you did for Abbey, telling her about a heaven filled with magic and miracles . . .'

'I'm sorry, I spoke out of turn.'

'No, you helped her a lot.' Her eyes held his. 'I think you helped me too. Is that an Islamic belief?'

He bowed his head, suddenly shy. 'No, it is only my belief.'

'Well, now it's mine too.' Kim caught his large, rough hand in her small one. 'There was a time I didn't want Dusty. Now I'd sell my soul for one more day.' She squeezed his hand. 'Find out who did this.'

Taj couldn't remember driving home. Dusty's death had dredged up memories of a time in his life that he'd crossed the world to forget. He settled the dogs, then went inside. In his bedside drawer was a pouch he hadn't looked at since coming to Australia, though for many years he'd carried it in a shirt pocket, close to his heart. He took it out now. Inside was a handful of sand, and the photo of a black wolf with piercing yellow eyes. Aakil. Taj lay on the bed, allowing the tide of emotion to wash over him. A surrender. He let his eyelids fall, and he was back in the shadowy forest of the Hindu Kush, following a wolf trail through stands of cedar and blue pine.

Taj pulled off his muddy boots, and pushed through an ivy curtain at the back door. Spring in Nuristan had come early this year, the garden bursting with new growth. Camila sat at the table, stuffing small plastic gift bags with toothpaste, toothbrushes and floss. Freebies for patients coming to the mobile dental clinic the following week.

She looked tired. Taj swept back the lock of fair hair escaping from her scarf and kissed her. Camila laughed, and pushed him away in mock distaste. 'Can't you wait until you wash up?'

'No.' Taj hungrily reclaimed her lips. As much as he loved his job, being away from Camila so much was pure torture. He released her, flushed and smiling. He wanted to take her to bed then and there.

Instead he went to the kitchen and washed his hands in a bowl at the sink. 'Poachers are on the move,' he said. 'Malik found an abandoned camp, the remains of a moon bear and her cub. He said they were heading for Wadi Gorge.'

Camila's lovely face creased with concern. 'Aren't your wolves there?'

Taj nodded. 'They've denned in readiness for Zahra to give birth. Malik and I will hike out to check on them in the morning. But first, I must take you to your parents' house.'

'You just want an excuse to visit Aakil.'

He couldn't deny he was looking forward to seeing the orphaned black cub he'd raised from birth. Aakil may be grown, and leader of his own pack now, but they were still brothers. Camila glided over, pressed against his back and put her arms around his waist. 'I don't want to stay with Amma. She fusses over me, makes me drink milk.'

'Good.' Taj spun her round, stroked her growing belly. 'I'll be gone just a few days, a week at the most.'

'That long?' Camila's lips found his, feather-light at first, then more demanding. He swept her into his arms, and carried her to the bedroom.

He and Malik set off at first light. Their driver took them as far as he could. At the end of the road they unloaded guns and gear, hefted their packs and hiked off into the wild western forest. Sunshine glanced off snow-capped peaks. Wildflowers bloomed in grassy clearings. Delicate buds of alder and birch unfurled in bursts of emerald green, and the air was aromatic with pine needles. A place of vast beauty.

The poachers' camp lay a two-hour march from the road. No attempt had been made to hide it, nor the skinned bodies of the bear and her tiny cub, whose heads and paws had been cut off. These were brazen men. Taj examined the carcasses, no more than two days old. The meat had been abandoned, not something opportunistic locals would do. This was a well-organised hunting party, and he and Malik were outnumbered. They counted the tracks of five men. It would take all their ingenuity to arrest them, but they'd done it before. The element of surprise was on their side.

Rugged Wadi Gorge was a two-day hike away, at the tip of a remote valley, where the broad Pashtu River flowed between high granite cliffs. Zahra's tracking collar told Taj the hand-raised pack had selected Wadi for their den site. A wise choice. The valley boasted an abundance of wild goats, hares, markhor and ibex. It boded well for the wolves first breeding season.

It was a hard climb at first. They needed ropes to navigate the narrow rocky overhangs. At one time Malik slipped, falling metres down a shaly scree, his fall broken by a spindly juniper tree, clinging recklessly to the cliff face. Yet, despite these setbacks, they were gaining on their quarry, who were laden down with skins.

The poachers had set snares as they went. Taj removed them one by one. He released a little beech marten, and two jungle cats trapped by their paws. At lunchtime they passed where the poachers had camped last night, a level clearing below a cliff face. They exchanged tired smiles – they were only half-a-day behind. Flayed bodies lay scattered on the ground: ibex, foxes, even a rare Marco Polo sheep, Afghanistan's national animal. Its severed head, with two-metre spiralling horns, was tied to the fork of a tree: a prize to be retrieved on the return journey. A frowning Taj carried it to the top of a jagged outcrop, and cast it over the edge.

They camped that night beside a swirling confluence of rivers, running high with snowmelt. Taj had hoped the trail might veer west, towards the headwaters of the Siah. But no such luck. The poachers were following the Pashtu, heading straight for the gorge, and wolf pelts were worth big money in the markets of Kabul.

Next morning – disaster. Malik's fall had been worse than they thought, his ankle swollen like a balloon overnight. He could barely stand. 'I can manage with a stick.'

'You'll slow me down.' Taj began packing his gear.

'You can't go on by yourself.'

'Watch me.' Taj shrugged on the rucksack and grabbed his rifle. 'You head back and report what's happened. Keep out of sight. They'll return this way.'

Taj shunned the easy path along the river, reaching Wadi Gorge that afternoon well ahead of the poachers. He took up a sheltered position on a ridge to wait. Once he stopped moving, the cold seeped into his bones. Hours later, when a line of armed men appeared below, every part of him was numb. They picked their way along the stony river-bank. Too many to take single-handed. Driving them off would have to do for now.

From his vantage point, Taj had a good view as they made camp. He couldn't pick out faces, but a tall grey-bearded man seemed to be their leader. Hours ticked by, and at last the cold sun dipped behind the mountains. When it was almost dark and they were cooking meat on their fire, Taj made his move. Lying on his stomach, he aimed the rifle and shot the canteen from the hands of Grey-beard. He shot the pot hanging over the flames, spilling boiling water over the nearest two men. Screams, as he made mincemeat of their bundles of animal skins.

Wild volleys of return fire rang around the cliffs, but in the failing light the frantic men could neither spot him, nor identify where the bullets came from. They were sitting ducks, and knew it. Taj's next shots strafed their tents, and the men had had enough. They fled back along the river.

In the morning Taj crept down to investigate the deserted camp. The poachers' tracks in the damp earth showed the story of their panicked flight. With any luck, Malik and his men would be waiting when the poachers tried to escape the forest. He threw their bundled skins and trophies into the dark, swift-running waters of the Pashtu, and set off up the gorge.

His electronic tracker revealed the wolves were close. So as not to alarm them, he cupped his hand to his mouth and howled, a long, double-toned note that swelled in volume and echoed off the ravine walls. The howl of a lost pack member. An answer came swiftly. Minutes later, a large, black wolf appeared on a ledge above him. Aakil. A second wolf appeared, and a third and a fourth.

One bound and they were upon him in a frenzy of greeting, nuzzling his mouth and rubbing themselves along his body. With a jaunty sweep of his tail, Aakil led him to the den, a roomy, well-concealed fissure in the cliff-face. Zahra was curled around six fat pups, two of them jet-black like their father. She was not pleased to see Taj, flattening her ears and baring her teeth.

'I won't bother them, mama bear.' He backed off, his grin as wide as the mighty Pashtu. Proud as any father. His assortment of waifs and strays had grown into a tight-knit, functional pack. The cubs were proof of that.

Suddenly the hairs on the back of his neck stood up, and Aakil raised his hackles, sensing an approaching threat. The pair stole from the den.

What a fool he'd been, reckless and over-confident. An armed poacher had followed them into the gorge. Taj and Aakil sought cover behind a pile of boulders, as the man took aim. The rifle roared. Bullets smashed into the rocks around them, raising puffs of dust, yet missing their mark. Taj aimed his own weapon, but the poacher was well protected too, ensconced behind a stony buttress. They exchanged pointless fire, both pinned down to their positions: a stand-off.

Taj recognised the new danger too late. A second shooter. He whirled to see a rifle barrel clear the boulders behind him. In a flash Aakil had launched himself over the barrier, whacking the weapon aside as he went. The rounds intended for Taj slammed into the wolf. With an anguished cry, Taj scaled the boulders, firing again and again, until he was sure the poacher was dead. He turned to see the first man running from the gorge.

Two bloodied bodies lay at the foot of the scree. Aakil and the poacher, side by side in death.

Taj knelt beside his fallen friend and bowed his head. One by one the wolves emerged from the den. Each in turn touched noses with Aakil. Last came Zahra. She lay beside him for a while, head across his bloody neck. Then as one, the wolves tipped up their muzzles and sang their sadness to the sky. Taj joined in the melancholy cry. The pack could not afford to be sentimental. Soon other males would fight for the right to mate with Zahra, but for now they were united in grief.

At some invisible signal, the wolves melted away, leaving Taj alone. He would bury Aakil by the river where he loved to play. Taj turned his attention to the dead man, lying face down in the dirt. With an effort Taj rolled him over and tugged the shemagh from his face. He blanched. Grey-beard — and Taj knew him.

Aakil must remain where he fell. Taj scrambled down to the Pashtu and lay face down, drinking his fill of its sweet life-giving water. He took two handfuls of river sand and, returning to the scree, cast one over the dead wolf.

'Goodbye, Aakil, my brother. Forgive me.'

Taj slipped the second handful into his pocket, and set off. He had to get back to the village before it was too late.

CHAPTER 38

When Ben arrived that afternoon, he found Kim in her bedroom, packing.

'You're leaving?' He paused. 'Not because of last night?'

'Oh, Ben, I don't know. Because of last night, because of today . . . because of a lot of things.'

'Are those tears?' He took her hand and led her into the kitchen. 'What, you're leaving for good? You sit. I'll make a cuppa.' He handed her a wad of tissues from the box on the bench.

She blew her sandpaper nose. Her whole face hurt, dry and salty from crying.

'I reckon we can get past last night.'

'Thank you, Ben, you're very sweet. But the truth is, I don't want to. I thought I did, but apparently I'm not ready. I'm just as surprised as you are.'

Ben's laugh was hollow. 'I doubt that.'

'There's something else, something terrible – Dusty was shot last night, down by the billabong.'

'I'm so sorry Kim. Is he . . . ?'

'Yes.' This bald statement of fact almost provoked fresh tears. She knuckled them away. 'I can't stay here.'

'Give it a few days.'

'Why? What will change? There's nothing for me.' Her words came out in a rush. 'You and I haven't worked out. Mel hates me. Loonies with guns are roaming the place at night. The town's turned against us. Geoff Masters is making threats. I don't want to check my messages. I'm scared every time I come home that there'll be a disgusting sign on the gate. I'm suspicious of everybody. The kids are copping it at school. The last thing Jake needs is to become a pariah again, especially for something that's not even his fault.' She paused for breath. 'And now some bastard's shot Dusty dead. The truth is, I don't want to spend one more minute in Tingo.'

'Sounds like you've made up your mind.'

'If it wasn't for the kids, staying strong for them, I'd fall apart. It'll be easier in Sydney.'

She'd never seen Ben look sad before. 'I care a lot about you, Kim, you and your kids. Even Abbey.' This said with the hint of a smile. 'What a stinking, rotten thing to happen. I know how attached kids get to dogs. If there's anything I can do, just say the word.'

'There is something,' said Kim. 'Find me a very special buyer for Journey's End. Someone who appreciates a unique conservation opportunity when they see it, and who'll put up with the dingoes. I don't care about the price. I'd happily give it away to the right person.'

'You're sure?'

'Certain.'

'I've got someone on my books right now. An older lady, very private. She's looking for a bushland retreat, somewhere with plenty of wildlife. She doesn't want to farm, so the conservation covenant won't be a problem. The thing is, she doesn't have a big budget, and is in a hurry. Do you want me to give her a ring?'

'Sounds perfect. I'm in a hurry too. Can I meet her, do you think, if she's interested?'

'I don't think that'll be possible. As I said, she's a very private person.'

'Then could you give her a letter? I'd want her to know about the history of the place, about the plants and animals.' Kim's hands started to shake. Her insides were twisting at the thought of leaving Journey's End, but twisting even more at the thought of staying. 'Call me and let me know.'

'Why don't I come over after work on Monday? Tell you how I got on?'

Kim tried to speak, but instead made only a strange choking sound. She tried again. 'We're leaving for Sydney tonight – going to stay with Daisy.' She stood and wrapped her arms around Ben's solid warmth one last time. 'I'm going to miss you.'

Ben hugged her back, a little awkwardly. 'What about Mel?' he said. 'And Taj, and Jean? Do they know you're leaving? Does anyone?'

'I've been trying to ring Taj, but he's not answering. Will you tell him I'm sorry I didn't say goodbye? And Mel too? Tell them I'll ring them, and that they can have the plants in the rainforest nursery. And let Jean know the kids aren't coming back to school.'

Jake came into the kitchen, looking naked without Dusty by his side. He seemed to have shrunk. He wouldn't speak, or eat, or cry – he was just a blank thing.

'See ya, champ,' said Ben, with a final salute.

Jake watched him leave with dead eyes. Kim knew that look. Her son had crawled back to a place where Dusty was still alive, and she wanted to join him there.

By three o'clock the possums, wallabies and quolls were rounded up and delivered next door to Mel's astonished sister. By four o'clock the car was packed and ready to go. Kim did a final check of the house, slipping Scout's ashes into her pocket before she pulled the back door shut. By five o'clock, they were nearing the coast road turn-off, and speeding straight for Sydney.

CHAPTER 39

aj had been crouching on a rise above Granite Hills homestead since lunchtime, waiting for Ben to leave. When the red land cruiser started off down the drive, he wasted no time. Moving at a scrambling run, vaulting the post and rails, he made a beeline for the vehicle shed.

Ben's old ute, with its remote-mounted spotlight, was parked outside. Taj pulled back the tarp. Just as he'd thought. Ben didn't believe firearm regulations applied to him. A rifle and boxes of ammo lay carelessly strewn in the tray under the tarp. Taj took up the Browning, a classy-looking rifle with a tactical scope. A precision weapon.

Taj worked quickly, with no idea how much time he had. At least Ben had the decency to leave the gun unloaded. Taj opened the breech, retracted the well-oiled bolt, thumbed bullets into the magazine and slid it home again. He put a log of wood underwater in the deep concrete trough at the cattle yards as a makeshift recovery tank, and shot four rounds into it. Cartridge shells arced to the ground, and he could smell burnt cordite.

Taj picked up the shells. Two of the bullets lay on the bottom, in perfect condition. The others had penetrated the log. He dug them out with a penknife. Mission accomplished. He stowed the rifle back in the ute, and made a swift getaway.

Back home, Taj set up his seed-identification microscope on the kitchen table. He possessed a good, working knowledge of ballistics, and had often matched bullets to poachers' weapons in Afghanistan. Who'd have thought such knowledge would prove useful in his new country?

He collected the bullets and cartridges for comparison: one from his test fire, and one that he'd gouged from Dusty's skull. The calibres matched. He compared the spent cartridges he'd found, and examined their micro-stamps under the microscope. All marked *Rem** for Remington Arms Co., the same brand that Ben used. So far, so good.

He compared the rifling impressions, distinct to each make and model of firearm. Another match. Finally, he painstakingly scrutinised the pattern of striations and scratches on each bullet. These were caused by grooves and imperfections in the barrel. Under the microscope they looked a bit like bar codes, and were individual to each particular rifle. They matched too.

There was no doubt about it; Ben had shot Dusty.

Afterwards he examined the bullet he'd taken from the spine of Mel's pregnant ewe, along with the spent shells he'd found at the scene. The result was crystal clear. Dingoes hadn't killed Mel's sheep. Ben had shot them too.

Taj arrived at Journey's End just on dark. He'd been agonising over how to tell Kim the news. She liked Ben, and so did Jake. She'd formed an attachment, although he didn't know how deep it ran. It still made no sense. What possible connection could Kim have with such a man? Women were mysterious creatures.

As he pulled in the gate, a peculiar emptiness crept over him.

Something was wrong. Bonnie and Clyde weren't in the garden. No lights in the house. No car in the drive.

He pushed his way through the unlockable back door, wandered from room to room. The fridge – empty and off, a tea towel over the door to keep it from closing. To stop the mould.

Kim was gone.

Taj fought to control his despair. Things couldn't end like this. He wouldn't let them. The logging, the sheep, Dusty; she had to know. The need to tell her roared inside him like dammed meltwater in spring, seeking release. Where would the truth go, without Kim? What use, to scream it to the mountains?

When Taj reached Kim on the phone next morning, her voice sounded far away, farther than Sydney, the distance more than geographic.

No, she hadn't said goodbye and was sorry. Yes, he should bury Dusty in the garden, maybe beneath the waratahs. No, she'd changed her mind, and didn't want to dwell on his death. Yes, she was staying in Sydney. No, she wasn't coming back.

Taj ended the call. The things he knew about Ben Steele, these were not things to be shared in phone calls or emails. But what was he to do? He had no idea where to find her. No idea if she'd listen if he did. Taj slammed the wall, filled with wild, impotent rage. He had to calm down; he had to try. Kim must learn the truth, face to face, and Ben must pay. There would be a way.

CHAPTER 40

When Kim first arrived at Daisy's, she could hardly hold up her head. Her weariness ran bone-deep.

Daisy hugged her. 'Why not let me look after things for a while. You take it easy.'

The first two days Kim did just that: sleeping late, rising later, and starting a Tolstoy novel of almost fifteen hundred pages that she'd found on a shelf. Trying not to think about how the possums were getting on, or whether the quolls would bite Nicole, or whether Mel was okay, or how Taj and his dingoes had wrecked everything. She fought a terrible restlessness. When the worries got the best of her, Daisy lent a sympathetic ear. Dear, sweet Daisy. It was a mini re-run of when Connor died.

Staying with Daisy was a tonic. The house in Holsworthy was modest, but comfortable and not too crowded, although the kids had to bunk in together. It even backed onto a park, a civilised affair of bare-branched poplar and oak trees, and one of those plastic-fantastic playgrounds with loads of rubber matting and no monkey bars. There was a dog, a portly spaniel with allergies named Oscar. Stu and Grace helped take the kids' minds off Dusty – when they weren't at school, that was. And she had Daisy to do the same thing.

Ben had rung with details of his buyer, a woman named Karen Thompson. She was keen on Journey's End, but offering a full fifty thousand dollars less than Kim's already-low asking price. 'Draw up the contract,' Kim said. 'I just want this over with.'

By the third day, she wasn't wearing her nerves on the outside of her skin anymore. All this practice must be making her better at grief. At six o'clock, when Steve came home from the barracks, Kim helped serve the evening meal of pot roast and vegetables.

'Guess what?' said Daisy. 'Steve knows your Taj.'

Kim stopped dishing out carrots. The sound of Taj's name sent a quiver right through her. He'd been on her mind more than she cared to admit, distracting her. She kept forgetting her place in *War and Peace*, having to reread pages, over and over.

'Taj Khan worked with our unit as a translator and cultural adviser,' said Steve as he carved the meat. 'Was that bloke ever fearless? No idea why, but he hated the Taliban more than we did. I helped arrange his Australian visa a few years ago under the interpreter immigration program. Connor knew him too.'

Kim tried to take in the information. Jake too, hanging off every one of Steve's words.

'Dad knew Taj?' A look of shame crossed his face. Kim felt for him through her own shock.

What a thing to find out. All this time practically living next door, working with Taj, pumping him for information about Afghanistan, and this connection had existed all along, right under her nose. Trust Daisy to find out more in five minutes than she had in nine months.

Connor had told her about the Afghan interpreters and the program to resettle them. 'They patrol with us, trudge the same stinking, booby-trapped tracks as us. Bleed the same blood. They're our lifeline, but to the Taliban they're traitors. We owe those blokes bigtime.' He and his mates had been fiercely loyal to these allies. One member of his unit had been awarded the Victoria Cross for risking his life to rescue a wounded interpreter under enemy fire.

'It's serendipity, that's what it is.' Daisy gave Kim's arm an affectionate squeeze.

Kim was quiet during dinner. Afterwards she helped Stuart and Grace do their homework, making her children join in, so they wouldn't be living in a totally education-free zone.

After the kids were in bed, Steve excused himself.

Daisy brought out a bottle of tokay, and poured them both a glass. 'You look like you could use a drink.'

'I can't believe it, about Taj I mean.'

'Oh, I know what you mean, alright.' Daisy stretched back in the armchair. 'I can't believe it either.'

That tone. Kim cocked her head. 'What?'

'That you don't know you've got a thing for him. He's all you talk about. *Taj this, Taj that, Taj ruined my life*. You're like a broken record.' Daisy wore her smuggest I-know-you-better-than-you-know-yourself smile. Kim opened her mouth to defend herself, but no words came.

CHAPTER 41

$\mathcal{K}$im woke to the sound of Oscar's steady barking, with the sun streaming in the window. A little groggy. All that tokay last night. She sat up in bed, sending her book sliding to the floor. She could hear the murmur of voices. Who was Daisy talking to?

'Come on, lazy-bones.' Daisy poked her head round the bedroom door. 'You have visitors. Don't keep them waiting.' She cast Kim an appraising glance. 'And you might want to brush your hair.'

'Who is it?' she whispered, but Daisy had disappeared.

Surely not her parents. They didn't know she was here, did they? Unless Daisy had told them. She wasn't quite ready for her mother to say 'I told you so.'

When Kim walked into the lounge room, an improbable sight greeted her. Taj and Mel sitting awkwardly together on the couch. Mel looked nervous and nursed a manila folder on her lap. Her hair was as messy as on the first day they met, a tangle of dark curls. Taj nodded a greeting, his dark hair falling over one eye like usual, following the angle of his scar. Muscles tense beneath his clothes, as if at any moment he might leap to his feet. He looked entirely out of place drinking coffee in Daisy's neat lounge room on her gold-and-white striped couch. Too large and alive. Too wild. Like a wolf masquerading as a family pet.

Her heart slowly tumbled in her chest.

'It's terrible about Dusty,' said Mel. 'I bawled my eyes out when I heard.'

Kim nodded, not trusting herself to speak. Was this why they'd come all this way? So Mel could express her sympathies? How did they even know where to find her? She went over to Mel, drew her into a hug.

'Are you okay?' she managed. 'I've been so worried. Where were you?'

'Doing an advanced training course in rehabilitating raptors.'

'Raptors?'

'Birds of prey,' said Mel. 'I want to specialise in eagles.'

'That's awesome,' said Kim. 'You're amazing.' Mel's cheeks flushed at the praise. 'We brought your mail. Winnie gave me your address off the redirection notice.' She took a single letter from the folder and held it out. 'I thought it might be important.'

Kim thanked her and put it on the coffee table. A promotion from the Rural Fire Service.

'There's something else,' said Mel.

Oh. Kim thought there might be. Jake came into the room and saw Taj. There was no more resentment in his eyes. Taj gravely nodded to Jake, who returned the gesture.

'Kim,' Mel continued, 'your dingoes didn't kill my sheep. It was Ben.'

'It was Ben what?'

Mel bit her lip and glanced at Taj. He shifted in his seat, but his face remained impassive. She went on. 'Ben shot the sheep. He shot Dusty too.'

The air grew thick. 'Wait a minute . . .'

Taj put a hand in his pocket and pulled out three sandwich bags. 'Bullets. This is from the spine of Mel's sheep.' He tossed it on the table. His tone was low and deliberate. 'I found this bullet lodged in Dusty's skull.' She flinched as it hit the table, saw Jake whiten. 'And these' – he held up the final bag – 'are bullets test fired from Ben's rifle. All a perfect match.'

'There must be some mistake.' She looked from one to the other, hoping. The knot of tension in the room twisted tight.

'No mistake.'

Kim swallowed, her throat a lump of sawdust as she put a hand on Jake's shoulder. Despite the absurd improbability of it, despite the shock and regret and terrible hurt, Kim did not doubt Taj for a moment.

Daisy stood up. 'How about I get us all a coffee?'

Taj drew something else out of his pocket. 'This is for you, Jake.' A photograph of the garden at Journey's End, the waratahs, upturned earth beneath them and a carved cross. 'I knew you would like to know where he is.'

Jake took the photo, eyes filled with tears.

'I'm going to the park.' He stopped at the door and turned to Taj. 'Thank you.' And then he was gone.

Mel put the manila table on the folder and opened it. 'There's more.'

Kim felt hollowed out. Bring it. Nothing could be worse than the treachery revealed so far.

'Ben's been buying up tracts of protected forest for a song, faking logging permits, clear-felling the land and selling the timber to a dodgy saw mill. He's raking in a fortune.'

Kim leafed through the documents, cautiously, as though they might bite. Purchase orders for vast tonnages of premium logs, the dollar amounts staggering, and the vendor's name – Ben Steele. She held up a form. 'This permit number . . . ?'

'It belongs to another property altogether.'

Something else caught her eye in the folder: a sworn valuer's report for Journey's End. 'Where'd you get this?'

'From Ben's home office,' said Taj. 'Don't ask.'

"This valuation's crazy. My land's not worth anything like that much.' The figure was twice what Karen Thompson had offered.

'It is if you count the standing timber as an asset,' said Mel. 'And that valuation doesn't mention any conservation covenant. Did you ever do a title search to check that it was registered?'

'Well no. I always left things like that to Connor.'

'Who arranged it for you?'

Kim slapped her forehead. 'Walter Steele. Ben's father. Looks like Ben inherited his dodgy from dear old dad.'

'I'm sorry, Kim. This must be hitting you pretty hard,' said Mel. 'We know you're sweet on him.'

Of course. They didn't know she and Ben were no longer an item.

'Taj!' Abbey cannoned into the room like an excited puppy, Daisy right behind her. 'Have you come to take us home?'

Mel's eyes widened with hope. Kim whet her lips and looked at Taj. For a long moment, they held each other's gaze. Daisy raised her brows and gave Kim a what-do-you-reckon? kind of smile. And Kim was no longer lost. She knew exactly what she had to do.

CHAPTER 42

Kim walked into the Taree office of Steele & Son. Gleaming chrome, lots of glass and bold abstract prints on the wall. Very swish for a country real estate agent. A thin, heavily made-up young woman sat at reception. 'Can I help you?'

'Would you tell—'

'I know that voice.' Ben sauntered round the corner, files in hand. 'Kim.' He gestured for her to come through. 'What a lovely surprise,' he said, once they were seated in his spacious office. 'How are things?'

'Much better for seeing you.'

He flashed her a dazzling smile. 'That's the shot. The contract's ready, by the way. We could grab some lunch and go over it?'

Kim looked at him. Why had Ben wanted her? Were there dollar signs in his eyes every time he'd been at her house? How had she missed them? She could barely see the resemblance to Connor now. And knew that there was none of Connor's goodness in him. She wished with a sharp powerful ache that Connor could see her. He would be cheering her on.

'The contract with that sweet little old lady who hugs trees and wants to retire to the bush?' she asked. 'Who is she really, Ben? Your secretary, your sister – your girlfriend?'

Ben's smile slipped and he got up to shut the door. She could see his mind working, trying to gauge what she knew.

'You shot Mel's sheep. What was that about? An accident? Or did you hope my dingoes would get the blame, because that's exactly what happened, isn't it?' A pause. 'And then, of course, there's Dusty.'

Ben held up his hand. 'Whoa, that was a mistake. After you chucked me out of bed that night, Geoff and I went hunting. I shot a dingo. You can't blame a man for that, they're vermin. I didn't know it was Dusty until the next day when you told me. But I did you a favour, Kim. He was bound to turn savage.'

'You knew?'

'Oh, I knew he was a dingo all right,' said Ben. 'From the moment I spotted that black and tan dog on the scalper's truck. Spitting image of Dusty.' His confidence was returning. 'Why not let me organise a well-bred kelpie for Jake? That's if you have room for a dog in Sydney.'

Kim stood up. 'I'm not going to Sydney. As a matter of fact, the kids and I are on our way back to Journey's End right now. It's officially off the market. And if you ever set foot on my land again, it might not just be defenceless animals that get shot.'

The sun lay low in the sky when Kim sank down on the frayed verandah chair. How she'd missed this place: the transparent sky, the mountains soft with purple haze. Jake, Abbey, Todd and Nikki were making a tree house in the old willow peppermint. She loved seeing them like this, four friends together.

Kim studied Mel as she poured the champagne. She looked very beautiful. Dark curls framing a face full of character and warmth. Skinny jeans that showed off her trim figure, with bling on the back pockets. Those gorgeous dark-red boots. Mel seemed to live in those boots nowadays. How badly Kim had underestimated her when they first met. She hadn't recognised the loyal, brave, clever woman behind the plain façade.

Mel held up her glass. 'To homecomings.'

The perfect toast. That's exactly what Journey's End was now – home.

Kim took a big sip, and let the tingling bubbles slip down her throat. It had been quite a day. The long drive from Sydney. The stopover in Taree to confront Ben along the way. Unpacking. The fun and confusion of rounding up their menagerie at Mel's place and bringing them back where they belonged. She should be exhausted, and she was, physically at least. But Kim couldn't shake the restlessness that had plagued her in Sydney.

Mel must have read her mind. 'I'll feed the kids,' she said. 'You go see Taj.'

She found him on the hill above his house, driving post-holes and stringing wire. Her body came alive at the sight of him.

Taj put down his tools and came to meet her, the dogs bounding ahead of him. He stopped short of her, seeming hesitant. 'It's good to see you.'

'We need to talk,' said Kim.

'What about?'

'Not here,' she said. 'I mean we need to sit down together, with no distractions and *really* talk. And we need to do it now.'

He followed her to the house. Kim took a seat in the kitchen, and indicated the chair opposite. Taj sat down.

'Why did you leave Afghanistan?'

His response was short and swift. 'The war.'

'No, that won't do. It's like me telling people I'm a widow, so they don't ask any more questions. What was the actual reason?'

He looked a little lost. 'My life there was over.'

'Right . . . you see, that doesn't tell me anything. I know you worked with the Australian forces. Did you know my husband, Connor Sullivan?'

'I remember the name.'

Kim took a moment. 'Okay, we'll definitely go back to that one.' She sat forward in her chair. 'But what about before?' He looked out the window. She wanted to scream and shake him. 'What about your life, your family? What about the money and toys you send to Kabul each month? For God's sake, Taj, tell me something important, something that matters.'

'Why?' He leaned close and brushed her cheek with his fingers. 'Why do you want to know.'

'You know why, don't you? By now.'

Taj let his hand drop and his expression changed, growing sharp and focused, like a filter had fallen from the lens of his eyes.

'You can't un-hear it, Kim. That is the thing.'

'Go on.'

He began to speak, the cadence of his voice spellbinding.

He told her of a wild forest, dangerous beyond imagining, that sheltered the world's most mythical animals. Creatures from fairy tales: moon bears, lynx, wolves and snow leopards. Of Aakil, a black wolf he'd raised from a cub and loved as a brother. A wolf who'd died to save his life. And of how he'd killed a man. His story moved her to tears.

Taj didn't try to comfort her. He let her cry.

Kim blew her nose. 'So that's why you quit your ranger job?'

Taj looked up at her. No, he looked through her. Perhaps he didn't see her at all. He was somewhere else. 'The man I killed was the father of Abas Abid, a local Taliban commander. When I returned home, my wife Camila was dead. Her mother and father, dead. Our unborn child, dead.'

Time stopped.

This was what she was after; this terrible truth of the heart, a truth he'd revealed to no one, maybe not to God himself. A truth that made sense of Taj's life. The trust it took staggered her.

Kim reached across the table for his work-roughened hand, a hand with dirt beneath the fingernails, and embedded in the fine lines of skin. A most beautiful hand. She touched his face, traced the raised, silvery scar down his cheek. Her eyes asked the question. A vein throbbed at his throat.

'I died that day. My friends were deceived because I still breathed, and spoke, and rose from my bed in the morning. I ate and drank and buried my family. But it was an imitation of life. I was already in hell, and my one desire was for Abid to join me there.'

Kim let out a cry. She'd been in that same vengeful place. Anger burning in her bones. Jealous of the soldiers who'd tracked down Connor's killers, because she wanted to murder them herself.

'I discovered where Abid lived, and disguised myself as one of his men. He invited me in. It felt good to know his death was as close as the pistol in my pocket. When Abid realised, he snivelled and begged like a coward. I made him say Camila's name, so he would know why he died.'

Taj's voice faltered. He shoved back his chair, and walked to the window.

Kim went to him. 'Tell me.'

'Then I saw her, a young woman, belly big with child. A tiny boy too, wide-eyed while I put a gun to his father's head.'

Kim remembered to breathe. 'You couldn't do it, could you?'

'This girl and her son were as innocent as my Camila. Afghanistan is a dangerous place for women without husbands and children without fathers. As I turned to go, she called a warning. Abid had pulled a knife from his robes. He slashed my cheek, before I shot him.'

Kim wrapped her arms around his shoulders and held him like she'd never let him go. 'And the girl who warned you?'

'Damira was only seventeen. She hated Abid. I took her and the boy with me to Kabul. Eight weeks later she gave birth to a daughter.'

'The money and presents are for her.'

He nodded. 'School fees and some extra besides. Damira works in a shelter now, helping child-brides escape their husbands.'

Kim blinked and looked around. The room was the same as an hour ago: the same rough-hewn table, bentwood chairs, cast-iron stove. The same forested slopes beyond the windows. Yet the world was changed, utterly and forever. 'Now you've told me something important.' She held his hand. 'Take me to the mountains.'

They stood on the lookout under a painted sky. An ancient tract of rainforest stretched out to the south - safe now, because of Taj. Sunset had turned Devil Falls to a ribbon of fire. Taj touched her arm, and the fire was on her skin. He pointed to the replanted paddock below them, with its thriving jungle of saplings. 'Look.'

Last time it was goats. This time it was dingoes – five, six, seven of them, fanning out on a hunt. A timeless scene, played out the same way for thousands of years. Red turned, before melting into the trees, seeming to look straight at them. He raised his head and howled. The cry echoed round the hills, wild and triumphant, a king reclaiming his country. Creatures of the bush shivered at the sound. Kim shivered too.

They moved nearer to the edge as the western sky flamed crimson and gold. She could hear Taj breathe, feel his heartbeat. The pull grew stronger. Her whole being ached with the waiting, the wanting. Surely he felt it too?

'You asked me if I will stay married to a ghost,' she said. 'What about you?'

Just as she thought she could bear it no longer, Taj gathered her into his arms. They kissed, soft at first, his lips like velvet. Then urgently. He tasted of earth and smelt of the forest. A surge of wild pleasure ran through her. This is what had been missing with Ben, this electricity, this perilous leap of the heart. Strong hands encircled her waist, lifting her down from the ledge.

Kim knelt on the grass and tugged him down beside her, under the dome of the sundown sky. Her fingers found bare skin beneath his shirt. Slowly she unbuttoned it. The tattoo of a wolf on his chest. She traced it with her fingertips. Felt him shiver. She marvelled at the breadth of his shoulders, the strength of his thighs, his hard maleness. And still he hesitated, his lean body tense and trembling. She stripped off her top, took his hand and put it to her breast. She said his name, as if it was a miracle.

His doubts evaporated. He caressed her, explored her body. Each brush of his hand, a delicious shock. Time stood still. And when at last he moved inside her, she was ready. In synch, lost in his touch, urging him deeper.

Afterwards she lay in the curl of his arm as twilight fell. Her body still craved him, would always crave him. His lips sought hers. The kiss said he believed in her, that she mattered above all else, that her truth was his truth. Kim breathed him in. This was love.

This was knowing someone by heart.

CHAPTER 43

Kim woke to sunshine streaming through her window, uncertain for a moment if yesterday had really happened. She took a while to sort through the memories. Taj's story, the lookout at sunset, their bodies entwined in a declaration of love. A new world. Ben's betrayal, the hostility in town, even the pain of Dusty's death couldn't touch her. The thought of Taj turned despair into a heavy dose of hope.

Footsteps in the hallway … Jake came in. 'I want to go to school.' And she'd thought life couldn't get any better. 'Todd said I can be his partner in the new class assignment. We're getting the ducklings today.'

'I want to go too,' piped Abbey, pushing through the door.

'If you're both sure.'

Jake rolled his eyes. 'Hurry up, will you Mum?'

Later that morning, Kim, Taj and Mel were hard at work, putting up nest boxes of various sizes in trees above the dam: part of the future wildlife corridor which would connect Cedar Creek to the national park. Mel was more enthusiastic than ever about the project. Taj had shown her foxes killed by the dingoes. This, and the truth about Ben, was enough to bring her back on board.

Kim looked round for Taj. He was never far away, and always showing her things. A family of tiny pygmy possums in one of last season's boxes. A pair of owlet nightjars in another. Pardalotes excavating nests in a bank of earth. The willy wagtail's courtship dance. Spring was right round the corner, and everyone from the lowliest beetle to the mighty eagle were seeking their mates. Kim stood a while, observing Taj in profile, studying the lines of his face. Secure in the knowledge that she'd found hers.

Kim turned to find Mel staring. She hadn't missed the look, or its significance. Kim grinned. So what? She was with Taj now, and didn't care who knew it.

'I meant to tell you,' said Mel. 'Some bloke from Parks and Wildlife came looking for you on Monday.' She took a card from her pocket and handed it over.

Kim read the plain printed card. *Noel Fullerton, Senior Project Officer.* It told her nothing.

'Did he say what it was about?'

Mel wore the tight-lipped, apologetic smile of somebody delivering bad news. 'He said dingoes.'

Kim's stomach lurched. She and Taj had always lived under the fear of a Wild Dog Eradication Order. Well, if the department planned to issue one now, they'd have a fight on their hands. One that Kim intended to win. She looked at the card again. 'I'd better give him a ring.'

'A trial,' she said. 'How would that work?'

Taj had followed her down to the house. He stood close by as she talked on the phone. By the time she finished the call, he looked ready to explode with impatience.

Kim reassured him with a smile, eager to wipe the worry from his face. 'They want to settle the dingo debate with a trial reintroduction. Noel read Del's article. He wants to use Journey's End as a test site.'

. . .

Tingo Memorial Hall was packed with people. Everyone wanted to know about the proposed dingo park, and how it might affect them. Everyone except Geoff Masters. The police had traced the threatening texts to his phone and wanted to speak to him. Last week he'd gone to visit his sister in Sydney, and nobody had seen him since.

Winnie was doing the rounds, dropping a snippet of gossip here and a snippet of gossip there. 'Did you hear about Ben Steele?' she said to Kim. 'He's up before the Estate Agent's disciplinary panel. And I heard something about the police. I wonder what that's about?' A pregnant pause, but Kim didn't bite.

Kim excused herself and went over to where Todd was admiring Jake's new cricket bat. 'Taj made it for me,' said Jake proudly. 'Come over tomorrow. We should start practising. The season's only a month away.'

Abbey was running round with the carved figure of a poodle that looked remarkably like Percy. Telling everybody that Bibi had puppies and they were getting one. Kim had no doubts this time about a new dog. They'd never forget Dusty, but he was safe beneath the waratahs, and this time her life would move on. She slipped a hand in her pocket and rubbed Peri, the mountain fairy figurine Taj had given her as a token. Smooth and reassuringly solid to touch – her new good luck charm. Kim would need all its magical powers if they were to win over the locals.

Noel Fullerton stepped onto the stage to explain the plan. 'A growing body of evidence suggests the reintroduction of dingoes can restore damaged ecosystems to balance. They keep predators in check, like foxes and feral cats. This benefits native species. Dingoes control overgrazing by feral goats, deer, and native herbivores like kangaroos, wallabies and emus. This allows plants to regenerate.'

Kim took a deep breath. Good, the crowd was quiet, hearing him out.

'We plan to test this theory at Kim Sullivan's property on Bangalow Road.' Noel went on to describe the scheme in more detail:

length of trial, monitoring processes, control sites and so on. 'The major hurdle to a successful dingo reintroduction trial is convincing farmers and the local community to support it. That's why I'm here. Any questions?'

Mel stood up and broke the ice with a Dorothy Dixer. 'I own the farm next door to Kim's place. What happens if dingoes kill my sheep?'

'This project is well funded. We'll generously compensate landholders for stock losses.' There was a murmur of approval from the floor. 'However in an area of abundant game, this shouldn't be a major problem. I believe you've lived next door for some time, Mel, and haven't lost sheep.'

'That's right. Not to dingoes at least.'

Half-a-dozen hands went up.

'Won't they breed up too quickly and overrun the park?' asked Shirley.

'No chance of that. Dingoes come in season only once a year, not twice like domestic dogs,' said Noel. 'And in a stable pack, only the alpha female has puppies.'

He was a great communicator, responding fully to each question, allaying doubts and calming fears. 'And in conclusion, don't forget the ecotourism potential of a project like this. It could put Tingo on the map.'

Kim wanted to clap. Noel was a master of public relations, and she could feel the positive energy in the room. 'Thank you, Peri.' She gave her pocket fairy an appreciative rub. The town was on their side.

The first glorious day of spring. A sapphire sky shone with Tingo's peculiar clarity of light. Kim dropped the kids at school and they ran off through the gate. Abbey and Jake had well and truly been welcomed back into the fold.

Jean waved and came over to the car. 'I was wondering . . . could you reconsider your decision to take Abbey away next year? I have a funding report to write, and you know how important student numbers are. They're always threatening to close us down, and ...'

'Done,' said Kim. 'I'm starting a new job next week with the Environment Department. Noel put me onto it. Advising landholders on bush regeneration. Who'd have thought that was even a thing? Anyway, we're staying put.'

'That's wonderful news,' said Jean. 'And not that it's any of my business, but I'd like to say how pleased I am for you and Taj. He's a good man, Kim, one of the best. You're made for each other.'

'Thank you, Jean. Now if you'll excuse me, I have something important to do.'

Kim stood with Taj by the rapids on Cedar Creek, holding Scout's silver urn. Above them the orchids were making a comeback, the cliffs scattered with fresh, green shoots. She cast the ashes to the breeze, and Taj threw his handful of sand. Two puffs of dust, merging, mingling, landing who-knew-where? Setting them all free.

ACKNOWLEDGEMENTS

Thanks to the team at Pilyara Press for making *Journey's End* available globally, and to my agent, Clare Forster, of Curtis Brown Australia.

Thanks to my patient family for enduring my absences while I was locked away writing, and for believing in me. You are all stars!

Thank you to my literary friends, talented writers themselves, who encourage me, and understand like nobody else the joys and pitfalls of this journey.

Perhaps the most special thanks of all goes to to my old school friend Kim Gollan and her husband Pete. *Journey's End* is based on their magnificent Dingo Creek Rainforest Nursery. I'll never forget that trip we took together to Tapin Tops National Park. Kim, you are my real life inspiration for the concept of bush regeneration and rewilding.

Last but not least, Thanks to Rewilding Australia for tirelessly supporting the restoration of Australia's natural ecosystems.

ABOUT THE AUTHOR

Bestselling Aussie author Jennifer Scoullar writes page-turning fiction about the land, people and wildlife that she loves.

Scoullar is a lapsed lawyer who harbours a deep appreciation and respect for the natural world. She lives on a farm in Australia's southern Victorian ranges, and has ridden and bred horses all her life. Her passion for animals and the bush is the catalyst for her bestselling books.

Visit Jennifer's website to enter the monthly prize draw! If you enjoyed this book and have a moment or two, please leave a rating or review. Reviews are of great help to authors.

www.jenniferscoullar.com